DOUBLE VISION

A Quantum Suspense Novel

RANDY INGERMANSON

Ingermanson Communications, Inc.

THERE'S A CODE EVEN THE NSA CAN'T CRACK

But Dillon Richard can. Dillon is a straight-arrow genius with Asperger's syndrome. He's never told a lie. He's never been kissed. And he's never had a badass quantum computer for cracking codes. Until now.

In just a few days, Dillon will finish the software to crack the "unbreakable" code that banks and terrorists use to protect their most valuable secrets.

Everybody's going to want a piece of Dillon. The Mafia. The NSA. And his two beautiful co-workers, Keryn and Rachel.

Who'll get him first?

AUTHOR'S COMMENT

This novel is set in the summer of 2004. I wrote the first draft in 2003 and published it the following year.

In this second edition, certain slang, clothes, and technology already seem remarkably out of date. I have resisted the urge to update them, because the story has to be set in 2004.

This is the way things were during that fateful summer when a remarkable new technology was born in a desperately hungry startup company in San Diego.

But the story isn't about the tech stuff. It never is.

The story is about the people.

A word about the central character, Dillon Richard, who has Asperger's syndrome.

My man Dillon would insist that every Aspie is different, that nobody is a mere concrete instance of an abstract syndrome. I consider Dillon to be neither typical nor atypical. He is his own man, and some of his quirks have absolutely nothing to do with Asperger's. I had fun writing him, and many of my readers have told me they enjoyed spending time with him.

I hope you will too.

PART 1: POINT OF KNOW RETURN

Consequently, the development of a fully operational quantum computer would imperil our personal privacy, destroy electronic commerce and demolish the concept of national security. A quantum computer would jeopardize the stability of the world.

Simon Singh
The Code Book, p. 331

CHAPTER ONE

Keryn

Keryn Wills was in the shower when she decided how to kill Josh Trenton.

Her best ideas usually came that way, letting the white noise of the pelting spray drown out the outside world. Josh had to die. That was just the way things were. If you were the designated corpse in a Keryn Wills murder mystery, your mission was to die—whether you agreed to accept it or not. The only question was how, and now Keryn had the answer.

All that remained was to slam it all down on paper before she lost it, and she had the whole Saturday ahead of her for that. Keryn twisted off the water and shoved back the shower curtain.

Smiley was sitting on the floor watching her, his blue eyes wide and glittery.

"What are you staring at?" Keryn grabbed her towel and began drying off.

Smiley yawned widely.

"You think I'm boring, is that it?" Keryn scowled at him. "Go on, admit it. I won't be hurt."

Smiley meowed and scurried out.

Keryn wrapped the towel around herself and dashed through her bedroom into her office. She grabbed a pen and began scribbling ideas on a white pad. *How Josh Dies. Must look like accident.*

The phone rang.

Keryn looked at the number on the caller ID. Mom and Dad. Not now. Just let it ring.

Botulism poisoning.

The phone kept ringing.

Keryn reached for her copy of *Deadly Doses: A Writer's Guide to Poisons.*

The answering machine picked up. "Hello, this is Keryn Wills. I'd love to talk to you, but I'm out. Leave a message and I'll call you back as *soon* as I can."

A click, and then her mother's voice. "Hi, honey, it's me. Rusty's still asleep. Long story, but just between you and me and the fence post, he got plastered again last night. Anyway, I just wanted to see how your big date went. Come on and pick up the phone, sweetheart. I know you're there. I want details—big, luscious, foaming details. You *are* home, aren't you? I swear, if you shacked up with that man on the first date, I'm going to call your preacher-creature and tell him you're nothing but a hypocrite, so pick *up* the phone or—"

Keryn snatched up the phone. "Hi, Sunflower." This was going to be horrible, but hell hath no fury like a mother scorned, so the only way through this was straight ahead, with all shields up.

"Sweetheart, I knew you were there. Now spill. Details. Remind me ... what's the name of Mr. Possibility again?"

Keryn took a deep, calming breath and exhaled slowly. "Dillon."

"I thought it was Rick or something."

"That's his last name. Richard." Keryn tapped her fingers on the desk, itching to grab *Deadly Doses* and start flipping pages.

"Dillon Richard." Sunflower pronounced it like a disease. "Sounds backwards. What kind of parents would name their boy Dillon Richard?"

Keryn ran her fingers through her wet hair and looked at the picture of her parents on her desk. The picture was five years old, and even back then, Sunflower's hippie ponytail had gone a dull and streaky gray. Rusty's hair wasn't rusty anymore. Mostly it just ... wasn't. Sunflower and Rusty. Locked in a time warp where the sixties were still groovin' and life was free acid and psychedelic VW buses and Grateful Dead concerts.

"So hit me with some details, girlfriend," Sunflower said.

Keryn sighed deeply. *Please, please, please grow up, Mom.* "We went to a play in La Jolla."

A pregnant pause, and then the world's most disbelieving voice. "That's it? A *play*? You didn't eat?"

"We ate. We went to a play. Dillon drove me home."

A moment of horrified silence. "And ... ?"

"It was a first date."

"And you invited him in? Please tell me you had the sense to invite him in for coffee."

Keryn didn't say anything. It had been late, and Dillon said something about going shooting in the morning. *Shooting.*

"What's wrong with him?" Sunflower's voice had a note of desperate resignation.

"Nothing's wrong with him. He's a perfect gentleman." Who just happened to look like a young George Clooney and made Keryn's brain turn into oatmeal every time she looked at him.

"He's *how* old? Thirty-five? Got to be something wrong with him if he's never been married."

"He's ... shy." *Shy* wasn't quite the right word, but if Keryn tried to explain, Sunflower would go into hysterics.

"He asked you out, didn't he?"

Keryn hesitated. "Really shy."

"You're telling me *you* asked *him* out? Not a good sign, girlfriend. Looks bad. Like you know your clock is ticking."

"My clock *is* ticking. It's a biological fact. I'm going to get old and die someday. And so are you. Have you ... read that book I sent you?"

"I don't read books by preacher-creatures."

"Mom, please!"

Shocked silence.

Keryn regretted it immediately. That was the only way to shut up Sunflower. Hit her with a chunk of her own maternity. That bothered her way more than her mortality.

Keryn heard a call-waiting blip on her line. She checked the caller ID. "Hey, um, Sunflower? I've got a call incoming from my boss. Can I call you back later?"

Sunflower slammed the phone down.

Keryn clicked the button on her phone to pick up the incoming call. "Hello, Grant. What's up?"

"Bad news." Grant O'Connell's gravelly voice sounded tired. "I know it's Saturday, but can you come in to work for a couple hours? We need to strategize."

Keryn looked at her scribblings on the paper and tried to remember exactly how Josh was going to die. "Um ... sure." *I guess.* It had to be bad if Grant wasn't out golfing on a Saturday. "Can I ask what it's about?"

"Not on the phone," Grant said.

Keryn felt her pulse quicken. *Not on the phone?* This was starting to sound like one of her mysteries. Or maybe a John le Carré. "I'm not dressed yet. What time do you need me?"

"Ten-thirty," Grant said. "I've already called the others. Dillon can't get in any earlier. If you can believe it, he's out shooting right now."

Keryn wondered why she and Dillon would be invited to the same meeting. He was a Senior Engineer and she was Chief Financial Officer, and that didn't give them a whole lot of common turf. "I'll be there."

"Don't panic," Grant said. "Everything's going to be all right. There's got to be some way out of this mess." He hung up.

Keryn stared at the phone in her hand. It hadn't occurred to her to panic until Grant told her not to. All of a sudden, she had a pounding headache, and her heart was hammering as fast as one of those old-fashioned typewriters. She put the phone down and headed back to her bedroom to get dressed.

She could already see that she wasn't going to kill Josh Trenton today.

Dillon

Dillon drove carefully into his favorite parking spot. The lot was empty. He stepped out and locked his minivan, setting the alarm. He walked once around the vehicle and inspected each tire. A knot of anxiety clutched at his stomach. It was highly unusual for Grant to call a meeting on a Saturday. Highly unusual.

Dillon strode across the lot to the bridge. A thin trickle of water ran through the gully. Again, highly unusual. In June the gully should be dry. But this was no ordinary June. It had rained twice already, and it might rain again before the month was over.

"Hey, Dillon!" Clifton Potter leaned out of his SUV and waved at Dillon.

Clifton was the Chief Technology Officer of the company and Dillon considered him technically competent. Mostly.

Clifton pointed at Dillon's minivan. "Dude! Why'd you park way over in the main lot? There's plenty of spots right here by the building."

Dillon did not know how to explain, so he shook his head and shrugged. He had parked in his favorite spot because ... it was his favorite spot. But Clifton was a Normal, and he could not be expected to understand.

Clifton shoved his door open and hopped out. He slammed the door and turned to Dillon. "Do you know what's going down?"

"You forgot to lock your door." Dillon pointed at Clifton's SUV.

Clifton shook his head. "Chill it, Dillon! There's nobody here on a Saturday to mess with my car." His long blond ponytail swished back and forth.

Dillon found this unnerving. He did not know why Clifton wore his hair so long. Nor did he know why Clifton used so much slang. Slang made a person hard to understand. After thinking for a moment, Dillon remembered that *chill* had a secondary meaning—something about relaxing. It made no sense to Dillon, but it made sense to Normals, and therefore he made an effort to learn such things. But he would rather that people said what they meant in the first place.

Dillon put a hand on Clifton's SUV. "Last year, 23,378 cars were stolen in San Diego County. The most popular makes among thieves are Toyotas and Hondas. Eighty percent of all cars stolen were left unlocked. You should lock your car."

Clifton's grin left his face. "Twenty-three thousand?"

"No. 23,378," Dillon said. "Approximately 8.3 stolen cars per thousand residents."

"Dude!" Clifton pulled out his keys and pressed a button. The car beeped and the door locks clicked with a satisfying chorus of *thunk*s.

Dillon smiled. You could never be too careful about such things.

"So how was your hot date with our famous author last night?" Clifton said.

Dillon paused for a moment, then remembered that *hot* had a secondary meaning that had nothing to do with temperature. "It went extremely well. We had dinner and saw *The Tragedy of Hamlet, Prince of Denmark*."

"Spiff!" Clifton said. "'To be, or not to be,' huh?"

Dillon often felt off-balance when speaking with Clifton. Clifton used many words that even most Normals did not. It made Dillon feel uneasy. Very uneasy. However, Dillon saw that he could easily change the subject to quantum mechanics, one of his favorite topics. "After the play, we talked about quantum mechanics and multiple universes."

Clifton's face took on an expression Dillon could not parse. "Dude! What's all that have to do with *Hamlet*?"

"'To be, or not to be,'" Dillon said. "The question Hamlet asks implies that he has a choice, correct? But all choices must be quantum mechanical in nature."

"Um, Dillon, have you been smoking something?"

"Cigarettes are very unhealthful." Dillon could not understand why Clifton kept changing the subject. "I explained to Keryn that all of physics is deterministic, with one exception. When you make a quantum measurement, the result is not determined. The only rational conclusion is that, if we truly have free will, it must be because our thought processes are quantum mechanical. Making a choice is equivalent to performing a measurement on our own brains. A decision defines who and what we are."

"Dude, I bet Keryn thought that was real interesting."

Dillon nodded. Keryn had found it highly interesting. "She had never heard that making a quantum measurement causes the universe to split into several parallel universes. In each of those universes, the result measured is different. Hamlet poses himself a two-state question: 'To be, or not to be.' When he makes his choice, his future splits in two. In one universe, Hamlet chooses to live. In a second universe, he chooses to die."

Clifton was staring at Dillon with his mouth open.

Dillon felt calm again. The multiverse interpretation of quantum mechanics was logical. It was still not as popular among physicists as the old-fashioned Copenhagen interpretation, but the Copenhagen interpretation was not logical. When all physicists became logical, they would believe in the multiverse interpretation.

"Well, whatever, dude. And while you were talking about multiverses, did you also happen to notice that Keryn is one massively hot babe?"

Dillon took a few seconds to parse this. Keryn was an adult woman. Therefore, she could not literally be a baby. Therefore, *babe* must take on its secondary meaning—an attractive woman. Furthermore, Keryn's body temperature was normal, so the word *hot* also took on its secondary meaning. Dillon thought it was insulting to call a grown woman a hot babe, but he did not know how to explain this to Clifton.

He felt his face getting warm. Yes, Keryn was highly attractive. Whenever Dillon looked at her, he felt an odd fluttering in his stomach, and he sometimes found it difficult to talk. Last night, sitting next to her at the play, he had felt light-headed.

But Keryn had a kind way of looking at Dillon that made him feel warm and comfortable. She knew he was not a Normal, and yet she liked him anyway. That was far more important than the illogical question of whether a woman was attractive or homely.

Clifton's cell phone rang. He yanked it out of his pocket and pressed a button. "Yo, hello, this is Clif."

Dillon turned to look at the gully.

A mother duck and three ducklings paddled down the thin rivulet.

"Yeah, sure, Kendall's a buddy of mine," Clifton said. "You're the dude who hooked him up with HP? Spiff, man! He used to have this bogus boss who thought he was God's gift to lasers but didn't know his head from a hole in the wave function. Know what I mean?"

Dillon was beginning to feel uncomfortable again. Clifton's illogical style of speaking grated on him.

"Hold on a sec." Clifton's voice had taken on a peculiar tone. He began walking away toward the corner of the building. When he reached the corner, Clifton looked back at Dillon. Then his head jerked around as if he were embarrassed by something.

Dillon put his hands behind his back and thought about his time talking with Keryn last night. Keryn Wills was a writer. An intelligent woman. He had enjoyed talking with her. She was not a physicist or an engineer, but she had been extremely interested in how quantum mechanics tied in with *The Tragedy of Hamlet, Prince of Denmark*.

She had a quiet and comfortable way of talking that made Dillon feel as if he had known her all of his life, even though she had only been hired a few months ago. Also—Dillon felt his ears getting hot—she worked out at the gym every day and her clothes fit her extremely well. Of course it was shallow of him to notice such things, but he would be highly unobservant if he did not.

The important thing was that she was a kind and friendly person. She was not the type of person who snickered behind her hands at people who were not Normal. He hoped he could have many more interesting conversations with her.

A horn honked. Grant O'Connell's Lexus appeared at the far end of the building, gleaming in the sunlight.

In San Diego, a Lexus was not stolen as frequently as a Toyota, but that was because more people drove a Toyota than a Lexus.

Dillon made a mental note to remind Grant to lock his car.

The Lexus pulled up next to Dillon. Grant flung open the door and thumped out, his big ruddy face smiling. He had a large bald head with a rim of gray hair around the back. His huge white Santa Claus eyebrows made Dillon a little uneasy, but Grant was a good man and Dillon trusted him.

The passenger door opened and a petite young woman sprang out. She had shoulder-length silky hair of a golden blond color, and she wore a garish pink-and-blue tie-dyed shirt that stretched tight across her chest and did not reach down to her navel. Her faded jeans had a hole in one knee and did not reach up to her navel. She wore an old-fashioned leather fanny pack low around her hips.

Dillon thought she looked like one of those supermodels on the covers of magazines in the supermarket. For a second, he simply stared at her. Then he caught himself and looked down at the ground. A wave of dizziness washed over him and he thought for a moment that he was going to fall over.

Grant came around the car and pounded Dillon on the shoulder. "Dillon, I'd like you to meet our off-site employee, Rachel Meyers. Rachel, this is Dillon Richard. He's the one I was telling you about— our hotshot in C++ and hardware/software interfaces. Dillon, Rachel just got her Ph.D. from Caltech last year and eats that multiverse thing for lunch. Believe me, you two are gonna have a *lot* to talk about."

Dillon looked at Rachel with surprise. Apparently she was not a ditz. "You are a physicist?"

"Biophysicist." She reached out a hand. "Glad to meet you, Dillon. Uncle Grant's told me how brilliant you are, and I'm *really* looking forward to working with you."

Dillon shook her hand. It was soft and warm and sent a bolt of electricity up his arm and into his brain. He swallowed a large lump in his throat and forced himself to look at Grant. "Rachel is your niece?"

Grant bellowed with laughter. "Virtual niece. She's the daughter of the kid brother of my roommate at MIT. I changed Rachel's diapers when she was a baby and watched her grow up, and she's every bit as smart as her daddy, who happens to teach string theory at Rutgers. Anyway, you're gonna love her, Dillon."

Another horn honked behind them. Keryn's old Honda came jouncing over a speed bump. She pulled in next to Grant's Lexus and scurried out. "Am I late?"

"Looks like we're all here," Grant said. "Let's get this show on the road. Sorry to make you all come in on a Saturday, especially a great day like today, but let's get it done."

Keryn stood there without moving, looking at Rachel with an odd expression on her face which Dillon could not parse.

"You should lock it," he said.

"What?" Keryn stared at Dillon blankly.

"You should lock your car," he said. "Hondas are one of the two most commonly stolen cars in San Diego County, and Civics are among the most popular models."

CHAPTER TWO

Keryn

Keryn did not like the way the blonde was staring at Dillon. Ogling him. Which was what every woman did the first time they saw Dillon Richard. If any guy on the planet ever deserved the word gorgeous, it was him. And the amazing thing about Dillon was that he had no idea how he affected women.

Keryn felt her nails digging into her fists. The blonde couldn't be much over twenty-two. Dressed like an airhead. Retro clothes, but apparently she couldn't figure out what era she wanted to be from. The tie-dyed shirt screamed sixties. The leather fanny pack suggested eighties. The pants looked more like nineties.

Probably fresh out of college. Grant's daughter? No, she had heard he didn't have any kids. So maybe a new receptionist or something. But that was crazy. There wasn't money to hire a new receptionist. Whatever. Keryn didn't like the way the airhead's flirty green eyes were drinking in Dillon.

Grant shot Keryn a huge smile. "Keryn, I'd like you to meet our off-site employee, Rachel Meyers. Rachel, this is Keryn Wills. She joined the team part time back in March to help with the financials.

She's our CFO and a really good one. Remember I told you about her? She's our author—written four or five books."

"Three," Keryn corrected him. "Number four is due in August." *And I'm way behind schedule.*

Rachel extended her hand. "Hi, Keryn. I'd love to read one of your books sometime."

Keryn shook hands with her. "Um ... right." Rachel was not wearing a bra. It was some consolation that she clearly didn't need one. Keryn shifted slightly to her right and smiled at Dillon. "Good morning, Dillon."

He was wearing a cream-colored cotton shirt and dark gray wool pants and a muted blue-gray tie. Shiny leather shoes. Every other engineer in the company wore blue jeans and wrinkled T-shirts, but Dillon was ... different. Not weird different. *Different* different. If guys had *any* idea how hot they looked when they dressed up a little, you'd see more guys in ties.

Grant was striding away toward the corner of the building. "Hey, Clifton? Ready to go inside? We've got a lot to talk about!"

Keryn edged a little closer to Dillon and smiled at Rachel. "So, um, Rachel, what do you do for CypherQuanta? Marketing?"

Rachel gave her a little-girl smile. "Research."

Keryn nodded. *Market research.* Grant was probably paying her chicken feed to call up banks and brokerages to find out what their data encryption needs were. Which was fine, except for one teensy little detail—CypherQuanta didn't *have* chicken feed.

Keryn had discussed this nicely with Grant twice in the last month, and she had understood that he agreed. Absolutely no more employees until the next round of funding came through. Cash flow right now was tighter than a Tom Clancy story line, and there was not one extra dime. And now there was some new crisis, which was the reason she had to come in to work today instead of killing off Josh Trenton.

Grant came steaming back with Clifton in tow. "Okay, now we're all really here. Rachel, meet Clifton Potter, our Chief Technology Officer. Clifton founded the company with me six years ago, and it's thanks to him we haven't folded yet. Clifton, this is Rachel Meyers, girl genius."

Clifton's eyes widened and he looked Rachel up and down appreciatively. "*Very* glad to meet you, Rachel. What kind of genius are you, exactly?"

"She is a biophysicist from Caltech," Dillon said. "You will like her, Clifton. She knows all about the multiverse."

Keryn blinked twice, feeling horribly stupid. *A biophysicist? A girl genius?* A large lump settled in her throat.

"Let's get inside, people." Grant looked around nervously. He leaned close to Clifton. "Rachel's made a breakthrough, Cliffie baby. A grade-A, gold-plated breakthrough that is gonna save our cookies if it pans out."

"Spiff!" Clifton said.

Dillon was beaming at Rachel.

Keryn suddenly felt very ill.

∾

Dillon

Dillon sat down at the circular glass table in Grant's office. He laid out a clean white pad of paper and a black Uni-ball pen. Keryn sat on Dillon's left. Grant and Rachel sat across from him. Clifton took a seat on his right.

The configuration felt asymmetric to Dillon. Better to have Rachel on his right and Clifton across from him. Then it would be—

"Let's get started." Grant's voice sounded like a wheelbarrow crunching over gravel.

Dillon wondered if Grant had been getting enough sleep.

Grant began clicking a ball-point pen in his hand. *Click-click. Click-click.* "Lost Angels met yesterday, and I gave them a presentation."

Rachel's eyebrows went up. "Lost Angels?"

"Our angel investors," Keryn said. "A Los Angeles high-tech investment club. They funded us for another year last December. Right now they own forty-two percent of CypherQuanta."

"Correction," Grant said. "They funded us in two tranches, contingent on meeting sales milestones."

"What's a tranche?" Rachel said.

"A pile of money." Grant clicked on his pen. "In our case, not a very high pile."

Dillon did not like the Lost Angels investors. They were abrasive and rude, and they had taken unfair advantage in the negotiations last December. For a week, Dillon had been afraid Grant might have a heart attack.

"We're ahead of our sales mark," Keryn said. "We needed to place ten units in Q1 and Q2, and we placed thirteen."

Grant's face twisted as if he had just drunk a glassful of vinegar. "San-D-Bank is returning four units."

A hiss ran around the table.

Dillon felt as if he had been slapped. He had worked overtime to customize the software on those machines. Speed had been a major issue on that contract, and he had found a clever algorithm to get an extra factor of 2.1 in throughput.

Grant *click-click*ed the pen again. "According to them, the units, quote—do not meet our requirements—unquote."

"And that means ..." Keryn sounded like she was being strangled.

Grant slammed his open palm on the table. "Lost Angels is cutting their losses. They're canceling the second tranche and putting the word out that CypherQuanta is a lost cause."

"That's totally bogus," Clifton said.

Dillon felt his stomach tighten into a hard, boiling knot. This was exactly why he did not like Lost Angels. They could pull out and destroy the company at any time. And if CypherQuanta went bankrupt and had to sell off its assets, Lost Angels would receive compensation first, before any other investors. It was written in the contract.

Keryn was clenching her pen so tightly Dillon could see the whites of her knuckles. "Um, Grant, how are we going to make payroll at the end of the month?"

"That's ..." Grant cleared his throat and looked around the table. "That's why I called this meeting. We won't be getting that second tranche, and we're also not going to get paid on the invoice from San-D-Bank. Plus, we're out the cost of parts for those four units."

Clifton leaned back in his chair. "Man, that is so bogus! We met the acceptance criteria on that contract!"

"There was a clause that it had to meet spec for ninety days," Grant said. "They claim its performance has degraded."

"Bunch of wallies," Clifton said. "Let's send Dillon over there. He'll get it working."

Keryn drummed her fingers on the table. "Right, let's send Dillon."

Dillon sat straighter in his chair and his pulse sped up. Yes, he was certain he could fix the problem. A machine was a machine. If it met specifications in the lab, then it should continue to meet specifications forever, unless some part failed. And a part could be easily replaced.

Grant shook his head. "It won't do any good. I've heard something —back-channel, but I think it's accurate. Somebody on the Lost Angels board has it in for us and is chummy with someone at San-D-Bank. We're doornails."

Dillon did not see how they could possibly be doornails. This must be some metaphor he had not learned yet. He did not like metaphors, because they asserted things that were not true. There was often an interesting explanation for a metaphor, but today he did not have time to ask for an explanation. He must focus on solving this problem.

This disaster could bankrupt Grant, and that was not acceptable. Grant had spent a fortune of his own money to start the company. Had it not been for the recession, they would have gone public by now and Grant would have earned back his investment. Dillon could find a job somewhere else, but Grant was almost ready to retire, and his only marketable skill was that he knew how to take risks and make money. Now he had taken an enormous risk and might lose all his money.

Keryn sucked in her breath. "Listen, I know this is going to sound harsh, but ... I think we need to take steps to maintain the financial integrity of the company. Right away."

"Meaning layoffs," Clifton said in a glum tone.

"No possible way," Grant said. "I've earned the team's loyalty, and I'm gonna be loyal to them. We are not doing layoffs except over my cold, reeking corpse."

Keryn sighed deeply. "Grant, I really think we have to worry about keeping our nose above water."

Dillon remembered that Keryn used this metaphor when she

meant that they must stay financially solvent. A nose had nothing to do with money, but it was Keryn's way of talking.

Grant looked steadily around the table, and there was an odd gleam in his eyes. He smiled. "There may be a way out. I'm pretty sure there's a way out. Keryn, how long could we stay afloat if we didn't write paychecks?"

Keryn's eyes opened wide and her cheeks turned pink. She bit her lip. "Probably through the end of August. It depends on if we can sweet-talk the landlord. Remember, our energy bills go up during the summer. But if we miss payroll, we're dead. CypherQuanta *is* our employees. That's your company motto, Grant. The minute you miss payroll, our engineers will be e-mailing resumés. The economy's not on life support anymore. In three weeks, they'll all be gone."

Grant *click-click*ed his pen. "How about if we pay everybody in stock for one month? With a bonus—we'll offer them double their salary-equivalent in stock."

Clifton shook his head. "That ain't gonna fly. If we miss payroll, our stock isn't worth toilet paper."

Dillon nodded slowly. "Grant, it would not be honest to pay them in stock if the stock has no value. If you intend to miss payroll, you are obligated to notify the employees right away."

Grant's eyes narrowed as he looked first at Keryn, then Dillon, then Clifton. "Point taken, people, but before you three bears run off into the woods, Goldilocks here has a little story to tell you." He pointed a stubby finger at Rachel. "Tell 'em, girl genius."

Rachel leaned forward in her chair and her bright green eyes lit up. She pulled Dillon's tablet across the table and held out her hand for his pen. "May I?"

Dillon gave her the pen. He noticed that she had small, clever hands. The nails were polished an emerald green that matched her eyes, with golden sprinkles the exact color of her hair.

Rachel drew a triangle on the paper and labeled the three corners. *Fast. Cheap. Good.* She looked straight at Dillon. "This is the classic engineering triangle. Even in the best case, you can only choose two of these three. NASA is wrong when they say faster-better-cheaper. You can never have all three, right?"

Dillon nodded. "Never."

Rachel tapped her pen on the triangle. "Where does Cypher-Quanta stand on this triangle?"

"We're in the *good* corner," Clifton said. "Our quantum encryption is the spiffest thing out there. Nobody does it better, nowhere, nohow. Even God can't do better."

Dillon did not like the way Clifton said this. It was a theorem of quantum mechanics that nobody could do better, but even so, Dillon did not like to place bets on what God could not do. That was an interesting metaphysical question, but it was not science and it was not engineering.

"And what else are we?" Rachel said. "Besides the *good* corner, do we have anything else?"

Nobody said anything for a long moment.

"We're not *fast*, that's for sure," Clifton finally said. "No offense, Dillon. You did the best you could, but we're still only getting kilobits per second. Conventional RSA encryption gets gigabits."

"But our encryption is better," Dillon said.

"Better doesn't always win," Rachel said. "If it did, everyone would have bought a Mac in 1984—and Bill Gates would have gone into shining shoes."

"Which brings us to our other problem," Grant said. "We aren't *cheap* either. RSA encryption is free."

"But our encryption is *better*." Dillon's hands were clenched so tight, his knuckles had gone white. He could not understand why people did not care about quality. "Quantum encryption is unbreakable. You can prove a theorem—"

"Theorem, shmeorem," Rachel said. "Our competition is RSA encryption. People *perceive* it to be just as good as ours. *And* it's faster. *And* it's cheaper."

"You're telling us our business model is majorly biff." Clifton leaned back in his chair and crossed his arms.

Biff was one of Clifton's special words. Dillon knew it meant *bad*, but he had never understood why Clifton could not simply say *bad*. And *majorly* was not a real word either. It was one of the most ridiculous slang words ever invented, and Dillon hoped it would go away soon.

"Listen, guys, I'm just telling you the reality," Rachel said. "Right, Uncle Grant?"

Grant grunted agreement. Then he exploded in laughter. "All right, stop playing with them, Rachel. Give 'em the good news."

Rachel put the pen down in front of Dillon. "In principle, RSA encryption can be broken."

Dillon stared at her, wondering what her point was. "In principle, yes. Everybody knows that *if* you can factor large numbers, you can break RSA encryption."

"Not *everybody*," Keryn said. "I didn't know that. Can you give me the *Dummies* explanation of what factoring large numbers has to do with encryption?"

Dillon took the pen and wrote down the number fifteen on his tablet. "Any schoolchild can factor small numbers. Fifteen is *what* times *what?*"

Keryn shrugged. "That's easy. Fifteen is three times five."

Dillon nodded. "Correct. But if I give you a ten-digit number, you will find it very much harder to factor."

"Can't a computer do that?" Keryn said.

"For ten digits, yes," Dillon said. "But as you add digits, it gets exponentially harder. For a hundred digits, it takes a long time. And no computer in the world has ever factored an arbitrary two-hundred-digit number."

Keryn still looked puzzled. "Fine, but what does this have to do with us?"

"Everything." Dillon wondered how to explain to her about the Euler totient function. "The RSA encryption scheme depends for its security on the fact that it is easy to multiply two large numbers together, but it is extremely hard to factor the resulting product without knowing one of the original two numbers."

Rachel blew him a kiss. "You get a gold star, Dillon. It boils down to this. If you could factor large numbers, then conventional RSA encryption would be broken. It would still be cheap and fast. But it would be worthless. Which would mean that anyone who needs encryption wouldn't have a choice. They'd have to buy our machines, because we'd be the only game in town. *If* we could factor large numbers, every bank, every brokerage, every government—*anyone* who needs to protect their data in transit—would have to buy our quantum encryption system."

Clifton shook his head. "That's one majorly bogus *if*. You can't factor large numbers. They use two-thousand-bit keys for RSA encryption. Factoring a number that mondo would take like billions of years."

"Billions of years on a conventional supercomputer." Rachel leaned forward. "Think different. Think quantum."

Dillon felt his heart thump. "There *is* a quantum algorithm to factor large numbers. Shor's algorithm. But ... you would need a quantum computer with thousands of qubits."

"Whoa, time out," Keryn said. "I'm lost. Thousands of what-bits?"

"A quantum bit," Dillon said. "Q-u-b-i-t, pronounced *cubit*."

Keryn shook her head. "And what are these qubit things used for?"

"It's all very simple," Rachel said. "Everybody in the world uses RSA encryption, which could be broken—if only you could factor huge numbers. In 1994 Peter Shor at AT&T showed that you *can* factor large numbers—if you have a quantum computer with thousands of qubits. In 2001 Isaac Chuang's team at IBM demonstrated that Shor's algorithm worked on a quantum computer with seven qubits. In fact, he used it to factor the number fifteen. It was big in the news. So the only remaining glitch is to construct a quantum computer with a few thousand qubits."

Glitch? Dillon did not see how this could be considered a small matter. "That is like saying you can run a mile in four seconds. All you have to do is run nine hundred miles per hour."

Rachel just smiled at him.

Dillon felt something funny wiggle in his stomach. Rachel had a nice smile and her eyes sparkled when she talked. When beautiful young women first met him, they often smiled at him with sparkly eyes. But when they found out he was not a Normal, they might smile at him sometimes, but their eyes never again sparkled.

Clifton gave a nervous laugh. "Dillon's right. We had a tough time commercializing quantum encryption, and that only needs *one* qubit.

Seven qubits is the record, but IBM had fits making that work sorta-kinda-maybe in a *research* lab. It'll be like thirty years before anybody gets a thousand qubits to play together."

Dillon shook his head. "It will not happen in our lifetimes."

Keryn's eyes glittered with a look that Dillon could not decipher.

"Tell 'em, Rachel," Grant said.

Rachel reached inside the fanny pack at her waist and pulled out a sealed tube filled with a greenish liquid. "Here are the qubits."

Dillon stared at it. A dizzy feeling washed through his brain. Was it possible that Rachel had found a way to create hundreds of qubits? Or as many as a thousand? How? When?

"That?" Keryn's voice cracked. "That's a computer?"

Rachel shook her head. "Not the whole computer. Just the hard part. The qubits."

"How can a tube of ... green goop be a computer?" Keryn said. "That doesn't make any sense."

Rachel's face flushed. "The qubits are the spin states of the nuclei in certain molecules in this goop. You manipulate the qubits by radio signals. It's an NMR-based quantum computer, not too different from the one IBM built."

Keryn was looking lost. "NMR?"

"Nuclear magnetic resonance," Dillon said. "Like in MRI machines."

Keryn did not look at all convinced. "A test tube? That's not a computer."

Rachel gave her an intense look that Dillon could not parse. "Listen, Keryn, you just write the checks, okay?"

Grant put a hand on Rachel's arm. "Keryn's not questioning your work, Rachel. It just doesn't look like a regular computer." He turned to Keryn. "You'll have to take this on faith. I realize this is pretty weird looking, but it really is well-established technology."

Dillon raised his eyebrows. "Seven qubits is established technology. A hundred qubits would be extraordinary technology. There was a paper published in *Science* some time ago saying that a hundred qubits using NMR technology was impossible."

"That paper was probably right, if you're doing it the usual way,"

Rachel said. "But I'm doing it a different way, and I've got ten thousand qubits."

A rush of adrenaline shot through Dillon's chest. Suddenly, he could not breathe. "Ten ... *thousand* qubits?"

"Plus or minus a few hundred." Rachel gave him a dazzling smile. "Impressed?"

Dillon could hardly swallow. Ten thousand qubits was impossible. *Impossible*. Ten thousand qubits would save the company and make it rich overnight. But it was still impossible.

"It's only missing one thing," Rachel said.

"What's that?" Clifton's hands were trembling on top of the table.

Grant cleared his throat. "So far, all we have is the core of an NMR quantum computer. Rachel finished it quicker than we expected, and we've got the NMR hardware to drive it, but we need some custom software to drive the hardware. Dillon, you're the best hardware/software guy we've got. We need you."

Dillon's tongue felt parched. "Custom software? That could take months of development time. Design reviews. Implementation. Testing."

"We don't have months," Keryn said. "In less than three weeks, we're going to miss payroll."

Grant put his hand on top of Dillon's on the table. "Can you do it?"

Dillon's heart was thumping in his chest. He had a chance to work on something extraordinary. It would save the company. It would keep his friends employed. It would save Grant's investment. And it would force the entire world to begin using unbreakable encryption technology. The world would be a more secure place. If he could make the device work.

"I ... I need more information," Dillon stammered. He wanted desperately to think about something calming. The multiverse. Hamlet. Keryn's soft and quiet voice.

"Dillon, as of today, I want to reassign you to work with Rachel," Grant said. "She's got a bio-lab set up off-site. I want you two working around the clock on this thing. Your first task is to tell me how long it's going to take. Do you want the assignment or don't you? Because if you don't, we're dead. Nobody else can write code as fast and clean as you can."

Dillon swallowed hard.

"Dude, you the man," Clifton said.

Keryn sat very still.

Rachel gave him an encouraging smile.

Dillon's heart quivered in a way he had never felt before. Rachel was exceptionally intelligent. He did not see how he could do this job in only three weeks, but ... possibly with her help? And they would have many interesting conversations also.

"Will you do it?" Grant asked. "I'm begging you, Dillon."

Grant was like a father to Dillon. More than a father. The schedule would be almost impossible, but ... Dillon could not say no to Grant.

Dillon nodded. "I will try."

CHAPTER THREE

Rachel

Fifteen minutes later, as Grant was parking his Lexus outside the bio-lab, Rachel felt a rush of butterflies. She desperately wanted to make a good impression on the others, her new teammates. She'd been working in isolation for six months now, and it was driving her nuts. But Grant had said he couldn't afford to break security by introducing her to the other employees. Until now. If she went splat, it was going to be horrible. Worse than horrible.

All five of them climbed out of Grant's Lexus.

"Whoa, spiff!" Clifton strode over to Rachel's bright red Miata convertible. The top was down and Clifton ran his hands over the leather interior.

"Like it?" Rachel said. "I got it when I came to San Diego."

"It's very nice," Keryn said in that cool and quiet voice of hers.

Rachel liked watching people, trying to dice out their relationships. She had already figured out that Keryn and Dillon were an item, or an almost-item, or ... something. They were alike in a lot of ways.

And yet different. Dillon was simply delicious looking, with the arms and shoulders of a gymnast, but the height and proportions of a swimmer. He had a direct way of talking, and yet there was something about him Rachel couldn't pierce—mysterious and self-contained.

Whereas Keryn was so ... dull. Boring dark brown hair, cut to her shoulders and very eighties. Tall, thirtyish, not quite slim, but nicely proportioned, a terrific rack, and a pleasant smile. Not too quick on the uptake. So besides the fact that all her brains were in her bra, what *exactly* did Dillon see in her? Or ... did he? It was obvious that Keryn saw a whole lot in Dillon.

There was clearly some sort of connection between the two, but Uncle Grant hadn't said anything about them being a pair. Of course, he missed a lot of that kind of thing, but still.

"Come on, people, we can admire Rachel's car later," Grant said. "Dillon, I want you to see the bio-lab."

Dillon was staring at the car, frowning.

"Hey, Dillon, check this out!" Clifton said. He was standing behind the car, pointing at the license plate holder.

Dillon didn't move.

Keryn went around to look. Her eyes widened and she covered her mouth with her hand.

Rachel wanted to laugh. The plate holder said, *Sometimes ... I go topless.*

Dillon leaned inside the car and inspected the flashing red alarm light. "This kind of alarm is extremely simple to defeat."

"People, come on!" Grant stood at the top of the stairs, waiting.

"Relax, I've got LoJack." Rachel leaned in next to Dillon, brushing against his right sleeve with her bare arm. "Not to mention, that alarm's a dummy. The real one detects tampering and calls me on my cell phone."

"Miatas have a very low theft rate," Dillon said. "Now I understand why."

Rachel leaned in farther and lost her balance. "Oh!" She grabbed Dillon's arm and caught herself.

Dillon's arm seemed to be made of steel. Rachel held it in a death grip and kicked her legs, but her feet couldn't find the ground.

"Hold still." Dillon's left hand came around underneath her and gripped her right shoulder. He effortlessly lifted her and set her back on the ground. "Are you all right, Rachel?"

Rachel felt much more than all right. A rush of heat seemed to be flowing out of Dillon's hand into her shoulder. "I'm ... fine. Just lost my balance. These stupid flip-flops don't have any traction."

Dillon pointed at a horizontal red line across Rachel's bare midriff where she'd fallen across the hot metal on the top of the door. "Does that hurt? Should we take you to a doctor?"

"It's fine."

"Your shirt is too short. You should buy the next larger size."

This was so stunningly inappropriate that Rachel stared up at him with her mouth hanging right open. She wanted to laugh, but she didn't dare. Uncle Grant had said there was something ... weird about Dillon, but she hadn't been paying attention.

"I hope you haven't hurt yourself," Keryn said.

Rachel turned to look at her.

Keryn wore a skeptical face that clearly said, *You planned that whole thing, didn't you?*

Well, duh.

"People, I hate to interrupt the car festival, but Rachel says she's fine and we've got work to do." Grant limped down the stairs, wincing each time he put weight on his trick left knee.

"We're coming," Rachel said.

"Right behind ya, Grant," Clifton said. "Great car, Rachel."

Grant turned and hauled himself back up the stairs to the door. He punched in the five-digit security code. "Dillon, I'll give you the code so you can come in anytime. Sorry, Keryn and Clifton, but you don't need to know it, and we're keeping tight security on this place." He turned the knob and pushed the door open dramatically. "Behold ... the bio-lab! Rachel, go ahead and give us all a tour."

Rachel stepped in past him. The suite was actually two moderately large rooms. In the outer office, she had a desk overflowing with photocopied papers, along with an empty filing cabinet. A stack of pizza boxes was mounded in the trash can. "Sorry about the mess. I don't eat in the lab because I culture live cells in there. They're not infectious, but still. There's a bathroom over there." She pointed to the corner. "It's kind of a mess in there too. Sorry. I'm not real big on cleaning."

Rachel pointed to a pair of metal double doors. "In through here is the actual bio-lab. We maintain it at a slight negative pressure, relative to this outer room. Not enough so you'll notice, but enough to keep stuff from blowing out. Not that anything could actually blow out. I do all the biology work under a hood, and it's vented."

"Biology?" Dillon said. "What does biology have to do with a quantum computer?"

Rachel pushed open one of the doors. "Come on in and I'll explain."

The others trooped in.

Rachel led the way to a wet bench. "Okay, here's the deal. The problem people have in making quantum computers is that the qubits are small." She grinned at them all. "I hope that's not a surprise."

Grant gave her a big smile. Keryn was gawking around the room. Clifton was sneaking a peek at Keryn's butt. Dillon was looking at the MagTec NMR machine in the corner.

Rachel joined him. "I guess you're familiar with conventional NMR quantum computers, right?"

Dillon nodded. "I know the basic idea. You control an ensemble of qubits by radio pulses. It is old technology."

"And the problem with that is ... ?" She touched his arm.

"The problem is that each qubit requires its own resonant frequency," Dillon said. "So if you want thousands of qubits, you will need thousands of resonant frequencies. But since the nuclei of every molecule have a characteristic set of resonant frequencies in a given magnetic field, this means that you require thousands of species of molecule, and that is impossible."

"Right," Rachel said. "It's a hard problem. I've solved it."

He gave her a probing look.

Rachel felt a shiver run down her frame. She could get lost in those deep, chocolate brown eyes.

"You have solved it?"

"Um ... right. I decided that if you can't bring Mohammed to the mountain, then you should bring the mountain to Mohammed."

For an instant, Dillon's eyes went blank. Completely and totally blank.

Rachel blinked, astonished. What had caused that response?

Grant stepped in. "Say, Rachel, maybe I better explain something to you before you get lost in metaphor-land. Dillon has kind of a special mind. I told you that, right? He thinks different than anybody else. So you need to take care how you talk to him."

Rachel vaguely remembered. She'd been too excited on the way to the meeting this morning to pay much attention. "Uh-huh." She had a sudden urge to turn around and run.

A pained expression crossed Dillon's face. "Grant, Asperger's syndrome is not a disease, and you will please not treat me like a cripple."

Rachel felt her mouth drop open. "Um, what's this all about?"

Dillon's face tightened. "I have a form of autism known as Asperger's syndrome. It is named after Dr. Hans Asperger, an Austrian physician who wrote a paper in 1944 describing—"

"Autism?" Rachel said. "You mean like Dustin Hoffman in *Rain Man?*"

"High-functioning autism," Dillon said. "I do not babble, nor do I slobber, nor do I require institutionalization. I am a contributing member of society with a special kind of brain."

"That is so cool! Can you count cards like in *Rain Man?*" Rachel put her hand on his arm. "Dillon, now I get it! Uncle Grant told me you were one in a million, but I thought he was exaggerating."

Dillon looked pleased. "Every autistic is different. I cannot count cards. That is a rare talent. But I have an unusual ability to concentrate. Like Einstein. Like Newton. Both of whom are thought to have possibly had Asperger's."

Grant put an arm over Dillon's shoulder. "Dillon comes up with some amazing out-of-the-box design solutions. But here's the thing. He tends to take things ultra literally. When you say 'out-of-the-box,' he thinks you're talking about an actual box."

Rachel giggled. She felt terrible for giggling, but ... it was *funny*.

"You saw his face go blank when you trotted out that thing about Mohammed and the mountain?" Grant said.

Rachel nodded. "You're telling me ... he thought I was talking about a real mountain and a real Mohammed?"

Dillon's face colored slightly. "My brain is just wired differently. You may think that I am weird, but in my reference frame, I am being logical and the rest of the world is not."

"I don't think you're weird," Rachel said.

Dillon's face relaxed. "Really?"

"Dillon, you're a stud."

His eyes opened wide.

Rachel giggled. "That's slang, sorry. It means you're ... brilliant. Um, it means you're really, really smart."

Dillon smiled. "Thank you. Now please explain to me how you solved the qubit problem."

"Um ... right." Rachel took a deep cleansing breath and tried to get her mind back on track. Which was practically impossible when what she really wanted to do was just stare at Dillon for a couple of thousand years. If ever a guy deserved to be called *beautiful*—

"Qubits, Rachel. Focus," Grant said.

"I don't do focus," Rachel said. "That's just the way *my* brain is wired. So, anyway, here's what I did. I asked myself why we should worry about making thousands of qubits, all different. Why not make them all the same but change their environment instead?"

"Environment?" Dillon looked puzzled.

"You know," Rachel said. "Embed each qubit in a little cage with slightly different magnetostatic properties. Just a small amount, but enough to change the value of the applied local magnetic field. In MRI, you vary the applied magnetic field spatially and therefore you get out spatial information from the signal. Here, you vary the magnetic field inside each type of cage, and that lets you drive the qubits in each cage independently."

"Oh." Dillon's face lit up. "I see it. It requires a different external frequency to drive each qubit, even though all the qubits are identical."

"Slow down," Clifton said. "I'm not getting this."

Dillon stepped to the whiteboard and wrote down the equation for the resonant frequency in an applied constant magnetic field. Then he added subscripts to each side. Clifton stared at the equation for a few seconds. "Oh yeah. Right. Hey, that's clever."

"How do you change the magnetostatic properties for each cage?" Dillon asked. "That is a difficult nanoconstruction problem."

"Biological cells do nanoconstruction all the time," Rachel said. "It's kind of a long story but the bottom line ... I mean, the summary ... is that I concocted a string of DNA that encodes the pattern for a particular class of proteins that fold themselves into perfect little ferromagnetic cages. I got the idea from rubredoxin, which occurs naturally. This class has millions of degrees of freedom in one particular string of nucleotides, so in principle I could make millions of qubits. I inserted the DNA as an artificial gene into a cell line and forced the cells to express ten thousand different proteins, each in large quantities."

Dillon's face was shining now. "Beautiful. Very, very beautiful."

Rachel felt her pulse speed up. Coming from Dillon Richard, that was quite a compliment.

"Okay, I'm thinking we need to leave you two to work," Grant said. "Dillon, you like what you see?"

Dillon's eyes were looking right at Rachel—or right through her— she couldn't tell which. "Yes."

"Great, then. I want you two to report directly to Clifton. Give him a daily update. If you need anything, ask him." Grant turned to Keryn. "And if they need to spend any money, give it to them. No questions asked."

Keryn's eyes were boring like lasers into Dillon's skull. "Um ... right, Grant." Her face colored, and she turned toward the door. "Right, let's let Rachel and Clifton and Dillon get to work, and I've got a couple of questions for you outside."

Grant went to the door and opened it. "We need to give Clifton a ride back, remember? We all came in my car. Come on, let's go, Clifton. Rachel, when you lock up for the night, take Dillon back to his car at CypherQuanta, okay?"

"Sure thing, Uncle Grant."

Grant put a hand on Keryn's elbow. "Let's be on our way so the geniuses can work."

"Of course." Keryn had a tight look on her face as she went out the door. Clifton followed her out, his long blond ponytail swishing behind him.

Grant threw a last look inside. "Pedal to the metal, Rachel."

"Vroom, vroom," she said. A rush of excitement ran up through her belly. She'd been locked away in this awful place for six long, horrible months, working alone. Finally, *finally*, she had a chance to work with someone. Not just anyone. A brilliant guy who appreciated her work. And just happened to be hotter than your average supernova. The next three weeks were going to be *fun*.

Dillon sat down next to the NMR machine. "Tell me what I need to do. I know very few details about NMR quantum computers."

"All we need to do is drive my bio-computer with this NMR machine," Rachel said. "This is an off-the-shelf component made by MagTec for biological applications. I've tested it on the bio-computer in manual mode, and I verified that my qubits respond to resonant frequencies spaced out roughly every hundred hertz, over a range of a megahertz. The signal is pretty weak, but it's detectable. That gives us ten thousand qubits. The first thing we need to do is write a calibration program to find the exact resonant frequencies. Then we have to implement Shor's algorithm."

"Actually, I believe the first thing I need is the manuals for this machine." Dillon said this in the same tone of voice that a small boy would use to ask to eat his ice cream first.

Rachel hated manuals and would rather eat crushed glass than read one of the horrid things. She found three thick volumes in the box, tore off the shrink-wrapping, and handed them to Dillon.

His eyes lit up. "Thank you." He opened the top manual and began reading the preface.

Rachel slumped into a chair. *Great. What am I going to do while he spends a week plowing through six inches of manuals?*

Keryn

Keryn marched down the steps and sat back against the hood of Grant's Lexus, folding her arms across her chest. "Grant, I think I'd like an explanation about Rachel."

"Hey, she's some kind of chick, isn't she?" Clifton said. "She's got the mondo right brain. Dillon's got the humungofied left brain." He threw a longing glance at the Miata. "Put 'em together, you've got one well-oiled machine."

Grant grinned. "That's about it, Clifton. Between the two of them, they can do anything. *Anything.*"

Keryn wanted to scream, but she didn't see how that would help. "Grant, my real question is how are you going to pay this girl genius? Last time I checked, Caltech grads were pretty pricey. I've been squeezing the jugular of every penny you've got. Didn't we agree to a hiring freeze?"

"Yes, of course." Grant limped past Keryn to the driver's side. He turned to look at her. "Ready to head on back?"

No, I am not. Behind my back, you've gone and signed on a senior-level scientist, and now you want to go on with business as usual? Keryn wished she dared to yell at him, but she just ... couldn't. Instead, she said in a calm and quiet voice, "Really, Grant, I need to know how much you're paying her."

Grant shot an uncomfortable look at Clifton. "Keryn, that's not something I want to—"

"Um, Grant ..." Clifton was looking very interested. "That is a gonzo good question. I don't recall you bringing up a new hire to the board."

Keryn felt her pulse pounding. "More important, you never mentioned her to me, and I'm supposed to be paying the bills. How in the world did you hire her without me knowing? And how much is this costing us that I don't even know about?"

Grant held up both hands. "Peace, okay?" He wiped his sweating forehead on his sleeve. "Keryn, the answer to your first question is that I didn't hire her without telling you. She's been employed by Cypher-Quanta since last December, and you've only been here since March."

"Oh." Keryn felt deflated. "And how much are you paying her?"

Grant pulled out a business card and wrote a number on it.

Keryn stared at it. "You're kidding me. That's way less than I make, and I only work half time. That's less than the going rate for a receptionist. How do you expect her to live on that in San Diego?"

Grant took a deep breath. "That's not her annual salary."

Clifton grabbed the card and stared at it. "You're paying her this much per *month*?" He glared at Grant.

Keryn winced. Unbelievable. If that was her monthly paycheck, Rachel was earning more than Grant and Clifton combined. "Grant, how are you cooking the books to do this? It's not possible to sneak that much money past me."

Grant gave them a shrug. "Keryn. Clifton. Listen to me. We *needed* Rachel. She's brilliant. When I talked to her last December, she was ready to quit her research, give the whole thing up. So I ... took out a loan on my house and put her on the payroll, unofficially. I'm paying her out of my own pocket."

Keryn narrowed her eyes and studied Grant. "You hocked your *house*? You must have been pretty confident."

"No, I was desperate," Grant said. "I've been hearing for months that Lost Angels was looking to break us. Somebody in there hates us, and whoever it is has picked up enough votes now to take us to the cleaners. I had to preempt that."

He stood up to his full height and gave them a defiant look. "Guys, it worked. Rachel broke the whole thing loose. She's hit it big, and we are gonna be the Microsoft of encryption by Christmas. Bigger than Microsoft. Uncle Bill sells his twerpware for a hundred bucks a pop. We sell ours for fifty K, and everybody's gonna need us."

Clifton began pacing back and forth. "Why'd she come to us? If this is so spiff, why didn't she go to IBM? They're deep into quantum computing."

"They're deep in the government's pocket." Grant looked around and then lowered his voice. "Listen, you may have noticed Rachel's a little unconventional."

"She doesn't seem to live with too many restraints," Keryn said.

Grant gave her a puzzled look. "Whatever. She hates Big Brother. If she worked for IBM or any of those other blue-chippers, anything she created would have wound up at the National Security Agency. And we all know the NSA would have taken it black and nobody would ever get to use it and we'd all be stuck with the same crappy encryption we've been using forever. Which I'll remind you, the NSA has probably broken a long time ago. That's the whole point of Cypher-Quanta. We make Big Brother impossible. Even God can't break our encryption, much less the NSA sleazeballs. I explained all that to Rachel and … gave her a decent offer, and she came here. Now it's paying off."

Clifton was pacing back and forth, his eyes on the Miata.

Keryn's stomach felt like lava and she could feel the blood rushing through her temples with every thump of her heart. She wished she had the guts to yell at Grant. Or quit. Or … something. She swallowed her anger. "Grant, you need to keep me apprised of financial matters a little better than that. Okay?" Which was a wimp-out, and she knew it, but she couldn't afford to lose her job right now. Why was she such a wuss?

Clifton stopped pacing and came up beside Keryn. "Ditto that on the technical stuff. Rachel's real spiff, but I should have heard about her six months ago."

Grant's eyes glowed with deep inner pain. "Keryn. Clifton. I see things from your point of view and I'm sorry. I just wanted so *bad* to not lose the shirt off my back. Somebody's trying to wreck my company and I did what I had to do to save it. I kept Rachel secret as a matter of security. It was a gamble, because I didn't know how long it'd take her to grow those qubits. I didn't even know for sure if she *could* do it. If word had gotten out … Lost Angels would have panicked and found some way to pull funding on us and grab the whole pie months ago. As it was, we kept them on board all the way till the end."

Keryn didn't put much stock in conspiracy theories. "Oh, be serious, Grant. What would Lost Angels do with our technology? They're *investors,* not techies. If they stole that technology from us, they'd have to find somebody else to commercialize it. Why wouldn't they work with us?"

"All I know is what I hear," Grant said. "This is from a source I can't reveal, and all I can tell you is that somebody on Lost Angels wants CypherQuanta drilled right through the skull. I don't know who it is, but they want the company dead and they need it to look like a natural death. Even paranoids have enemies, right?"

Keryn shook her head. That was just plain crazy. "You've been reading too many spy novels, Grant."

"Just do me a favor, both of you." Grant's face lost all trace of humor. "We need tight security on this thing until Dillon does his magic and gets that thing working. Clifton, you come over once a day and get a report from them, and give it to me, privately. Keryn, I'll keep you abreast of progress, on a need-to-know basis. But I don't want either one of you talking to anyone else about it, not even the other CypherQuanta employees. Got it?"

"Got it," Clifton said. "Loose lips sink ships. Right, Keryn?"

Keryn nodded. She had just realized something.

Six weeks from now, if this thing worked, CypherQuanta could be huge. Bigger than Microsoft. Bigger than IBM. Bigger than Google. Combined. And her eight thousand shares of CypherQuanta stock would be worth ... lots.

At which point, she could retire. Buy a little cottage by the beach. White picket fence. Drop the day job and write full time. She could live the life every writer wanted, and all she had to do was stay calm and not yell at Grant.

And make sure Dillon and Rachel worked together like a well-oiled machine.

CHAPTER FOUR

Dillon

Dillon finished reading the last manual. He turned to Rachel. She was pacing beside the biology wet bench. When the book snapped shut, her head spun around to stare at him.

"I am finished," Dillon said. "Those were excellent."

Rachel's eyes narrowed. "You've finished skimming through them?"

He shook his head. "I have finished *reading* them. The third one was especially fascinating."

Rachel looked at her watch. "You've only had those horrible things for an hour and ten minutes. What can you learn in seventy minutes?"

"Enough to know how it works and how to drive the hardware. The software has a peculiar interface, and I do not like their naming conventions, but it will be sufficient. Show me your development environment."

Rachel wore a most unusual expression on her face. Dillon found women unreadable at the best of times, but Rachel seemed even more inscrutable than most. She sat down at a Dell workstation and double-clicked on an icon. "I've installed Visual C++ for you. Grant told me that's what you use."

The familiar user interface popped up on the screen. Dillon took ten minutes customizing the environment to his satisfaction. Then he closed the program. "Excellent. Now I need to set up the source control package."

Rachel waved her hand in the air. "I never use source control. It's a waste of time."

Dillon held out his hand. "We need it. Hand me the CD, please."

"I don't have a CD. Relax. We don't need it."

He gave a deep sigh. "Do you drive without insurance on your car?"

"It's not the same thing."

"Rational people insure their cars. Rational programmers use source control."

"There's only the two of us, and we'll be working together on this. We don't need it."

Dillon stood up and went to the door.

Rachel's mouth gaped open. "Where are you going?"

"We are going back to CypherQuanta in your car to get the installer CD for SourceSafe."

Rachel muttered something under her breath and followed him outside. She showed him how to set the alarm on the outside door.

Dillon climbed into the passenger side of her car. He had never ridden in a convertible, and he felt … exposed. Naked. He carefully fastened the seat belt.

Rachel hopped in and punched in a combination on a keypad. The engine started. She looked at him and grinned. "Ever ridden in a Miata?"

He pointed at her chest. "You forgot something."

She gave him an offended look. "That's hardly any of your business."

Dillon could not imagine what she was talking about. "It is illegal to drive in California without a seat belt."

"Oh … that." Rachel grabbed the belt and buckled it.

Dillon took sunglasses out of his shirt pocket and put them on.

Rachel put the car in reverse and squealed backward out of the space.

Dillon jammed his foot against the floorboard.

Rachel braked hard, shifted into first, and roared forward. A minute later they were on Miramar Road, speeding west. The speedometer needle sprang past eighty. The wind roared in Dillon's ears.

He held his sunglasses in place with one hand and clutched his seat with the other.

"Like the car?" Rachel shrieked. Her face shone with glee.

Dillon hated it. The car would be completely unsafe in a rollover, and that was not at all improbable, considering the reckless driving style Rachel was using. "Slow down!" he shouted.

"What?" Rachel downshifted into third and veered onto the on-ramp to Highway 805.

"Slow down!" Dillon shouted again.

She shook her head. "Can't hear you!" She punched the gas and the wind rose to a roar.

Dillon gritted his teeth and held on.

Rachel flitted left and passed a couple of trucks and a minivan, then slid across two lanes of traffic and onto the Sorrento Valley Road exit. She downshifted smoothly to the corner and zipped through a right turn without stopping for the red light. She did the same at the next light.

Dillon promised himself he would never, ever ride in a car driven by Rachel Meyers again. This was beyond reckless. This was foolhardy.

Rachel accelerated under the 805 overpass and flitted into the left lane, skidding through a left turn in front of the nose of an oncoming Mercedes. She raced down a steep slope, veered left, roared forward, and shrieked to a stop in front of Suite A. She put the gearshift in neutral and left the engine running. "Run on in and get the CD. I'll wait for you out here."

Dillon unlatched his seat belt and climbed out. His heart was hammering on his ribs. It was fortunate to learn on such a short trip that Rachel drove like a maniac. He would not make the same mistake again.

After getting the SourceSafe CD from his desk in CypherQuanta, Dillon walked out the back door and across the bridge to his parking spot. Slot number 314—his favorite—the first three digits of the number pi. He unlocked his Toyota Sienna and buckled himself in, feeling very safe. Minivans had poor gas mileage, but they had an excellent safety record, especially if the driver was cautious. He drove out of the lot and around the building, waving to Rachel to follow him.

Her mouth opened in a big O.

In his rearview mirror, Dillon watched her squeal around in a tight U-turn and follow him out. He climbed the hill to Sorrento Valley Road.

Rachel roared past him and skittered through a right turn at the stop sign without slowing. By the time Dillon stopped and checked traffic on his left, Rachel's car was disappearing onto the 805 on-ramp.

Ten minutes later, Dillon arrived at the bio-lab.

Rachel was leaning back in her seat, her eyes closed, the sun beating down on her.

For an instant, Dillon felt like he had in high school, when he had been forced to work in chemistry lab with a vivacious cheerleader. Blonde, with blue eyes, and ... Dillon felt his cheeks warming ... she sometimes failed to wear a bra. In the lab, she smiled at him and talked incessantly about what a genius he was, and she sometimes brushed up against him in a way that made his brain stop functioning correctly. Her knowledge of chemistry was minuscule, but both of them received an A+ each semester for their lab work. Later, Dillon learned that among her friends, she referred to him as "the social retard from hell."

Dillon's stomach felt like ice water.

Rachel yawned. "Give me another five minutes and then we'll get to work, big guy."

"Excessive exposure to the sun causes skin cancer."

"Too late. I've been waiting forever. Your car drives like a tank."

"Besides its excellent safety record, minivans are rarely stolen."

"I can't imagine why."

Dillon was not sure how to interpret this cryptic remark, but he let it pass. Normals often made illogical comments. It was not important. He unlatched Rachel's door and held it open for her.

"Um, thanks." She gave him another strange look as she got out. "Okay, let's see if you remember how to unlock the lab."

"You forgot to secure your car."

Rachel rolled her eyes and leaned in to punch a number on the keypad.

Dillon did not mean to spy on her, but he inadvertently saw her combination. "Rachel, that is insecure. You are using the same combination for both your car and the lab."

She stood up and an amused smile covered her face. "So litigate me."

Of course this made no sense at all, since Dillon was not a lawyer, but she was smiling, so he smiled back. If someone was smiling, it was best to assume their meaning was friendly, even if it was incoherent. But you should always remember that sometimes a smile was a cover for secret scorn. Normals could not be trusted. He went back up the stairs, punched in the combination, and stepped inside.

Rachel followed him in. "So how long will it take to install SourceSafe?"

He shrugged and pointed at the desk. "Your desk is a mess. It will take less than an hour to clean it, and by then the software will be installed."

Rachel's eyes went wide.

Dillon could not begin to parse what that might mean. He spent the next half hour installing SourceSafe. When he came back out to find Rachel, her desk was still covered with papers and she was lounging in her chair with her feet on the desk, reading a magazine called *Cosmopolitan*. Dillon had seen this magazine at the supermarket, but it had never occurred to him that an intelligent woman would read such a thing. The cover had a picture of a blond woman in a red dress with a plunging neckline.

"All done?" Rachel tossed the magazine on top of the stack. "Okay, let's get to work."

Dillon picked up a plastic garbage bag and emptied the overflowing wastebasket into it. He tied the bag and took it outside to the dumpster in the side alley. When he went back inside, Rachel was sitting in a chair in front of the computer.

Dillon went to the whiteboard. "What can I erase?"

She blinked twice. "Nothing. Everything on that board is important."

"We need to design the software."

Rachel shrugged. "So design. Have a seat here and let's write some code."

Dillon opened his briefcase and pulled out a white pad of paper. "Writing code is not designing."

"Dillon, we're in a hurry, okay? Let's just skip the anal-retentive stuff and get to work. You've already wasted an hour installing a safety net we don't need. I want to see some code."

Dillon sat down beside her and took the cap off his Uni-ball pen. "The first thing we will design is the class hierarchy for our computational engine. What representation would you recommend for the qubit? Personally, I prefer the—"

"Dillon!"

Dillon looked up at her, astonished. She sounded angry. She looked angry. He could not understand why. If anyone should be angry, it should be him. Rachel had failed to adequately prepare the development environment, causing them to lose an hour. Now she was obstructing work on the analysis and design of the system.

"Put that paper away and let's write code," Rachel said. "Uncle Grant wants us to get this thing done as fast as possible."

Dillon sighed and leaned back in his chair. "Do you speak French?"

She stared at him with a look that told Dillon she thought he was an idiot. "What does that have to do with anything?"

"If you go to France and you do not speak French, what should you do?"

She sighed dramatically. "Speak English and hope somebody understands me, I guess."

"Wrong." Dillon had not expected her to be correct. "You take along someone who speaks French."

Rachel stuck out her tongue at him.

Dillon had no idea what this might mean. It was not logical, and therefore it was a waste of time to try to decipher her behavior. "Grant must have told you that I write software quickly. I know what I am doing and you do not. If you knew what you were doing, you would not need me. Please let me do my job."

"Okay, so *do* your job."

Dillon smiled. Excellent. She was going to cooperate. Sometimes people refused to cooperate, and then he could not work with them. This partnership was going to work out extremely well.

Unless ...

~

Clifton

Clifton sat on the beach at La Jolla Shores staring out at the waves. He could not believe how much Grant was paying Rachel. The chick was sharp, for sure, but Clifton was no dummy. It was his intellectual property that CypherQuanta was built on. His Ph.D. thesis they'd used ever since they founded the company. He was CTO. He owned six percent of the company, and he held stock options on another four and a half.

All of which would never pay off unless Rachel and the Dillon Dude got that thing to work. Meanwhile, somebody was trying to cut off CypherQuanta at the knees. Bogus, man!

Three girls in bikinis walked by in front of Clifton. He followed them with his eyes for a minute, until they left his field of view. It was just ... biff, the way Grant was paying Rachel so much. *And* she was getting stock options too. Clifton didn't mind that she got options. Everybody in a startup company got options, even the janitor. But those options would be toilet paper if the company went under.

Whereas cash in the hand was good, CypherQuanta or no CypherQuanta.

Clifton took out his cell phone and flipped it open. He pulled up the list of calls recently received and studied the top number for several minutes. Finally he pressed the Dial button and put the phone to his ear. It rang twice and then ...

"Ted Hunter."

Clifton cleared his throat. "Yeah, hey, Ted. This is Clifton Potter. You called me this morning."

"Oh, hey, Clifton! Great to hear from you! Are you interested after all in having me look around for you?"

"Um ... maybe. Just ..." Clifton swallowed hard. "Just be real discreet, okay?"

"I understand," Ted said. "That's my job, to be discreet. I'll need a little bit of information to get started. You're working for ... remind me?"

"CypherQuanta."

"I'm not familiar with it. You do what exactly?"

"Quantum encryption. My expertise is lasers. I've got a Ph.D. in laser physics from UCSD and six years' experience."

"Okay, sounds great. What's your job title there at CypherQuanta?"

"CTO."

A long pause. "I see. How big is the company?"

"It's a startup." Clifton tried to remember how many people were on staff. "I think we're down to forty-five FTEs. We've had a few financial problems lately and a couple of our engineers left to work for Cymer."

"Right. That happens. Listen, it may take a while to find something at your pay scale. May I ask what you're earning?"

Clifton told him.

Another long pause. "That's not bad in this economy. Ya know, if things keep ramping up in the county, it's not out of the question that you could get something better, but it may take a few months. Are you in any particular hurry?"

"Huh-uh." That was a lie, but Clifton didn't want to sound desperate. Besides, he was just checking. "Look, it's not that big a deal, okay? You just got me thinking this morning when you called and ... you know, I'm mainly just curious. Not a big deal."

"Gotcha, buddy." The sound of writing. "Listen, I'll check around, and you can rest assured that I'll keep it discreet until there's something definite. Now, maybe you can do me a favor?"

"Sure, if I can."

"Are you guys publicly traded there at, um, CypherQuanta?"

"Not yet." Clifton shrugged. "We were hoping for an IPO in the next couple years, but you know what the climate's like lately."

"Chilly." Hunter laughed. "Things'll get better. Reason I ask, by the way, is I'm always looking for new companies. I invest a little on the side, but ... if you're not on the Nasdaq ..."

Clifton snorted. "You want some stock? I can let you have some of mine."

"That bad, huh?"

"Um ... forget I said that, okay?"

"Right. Look, it's my job to keep things between my ears, so don't worry. I'll be discreet on that. Look, I'll put out some feelers and be in touch if anything comes up, all right?"

"Right." Clifton felt a queasy feeling deep in his gut. He hadn't worked for anyone but Grant since grad school. And he hoped he wouldn't have to jump ship, but it was always a good idea to keep your options open.

"Oh, one more question," Hunter said. "Can I call you in the daytime? I mean, will it compromise you if I call you at work on your cell phone?"

"I'm in a cubicle," Clifton said. "If you call, I'll just go out in the parking lot and we can talk. Everybody does that. Reception in the building is really biff."

"You're good with that? I don't want to do anything to damage your relationships there."

"I'm good."

"Great. Listen, Clifton, it's been a pleasure talking to you, and I hope I can help you like I did your buddy Kendall."

"Me too," Clifton said. "Catch ya later." He closed his phone and stared out at the waves. His gut felt cold and empty. It was just bogus, thinking about working somewhere else. He'd been loyal to Grant for a long time.

And Grant was paying Rachel Meyers twice what he was paying Clifton. Was that fair? No, it was not.

It was not fair at all.

CHAPTER FIVE

Rachel

A dozen sheets of white paper lay in Rachel's lap. Dillon was working on the thirteenth, his tongue just poking out of his mouth in concentration.

Rachel had seen a movie once that freaked her out. *Amadeus.* One scene in particular she could not get out of her mind. Mozart stood hunched over a pool table writing music. He would take the cue ball, idly send it rolling against one of the cushions, pick up his quill pen, and write a measure of music. As he wrote the notes, the cue ball bounced off each of the four cushions in turn. As he set down the pen and opened his hand, the cue ball came rolling back perfectly into his fingers. Mozart caught it, then sent it on the next circuit while he wrote the next measure.

Mozart was amazing, a genius, a prodigy, a ... machine.

Dillon Richard designed software like Mozart wrote music. Rachel could not believe what she was seeing. In a couple of hours Dillon had discussed a complete computational architecture with her, suggested several options, analyzed them for space and time efficiency, made his trade-off decisions, and begun producing a design document.

It was poetry and art and music, and there was nobody to appreciate it but Rachel. It was like watching Mozart compose a symphony that only she would ever hear.

Dillon finished the sheet of paper and tore it off. He handed it to her. "That should finish it. Do you have a stapler?"

Rachel went and rummaged around on her desk for several minutes. Finally, she found her stapler. It was out of staples. She yanked open several drawers. At the bottom of the third one, she found a box and refilled the stapler. She pushed the stack of pages into the stapler, then thought better of it. A work of art was a work of art. She straightened all the edges so they were exactly even, then stapled the document.

When she got back into the bio-lab, Dillon had pulled his chair up to the computer and created a Visual C++ workspace.

"Hey, Dillon, you forgot one thing."

He turned to look at her, his eyes two question marks.

She giggled and held out the design document. "You need to sign this."

"Sign it?" Dillon looked at the top page, his face mystified. "I have put our names and the date on the top of every page."

"Dillon, this is a masterpiece. Every artist should sign his work."

Dillon smiled—an innocent puppy-dog smile that made Rachel's brain melt. "Do you ... like it?"

"It's gorgeous." She pressed it into his hands. "Go on. Sign it."

Dillon uncapped the pen and signed his name at the bottom. His signature was square and precise, without frills or flourishes.

Rachel sat down in the other chair. "Hey, um, I'm sorry about ragging on you about SourceSafe. You're really good and really fast and ... I guess I'm learning a lot just watching you."

He smiled again. "Understood. Shall we begin coding?"

"Rock and roll, big guy."

Dillon gave her a completely blank look.

"I mean go ahead." Rachel suppressed a smile. Dillon had a different kind of brain. If there were some things he didn't get, well ... there were some things at which he was master of the universe.

Dillon reached into his pocket and pulled out his keys. Clipped to the key ring was a small USB flash drive. He inserted it into the USB port on the computer and waited for it to mount.

Rachel leaned forward. "What have you got there?"

"A few libraries I wrote," Dillon said. "Also some software templates for C++ classes." He dragged several folders onto the hard drive of the Dell and unmounted the flash drive.

Rachel stared at the screen, fascinated. "But ... Visual C++ already has class templates built in. It's got a wizard to write a skeleton of your classes for you."

Dillon returned to Visual C++ and opened one of his template files.

Rachel gasped. The file looked like poetry. She suddenly realized that the auto-generated class files of Visual C++ were unbearably ugly. "That's ..."

"Better?" Dillon looked at her.

"Yeah." Rachel looked into his eyes. There was depth in those eyes. And pain. She read the hurts laid on him by a thousand people who never saw beyond his pocket-protector geekiness to the soul of the artist that lived inside him. An artist who worked in for-loops and access functions and class hierarchy diagrams.

Dillon's ears turned red, and his eyes dropped to the design document. "I had better ... start coding."

Rachel felt flustered. Had she embarrassed him? She hadn't meant to, but ... it was a nice feeling looking into his deep brown eyes. She stood up. "Hey, I just realized my desk is kind of a mess. Maybe I'll, you know, clean it up a little."

Dillon nodded without looking at her. He began typing rapidly into the document he had opened. Mozart was back at work.

Rachel backed away to the door and pulled it open. She turned around and looked at her desk and suddenly felt ashamed. Dillon must think she was a pig. She stared at the enormous stack of papers. Revulsion swept through her. And panic. How in the world was she ever going to clear away this mess?

She swore at the stack and then opened the file cabinet. Dozens of empty folders sat there. Rachel took a deep breath. It didn't have to be perfect. Anything would be better than this. She grabbed a handful of papers. Dr. Chuang's reports on his implementation of Shor's algorithm in seven qubits.

Rachel straightened the papers into a neat pile and shoved them into a file folder.

~

Rachel

Two hours later, the desk was clear. It was a typical metal office desk. She hadn't seen its Formica surface since last January. It looked naked. Rachel felt a little lost. She liked clutter. Chaos was a good thing, wasn't it? The clean desk made her feel so linear and straight-edged and geeky, she wanted to shriek. She plopped into her chair and put her head in her hands. What was she trying to do anyway? Play Salieri to Dillon's Mozart?

Her cell phone rang.

It was an unknown caller. She flipped open the phone. "Hello?"

A slight pause. "Um, hi, this is Keryn Wills. Grant gave me your number. I just thought I'd, you know, check in on you two, see what's happening. How are you getting along? I mean, um, are you making progress?"

Keryn's voice sounded a little higher than normal. Rachel leaned back in her chair. "We're doing great. Dillon is just a *machine* at writing software. He read the manual in, like, an hour, and then he came up with this design that ... well, you wouldn't understand, but it's, like, brilliant. I mean, it's not like there's anything new there. Just qubit representations and hardware drivers and some high-level algorithms. But ... it's hard to explain...." Rachel let her voice trail off. Keryn wasn't a techie. There was no way to explain. It was like Einstein's equations. If you didn't know tensor calculus, Einstein didn't make any sense. But if you knew it, then looking at those equations was like looking at Michelangelo's David.

"Hey, sounds great," Keryn said. "Listen, it's getting on toward suppertime, and Grant wanted me to make sure everything's, you know, going smooth and make sure you guys don't work your fingers to the bone, so I was thinking maybe I could bring some pizza over so you won't forget to eat."

Rachel closed her eyes. Pizza sounded great. Keryn sounded uptight about something, but maybe she was just strung tight. She had struck Rachel as kind of a nervy woman today when they'd met. "Actually, I'm getting hungry and pizza would be awesome. I'm a vegetarian, and I like any kind of veggies. Shall I ask Dillon what he likes?"

Keryn laughed. "Dillon likes pepperoni and pineapple. It's kind of a company joke. He always wants the same thing. He's ... predictable, you know."

"I think it's kind of cute."

A moment of silence. "Um, right, then. I'll call in the order and pick it up on the way over. You want a soda or something?"

"Diet Coke," Rachel said. "Should I ask Dillon—"

"V-8," Keryn said. "It's very nutritious. See you guys in a while."

The line went dead.

Rachel sat staring at her phone for a moment, wondering why Keryn was in such a hurry. Whatever. She folded her phone and put it away, then slipped into the bio-lab.

Dillon sat just as she'd left him. She could hear him talking softly. He was dictating C++ to himself and typing it in as he spoke.

Rachel sneaked up behind him and listened.

Dillon's quiet voice muttered on.

Rachel stood there silently watching him. A feeling of awe settled over her. The bio-lab felt like a cathedral, with Dillon whispering his secret incantations that would turn a string of characters into a program that could tap the power of a zillion universes. It was kind of like one of those Catholic priests who believed he could turn bread and wine into the body and blood of Jesus. Rachel couldn't understand why anyone believed such nonsense. She had figured out that religion was a crock when she was twelve years old.

If you wanted to believe in something bigger than yourself, all you had to do was look around at the universe. You'd see Einstein's God. Truth. Beauty. Order.

Religion was for morons.

Keryn

Keryn pulled up in the parking lot next to Dillon's minivan. Something funny was going on. When they had all come here earlier in Grant's Lexus, Dillon had left his minivan back at CypherQuanta. So how had it gotten over here? Keryn climbed out of her car, set the pizza on the roof, and called Rachel.

She answered on the second ring. "Is that you, Keryn?"

"Hey, Rachel. Yeah, it's me. I'm outside and I don't have the combination. Can you let me in?"

"I'll be right out." Rachel hung up. A minute later the door swung inward and Rachel bounded down the steps. She gave Keryn a golden-girl smile. "Thanks for doing this, Keryn. That's awfully nice of you."

Keryn handed her the pizza box. "Grant's orders. Got to make sure you two don't starve to death. I'll get the drinks and lock my car."

Rachel grinned. "That's right, Hondas are one of the most commonly stolen cars in the county."

"Um ... yeah, I've heard." Keryn went back to her car and got two takeout cups and a pop-top can of V-8. She hurried up the stairs and into the lab and ...

Keryn stared at the clean desk. "Wow, what happened?"

Rachel opened the box and a puff of steam came smoke-signaling off the pizza. "Oh, I just, you know, got ambitious this afternoon. Dillon was writing code and ..." She waved her hand at the desk. "I just cleared out a little of the mess. Filed it away."

Keryn set the drinks down. "Good idea." All of a sudden, she felt less hungry. She looked at the door of the bio-lab. "Shouldn't we take the pizza in to Dillon? When he gets coding, he forgets to eat."

Rachel shook her head. "Can't. I culture live cells in there. They're harmless, but it's just a bad idea to take food into a bio-lab. I always eat out here. We'll have to bring Mohammed to the mountain." She went into the lab.

Keryn followed her.

Dillon sat at the computer, typing out code in a perfect rhythm.

Rachel went up and touched his arm. "Hey, Maestro! It's chow time. Keryn brought us some food."

Dillon turned around and looked up at them. As always when he came out of his private universe, he looked lost for a moment, as if wondering which Narnian world he had fallen into. Then his eyes focused on them. "Thank you, Keryn. Rachel and I are making excellent progress. We read the manuals and then we worked out a design."

"Oh," Keryn said. "That's great. Really great." She took a deep breath. "Are you hungry?"

Dillon looked at his watch. "It is already six-thirty. Yes, I am hungry."

Keryn wondered if he really needed to know the time before he decided if he was hungry. Rachel didn't wear a watch, and it was a good bet that she just ate when she felt like it. Way different from Dillon. Totally different.

They went back into the outer office. Rachel and Dillon rolled their chairs along with them. Keryn sat in the chair at the desk. Her head felt dizzy, disoriented. This was Rachel's territory, not hers. She grabbed a handful of napkins and handed them to Rachel and Dillon. "Sorry, I couldn't get any paper plates. We'll have to rough it."

Rachel peeled up a long strip of pizza. "Ooh, this looks good! Thanks for bringing this, Keryn."

Dillon took his can of V-8 and shook it exactly eight times, then popped it open and took a long drink.

Keryn took a long pull on her Coke and grabbed a slice of pizza. She felt like an intruder here, but Grant had specifically asked her to make sure Rachel and Dillon got fed, so she was just doing her job.

As they ate, Rachel told them her life story. Her father was a physics professor at Rutgers. Grant O'Connell was a longtime family friend whom she'd known ever since she could remember. For all she knew, Grant really had changed a few of her diapers, as he claimed. She graduated from high school a couple of years early and started at MIT when she was sixteen. Majored in biophysics, but earned enough credits that she could have gotten a degree in either biology or physics. After finishing her undergraduate work at MIT, she went to Caltech, where she'd worked on protein-folding problems, and got her Ph.D. in four years. Then she'd continued on there in a postdoc appointment and discovered a special class of proteins with interesting physical properties.

"And you did not publish it?" Dillon said.

Rachel shook her head, and her silky hair swished her shoulders. "I knew Big Brother was going to want it and Big Brother never shares his toys."

"Big Brother? You mean as in *1984*?" Dillon looked skeptical. "The governing authorities?"

"The clowns running Guantanamo Bay." Rachel wiped her mouth and slurped up the dregs of her Diet Coke. "Another few years, Big Brother is going to take quantum computing black and—"

"Black?" Dillon took a long drink of his V-8. "This is a figure of speech?"

"It means they're going to classify it and we won't have access to it," Rachel said. "The National Security Agency employs more mathematicians than anybody else in the world, and none of them publish. It's all classified, hush-hush stuff."

"They need to," Dillon said. "The NSA handles the federal government's requirements for encrypting sensitive data and decrypting the ciphers of other governments."

Rachel leaned back in her chair. "It doesn't bother you that they have a budget of, like, billions of dollars a year? You don't get a little steamed that for decades the Feds denied the NSA even existed? The joke was that the initials stood for No Such Agency. The exact budget is still classified and they don't allow visitors. The place is a black hole, and I'll roast in hell before I let my research go to Big Brother."

"So you came to work for Grant," Keryn said.

Rachel nodded. "Uncle Grant hates the NSA as much as I do. That's what CypherQuanta is all about—putting encryption in the hands of the people. Encryption means privacy. And it happens to be a theorem of quantum mechanics that Big Brother can't break our quantum encryption."

"What about conventional encryption?" Keryn asked. "Big Brother can't break that either, can they? Didn't someone in the government try to keep people from getting access to that? There was a big court case years ago."

"They took Phillip Zimmermann to court," Dillon said. "He created software that he called PGP—Pretty Good Privacy—that made it easy for anyone to use RSA encryption. The government opposed it because it lets criminals protect their data from the government."

Rachel scowled. "That's completely a smoke screen. A lot of cypherpunks think the NSA has an efficient way to factor large numbers. I betcha the Feds just made a big noise to lull people into thinking PGP is safe to use. In reality, they probably cracked it years ago and they're laughing up their sleeves about our Pretty Bad Privacy."

"But ... if your machine works, you'll be able to crack PGP too." Keryn had a queasy feeling in her stomach about that.

Rachel smiled. "If my machine works, everyone will *know* I can crack RSA, and nobody'll trust PGP or any flavor of RSA encryption ever again. That'll blow the cover off the NSA's smoke screen."

"And at the same time it'll make CypherQuanta a pile of money," Keryn said.

Rachel shrugged. "Money is beside the point. Money is nothing if you don't have freedom. And freedom can't happen if you don't have privacy. That'll be my gift to humanity. Privacy forever."

Keryn wiped her hands on a napkin. "I guess that's the sixty-four-billion-dollar question, then. Is your machine going to work? Dillon, what do you think?"

Dillon gave Rachel a look of unrestrained admiration. "The construction of the qubits is pure genius. There are going to be some problems writing the software, but—"

"But nothing." Rachel leaned back in her chair and locked her hands behind her head. "I can't believe how fast Dillon writes code. He'll have the drivers done in a few days. Keryn, it's like a work of art. I just wish you understood C++. You'd ... " She shrugged helplessly. "Sorry. It's like a sonnet. You either know how to appreciate it or you don't."

And I don't. Keryn felt cold. She was on the outside looking in, while these two geniuses got to huddle together, the Dream Team of CypherQuanta. Great. Wonderful. *Spiff,* as Clifton Potter would say.

"Well, hey, I'm keeping Dillon from working." Keryn slapped both hands on the desktop. "I better head on home." She folded up the pizza box and stuffed it in the trash can, then went into the bathroom. The toilet stank and a line of mold ran down the wall from the sink. Gagging, Keryn washed her hands and then came out. "Say, Rachel, have you got any cleaning supplies? That room is *disgusting.*"

Dillon's eyebrows raised. "Really? That is extremely unhealthful."

Rachel stood up, and her cheeks pinked. "You go ahead and write code, Dillon. Thanks for pointing that out, Keryn. I'll take care of it." Her eyes were lasering holes in Keryn's brain.

Dillon went into the bathroom and stepped back, alarm scrawled across his face. "That is definitely a health hazard."

Keryn headed for the door. "Want me to go pick up some cleaning supplies at Ralph's? They've got the best prices—"

"I said I'll take *care* of it." Rachel took Dillon's arm and guided him back to the bio-lab. "You keep writing code. I'll take care of the cleaning. See you Monday, Keryn, and thanks for catering supper for us drudges."

Keryn slipped outside, but not before she caught a look of silent fury in Rachel's eyes.

Fine, let her be furious. Rachel was all wrong for Dillon. All wrong. The two of them were total opposites. The sooner Rachel figured that out and got over it, the better.

CHAPTER SIX

Dillon

D illon sat down at the keyboard and picked up his design documents. It took a moment to remember where he had been before eating. He had finished the pure virtual interface class for the NMR driver. The next part would take more effort. He needed to write an abstract class to do a partial implementation. He had been thinking about the autocalibration function while he ate the pizza, and he thought he had worked out the main algorithm. Of course there would be some low-level details specific to the MagTec NMR machine, but he intended to wrapper those in a concrete subclass so it would be simple to use a machine from a different manufacturer if CypherQuanta decided to change vendors. Then he would only need to write one new concrete subclass and his code would work with the new device.

If manufacturers were intelligent, they would all use the same standard interface for their machines. But they were not intelligent. In the name of competition, they insisted on each creating a different and incompatible interface. They could make life easier for all their users if they would cooperate, but they would never do that.

Dillon took a moment to add some comments to his design document to sketch out the algorithm. Then he began typing. It felt relaxing and soothing to be writing code. He had not felt relaxed or soothed while he was eating, and this puzzled him. Dillon found it pleasant to be around Keryn. And around Rachel also. Yet eating with both together had not been nearly as pleasant as he had expected, and he could not think why.

Last night had been a wonderful evening. Keryn had invited him to dinner and a play in La Jolla. Dillon liked Keryn very much. The books she wrote were smart, logical mysteries that made Dillon think. And she reminded him of his favorite comic strip character.

On the advice of his counselor, Dillon regularly read all the comic strips in the newspaper. It was supposed to help him learn the slang and double meanings most people understood so easily. Dillon's favorite character was Sally Forth. Sally was a likeable woman, honest, good, humorous, intelligent. Keryn was like Sally, and she had a quiet way of speaking that made Dillon feel at home. She had treated Dillon well ever since he met her, and that was not usual for a female.

Dillon had three brothers, all Normals, and they had treated Dillon extremely badly when he was growing up. But his brothers were saints in comparison to the girls he had known in school. Dillon had only bad memories from high school.

But Keryn was different from most females he had known. Keryn did not mind that he was not a Normal. Keryn was a kind person, and her eyes made Dillon feel warm inside. She asked his opinion about things and then listened. He hoped they could have many interesting conversations together.

Whereas Rachel was something entirely different, and Dillon did not know how to think about her. She ... excited him, and she terrified him, both at the same time. It was like quantum mechanics, in which a qubit could represent both 0 and 1 simultaneously.

In Dillon's experience, a woman who talked and dressed and acted like Rachel was what Clifton called an airhead. Dillon did not know why such women were called airheads, but he knew that they despised him because he was not a Normal. Yet clearly, Rachel was not an airhead. She did not treat him like a fool. She was interested in his ideas.

Furthermore, Rachel was brilliant. Her solution to the qubit construction problem was clever and profound. How could that be, in a woman so undisciplined, so chaotic? A childish woman who drove like a maniac and lacked the sense to clean the toilet? She was deeply disturbing to everything Dillon believed in. She was chaos to his order. Working with her was like mixing fire and ice.

But whenever she touched his arm, Dillon felt something hot rush through his heart. He did not understand this, but he felt sure it had an excellent biochemical explanation. He would ask his friend Robert about it the next time they talked on the phone.

A hand settled on his shoulder.

Dillon felt an electric jolt through his body. He did his best to show no reaction. It would be highly inappropriate to react. Highly inappropriate.

"How are you coming along, Dillon?" Rachel took her hand off his shoulder. Its absence felt like the vacuum of deep space.

Dillon took a deep breath and tried to calm his heart. He pointed to the monitor. "I have written most of the autocalibration routine in terms of pure virtual functions that we will implement in the concrete subclasses. When that is—"

"What's this?" Rachel pointed at a line. "You misspelled a word in your comment!"

Dillon felt his ears getting hot. He had spelled "magnetic" as "mangetic." He double-clicked on the offending word and retyped it. "I am very sorry."

Rachel looked down at him and giggled. "It's okay, you know. Nobody's perfect. Anyway the compiler won't care because it's in a comment."

"But I care," Dillon said.

Rachel sat down and flashed him a smile. "That's what I like about you. You *care*. That's really awesome, you know that?"

Dillon felt like a piece of ball lightning had gotten stuck inside his chest.

Rachel leaned back in her chair and locked her hands behind her head. "Most people are such ... muggles."

"Muggles?" Dillon had never heard this word.

Rachel shrugged. "You know ... they're so boring, so ... *normal*."

Dillon's heart double-thumped. "You make being Normal sound bad."

"It *is* bad," Rachel said. "It's horrible. I'd hate to be normal."

Dillon did not know what to say, but he liked the way Rachel's soft green eyes were looking at him. Finally, he said, "I am very not-Normal."

She leaned forward and slapped his knee. "You're a stud, Dillon."

Dillon's whole leg felt like it was full of molten metal.

Rachel stood up. "Well, hey, time for you to take a work break. How many lines have you written?"

Dillon opened up his line-counter program and checked his work. "Over three thousand." Had they not lost an hour fetching the Source-Safe program, it would have been over four thousand, but Dillon did not want to say so.

"Rock and roll, big guy."

Dillon smiled and looked down at his design document. After a brief recalibration of his mind, he began typing again. But now he found it much harder to concentrate. *Rock and roll*.

Being around Rachel did something to his mind that he did not understand. Dillon desperately wished that this phenomenon would go away. And he desperately hoped that it would not.

Rachel

R achel would have been happy to sit and watch Dillon write code forever, but at precisely 10:00 p.m. he pulled out his flash drive and inserted it into the USB port on the computer. "All done for the night?" she asked.

He nodded. "I am making a backup, and then we can go home. We have almost five thousand lines. At this rate, we should be ready for testing in a week."

"A week?" Rachel felt a huge weight lift off her heart. "That's incredible." She opened her fanny pack and took out the vial containing the bio-computer. "I'll just put this in the safe. Come here and watch this. You need to know the combination. It'll reduce my truck factor."

"Truck factor?" Dillon joined her at the safe.

She gave him a sly grin. "Sorry. That's my private slang. It means the risk to the company if I get hit by a truck."

"If you drove a safer car, you could reduce that factor substantially."

"I'm sure you're right." Rachel dialed in the combination and put the bio-computer in the safe. "Did you catch all the numbers?"

"It is the same as the combination for the keypad outside." Dillon sounded disappointed. "That is a security risk. If somebody can break into one, then they can break into the other."

Rachel flipped the door of the safe shut and spun the dial. "If I used a different security code for everything, I'd have to write them all down, and that would be an even bigger risk."

"Why not just remember them all?"

"Did you encrypt the information on your flash drive?" Rachel didn't want to argue, so she figured the best defense was a good offense.

"Of course."

Rachel shrugged. "Well, whatever. Listen, you're good at that kind of thing. I'm not. So I'm just going to do things the way that works for me, and you do what works for you. Deal?" She stuck out her hand.

Dillon shook it. His hand felt strong and warm. "Deal."

"Great." Rachel looked at her watch. "It's still early. Go home and get a good night's sleep and let's try to get in early tomorrow. What time works for you?"

Dillon gave her an indecipherable look. "Tomorrow is Sunday."

Rachel wondered what that had to do with anything. "Listen, Grant's in a real panic over all this. I'm sure he'll give us some comp time when we get this baby in the bank, but right now we need to work every spare minute till it's done."

Dillon looked offended. "I am not objecting to working extra hours."

Rachel saw that she'd hit a nerve, but she had no idea what it was. "Then what are you objecting to?"

"Sunday is the Lord's Day. I do not work on the Lord's Day."

Omigosh, a religious kook. Rachel felt sick to her stomach. She ought to have seen this coming. Uncle Grant had said something about Dillon and she had blown it off. "You don't work on Sunday even in an emergency?"

Dillon sighed. "Do you change your oil every three thousand miles —even in an emergency?"

Rachel gave a nervous titter. "Now that you mention it, I think I haven't changed the oil on my Miata at all."

"If you change your oil on the recommended schedule, your car will last forever. If you give yourself a break on the Lord's Day, your soul will last forever."

Oh, crap, he was really serious about this. A whole flood of emotions cut through Rachel. Pain. Rejection. Hate. Rage. It shocked her. She wanted so much to be over all that. Fat chance. She had been born right smack in the middle of a religious fault line that was two thousand years old. How was anybody supposed to get over that?

Dillon was still looking at her, and there was concern in those chocolate brown eyes of his. "Are you all right?"

"I'm ..." Rachel wanted to say she was fine, but that would be a big fat lie. And somehow she didn't want to lie to Dillon. She sat down in a chair. The polite thing to do was just to let it drop. Nice people didn't talk about religion. But Rachel had been run over by religion once too often and she wasn't going to get run over by it again. Ever. If Dillon was the kind of person to run her over, then he was off the project—or she was. And she wasn't going to waste one more minute finding out. "Can I ask you a question?"

Dillon sat down too. "Of course."

Rachel hoped she wasn't going to hurt his feelings, but she really had to know. "You believe in science, right?"

"Yes."

"And you believe in ... God and all that."

"I believe in God. I am not sure what 'all that' is."

"You know. Creationism. The Flood. Jonah and the whale. Water into wine. All that."

Dillon flinched. "The epistemic status of each of those must be investigated independently."

"The ... *what?*"

"There are good philosophical arguments for the existence of God. There are no such arguments for young-earth creationism, and there are strong scientific arguments against it. Therefore, the epistemic status of young-earth creationism is infinitesimally smaller than the epistemic status of the existence of God."

"Really? Good philosophical arguments?"

Dillon's eyes were steady, but there was pain deep inside them. "Are you really interested or are you just wanting to make fun?"

Rachel put a hand on his arm. "Dillon, I'm not trying to be rude. It's just ... I've been burned. How do you believe in science and God with the same brain? Don't you worry about all the contradictions?"

"Contradictions?"

"Like Genesis and the Big Bang."

"There is no contradiction between Genesis and the Big Bang. The universe began to exist 13.7 billion years ago. Everything that begins to exist has a cause. Genesis asserts that God is that cause, but it says nothing about when or how."

Rachel stared at him for a moment. Okay, that was acceptable. Weird, but acceptable. Also conveniently unfalsifiable. "Well then, if God is good, why did he allow Hitler? The fact of evil pretty much rules out the existence of God, wouldn't you say? There's a contradiction, if I ever heard one."

"The fact of evil rules out metaphysical naturalism."

"What?"

"Metaphysical naturalism asserts that there is nothing but matter and energy. On this view, Hitler was a piece of meat who interacted with other pieces of meat. There can be no moral significance to the interactions of meat. Moral values apply only to conscious agents, which are explicitly ruled out by metaphysical naturalism. So if you grant the objective reality of evil, then you cannot also accept metaphysical naturalism."

"Well, sure, but what I'm saying is that a good God who allows massive, uncontrolled, purposeless evil is a contradiction in terms."

A muscle twitched in Dillon's cheek. "That is possible but not proven and it may be unprovable. In any event, contradictions can be extremely useful."

"In what possible way?"

"Do you believe in Einstein's theory of general relativity?"

Rachel couldn't see where he was going with this. "Well, obviously. The evidence is overwhelming. Gravity. The expanding universe. The cosmic microwave background. General relativity is just about the best-supported theory ever constructed."

"Do you believe in quantum mechanics?"

"Well, duh. Everybody believes in quantum mechanics." She pointed at the safe. "If I didn't believe in quantum mechanics, I wouldn't have spent the last six months building that bio-computer. What's this all about? You must believe in quantum mechanics."

"Yes, I believe in quantum mechanics." Dillon studied her for a long moment. "The evidence for quantum mechanics is overwhelming. It is, as you said, one of the two best-supported theories ever constructed. Einstein's general relativity is the other. But those two excellent theories contradict each other. They cannot both be exactly true."

Rachel shrugged. "Well ... of course. Everybody knows that."

Dillon leaned forward. "How can you believe in both of those theories with the same brain?"

"It's ..." Rachel didn't know what to say. "That's the big unsolved question from the twentieth century. How to arrange John Wheeler's 'fiery marriage' of gravity and quantum mechanics. Maybe it's superstrings. Maybe it's quantum loop gravity. Maybe it's something we haven't thought of yet."

"But you believe they can be married," Dillon said. "Why not just throw out one of them?"

"Because they're both true," Rachel said. "I can't give up relativity.

It's too perfect. Too good. Too beautiful. And the same goes for quantum mechanics. I *know* quantum mechanics is true."

"You have strong warrant for your belief in quantum mechanics."

"That's what it means to know something."

"And you have strong warrant for your belief in general relativity."

"Right. They're both true—essentially true—so I'm confident there's a way to resolve the contradiction. We'll find a quantum theory of gravity that makes predictions we can test."

"Agreed. But even if we never discover the quantum theory of gravity, we know that it must exist, because we have strong warrant for both quantum mechanics and relativity. What if you had strong warrant to believe that God exists?"

Rachel shook her head. "Well, I don't, so it's a moot point. Look, God is just some kind of cosmic father figure."

Dillon stiffened as if she'd slapped him. For a moment, something flickered in his expressionless face.

"I'm sorry. That came out wrong." Rachel wished she could just back up and start over. "Listen, I'm not into religion or God or any of that stuff. If you want to believe in the church, I don't care, as long—"

"I said I believe in God. I did not say I believe in the church."

Rachel saw a flicker of pain in Dillon's eyes. Okay, good. He'd been steamrollered too, somehow. He was weird, but he was obviously not going to steamroller her, because he knew what it felt like. She could work with that. Whatever he believed, he was going to keep to himself unless she asked. And she wasn't going to ask. "Well, then, we have a lot in common. Because I don't believe in the church either. So let's just leave it at that and work like mad on this project."

"I will not be working tomorrow."

Rachel sighed. "Fine. Let's both take a nice break tomorrow. We'll come in on Monday all fresh and rested and we'll jam out some code. Okay?"

"Jam out code?"

"We'll write it really fast." Rachel smiled at him. "You'll write it really fast and I'll watch. Okay?"

"Okay." Dillon turned and picked up his briefcase. "See you Monday."

The way he said that, it sounded like a thousand years. "Right," Rachel said. "Monday."

~

Rachel

Driving home on Miramar Road, Rachel let the wind wash through her brain. It had been a weird, weird, weird, whacked-out day.

Uncle Grant was a big teddy bear who didn't want much except to save the world. Right now he'd be lucky if he could save the company.

Clifton Potter was a lech and a half. She'd need to keep an eye on him, because for sure he'd be putting his eyes all over her.

Keryn Wills was a sweet, literary, gracious, backstabbing pain in the butt, who was going to keep wedging her way in every chance she could because she thought Rachel was competition. As if Rachel would want in on her game. As if Keryn could even remotely compete if Rachel was interested. Which she was not.

Dillon Richard was a big bundle of contradictions—a Mozart of a programmer, some sort of religious nutcake. A socially inept guy who just happened to connect with Rachel like a Vulcan mind-meld whenever she looked deep into his gorgeous brown eyes.

Well, that wasn't going to go anywhere. Religion and Rachel didn't mix.

But what about Keryn? She was clearly gunning for Dillon. Fine, she could have him. But she might be getting less than she'd bargained for.

Keryn had all the earmarks of one of those earnest, clean-living fundies that you found all over southern California. How was she going to react when Dillon started talking about the epistemic status of creationism? That was going to be extremely interesting.

Rachel laughed out loud into the night wind.

Working at CypherQuanta was going to be a lot crazier than she had bargained for.

CHAPTER SEVEN

Keryn

Keryn couldn't think of an excuse to call Dillon on Sunday. Monday morning, she pottered around her home office all morning, unable to focus on her novel. She needed to drill out ten thousand words this week, and it was going horribly. She couldn't concentrate, knowing that Rachel was holed up in that bio-lab with Dillon, getting chummy and doing the well-oiled machine bit.

Around noon, she couldn't stand it any longer and she went in to work early. Grant was on the phone with his door shut, and he didn't look up when Keryn peered in through the little glass square on his door. His forehead looked shiny, and he was scribbling furiously on a pad of paper while he talked.

Nobody else in the company was in on the secret, other than Clifton. It was his job to keep tabs on progress, so Keryn went looking for him. He wasn't in his cubicle, or the coffee room, or the weight room. Keryn poked her head in the assembly room. A couple of engineers were working on a CypherQuanta encryption device. It was the size and shape of a shoebox and was connected to a Dell workstation.

Keryn sauntered in. "Hey, Bill and Jill, have you seen Clifton?"

Both of them turned around. Bill and Jill were twins in their early thirties. Bill had a blond crew cut and Jill had a short brown ponytail tied with a rubber band, but other than that, they looked amazingly alike. They both wore No Fear T-shirts and faded Levi's. Jill had a tattoo on her right arm that said *Bill*. Bill had a *Jill* tattoo on his left arm. They drove identical white Saturns. Keryn had heard they lived in a house they had bought together, which was kind of weird, but whatever.

"I," Jill said.

"Saw," Bill said.

They continued the sentence, alternating words. "Him." "Going." "Outside." "Talking." "On." "His." "Cell." "Phone."

Keryn laughed. Bill and Jill were always trying to do that. Occasionally, they actually made sense. "You two are nuts."

"Thank."

"You."

Keryn went back outside, wondering what it was like to be that in tune with another person. A deep ache settled in her chest. As she reached the door to the parking lot, it swung open.

Clifton Potter stood there. His eyes flicked down for a second, then back up to her face. "Whoa, hey, Keryn. You're in early today. Finished killing off the bad guys already?"

Keryn felt flustered. She wanted to know how Dillon and Rachel were getting on, but she felt awkward asking. "Bill and Jill said you were out here."

"Phone call," he said. "You know how biff the reception is inside."

Keryn knew. "Listen, I came in a little early to talk to Grant about ... you know. The financials."

Clifton pulled the door all the way open. "Right. Let's step outside, if you don't mind."

Keryn followed him.

Clifton plunked himself down at a picnic table looking out toward the gully.

Keryn sat across from him. "Listen, there are financial integrity issues we need to deal with. I need to know what the probability is that we're going to do layoffs this month."

Clifton looked all around, his alert blue eyes sweeping the whole parking lot. "I hear ya on that. I'm still chafed that Grant didn't tell us about Goldilocks for six months. We needed to know that. Know what I mean?"

Keryn knew. She hadn't gotten over it herself.

Clifton grabbed his long blond ponytail and held the end of it in his fist. "I mean, this thing Rachel's found is quite the breakthrough. A CTO ought to know about things like that."

"Do you think it'll work?"

Clifton pursed his lips. "Saturday, I wasn't sure. We've never done anything like this before. But I talked to the Dillon Man this morning, and he's on target. Thinks they'll be ready for testing by Friday, next Monday at the latest."

"That soon?" Keryn felt a rush of relief. The less time Dillon was cloistered with Rachel, the better.

"Those two are the Dream Team," Clifton said. "Between the two of them, we're gonna put the wallies of the world on the run."

"The what?"

"The wallies. The doofuses. Like Wally in Dilbert. Everybody's gonna come running to us when they find out about this thing."

"We'd better start gearing up production."

Clifton gave her a look that told her she was missing something. "You got the money to hire another ten thousand Bills and Jills?"

"Ten thousand?"

"Every bank's gonna need a bunch of our machines," Clifton said. "Anyone who transfers money. Every ISP. Every—"

"ISPs?"

"Internet service provider."

"I know what an ISP is. Why would they need one of our machines? Our business plan targets financial institutions, not ISPs."

Clifton just looked at her. "You ever bought a book on Amazon?"

"All the time."

"And you never worried about typing in your Visa number?"

Keryn shook her head. "Everybody does it."

Clifton narrowed his eyes. "You do know that Internet traffic goes through about a bazillion unsecure computers on the way between you and Amazon?"

"Yes, but ... everybody does it. That info gets encrypted, right?" Keryn suddenly got it. "What kind of encryption do Web browsers use?"

Clifton gave her a sardonic smile. "Every web site in the world that does e-commerce uses something called Secure Sockets Layer. Which is just a fancy way of saying RSA encryption. And which we will soon demonstrate can be broken. So every ISP in the country is going to need to come to us to get their quantum encryption. Eventually, every business and every home user. We'll be a commodity."

Karen's heart started pounding. "That means we need a whole new business plan."

Clifton grinned. "Right, I talked to Grant about that this morning. If this thing flies, we'll be the only encryption game in town, and we aren't going to be able to meet the backlog without some *serious* capitalization. Which means we are going public real soon now and we'll be sitting on a market cap of a big pile of gigabucks."

Keryn thought about that for a few seconds, and the implication slugged her in the stomach. She sucked in her breath. *God have mercy on us all.*

"You're looking a little green around the gills, sister. Chill, Keryn! Hey, this is *good*! We're gonna be rolling in green when this takes off. E-commerce moves like a hundred billion dollars a year. The banks and brokerages move trillions. And we'll be sitting there taking our cut."

"Not right away," Keryn said. "You already said we can't gear up that fast. It's going to be months before we can ramp production. In the meantime, everybody will know we've got this technology that makes it all ..." She was too scared to finish the sentence.

"Makes it all naked as a jaybird," Clifton said. "I thought Grant went over all this on Saturday."

Keryn shook her head. "I didn't realize it went beyond the financial industry. We've been selling a few tens of our encryption units per year. I was thinking that would go up to thousands, which would be huge for us. You're talking ..."

"Millions," Clifton said. "Eventually, hundreds of millions."

Keryn was sweating now. "What if our new device gets into the wrong hands?"

"It won't," Clifton said. "Here's what'll happen. We make a public demonstration. The Feds take it over on grounds of national security. But by then the cat's out of the bag and everybody knows Big Brother can read their mail, so they switch over to using our encryption. We sell a bazillion machines, get huge economies of scale, and cut the price way low, grabbing market share before anybody else can move. We *talked* about all this, remember?"

"You didn't explain about the ISPs," Keryn said.

"I thought it was obvious."

"And what if somebody finds out about this before we make our public announcement?"

Clifton shook his head. "You mean like Big Brother? Won't happen. Rachel made her crucial discovery back in November. She didn't publish it. Didn't tell anybody at Caltech. Didn't tell her funding agency, which is probably legal grounds for the Feds to take it over as soon as they find out. Lucky for us, she called her daddy, who told her to talk to Grant. The rest is history."

Keryn lowered her voice. "But what if somebody else finds out first? Think like a novelist for a minute. What if organized criminals found out we had this?"

Clifton gave her a sick smile. "I guess we'd have to call in the Feddies on them."

"Don't be an idiot." Keryn felt prickles of fear all over her body. "Before we picked up the phone, they'd kill you, me, Grant, Rachel, Dillon. They'd kill their own mothers to get this technology. If the crooks find out about this thing ... we're dead. I mean, literally dead. Large-caliber-bullet-wounds-to-the-head dead. They could use it to rip off the whole world, and nobody would know until they had a few trillion sitting in Swiss bank accounts."

"I didn't think of that." A sheen of sweat appeared on Clifton's forehead. "Makes me wish we could just ... get Rachel to forget how she made those qubits."

Keryn shook her head. "Grant would never let her do that. Once you know something, you can't unknow it."

Clifton swore softly. "So we've passed the Point of Know Return, is that it?"

"Cheesy, but yeah, something like that." Keryn shivered.

The CypherQuanta door burst open and banged against the wall.

Keryn jumped and screamed.

"Relax, Earthling," Jill said.

"It is only us Martians." Bill stuck his fingers behind his head like an antenna.

Keryn fanned herself rapidly with her hand. "Sorry, BillJill. I just ..."

"She was just telling me her latest ghost story and got herself all excited." Clifton studied them. "What brings you two geek-meisters outside in actual daylight?"

"Lunchtime," Bill and Jill said simultaneously.

Clifton looked at his watch. "Oh. Right. Well, don't let us keep you from your appointed rounds."

Keryn watched until Bill and Jill climbed into one of their Saturns and drove away.

Clifton stood up. "Okay, Lit-chick, I think you and I better go have a chat with the Grant Man. He's been paranoid about Uncle Sam finding out, but I don't think he ever considered the commercial appeal to Cousin Vinnie."

Keryn followed him into the building. Her head felt hollow and her skin prickled. She'd written three and a half novels, in which a total of six people got themselves killed and fifteen others narrowly escaped death. She'd often wondered what it was like to be in one of her books. Now she knew.

And she wanted out.

Grant

Within half of an hour of hearing Keryn's fears, Grant was in the bio-lab, pacing back and forth while Keryn and Clifton explained the situation to Rachel and Dillon. This was horrible. The whole thing could blow up in his face. Everything he'd worked for could be taken away from him. An iron fist tightened on his chest.

"... if organized criminals were to find out about this, we'd be dead," Keryn said.

Rachel's face went white. She was a great kid, and Grant had never meant to put her in danger.

Dillon stood up and his face showed no expression at all. "There is only one solution."

Grant didn't think he was going to like Dillon's solution. "What might that be, Dillon?"

Dillon took out his cell phone. "We need to talk to the FBI. If criminals get hold of this information, it would be a disaster. Nothing would be safe. The whole economy would stop. And an economy is driven by money flow, not by money. Once that flow stops, it cannot simply restart. The world economy would collapse."

Grant stepped to Dillon's side and put his hand on the phone. "Dillon, listen. We're not going to call the Feds."

Dillon blinked. "We have to. This is too big for us."

Grant felt sweat running down his sides. He could not let Dillon call in the government. That would ruin everything.

Rachel edged up beside Grant and put her hand on Dillon's. "Give me the phone, okay, Dillon? Just for a minute while we talk."

Dillon's hand spasmed. His face didn't move a whisker, but he released the phone.

Rachel was wearing a brilliant pink silk blouse today. She slipped the phone inside it and smiled at Dillon. "Listen, the reason I left Caltech was to keep Big Brother from getting his claws into my research. I am not—"

"Big Brother?" Dillon said. "You mean the governing authorities? That is ridiculous. We have a free press. We have the Internet. The free flow of information is the best protection against a government dystopia."

Which was so naive it was pathetic, but Grant didn't want to say so. And anyway he had a hunch Rachel would be a whole lot more persuasive.

Rachel's eyes were glittering. "Dillon, use your head, will you? This technology is going to force people to go all the way with encryption. They'll have to use quantum encryption. They'll get their privacy back."

"Get it back?" Dillon looked skeptical. "What are you talking about? The government does not spy on people. It is a violation of the Fourth Amendment."

"The Fourth Amendment lets them spy on people if they get a warrant," Rachel said.

Dillon was shaking his head. "No, not even with a warrant. If people want privacy, they can use encryption. Until now, RSA encryption has been unbreakable."

"You know that for sure?" Rachel said. "You have a theorem that the factoring problem can't be solved in polynomial time?"

"Well ... no," Dillon said. "But it is widely believed."

Rachel gave a harsh laugh. "It's widely believed by gullibles. Before the RSA paper in 1977, it was 'widely believed' that asymmetric encryption was impossible. But you know what? It had already been invented four years earlier. By British intelligence. And they didn't tell a soul. Why not? Because they didn't want us proletarians to have good encryption. All intelligence agencies think alike—they deserve the best encryption, whereas we deserve the worst."

"I don't understand what you're talking about," Keryn said.

Rachel gave a thick sigh. "The British cryptology agency GCHQ discovered RSA encryption in 1973, but they kept it classified. They never said a word about it until years after it was commonplace in the private sector, because they knew people could use it to shut out Big Brother. In 1997 they came clean. You want to know why? Because either their guys or our guys finally cracked the factorization problem. A lot of cypherpunks think so, anyway. The NSA has some of the world's best mathematicians, experts in number theory. If anybody knows a classical way to factor large numbers, it's them. They'd share it with the Brits, but nobody else."

"So ... what's the problem, then?" Keryn asked. She looked at Grant. "If the NSA already knows how to factor big numbers, they can ... Oh, I get it."

"They can read our mail," Rachel said. "They can spy on us. Everybody who uses RSA encryption thinks their secrets are safe, but they aren't. It's all an NSA con job."

Dillon looked puzzled. "Rachel, how can you know this for sure? A great many mathematicians in academia have looked at factorization. None of them have solved it."

Rachel tapped Dillon lightly on the nose with her forefinger. "I can't know it for sure. It's plausible, but there's no way to prove it. So assume the opposite. Assume the NSA can't factor large numbers. If we go to the FBI for protection, they'll turn this over to the NSA and *then* they'll have the secret. And nobody else will know."

"But we could tell people," Dillon said.

Rachel shook her head. "Dillon, that is so absurd. The NSA would make us sign some kind of confidentiality statement. So they can prosecute us if we talk. And if they get really upset with us ..." She drew her finger across her throat.

Dillon's lip curled. "That is ridiculous. The U.S. government does not kill its own citizens."

Keryn came and put a hand on Dillon's shoulder. "Dillon, I'm not sure I'd want to bet my life on that."

"Dude, no way," Clifton said. "This nice government of ours could not care *less* if you die. They did all those syphilis experiments on that bunch of African-American dudes in Alabama. You ever heard about that? Plus, they lied about those radiation experiments in Nevada."

"Not to mention they covered up the fact that Elvis is playing checkers with the aliens who landed in Roswell," Dillon said. "It says so in the National Enquirer, so it must be true."

"Be serious," Rachel said. "Dillon, I am not going to let the NSA get my bio-computer. I am not."

"She's right," Keryn said. "The NSA is bad news, Dillon."

"Dude, I'm with the ladies on this one." Clifton began pacing. "Grant, tell him we're not going to the Feds."

Grant coughed softly into his hand. "Dillon, listen. I'm not a conspiracy buff, but I'm cautious about the NSA. Clif and I talked about it this morning. We intend to do an end run on the Feds."

Dillon's eyes went blank. "A what?"

Grant sighed. Dillon could be a royal pain sometimes. "We can beat them at their own game. Here's what we're gonna do. You and Rachel finish this machine up as quick as you can. How much longer do you think it'll take?"

"By Saturday," Dillon said. "If we start testing Friday."

"Fine." Grant thumped Dillon on the shoulder. "Look, there are five people in the world who know about this thing, and we're all in this room. We're all at the same risk. If this secret gets out, we're Alpo and the bad guys are Clifford the Big Red Dog. So we better not talk—any of us. But we can all keep a secret for five days, right?"

Keryn nodded.

"Better believe it," Rachel said.

Clifton's face was so tight you could play a drum on it. "Of course."

"Right, Dillon?" Grant said. "You agree we can keep it quiet for five days?"

"Yes."

Grant felt the tension in his gut ease. "Good, so we test the machine, prove that we can factor a big number."

"And then?" Dillon kept his poker face.

"Then we hold a press conference. We bring in all the honchos and let 'em examine the instrument. We demo the thing factoring large numbers."

Dillon's eyes narrowed. "If the government is as evil as you say, then they will confiscate the machine."

Grant nodded. "Exactly. They take the machine, but then what happens? Then everybody in the world knows that Big Brother really *is* watching them, and they all beat a path to our door to buy the better mousetrap. That's just what we wanted, isn't it? CypherQuanta goes public, we all get filthy rich, and the world gets a decent level of encryption." Grant thumped Dillon on the shoulder. "Now explain to me the downside of that."

Dillon stood motionless, his eyes revealing the wheels turning in his brain. Grant held his breath. Dillon had to see the logic here. He was a smart guy. He had to see that this was the best solution. The only solution.

Finally Dillon nodded. "All right. Five days. If we do not have it working by then, I want us to go to the government."

Grant shook his head. "Nice try, Dillon, but no. You're the bottle-neck in this process. You can just stall for five days and then force us to go to the Feds."

Dillon looked shocked. "Grant, I give you my word of honor that I will not stall. Before the Lord, I give you my word."

Which was just about as ironclad a guarantee as Grant could think of. Dillon was one weird duck about religion. If he made a promise like that, then his word was good.

"Five days," Grant said. "Everybody agree on that?"

Heads nodded all around.

Grant felt relief rush through his veins. He had just dodged a cannonball. "Okay, we'll let you get back to work, then. But everybody, remember one thing. This isn't just a business deal we're talking about here. If one syllable of this gets to the wrong ears, we're dead. All of us. Everybody clear on that?"

Everybody was.

"All right, then. Keryn, Clifton, let's get back to CypherQuanta." Grant herded them toward the door.

It was going to be a long five days.

CHAPTER EIGHT

Dillon

By Tuesday afternoon Dillon felt as if he had been flogged. He and Rachel had worked until midnight in the lab yesterday, then come back in at 8:00 a.m this morning. Now his back felt kinked and his brain felt muzzy.

Somebody pounded on the outside door of the bio-lab.

Rachel went to answer it and came back with Clifton.

"Hey, Dream Teamers! What's the word on progress?"

Dillon stood up and stretched his aching back. "Actually, we are a little behind schedule. There was a problem with the hardware libraries. Rachel called the manufacturer, and they promised to get a patch to us by tomorrow."

Rachel put a hand on Dillon's shoulder and leaned on him. "It's what they call a 'known problem.' I asked them why they haven't fixed it yet, and they said it only happens when you pulse the machine at rates beyond the spec. Then they wanted to know details about our application and—"

"You didn't tell 'em, did you?" Clifton's face went tight. "The Grant

Man would have a kangaroo if you told them a word. Not to mention that we'd all die in a hail of bullets. Or whatever."

Rachel shook her head. "I told them we're working on a handheld scanner at UCSD and we're gonna miss a deadline for the FDA if we don't get that patch by tomorrow, or Thursday at the latest. I also hinted that our device could double the installed base of NMR machines worldwide, once we take it to market."

Dillon felt his jaw tighten. It should never be necessary to use prevarication. Unfortunately, Rachel lived life by her own rules, and he had not been able to stop her.

Clifton pointed at the computer. "Can you show me where you're at?"

Dillon's cell phone rang. He checked the caller ID. Robert was calling again from Berkeley. Dillon stepped toward the door. "Excuse me, Clifton, but I need to take this call. My friend is getting married in August."

"Gotcha, dude." Clifton waved him out and sat down at the computer with Rachel.

Dillon stepped outside the bio-lab and opened his phone. "Hello, Robert. How are you?"

"Dillon! Sorry to call you while you're working." Robert's voice sounded wobbly.

"My reception is bad," Dillon said. "Can you hear me?" He went to the outer door and stepped outside into the late afternoon sunlight.

"I hear you fine," Robert said. "I'm ... kind of upset."

Dillon felt his stomach tighten. Robert must have had another fight with his fiancée. "Please tell me about it."

Robert spent the next fifteen minutes detailing his latest crisis. For the hundredth time Dillon wondered why people ever got married. It only led to fighting and unpleasantness. Marriage was illogical.

Finally, Robert finished.

"Have you talked to your priest?" Dillon did not like priests, but it would not be polite to say so to Robert. "Ask Sarah to go with you to see your priest."

"She said she'd go see him with me in the morning," Robert said.

"All things work together for good," Dillon said.

A long silence.

"So did you get that San-D-Bank thing resolved?" Robert asked. "They can't just send back four machines after they passed the acceptance test, can they?"

Dillon had forgotten about San-D-Bank. "I ... we have not gotten back to them on that issue."

"What?" Robert sounded shocked. "I thought that was your latest show-stopper."

"There has ... been a change of plans." Dillon looked around, suddenly feeling quite exposed standing outside in public.

"What are you talking about? Sunday you made it sound like a big deal. Now you guys are just going to politely drop it?"

"Robert, I am not able to talk about it." Dillon's heart began thumping. He hated prevaricating.

"What's wrong with your voice?" Robert said. "You sound sick or something."

Dillon felt like a thick rope was wrapped around his neck. "There is nothing wrong. I am working on a tight deadline and I need to get back to work. Please call me tomorrow and let me know if your priest can resolve things."

"Dillon, are you okay?"

Dillon looked around nervously. He had nothing to hide. Nothing except a trillion-dollar secret. He went back inside the building. "I am fine, Robert. I will call you tomorrow."

Clifton burst out of the bio-lab. "Dude, you rock! Rachel showed me your implementation of Shor's algorithm."

"Good-bye, Robert." Dillon hastily folded his phone and slipped it into his shirt pocket. "It is not really mine. I found it on the Web and made a small optimization. But if we cannot solve the hardware problem, we will need another vendor."

"We don't have time for another vendor." Clifton pointed to his watch. "Four more days until we all turn into pumpkins. You'll be done, won't you?"

"Probably."

"Dude, I don't want a probably, I want a yes."

Dillon shrugged his shoulders. "Probably."

Clifton swore and went out, slamming the door behind him.

Clifton

T he next day, Clifton burned the whole afternoon with Bill and Jill, going over the failed San-D-Bank machines. And there wasn't a thing wrong with them. San-D-Bank had lied to them.

Bill sat staring at the monitor. "Our data rates meet the spec, Clif." He ran his fingers through his blond crew cut. "They're blowing smoke up—"

Clifton's phone rang. He checked the number and saw that it was Hunter. "Hey, gotta take this outside. Okay, guys?" He strode toward the door without waiting to see if it was okay. On the third ring he flipped the phone open. "Clifton Potter."

"Clifton, *great* to get hold of you!" Hunter had a way of talking that made him sound like a long-lost cousin getting reunited after fifty years. "Are you in a place where we can talk?"

"Gimme about fifteen seconds and I will be." Clifton walked past his cubicle and out through the back door into the late afternoon sun. He continued to the far end of the parking lot. "Okay, I'm away from civilization. What's up?"

"I've been doing a few phone calls," Hunter said. "There's an interest over at Qualcomm."

"Oh." Clifton hadn't expected anything nearly this fast.

"Something wrong with Qualcomm?" Hunter asked. "They took a bit of a tumble way back when, but everybody did. I've got a few ears over there, and I think they're ready to take over the world."

Clifton didn't say anything.

"Hey, you still there?" Hunter said.

"Oh. Yeah, sorry."

"Listen, there's an opening at your level over there. Actually, it'd be a bit of a step up. Where you're at, you're a big fish in a dinky pond. Over at Q, you'd be a pretty big fish in a great big ocean. We're looking at maybe an eighty-percent pay raise, plus some equity options. The options aren't as fat as they were in the dot-com days, but they're real, not vapor. Can you do an interview over there on Friday?"

Clifton felt his heart racing. "I'm ... kind of busy right now."

"You're busy." It wasn't quite a question, but it wasn't quite a statement.

"Yeah."

A short silence. "Okay, how about Saturday? They're really interested in you, but here's the problem. They were about to make an offer to a guy at Ericsson. It's kind of time-sensitive, but you've got some way innovative stuff in your background. They like that quantum encryption you've been doing."

"I don't think I can make it Saturday."

"Some sort of a crunch over there at CypherQuanta?"

Clifton wasn't quite sure what to say. Either answer was bound to draw more questions. "I can't really say."

Hunter gave a long sigh. "That kind of puts me in a bind. One of the execs who wants to interview you is taking a flight out to Japan Sunday morning. Are you really sure you can't meet with them? What about Thursday? If they scrunch up their schedule, can you make it tomorrow, say, fourish?"

Four was the normal time to talk with Dillon and Rachel. "Sorry, got an appointment then."

"I thought you said you were in a work crunch."

"That's what I mean. A meeting."

"You can't reschedule?"

"No." Clifton could feel every molecule of adrenaline in his body. "Look, it's not a big deal."

Hunter gave a sharp intake of breath that hissed over the line. "Did I not make myself clear? This is the big leagues, Clifton. Qualcomm is a mega-billion-bones company. How much sales revenue are you guys doing over there at Cypher? Annual?"

"Two." Clifton felt like an idiot.

"You're kidding me, right? Two *billion*?"

"Million."

Hunter didn't say a word.

An Amtrak train roared by. Clifton waited for it to pass. "Listen, Ted, I'll think about it and get back to you, okay?"

"You'll think about it. That's it, you'll think about it?"

"Yeah."

A pregnant pause. "Say, Clifton, you still got any stock you want to unload on me?"

"Sorry." Clifton snapped the phone shut and put it in his pocket. An eighty-percent raise. Maybe a few thousand shares of QCOM. It sounded great, but ...

If the Dillonhead came through by Saturday, that would be chicken feed.

If.

~

Keryn

Keryn leaned back in her ergonomically correct chair and rubbed her tired eyes. It was 10:00 p.m. She had been typing for two hours and she had managed 384 words. A page and a half.

Of shlock.

This was not Keryn Wills fiction, this was junk. She was now about twelve thousand words behind schedule and getting further behind every day. A little nagging voice was playing in her head. *Train wreck. You're headed for a train wreck on this one, Keryn. You're going to crash and burn, and no editor will ever buy one of your books again.*

Keryn took a deep breath and stood up and went out to check the front door. The dead bolt was in place. All the windows were locked. The back patio door was locked. The kitchen door was locked. Fine. All secure. No problem. It was Thursday night. Two more days and Dillon would be done doing his magic. And Keryn could quit looking over her shoulder. She *hated* this.

The phone rang.

Keryn jumped.

Smiley meowed loudly from the couch. Keryn gave him a shaky

smile and went to check the caller ID. Mom and Dad. She scooped up the phone. "H-hello."

"Sweetheart, what's wrong?" Concern sugared Sunflower's voice.

"Nothing. Everything's fine."

"You don't sound fine, pumpkin." Rusty sounded a little drunk over the speakerphone. That was good, if he was only a little.

"I'm fine."

"You aren't acting fine," Sunflower said. "You always screen calls this time of night. Tonight you picked up on the second ring. What's wrong?"

Keryn realized she wasn't going to get anywhere by lying. "I'm just … nervous, that's all."

"Well, if you weren't always slicing up people and leaving a trail of corpses in your books, you wouldn't be so jittery."

"It's not that. It's …" Keryn remembered something she'd read in the newspaper the other day. "It's just that … a woman was attacked the other day. About three blocks from here. Everybody in my neighborhood's a little antsy."

"What does that mean, attacked?" Sunflower said. "You mean raped, say raped. I hate those stupid euphemisms. Anyway, didn't you get a permit to carry pepper spray?"

"Pepper isn't foolproof." Keryn had written a novel in which that was a crucial point. She sat down beside Smiley and began stroking his soft fur. "Anyway, I'm just … nervous. What if somebody broke in while I was asleep?"

"So go stay with Kathii and Allen for a few days."

"I don't think so." Keryn closed her eyes and leaned her head back. If it was just her sister, Kathii, that'd be fine. Kathii never asked her about work. But her husband, Allen, was an electrical engineer at SAIC, and he always had a ton of questions about CypherQuanta. Not to be nosy, he was just friendly. And curious. Maybe a little jealous that Keryn was getting great wads of stock options for working half time at a startup that just might IPO someday and just might pay off a few megabucks.

Keryn did not trust herself to face up to a barrage of Allen's questions about "how are things at CypherQuanta these days?" She wasn't good at evasion. If Allen guessed anything, it would just be horrible if he went back to SAIC tomorrow to speculate with his friends about what breakthrough Keryn couldn't talk about.

"I'm calling Kathii right now," Sunflower said.

"Mom, don't you dare!"

The line went dead.

Keryn wished just once she could find the backbone to stand up to Sunflower. What was wrong with her, anyway? She shouldn't just let Sunflower run over her.

Smiley yawned hugely. Keryn tickled his chin and slammed down the phone. "And how is Mama's big boy today?"

Smiley could have had a Ph.D. in relaxing, he was so good at it. He rubbed the side of his head against Keryn's hand and looked up at her with his big round Paul Newman blue eyes. Keryn stroked his fur. Smiley was an enormous bicolor Ragdoll cat, twenty pounds of warm, soothing, relaxed pleasure. A massive purr rumbled through his body.

The phone rang again. Keryn ignored it.

Three rings later, the machine in her office picked up and invited the caller to leave a message.

"Keryn! Sunflower just called! Are you all right? Please pick up the phone, Keryn. I'm *frantic*. Allen, she's not answering. You'd better go over there and—"

Keryn picked up the phone. "Hi, Kathii. Sorry, I had Smiley on my lap, and it's hard to get to the phone with a sack of flour across your legs." She tickled Smiley and he meowed in cooperation.

Kathii had this oozy, eager-to-please voice that usually made Keryn feel glad she had a big sister who cared.

Tonight it grated on her.

"Listen, Keryn, can we come over and get you? It's *really* no trouble. We can have you stay over tonight. Jason and Jordan are in bed already, so you could bring your laptop and write. Really, we'd *love* to have you."

"Thanks, Kath, but no. I'm fine. You know how Sunflower is— always reading in things that aren't there."

Allen's voice came in on the extension. "Keryn, are you *sure* you're okay? I can be there in five minutes and pick you up. Bring Smiley. The boys love him."

"Th-thanks, Allen, that's really nice of you, but I'm fine. I'm already in my nightgown, and I'm not going anywhere tonight. I'll paint Smiley orange and black—anyone who tries to break in will think he's a tiger."

Kathii and Allen both laughed.

Keryn was pretty sure she had won.

"How's the book coming along?" Kathii asked.

"Fine. Just ... great," Keryn said. "I'm a little behind, but you know, I'm getting all these really exciting ideas and just trying to get it all integrated in my head."

"Things still going hunky-dory at CypherQuanta?" Allen asked.

"Super."

"I'm having lunch with one of your investors tomorrow."

Keryn held her breath. "Um, really?"

"Yeah, one of the honchos over at Cymer. He's got quite a bit of money in Lost Angels. He's coming over to give a talk on some of the new lasers Cymer's using. Anyway, I've been thinking of cashing out some of my equity at SAIC and, you know, playing it somewhere with a little more action. I'm thinking of putting fifty K into Lost Angels and seeing what they can do. What do you think?"

Keryn held her breath. Allen wasn't probing, exactly. Not in an insider-trading kind of way. He was just nervous, that was all. He had socked away all of his money in SAIC stock during the crazy nineties, and that had done just fine, but he had missed the big run-up on all the highfliers. Of course, he'd also missed the bubble popping, but like everybody else who just said no, he was sure he should have said yes, that he would have cashed out at the peak. Now that the economy was turning up again, he was starting to look around for some of that greener grass he had missed the last time.

"Hey, are you still there?" Allen said.

"I'm here. It's just that I'm not allowed to talk about—" She stopped. Good heavens, what had she said?

"Oh." Allen's breathing sounded hoarse. "Sorry. I had no idea you were so close to doing an IPO."

"No, it's not that." Keryn bit her knuckle and wondered how to back out of this.

"Look, if you can't talk about it, I'll understand."

"Thanks. I really can't talk about it. And please don't mention it to anyone, all right? I mean, even the fact that I can't talk about it. Okay?"

"Sure, no problem. Whatever you say." Allen's voice sounded strangely light. Happy.

"I have no idea what you two are talking about," Kathii said.

"You don't want to know." Keryn opened her mouth and forced a yawn. "Listen, guys, thanks for your concern, but I'm fine and I need to hit the sack. I love you both. Kiss the boys for me, okay?"

"Love you!" Kathii said and hung up.

"Sleep well, and ... thanks." Allen rang off.

Keryn put the phone down so hard that Smiley jumped off the couch and raced into the bedroom.

Keryn got up and began pacing. "I'm an idiot. I am an idiot. I'm an *idiot*."

However you sliced it, she had let the cat out of the bag. Massively.

Rachel

At midnight on Friday, Rachel admitted to herself they weren't going to make it. Dillon had been hunched over the computer for nearly sixteen hours, his typing a steady drumbeat. Grant had called about fifteen times on his cell phone and asked in veiled terms if they were "there yet." They weren't. Keryn and Clifton had come by around 7:00 with pizza and drinks and tense small talk. Dillon had taken a few minutes to scarf some food and then zipped back into the bio-lab to continue typing flawless code.

The idiots at MagTec had set them back by two full days. Dillon was racing the clock, but even Mozart was human. He wasn't going to get it done tonight and he needed sleep.

Rachel stood behind him and put her hands on his shoulders. Thick knots stood out on either side of his neck. Rachel kneaded them gently. "Hey, Dillon?"

He continued tapping out source code, dictating it to himself in a low voice.

"Dillon?" She pressed harder.

Nothing.

She tightened her grip on his shoulders. "Dillon!"

"I am listening. You are distracting me." He continued typing.

She came around and stood beside him. "Let's break for the night. You've been at that thing since this morning. Let's go get some shut-eye."

"I could be done in another few hours." Dillon covered an enormous yawn. "We could be testing by three o'clock."

"You're going to give yourself a heart attack," she said. "What's the point? Let's go get some sleep, come back tomorrow, and finish it up."

Dillon looked irritated. "We had a plan. We were going to be testing by this morning. I want to stick to the plan."

She gave him an exasperated sigh. "So plans change. What's the big deal? You've done a miracle already. This is awesomely better than we had any right to expect. We'll be testing tomorrow and wrap things up Sunday ... um, Monday."

"The plan was to be finished tomorrow. We can do that, but I will need to work all night."

Rachel put both hands on her hips. "What is this nonsense? The plan was an artificial thing. We pulled a date out of our armpit. Saturday. So what's the problem if we slip till Monday?"

"We agreed to work until Saturday and then turn the device over to the NSA if we were not finished," Dillon said. "If I give it less than my best effort, Grant will accuse me of slacking and he will not be willing to live by the agreement."

"Dillon, read my lips! We lost two days because MagTec screwed us over! Let's just take that two days and add it to our schedule."

Dillon shook his head. "No. We cannot."

Rachel was getting tired of this stupidity. "Where do you get this *can't* business? Let's call Keryn and Grant and Clifton and tell them we need two more days. They'll give it to us."

Dillon just looked at her.

"Dillon, use your head. They'll give us two more days."

"I am sure they will. But I will not."

"What do you mean, you won't?"

"When I make a plan, I stick to the plan."

"Is this part of your Asperger's thing?"

"Syndrome. Not thing, syndrome."

"Is it?"

Dillon shrugged. "Maybe. Or maybe it is part of being Dillon. But I will stick to the plan."

"I thought you people were supposed to be rational, a bunch of Spocks running around," Rachel said. "Continuing to work until you keel over, just to stick to the plan, is the most irrational thing I've ever heard."

Dillon looked stung.

She leaned on his shoulder and pointed at the screen. "Look, you're making spelling mistakes again in your comments. You're tired. Get some sleep. Or at least let me type. You tell me what to type and I'll do it."

He shook his head. "I need to do it myself."

"I'm a pretty competent programmer."

Dillon's eyes narrowed. "I prefer to do it my way."

"You like to control things, don't you?"

"I am extremely good when I am in control."

Rachel was tired of this attitude thing Dillon had. "I bet you there's an error in that function you're writing."

"You bet me what?" Dillon said.

"If I'm right, we go home. If you're right, we stay till it's done."

Dillon reached up his hand. "Shake."

Rachel shook it.

Dillon held down the Ctrl key and pressed F7. The compiler ran through Dillon's source code. In the message window below, it showed the results: 102 errors.

Rachel dared to breathe.

Dillon double-clicked on the first error listing, and Visual C++ highlighted the error in the source code. He sucked in his breath. "That was stupid. Very stupid." Red lines of fatigue spiderwebbed the whites of his eyes.

She began massaging his shoulders. "Look, let's just go home and rest a little. We can finish it tomorrow and—"

Rachel's cell phone rang. She checked the display, then flipped it open. "Hi, Grant."

Grant's voice sounded like ground glass on asphalt. "Hey, Rachel, I've got Clifton here on a three-way. How are you two doing?"

"We're shutting down for the night," Rachel said. "We're getting close."

"How close is close?" Clifton said.

"Here, talk to Dillon." Rachel handed him the phone.

He pressed it to his ear. "Grant ... I am terribly sorry. I wanted to stay all night and work, but ... I am losing efficiency." He paused, listening. "No, probably not. Rachel wants to extend our deadline to Monday, but that is not part—"

Dillon winced and pulled the phone a couple of inches from his ear. Rachel could hear Grant shouting. Dillon handed her back the phone.

Rachel held the phone in front of her and whistled through her teeth, a long shrill blast.

That shut Grant up.

Rachel pressed the phone to her ear.

Clifton's voice broke through. "Listen, dudes, let's stay calm. I say we extend to Monday. What say, Grant Man?"

"I guess I'm good with that," Grant said. "Dillon, you good with that?"

"I'm good with it, but Dillon isn't," Rachel said. "But listen, it doesn't matter. We're spinning our wheels right now and we are going home. Right, Dillon?"

He nodded, his lips pressed together into a thin white line.

Rachel rubbed her tired eyes. "We're out of here, guys. We can talk about extending the schedule when we're fresh. It's really close. We might get it done tomorrow. We were just about ready to begin testing, but we're falling-down-on-our-knees tired."

Dillon's eyes shot open and he shook his head.

Rachel turned around so she couldn't see him.

"Go home and get some sleep," Grant said. "Tell Dillon that's an order."

"Roger dodger," Rachel said. "Sleep tight, guys. We'll get there. Monday at the latest."

Grant and Clifton rang off. Rachel closed the phone and put it in her pocket. She turned to look at Dillon.

"We are *not* ready to begin testing," Dillon said. "You prevaricated. We still have another two hours before we can begin testing."

"Which means we're just about ready," Rachel said, irritated. "Compared to how much time we've put in, we're there. Grant says to go home. That's an order, sez he."

Defeat washed across Dillon's face. He looked like his firstborn child had just been chosen to be sacrificed to the volcano.

"Let's go," Rachel said. "Tomorrow's a big day."

"Big." Dillon's voice sounded thick and tight. "Very big."

Five minutes later Rachel was driving west on Miramar Road toward home, watching Dillon's taillights disappear to the east. She was so tired she could barely drive, but it was okay.

Like Scarlett said, tomorrow was another day. Matter of fact, since it was after midnight, today was another day. Or whatever.

Grant

Grant hung up the phone and stood staring out at the Pacific. Dillon was going to cause problems. He was picky on schedules. Not just picky. Boneheaded. When Dillon Richard made a schedule, he stuck to it or split a spleen trying. And if somebody else made him miss it, he could get downright hostile. That blasted Asperger's thing or Dillon's perfectionism—Grant wasn't sure which.

That was the downside of Dillon. The upside was that Dillon was practically perfect. The only thing that could stop the guy was a Kryptonite cannonball. The snafu with MagTec was just an act of God. It was beyond anybody's control. Tomorrow, they'd all gang up on Dillon and talk sense to him until he gave in. If they missed the deadline, they'd just extend it till Monday.

"Honey, are you coming to bed?"

Grant spun around to see Julia in her nightgown.

She gave him a pouty smile that had looked a lot better on her when she was on the short side of thirty. Now she was pressing thirty-five, and the pouting put little crow's feet around her eyes that Botox would never erase. "It's after midnight, sweetheart."

"I'll be there in a minute." Grant turned back to stare out at the ocean.

"Who was that you were talking to?" Julia came up behind him and put her hands on his shoulders.

"Rachel."

Julia's hands froze. "Why is she calling you at midnight?"

"I called *her*, for crying out loud, and she's my niece, practically. I changed her diapers when she was a baby." Grant just did not want to deal with some stupid jealousy thing right now.

"What were you talking to her about at this hour?"

"Work."

"She works at midnight on a Friday night?"

Grant put his thick hands on Julia's. "Yes, she works at midnight on Friday. Matter of fact, she's working with Dillon Richard right now, and I think she's got a thing for him. You remember Dillon from the Christmas party?"

"How could I forget that amazing three-hour conversation about the multiverse?" Julia giggled. "You can't be serious. What's she see in him? He's so ... Dillon."

Grant turned around. "He's also brilliant and handsome."

"He's gorgeous, but he's boring as a barn door. He's nothing like her."

"She's brilliant and beautiful."

Julia grimaced. "She's totally different from him."

Grant shrugged. "Opposites attract. He's yin and she's yang."

"And you think they're doing some hanky-panky?"

"I don't care if they do the hokey-pokey, as long as they get that machine done before we go belly-up. We get that working and I'm gonna change my name to Trill."

Julia gave him a strange look. "Trill?"

"You know how Bill Gates is a billionaire? Ever think what he'd be worth if his mother had the sense to name him Trill?"

"Rachel's machine is worth that much?"

"More. *If* they get it done before our money runs out."

Julia's face tensed. "And what if they don't?"

"Then ... I'll have to make some layoffs and we'll lose the house and the Feds will get the technology and privacy in this country will go down the toilet. But other than that, no big deal."

"You can't just get a loan?"

Grant stuck his finger to his neck and slashed. "Right, let's just advertise to the whole world what we've got. Counting you, six people know about this, and that is five too many."

And if one of us lets it out to the wrong people, we all get sized for concrete boots.

CHAPTER NINE

Dillon

Saturday morning Dillon checked his watch when he parked in front of the bio-lab. 10:28 a.m. He had arrived two minutes before his schedule. This made him feel uncomfortable. He had meant to arrive at 10:30, and now he had an additional two minutes that were not scheduled. He sat in his car impatiently tapping his fingers on the steering wheel.

Rachel's Miata was not yet in her parking spot. Dillon had found her unreliable in the matter of scheduling. Some days she came earlier than he did. Other days she came later. Therefore he had already quit giving her a schedule, since she would not meet it. He did not need her until later today anyway. When it came time to test the bio-computer, then he would need her.

Precisely at 10:30 Dillon got out of his minivan and locked it. He went up the stairs and tapped in the keypad combination and went into the outer office. Rachel's desk had begun to look messy again, but that was not his problem. If it were his own desk, he would be angry, but Rachel could do as she liked with her own workspace.

He went inside the bio-lab and immediately saw that something had changed. His chair was now facing away from the computer. Dillon never left his chair like that. It reminded him of the story he had liked so much as a child, the Three Bears and Goldilocks. The story had a perfect three-fold structure: a beginning, a middle, and an end, each of which also had three parts having to do with the porridge, the chairs, and the beds, and each of which had three subparts having to do with Papa Bear, Mama Bear, and Baby Bear. It was a perfectly ordered story about a perfectly ordered world, and the only element of chaos was Goldilocks. The three bears easily detected her presence because she brought disorder to their world. Dillon liked Baby Bear, who epitomized the perfect middle ground. Mama Bear and Papa Bear represented the bounds of permissible behavior. He did not like Goldilocks at all. Goldilocks stood outside the bounds, and this was bad.

Somebody has been sitting in my *chair.*

Dillon knelt beside it, scanning for clues. He almost expected to find a long golden strand of hair, but of course that was absurd. The chair seat did not feel warm. He concluded that it had not been occupied in the past few minutes. Nor were there any other signs, such as food crumbs on the floor. After a careful inspection, Dillon sat in the chair and turned to face the computer.

He pressed the three-key combination—the Ctrl, the Alt, and the Del keys. A log-in dialog appeared.

Dillon sucked in his breath. The dialog initialized itself with the username *rmeyers*. Last night he had been logged in on his own account, not Rachel's. Evidently, Rachel had come in earlier today and logged in. Therefore, she was the person who had left the chair in the wrong position.

Dillon typed in his own username and then typed his password, which was an eight-letter random sequence of characters, of which five were lowercase letters, two were uppercase letters, and one was a numeric digit. This was a secure combination and could not be guessed by a hacker. He used this password only on this one machine, and he had never used it before. It was completely safe.

Dillon double-clicked on two icons, one to start up Visual C++ and one to start SourceSafe. He reopened the workspace he had been working on last night when Rachel had forced him to go home. The files he had been working on automatically opened. The one that had generated 102 errors was the topmost item. Dillon pressed the Ctrl key and then F7.

The compiler started up, and after a few seconds the results appeared in the message window: *0 errors*.

Dillon leaned forward and stared at the screen.

He distinctly remembered that there had been 102 errors last night. One hundred and two was the maximum number of errors that Visual C++ would tolerate before stopping the compiler. It usually meant there was a blunder early in the file that had continuing ramifications. Last night, he had seen the cause. It was a simple matter—he had forgotten to type a *#include* statement at the top of the file to import one of the interface files. An easy mistake to correct.

But he had not corrected it last night.

Therefore, Rachel must have done so. Dillon felt a surge of anxiety. Rachel might be a competent programmer. Then again, she might not. Either way, he did not want her making revisions on his code. When speed was so important, he needed to have the entire program clear in his own mind, and this he could not do if someone else was writing part of the code. He had made this clear to Rachel last Saturday.

Dillon pressed the Alt key and the Tab key. The active program switched to SourceSafe. He selected the folder representing the hardware library. A list of the files in that folder appeared in the display window. He pressed the column labeled *Date-Time*. The files sorted themselves in chronological order according to when they had last been changed, with the most recent first.

He saw at once that the file *MagTecNMRDriver.cpp* was at the top of the list. He clicked the right mouse button on this line and a contextual menu appeared. Dillon selected the *Show History* menu entry.

A dialog appeared showing when this file had last been worked on. It showed only three entries. Dillon had created the file on Tuesday and checked it in while still incomplete. He had checked it out again yesterday and checked it back in late last night when he finished.

The file had been checked out again at 2:14 a.m., but it was not checked out by *drichard*.

It had been checked out by *rmeyers*. Which meant Rachel must have done it, because nobody else would know her password in order to log on using her account.

Rage shot through Dillon's veins with such speed he felt dizzy for a moment. Rachel had argued with him and forced him to quit and go home. But it was all a charade. After the two of them had left, she had waited a couple of hours and come back.

She had come back to work on his code secretly. Why?

Dillon selected Version 2 and Version 3 together and then clicked on the Diff button. A window popped up showing the differences between the two files. New lines were marked in red. Dillon saw that Rachel had inserted a *#include* statement to fix the first problem. But there were several other changes. He felt his cheeks burning. He had made a number of elementary errors in his coding. He must have been quite exhausted. Rachel had corrected each one. However, she had not revised any comments, and this was annoying. Now the comments did not match the code. This was bad coding practice and would lead to maintenance problems in the future.

And furthermore ...

Dillon traced through the program logic and felt a deep ache in his chest. Rachel had made some changes that broke the logic or violated encapsulation. The program compiled, but it would not work correctly. This was inexcusable. It was obvious that Rachel did not know what she was doing, that she was simply guessing. The worst sort of programming. It made him feel sick, to see Rachel ruining the deep beauty of his program.

Somebody pounded on the outside door.

Dillon stood up and went to open the door.

Clifton Potter was waiting outside. "Dude! Sorry to bother you, but—"

Dillon raised his hand. "I will not work with Rachel anymore."

"Um, what?" Clifton's eyebrows went up.

Dillon had learned that this sometimes meant surprise, but it also meant other things depending on something called the social context. His counselor had given him a number of different social contexts and explained what raised eyebrows meant in each one, but Dillon had no time to parse the meaning of Clifton's eyebrows now.

Dillon pointed toward the bio-lab. "Rachel insisted that we should leave last night when I wanted to continue working. Then she came back later and made changes to the code. There is no possible honest explanation for this. Therefore, I do not intend to work with her anymore."

"Whoa, my man!" Clifton looked around. "Let's just go inside and try to sort this out. Sounds like there's some major biffosity afoot. Am I right?"

Dillon did not understand this question, but he stepped back and led Clifton into the bio-lab. He told him about the chair and showed him the changes in the source code, explaining why nearly all of Rachel's changes had actually made things worse, rather than better. Clifton had some skill in programming and he nodded as Dillon pointed out each error. "Biff." "Whoa, that's bonehead." "Bogus City."

When Dillon finished the litany, Clifton sat for a minute holding the end of his ponytail in his hand and staring at it. "What did Rachel say when you discovered this?"

Dillon shrugged. "She was not here when I came in. I have not talked to her yet."

"Dude, when did you get in, then?"

Dillon looked at his watch. "Twelve minutes ago."

Clifton's eyes narrowed. "You came in way later than normal."

"Today is Saturday."

Clifton stared at him. "I know. As in, this is our last day on the nominal schedule. I'd have thought you'd come in early."

"I go shooting on Saturday morning."

"Shooting?"

"I shoot target practice every Saturday morning at nine-thirty. One hundred rounds."

"You couldn't have maybe put it off till tomorrow?"

"I shoot on Saturday." Dillon did not understand why people did not see the value of making a schedule and keeping to it. When you were on schedule, then you felt calm and you did not make mistakes.

"Dillon Dude, listen, maybe a little flexibility would be good. That's why we put Rachel with you on this—"

"I will not work with Rachel anymore," Dillon said. "She did something dishonest."

Clifton stood up and began pacing. "Maybe she had a reason."

"There is no logical reason."

"She's not the most logical chick in the flock. Maybe she had an illogical reason."

Clifton's phone rang. He pulled it out and looked at it. "Hey, Dillon, 'scuse me but I'm gonna step out. Private call."

Dillon nodded and began working at undoing the damage Rachel had done. He did not care what Clifton said. He was not going to work with Rachel anymore.

～

Clifton

Clifton stepped outside and walked toward his car. His phone rang again. He popped it open. "Hi, Ted, how are you, dude?"

"Clifton, I have three seriously demented Qualcomm honchos on my case." Hunter's voice sounded tight. "Are you or are you not going to meet with them today?"

Clifton considered his options. Interviewing with Q wasn't an el slammo, but it was a great shot at a great company. If he passed on this one, Hunter would never talk to him again, and he'd probably pass word on to his headhunter buddies and none of them would give Clifton the time of day either. On the other hand, it was Crisis City here at CypherQuanta. There was a small chance that he could fix things. Small, but the payoff was *huge*. And Clifton wanted that payoff more than anything. It was high risk, high reward, and that was why a guy got into a startup in the first place. If this thing failed, he'd be out of a job, or maybe even dead. But if he won ... well, he'd pretty much own the world.

"Clifton, are you there? Hello?" Hunter sounded agitated.

"I'm here." Clifton took a deep breath and let it out slow. "Listen, Ted, I want you to know how much I appreciate the hoops you've been jumping through on my behalf."

Hunter didn't say anything, which meant he was seriously biffed about this.

Clifton saw no way out except straight ahead. "I wish I could say yes, but I have obligations I need to meet today. I'm just hoping the guys at Q understand that my loyalty is to my company for as long as I'm working with it. So I've got to say no for now, but I'd love to talk to them later, if that's possible."

"It isn't possible, and you are making me look bogus," Hunter said. "And it would kind of help if I had an excuse I could toss these guys, because you're gonna lose all credibility when I tell them you were hot to trot a week ago and now today you're loyal to your boss. Has there been some sort of major change in your situation that would explain why you've gone all wobbly on me?"

"Oh, hey, listen, my boss just pulled into the parking lot. Gotta go," Clifton said. "Catch you later, okay?" He hung up without finding out if it was okay and put the phone in his pocket. He looked all around him again. Not a soul in sight. The pressure was massively getting to him. He felt like somebody was watching all the time, and it was seriously creeping him out.

But there was no *time* for being creeped out. This was a royal biffosity, but for sure he could make things right. All he had to do was sit Dillon and Rachel down in the same room and straighten out the mess and get them back on track.

The sooner, the better.

CHAPTER TEN

Rachel

Rachel's tires spun on the gravel at the side of the road. She set the brake, armed the alarm, and jumped out of her Miata, slamming the door behind her. That stupid Dillon had ruined everything. She should never have agreed to work with him.

Grant was already waiting at the top of the steps, his face a picture of grandfatherly concern.

Rachel stormed up the steps to him. She reached into her fanny pack and pulled out a Ziploc bag containing her bio-computer. What remained of it.

Grant's face went pale when he saw it, and he looked nervously around. "Let's get inside the house before you wave that around." He shepherded her through the massive oak door.

Rachel flounced onto the leather couch and stared out at the Pacific Ocean far below.

"Hey, Rachel, how about if you come back away from the window?" Grant suggested. "They can shine lasers on the glass and pick up what we're saying on the bounce-back signal."

Rachel followed him through the house to the pool area. It was an enormous house, completely surrounding the pool. Grant's wife, Julia, was lying out in the sun on a lounge chair. Rachel knew that she was about thirty years younger than Grant. Grant's first wife had left him for an older man, and Daddy thought that had really got Grant's goat, to be left for some rich old coot. According to Daddy, Grant had snagged a young bimbo as a way of thumbing his nose at his ex. Rachel guessed Julia was about ten percent saline or silicone or whatever they used these days. She had that scorched-meat look to her skin that a lot of La Jolla people seemed to wear as a badge of honor.

Grant led Rachel to a pair of chairs next to Julia.

"Oh, hi, honey," Julia said in that phony saccharine voice of hers. She was always giving Rachel that weird look, like she thought Rachel was going to seduce Grant or something. As if.

"Hi, Aunt Julia." Rachel sat down in the chair and pretended to be relaxed. Inside, she was trembling with rage.

Grant sat between them. "Rachel, Julia knows all about the bio-computer, so anything you can say to me, you can say to her. Show me the vial."

Rachel took it out again. Most of the contents had leaked out. A few milliliters of it were left. "Dillon left this in the NMR machine upside down and it wasn't stoppered quite tight enough and most of it leaked out on the floor."

"Couldn't you sop it up somehow?" Grant asked.

"There's a slight tilt in the floor. Liquids flow right to the drain," Rachel said. "It's a safety feature."

Grant held it up to the light. "Is this going to be enough to run the tests?"

Rachel shook her head. "I don't think so. I synthesized enough to give a decent signal and no more." Which wasn't strictly true, but that was none of Uncle Grant's business. She had another vial in her apartment as insurance, but she wasn't going to tell anyone about that until she got this resolved.

"And you're sure Dillon spilled it?" Julia said.

Rachel gave an impatient sigh. "There were no signs of forced entry into the lab when I went in this morning. Dillon wasn't there, but I saw that someone had logged on to the computer using my account and was working on the NMR machine. I looked inside and found this. Then I checked the safe where the bio-computer is supposed to be kept, and it was empty. There are three people in the world who know the combination to the lab. Me, Dillon, and you, Uncle Grant. And I know you didn't go there in the middle of the night."

Grant's face looked pale and moist. "Bet your cookies I didn't. I went to bed after we called you last night."

"I know Dillon did it," Rachel said. "I didn't do it and you didn't do it, so according to Sherlock, that leaves Dillon. And it's real suspicious that he wasn't in when I got there. He was the one foaming at the mouth last night about working till we got it done."

"When did you go in?" Grant asked.

"Ten o'clock," Rachel said. "Maybe a little after."

Grant looked at his watch. "Dillon goes shooting every Saturday morning at nine-thirty."

"Shooting?" Rachel felt her pulse ratchet up. Guns were for ... criminals. Violent people.

"Right, shooting. He's kind of a gun freak. You know, some Asperger people are weird about trains. They can tell you everything you were ever afraid to ask about trains. They memorize schedules. They obsess on every mechanical detail. Dillon's that way about guns."

Julia gave a nasty smile. "Whatever you do, don't ask Dillon about nine-millimeter pistols at a party. He's even worse about those than the multiverse."

Rachel couldn't imagine why Dillon would take time out of an impossible schedule to go *shooting*. "You're telling me he's shooting while we're trying to get this project done?"

Grant didn't look perturbed. "Listen, Rachel, Dillon is a very weird bird. Yes, he goes shooting every Saturday morning at nine-thirty. He arrives exactly the same time every week, shoots exactly a hundred bullets, and then goes home. It's one of the things in his life that has some order to it. No matter how busy he is, he goes shooting on Saturday."

"And to church on Sunday," Rachel said. "He's some kind of a religious fanatic."

"Actually, Dillon never goes to church," Julia said. "Whatever you do, don't get him going on the evils of Catholicism."

"He has a brilliant obsessive mind," Grant said. "It takes all kinds, and he's one of the kinds it takes all of. He doesn't think like you and me. In fact, he thinks so far outside the box, he might be in a different universe. But what I care about is that he gets results."

Rachel held up the bio-computer. "Excuse me, but he just waxed six months of my work. That's not the kind of results I want."

Julia looked as if she was going to throw up. An activity she probably had some practice in, judging by her thin, thin waist.

Grant was sweating now. "Listen, innocent until proven guilty, right?"

Rachel leaned forward and let all the fury in her body funnel into her voice. "I don't think you're getting this. We already proved Dillon's guilty. You didn't do it and I didn't do it. Dillon's the only other possibility."

"It couldn't be somebody else?" Julia said. "Maybe somebody else knows the combination to the lab, somehow?"

"Oh right. Somebody who also magically knows my computer password?" Rachel said. "Dillon knows it—he sees me type it in twice a day. Even Uncle Grant doesn't know my password. So it's Dillon or me, and I didn't do it."

Grant took out his cell phone. "Okay, let's not panic. We need a meeting of the minds. I'm calling Clifton right now, and then—" He swore softly under his breath. "I'm getting shunted through to voice mail. He must be on the line." Grant waited a minute, then left Clifton a message to call back right away. He punched in another number and waited. "Hello, Dillon? I need to see you right away. Where are you?"

Grant listened for a couple of minutes, and his face showed a curious mix of emotions. Surprise. Shock. Puzzlement. "Okay, Dillon, let's not talk about this anymore over the phone. I get the picture, but it's an insecure medium. You and Clifton just sit tight. Rachel and I will be over as quick as we can. Do me a favor—call Keryn and have her meet us over there, okay? She needs to be in on this."

Grant hung up and put the phone in the geeky little plastic holster he wore on his belt. He narrowed his eyes and studied Rachel.

"Is something wrong?" she said.

"Real wrong," he said. "More wrong than I want to think about."

Rachel felt her belly tighten into a hard knot. "What is it?"

Grant stood up. "Dillon couldn't say much over the phone, but he did tell me he doesn't want to work with you anymore and that's final."

"Final?" Rachel's voice came out in a squeak.

Grant's lips were white. "And by the way, when Dillon says something is final, it's ... final."

~

Keryn

Keryn paced back and forth in the bio-lab and listened while Dillon explained the whole thing. Clifton kept walking out every two minutes to see if Grant and Rachel had arrived yet. None of it made any sense to Keryn. Why would Rachel send Dillon packing at midnight, then turn around and come back two hours later? What could Rachel expect to do that Dillon couldn't?

Clifton burst in. "Dude, they're here." He put a hand on Dillon's arm. "Listen, buddy, let's just stay calm, okay? I bet there's a rational explanation for it all. Let's give Rachel a chance to explain what she did."

Dillon's face was an unreadable mask.

Keryn had never felt so scared. This was not the *time* for Dillon to go getting principled on them. Time was critical. They needed to just move on and finish the software. A secret this big was too hard to keep under control. And once it got out ... they'd have no choice but to go to the Feds.

The outer door opened, and then the inner door. Grant strode in, his face gray with determination. Keryn thought he didn't look healthy. Then she saw Rachel, and fear kicked her hard in the gut.

Rachel looked furious. She fumbled in her fanny pack and pulled out a Ziploc bag.

Dillon stared at it with a blank expression. "That is supposed to stay in the safe."

"No kidding," Rachel said. "Is there any particular reason you were testing it in the NMR machine this morning?"

Dillon looked like she'd slapped him. "I was not testing it in the NMR machine."

Rachel pulled the vial out of the bag. "Excuse me, but there isn't any other interpretation of the facts. I came in this morning and—"

"And you interfered in my software," Dillon said. "What possible reason could you have for that?"

Rachel gawked at him. "Don't be stupid. I haven't got any reason to geek with your software. Look at this vial. You put it in the NMR *upside down*. Notice how much there is left? The rest leaked out. Do you have any idea how long it took to synthesize this? There is no excuse for this—"

Dillon stood up and his face looked like a mask. "I did not touch your bio-computer."

She put her hands on her hips. "You're lying. I didn't do it. Grant didn't do it. You're the only other option."

"I do not tell lies." Dillon's face had gone bright red.

Rachel scowled up at him. "So you're saying I'm a liar? Or Grant is?"

Keryn wanted to find some way to make peace, but she didn't know how.

Dillon looked at Grant, then back at Rachel. "I do not believe Grant did it. I know I did not do it. Therefore, *you* must have. Furthermore, I have proof you tampered with my software."

"Proof?" Rachel spat out the word. "What proof? I didn't do anything with your software. I wouldn't know how."

"That much is obvious from the bumbling attempts you made to fix it." Dillon sat down in the chair and pulled up a program.

Keryn stepped closer, feeling hopelessly out of her depth. "Okay, explain all this in slow motion, would you? I'm still not following what happened."

Dillon explained in great detail how SourceSafe worked. It kept a record of all changes that were made to a program. Each time you wanted to work on a file, you had to "check it out" from SourceSafe. When you were finished working, you "checked it back in." SourceSafe kept a record of the changes between the two versions. And it showed who made each change.

One thing was clear. Rachel had checked out the file at 2:14 a.m. and made some changes that allowed the file to "compile," whatever that meant. According to Dillon, the changes were wrong and had to be fixed again.

When Dillon finished explaining it all, Keryn turned to look at Rachel. She was sitting on a high lab stool at the wet bench with her arms folded across her chest.

Grant cleared his throat. "Um, Rachel, what about these changes here? You made those and—"

"I didn't make them." Rachel stuck her chin at Grant. "Somebody used my account to make those changes. But it wasn't me."

Dillon stood up. "Nobody can do that unless they know your password. Who knows your password?"

Rachel jabbed a finger at him. "You do, and nobody else does. You're sitting there every time I log in to check e-mail. All you have to do is watch me type it in."

Dillon looked shocked. "You know I would never do that. It would not be honest."

Rachel got off her lab stool. "Oh, excuse me! I would have thought it was perfectly innocent, as compared to sneaking in here at two a.m., logging in under my account, making a bunch of changes under my name, and then playing games with my bio-computer and losing most of the sample."

"Two-fourteen." Dillon said.

"What?" Rachel's mouth hung open.

"It was 2:14 a.m., not two a.m." Dillon pointed at the time stamp. "It says so right here."

Rachel stomped her foot. "I don't *care* what time it was. My point is that spying on me while I type in my password is pretty innocent compared to doing all the rest of it. So don't give me this crap about how it wouldn't be honest."

"You are saying I did all that?" Dillon's eyes glowed with anger.

"And you're saying I did it," Rachel said. "Don't give me all that holy-holy stuff. I didn't do it and therefore you did."

Dillon's mouth set like granite. "I demand an apology."

Rachel held up the nearly empty vial. "I demand my computer back. I'm beginning to think it wasn't an accident. What if you stole it —drained it off into another vial and left me a little bit so it looked like an accident? Tough-guy Dillon, coming in to work all night. Sorry, but I'm not impressed."

Dillon turned his back on her.

Clifton stepped to his side. "Dude, listen, I think you're kind of overreacting."

Grant put a thick mitt on Rachel's shoulder. "Rachel, let's not forget why we're in this thing. Privacy for the world. Protection from Big Brother. This is a lot bigger than any of us. I think you two need to just lay this aside for the good of—"

Rachel froze him with a look.

Keryn was sweating now, and praying. *Hey, God, if you're listening, it's me with another emergency. I know I've been kind of AWOL lately, but we're in trouble here. Help me figure out something. Help me get them back on track.* But she had a horrible feeling in her gut that God wasn't going to step in and fix it all up. Maybe God had gone AWOL too.

"Um, guys, could we take a time-out for a couple hours?" Keryn put a hand on Dillon's shoulder. "Clifton, why don't you and Dillon go grab lunch somewhere so you can talk? Grant, you can take Rachel home and do the same. Let's all just cool off and think about what this all means. We're sitting on a really valuable, really dangerous secret. Let's not blow it. We can meet back at CypherQuanta in a couple hours, all right?"

Grant nodded. "Good idea. We need to keep our eyes on the target, people."

Clifton wiped his hands on his T-shirt. "No kidding. Dillon Man, come on. Let's go chow and just talk things through with logic." He led Dillon out of the lab. Dillon looked back at Rachel. His eyes glowed with a deep, deep fury.

Keryn's stomach churned. Conflict like this made her physically sick. She had heard that Dillon could sometimes be as ridiculously stubborn as a three-year-old. This was the first time she'd seen it.

Grant waited a few minutes, until the sound of Clifton's engine had died away. "Come on, Rachel. I'll call Julia and she'll make some of her taco salad. You like that, right? Keryn, you want to come with us?"

Keryn shook her head. "I need to maintain neutrality here. I'll just ... go home and talk to Smiley and clear my brain. There's got to be an answer."

All three of them went out together. Grant armed the alarm and then got into his car and drove off with Rachel.

Keryn sat in her car with her head on the steering wheel and wondered how she was going to get her novel done when her life was getting deeper and deeper into a story line she wanted desperately to get out of.

CHAPTER ELEVEN

Dillon

Dillon sat with Clifton in one of the booths at Souplantation, a soup and salad buffet on Mira Mesa Boulevard. It was a very healthful place and on Saturday at lunchtime, it was a calming environment. On Saturday evenings, it was not calming. Dillon never came here on Saturday evenings.

Clifton took another bite of his pizza. "You've been hanging with Rachel an awful lot this week. Tell me what you think of her."

An image formed in Dillon's mind of himself and Rachel hanging together on a gallows. He did not think this was what Clifton meant, but he knew from experience that it was impossible to get a suitable explanation for Clifton's slang.

"I mean, I don't know the chick at all, hardly," Clifton said. "I'm just trying to get a line on her."

"She is exceptionally intelligent," Dillon said. "The bio-computer is extremely clever—a major advance. She is paranoid of the government."

"Hey, who isn't?" Clifton said. "With the technology now, they can spy on us and we'd never know."

Dillon shook his head. Such talk was silly. It was foolish to—

Dillon's cell phone rang. He took it out and examined the caller ID. Robert again. Dillon wanted to talk with Robert, but he also knew that he must not talk with Robert while he was upset. It would be unhelpful to Robert, and therefore it was illogical to talk with him now. He put the phone back in his shirt pocket.

"I mean, take that cell phone," Clifton said. "You got one of the new ones with GPS on it?"

Dillon nodded. It was a logical feature to have. If you had to call 9-1-1, the cell phone could help the dispatcher find you more quickly and accurately than if you tried to communicate your location verbally.

"So, what I'm saying is, Big Brother can tap into that and they know where you are at all times," Clifton said. "That's information, man. That's power. They could send out a drone to spy on you and you'd never know. They can tap your phone, steam open your letters, read your e-mail. Your whole life is like an open book to your friend, the government."

Be in submission to the governing authorities. "I have nothing to hide from the government," Dillon said.

"Well, it isn't just the government." Clifton took another bite of pizza. "Some fourteen-year-old kid could hack into the networks and ... Va-voom!—he gets your stuff. Steals your ID, or messes with your records, or takes pictures of you naked in the hot tub with your chick and puts them on the Web."

"I do not get in hot tubs naked with women."

Clifton grinned. "Well, maybe you'll get lucky with Rachel. I'll tell you, I wouldn't say no to her. She's a hot little number, isn't she?"

Dillon did not understand this at all. Rachel was not a number, nor was she hot. Therefore, this was some bit of slang that needed parsing, and he had no time for such nonsense. "But you have a girlfriend." Dillon had met Clifton's girlfriend once at a Christmas party. She was a redhead with a mole on her left cheek and her name was Cynthia. Clifton lived with her in a condo east of Highway 5, in a district that called itself La Jolla but was technically part of University City.

"Hey, it's a figure of speech," Clifton said. "I'm just saying, Rachel's kind of cute." He studied Dillon for several seconds. "I would have thought you noticed that, man. Aren't you, like, ever *attracted* to women?"

Dillon did not know how to answer such a personal question. Of course he felt a physical attraction to good-looking women. Just because he was not a Normal, it did not mean that he failed to notice attractive features of women. But it was an embarrassment to speak of such matters.

Yes, he had noticed that Rachel was unusually attractive. She had a vivacious personality and was incredibly intelligent. When he was around her, Dillon felt as if he were more *alive* than usual. Of course, this was a mere emotional observation. A person was either alive or not alive, and the quality of aliveness was not quantifiable. It was only an emotional reaction to her excellent personality.

He had already had several interesting conversations with her on quantum mechanics, and she also believed in the many-universe interpretation. However, she did not seem to be very knowledgeable about philosophy. She had told him she was raised Jewish and became an agnostic at the age of twelve. She did not seem to be a metaphysical naturalist, but neither was she a theist. Dillon guessed she had spent more time thinking about what she did not believe than what she did.

She did not seem to be disgusted with him for not being a Normal. In fact, she seemed to think that being Normal was a terrible thing. So Dillon felt extremely comfortable around her. Up till now, he had only ever known one woman who was not bothered by the fact that he was not Normal.

Keryn. She was very much more conventional than Rachel—much more like most women, and therefore Dillon sometimes felt awkward and shy around her. But she did not think he was weird, and that was very unlike most women. She was attractive and modest and intelligent. She was a theist, although Dillon did not think she had sound philosophical reasons for that position. He thought it likely that she went to a church he would not approve of. Dillon had never seen a church that he approved of.

Keryn did not make Dillon feel more alive when he was with her. She was not exuberant and vivacious like Rachel. But Dillon thought she had more depth to her character. She was reliable and kind and good, and he felt *calm* around her. *Calm* was not exactly the opposite of *alive,* and yet Keryn was very much the opposite of Rachel. Dillon felt warm and happy when he was with Keryn.

"Dude, I didn't mean to, like, *intrude* or anything," Clifton said. "It's just, hey, haven't you ever been in love?"

Dillon shook his head. From what he had seen, love made people do foolish things. And this was not merely his own observation, it was universally known to be true. Everyone could see when others made foolish errors of judgment. When a man left his wife and children for a fling with some young woman, all his friends could see that it was a tragic mistake, except he himself. Routinely, such men made extraordinary claims for the strength of their love for the girl. And just as routinely, within a year or two, they saw that they had made a blunder, but by then it was too late. Dillon had known many people who married obviously inappropriate partners on account of this mysterious thing called love. Soon enough, the love was gone and a messy divorce soon followed.

Love made people blind, deaf, stupid.

Dillon was not interested in such a thing.

Not interested at all.

Rachel

Rachel could not remember ever being so angry at anyone. Dillon had stolen her bio-computer and then had the nerve to call her a liar. And Grant wasn't getting it.

"... need to think of the endpoint of all this," Grant said. "Look, I know you and Dillon are kind of at loggerheads, but you need to just swallow your pride and work with him. Another couple days and we're done and the payoff will be huge. You know how many Miatas you can buy for a billion dollars, Rachel?"

Rachel stuffed in another forkful of taco salad. She couldn't talk with her mouth full, could she?

The phone rang. Julia went to answer it. Rachel kept chewing furiously.

Grant poured some more Diet Coke for her. "And a billion dollars will be chump change after we go public, Rachel. Maybe we'll hire Gates as our gardener, huh? We'll offer him a billion bucks a day to mow our lawn. Wouldn't that be a kick?"

Julia came back. "Grant, it's the people from RediChex again. They are getting *really* antsy because the direct deposits need to go out next Thursday, and that means money needs to be in the bank by then, and ..." She pointed her thumb at Grant's office. "They're on the line."

Grant huffed into his office and shoved the door shut hard.

Julia sat down across from Rachel. She was still wearing her bikini, and her brick-red skin looked as rough as the corn chips in the salad. Rachel shivered. Some melanoma doctor was gonna put his kid through college someday on Julia's suntan.

"I almost left Grant a few years ago," Julia said.

Rachel washed down her mouthful with a swig of Coke. "Oh yeah?"

Julia looked back toward the office door and gave Rachel that conspiratorial I've-got-a-secret-for-just-us-girls kind of a look.

Rachel leaned forward. Julia was just a dumb bimbo, but scuttle-butt was scuttlebutt. "So, um, spill."

"People think I married him for his money," Julia said.

Well, obviously. Rachel took another drink of Coke, which covered up what was probably a horribly skeptical look on her face.

"And people think he married me for his trophy case." Julia's eyes were gleaming now, and Rachel saw a look of deep hurt inside her. "Another piece of La Jolla arm candy. Wife 2.0, the new and improved version."

Rachel had never had much sympathy for Bimbo Bambis. She put her hand on Julia's anyway. "That must have been hard."

"Then one night we were at a party and Grant had had a few. When it came time to leave, he couldn't find his car keys, and he insisted he'd given them to me." Julia's face went hard and cold. "I didn't have them, of course. I hadn't brought a purse, didn't have my keys, didn't have his."

Rachel, despite herself, felt some pity for Julia. She'd been in exactly
that position a few times, only ... she was usually the one who lost her
keys. She was a little scatterbrained sometimes. That was why she got the
Miata fitted with a combination keypad. That way, she never needed keys.

"Anyway, he couldn't find them, and he was a little plastered, and he
made a scene." Julia closed her eyes. "By that time, the whole party was
watching us. A lot of hoity-toity people who think they're richer than
God. Anyway, Grant finally called me a dumb bim—" Julia's voice
cracked. She took a deep breath. "A dumb bimbo."

Rachel found she could not breathe. Because she'd never wondered
what it was like to be a vanity bride like Julia. Now she could imagine
it. People always looking askance at you, measuring you against your
thirty-years-older husband, giving you that pitying you-belong-in-
diapers look.

"So I called a taxi and we went home," Julia said. "I didn't talk to
him for three days, and then I called a lawyer. We have a prenup that
gives me practically nothing if I jump out, but I'd had it."

Rachel knew this story must have a happy ending, but she couldn't
imagine how. "So how... ? I mean ..."

Julia smiled and opened her eyes. "The hosts of the party found
Grant's keys down in the game room. He apparently dropped his keys
while playing pool with the men. The maid found them in the crack of
one of the chairs, and somebody put two and two together and called
Grant."

Rachel narrowed her eyes. "And that's it? That's the whole story?"

Julia shook her head. "No, of course not. Because here's the point.
When Grant found out he was wrong, he apologized to me. And he
called up every single person at that party and told them he was a
jackass and a fool and admitted that he'd been wrong and I was right
and that he was a king-sized jerk to call me a bimbo when I have a
bachelor's degree in Cognitive Science and a master's in Russian
Literature."

Rachel gaped at her. "You have a ... what?" She put her hand over
her mouth, embarrassed. "I'm sorry."

Julia smiled. "Appearances can be deceiving sometimes. Grant acts
and talks gruff, but he's really a big teddy bear. I can read Dostoevsky

and Tolstoy in Russian. And sometimes, even when people are in love, they say things they don't mean."

Rachel didn't say anything.

Julia gave her a sly look. "You like Dillon, don't you?"

Rachel sipped her Coke. "No."

"I think Keryn Wills has a thing for him."

"She can have him." Rachel felt a lump the size of France in her throat.

Julia shrugged and put on an unconcerned look. "Okay, if you say so. Honestly, if you ask me, Keryn's a better fit, anyway. I think they'd be quite compatible. A nice little cottage somewhere, a white picket fence, a neatly mowed lawn, 2.1 kids, a minivan, two cats in the yard. Wouldn't they be happy together?"

"She can *have* him. If he can stand her."

Julia patted her hand. "But take it from me. People aren't always what they seem. Life is full of surprises, and there ain't no logic in love, honey—you can quote Dostoevsky on that one."

Rachel just looked at her.

"Just try to make up with him," Julia said. "What can it hurt?"

Grant came out of his office and his face looked tight, very tight. "Rachel, look, we have till Wednesday to pull this thing back together again. Do you wanna play ball or don't you?"

Rachel studied the two of them for a long moment, first Grant, then Julia. Finally, she stood up. "I'll play." She moved to the door and waited.

Grant and Julia were exchanging a look that Rachel couldn't begin to read, and she suddenly realized with a deep ache in her heart that she wanted something like that.

Even if it was with a guy who infuriated the guts out of her.

Keryn

Keryn sat on her couch with Smiley in her lap. She had named him after George Smiley, the famous spy in John le Carré's novels. Like his namesake, Smiley was short and fat and had a truly pathetic love life. Unlike his fictitious counterpart, Smiley never took long walks in the rain.

Keryn ran her fingers through Smiley's long, soft fur. "Rachel says Dillon messed with her bio-computer. Dillon says he didn't, but he claims she made a bunch of changes to his software. Which she denies. It's a mess, Smiley, and we don't have time to figure it out and the whole company's coming unglued."

Smiley meowed and rolled over on his back.

Keryn petted his ruffly white belly.

He batted at her hands with sheathed paws.

She scratched between his ears. "Oooh, you love Mama, don't you?"

Smiley began purring in that deep rumble of his. All was well in this corner of the universe.

Except that it wasn't.

"Smiley, I realize you don't have any girlfriends, but you're a guy, so I need your advice. Dillon's hard to read. He's a really nice guy, and there's something ... tender inside that heart of his, if I could only get at it. But he's a great poker player. I can't tell if he likes me, and I can't tell if he likes Rachel. What do you think about that?"

Smiley closed his eyes to flat slits and purred.

"Hey, I'd pay big money if Dillon would purr for me, just once. I was barely starting to get some traction with him when that little chocolate chip cookie butted in on us. It isn't fair, Smiley. She flaunts her itty-bitty little body at him and hangs all over him for fifteen hours a day, and I see him twice a week. I bet she doesn't like Shakespeare. I bet she's a floozy. She's just going to use him and lose him, and meanwhile, I'm left standing by to get the leftovers."

Smiley yawned hugely.

"I know. I'm boring." Keryn sighed deeply. "Just once in my life, maybe I should do something risky. Something crazy. Act a little more like Rachel. Think that would get Dillon's attention?"

Smiley began purring again.

"I hate to admit it, but I'm ..." Keryn took a deep breath. "I'm almost glad they've had this big argument. Now he'll see what she really is—a flighty little flirt. And maybe he'll see me for what I really am. I'm calm and steady. Does that make sense, big boy?"

Smiley might have been asleep and he might have been awake. Keryn leaned over and sniffed the bunch of fresh daisies she'd cut from her backyard that morning. She pulled one out of the vase and stared at it idly. A childhood game came into her mind.

She plucked a petal. "He loves me."

Plucked another. "He loves me not."

One by one, she plucked the rest. "He loves me." Pluck. "He loves me not."

When she reached the last two, Keryn saw that she had gotten started on the wrong foot, and now she was doomed. Her heart felt like a brick inside her chest. "He loves me ..." She pulled on one of the petals.

The other came out with it. Keryn stared at the two petals, stuck together in her hand. She shook the two, but they resolutely held fast.

Smiley opened his eyes and looked up at her with all the love a cat could give. Which was not enough.

Keryn showed him the two petals. "Good news/bad news, Smiley. He loves me *and* he loves me not."

PART 2: BRIDGE OVER TROUBLED WATER

Shor's algorithm is extraordinarily simple and requires far more modest hardware than would be needed for a universal quantum computer. It is likely, therefore, that a quantum factorization engine will be built long before the full range of quantum computations is technologically feasible.

David Deutsch
The Fabric of Reality, p. 215

CHAPTER TWELVE

Grant

W hen they were all inside his office, Grant shut the door
and sat down at the round table where they'd all met last
Saturday. He could not believe how far they had come in
a week. Dillon had worked a miracle. Another couple days and they
could put a wrap on this thing.

"Okay, listen." Grant looked around the table. On his left sat
Dillon, then Clifton, then Keryn, then Rachel. "I know we all had a
little misunderstanding this morning, but I want us to get past that
and move on. We have a trillion-dollar opportunity in front of us, not
to mention the chance to do a good deed for the world. So let's do
it right."

An uneasy silence.

Grant hadn't expected this to be easy. Unfortunately, he wasn't any
good at warm fuzzies. He looked at Dillon, whose face showed nothing. Rachel's was a war of conflicting emotions.

"Okay, Dillon, let's start with you," Grant said. "Rachel is sorry for
anything she might have done, and—"

"I didn't do anything," Rachel said in a hiss.

Dillon's face was stone.

Grant put a hand on Rachel's shoulder. "Let's pretend like you did. And in exchange for that, Dillon is sorry for whatever he did."

"No."

Grant spun his head to look at Dillon.

Dillon looked perfectly calm, but a muscle was twitching in his cheek. "I did not put her bio-computer in that NMR machine."

Grant sighed. "Listen, I'm trying to mediate a peaceful—"

"With respect ..." Dillon took a deep breath, as if he was trying to work up his courage. "I do not think ..." He stopped, and something flickered across his face.

"Go ahead," Grant said. "I hardly ever kill employees anymore since they changed my medication."

Keryn and Clifton cracked smiles at that. Dillon seemed puzzled, as if trying to work out his meaning. Grant kept forgetting that Dillon didn't do irony.

"Uncle Grant, I think Dillon's saying that you're not exactly a neutral mediator." Rachel pressed her lips into a tight line. "And ... maybe he's right."

Grant hadn't thought of that. Yeah, well, maybe they had a point. He'd known Rachel's daddy and uncles since grad school. She was like a daughter to him, and that didn't make him exactly objective, did it? "All right. That's fine. Somebody else needs to mediate, but it needs to be one of us five, are we agreed on that? Unless we want to let our secret out to one of our twelve hundred best friends."

Everybody nodded.

"Okay, fine. That means one of you two." Grant pointed to Clifton and Keryn. "Anyone got any objections to either of these?"

Keryn was looking a little pale. "Really, I think Clifton would be better at that."

Clifton shrugged. "Whatever. Dillon, you good with that?"

Dillon nodded.

Clifton looked to Rachel. "What about you, Rache? Want me to mediate this thing?"

Rachel's eyes narrowed to slits and she studied Clifton for several seconds. Grant figured she had to say yes. Julia had already picked up on something that Grant ought to have seen himself—namely, that both Keryn and Rachel were kind of sweet on Dillon. No way in the world would Rachel let Keryn be the mediator.

Rachel shook her head. "If it's all the same to everyone else, I'd rather have Keryn."

Clifton shrugged. "No problem for me."

Grant saw Clifton's eyes flick down to Rachel's T-shirt, and he thought he could guess part of the reason. But it still didn't make sense. He pointed to Dillon. "Dillon, are you okay with Keryn mediating?"

Dillon as usual showed absolutely no emotion on his face. Grant wondered if he could maybe get Dillon some training in negotiation. The guy would be a killer if he could learn how to lie with a face like that. The hard part would be getting him to lie.

"I like Keryn," Dillon said.

Grant wondered if that meant what it sounded like. "Keryn, sounds like you're nominated."

Keryn hesitated, and Grant saw right away that she was going to refuse. Which didn't make sense. Furthermore, he could not afford to let her say no.

"Hey, time out." Grant made his hands into a T. "Folks, I want to have a chat with Keryn alone. Five minutes, okay?"

Clifton walked out looking puzzled. Dillon followed him, expressionless as always. Rachel went last, and when she looked back, Grant saw a knowing smile on her face. This did not make sense. It did not make sense at all.

Grant shut the door. "Okay, what's up, Keryn?"

Keryn pressed her hands against the sides of her head, as if doing so would squeeze out some thoughts onto the table. "I'm ... really behind on my book. Those two are not even close to an agreement—you must have noticed, right? Mediating could take days, and I'm a half time employee, and I'm on a deadline and my publisher is going to kill me if I'm late."

Grant had been afraid it was going to be something *important*. "Listen, Keryn, not a big deal. Your book's due when?"

"The middle of August." Keryn's face looked tense. "I really needed to work on it today."

"Okay, fine. Two months." Grant took out a pen and clicked it a couple of times. "This is going to take a day or two, max."

"I wouldn't bet on it."

"Max." Grant put the pen down between them. "You patch up this little spat and I'll give you paid time off to work on your book until you're done. That sound fair?"

Keryn considered this for about five times longer than Grant would have expected. She had a look on her face as if she wanted to say something, but finally she sighed deeply and nodded. "Okay. I'll try. For a week. After that, it's over and I want the paid time off, success or no success."

Grant didn't know what to say to that. If they got this thing fixed fast, there was that trillion-dollar payday right down the road. If it dragged on for a week, there was not going to be enough left in the kitty to pay a chicken, much less Keryn.

"Deal," he said. "Just remember how much is riding on this, okay? But no pressure."

Keryn got up and went out of the office without saying anything.

Grant sat there feeling a little sick in his gut that he'd lied to her.

The only consolation was that he could tell by the way she'd looked at him that she hadn't told the truth, the whole truth, and nothing but the truth either.

Keryn

Keryn wanted to kick herself. Why, why, why hadn't she told Grant the real reason she didn't want to mediate?

Because it sounded stupid and she didn't want to sound stupid, that was why. But she *was* stupid, and now she'd stepped into it with both feet. Rachel, the little vixen, had asked for Keryn to mediate because she believed that Keryn could sweet-talk Dillon to get concessions out of him, whereas she, Rachel, would be immune to all that.

Furthermore, Rachel knew good and well that Keryn's intrinsic sense of fairness would make her bend over backward to keep her from steamrolling over Rachel.

Rachel had read the situation and chosen the battlefield for maximum advantage. Now Keryn had to figure out a way to resolve the situation with two strikes against her.

Rachel sat in one of the comfy leather chairs next to Grant's office. Dillon stood stolidly looking out the window. Clifton was looking at the display on his cell phone with a funny expression on his face.

Keryn had no idea what to do next. The problem with geniuses was that they could be such *children*. First, she had to talk to both Dillon and Rachel separately—find out what their nonnegotiables were—and then she had to bring them together and find common ground. It sounded simple, but if negotiations were that easy, the Israelis and Palestinians would have kissed and made up fifty years ago.

Keryn put a hand on Dillon's shoulder. "Do you have a coin?"

He reached into his pocket and took out a quarter. Rachel came over to join them.

Keryn put the coin on her thumb and flipped it in the air. "Heads or tails, Rachel?"

Rachel waited till the quarter reached its apex. "Tails."

It landed on the carpet. Heads.

Keryn picked it up and gave it back to Dillon. "I'll talk with you privately first, Dillon."

He put it in his pocket. "Did you know that in another universe, that came up tails? This whole episode will end differently in that universe."

Keryn led the way to her office and opened the door. "Wish their universe well. We're stuck in this one."

Dillon followed her in and sat down. Keryn had a clean desk, but her computer sat square in the middle, so she rolled her chair all the way around to the other side and sat down next to Dillon.

A big lump formed in her chest. She wanted to reach out and grab his hand. Stick a flag in his head that proclaimed him her possession. Or something. Instead, she just smiled and crossed her legs. "Dillon, we need to get you and Rachel back working together." *Right, that's the last thing I want you doing.* "So, um, I'm not very good at this, but ... what will it take to get you going again?"

"She lied about me," Dillon said, and there was a note of pain in his voice. "I swear to you, Keryn, I did not tamper with her bio-computer. I did not."

Keryn believed him. Dillon did not tell lies. Maybe it was something to do with his Asperger's thing. Maybe it was just his own unique mental wiring. Whatever. Even bending the truth weirded him out. Telling a lie put a bend in his universe, and he couldn't stand having any lines that weren't straight.

Yet she couldn't see who else could have done it. There were exactly three people who knew the combination to that bio-lab. Dillon. Rachel. Grant. None of them made any sense as the suspect.

Keryn patted Dillon on the knee. "Okay, I believe you. I don't believe you tampered with it. But it couldn't be Rachel either."

"It had to be Rachel."

Keryn felt taken aback. "Um, why?"

"Because she is the only person who could have compiled the program, inserted the bio-computer into the NMR machine, and tried to calibrate the system."

Keryn stared at him. "How could you possibly know that?"

Dillon sighed. "Somebody logged on to Rachel's user account, *rmeyers,* using a password that only she knows. Only Rachel could have done this, unless she has an insecure password. The SourceSafe history shows that at 2:14 a.m. the user named *rmeyers* checked out a file and made several modifications to it. These were incorrect modifications, but this user succeeded in compiling the file and building an executable."

"A what?" Keryn was not following this completely and wished she knew more about software development.

"A program. There is an executable program on the hard drive of the system. It was created at 2:43 a.m. I saw the time stamp on it. Rachel created both a debug version and a release version."

"I have no idea what that means."

Dillon nodded. "My apologies. It is common to make two versions of software. One is optimized to run as fast as possible. This is called the release version. The other version is compiled with special information that lets a program execute it using a debugger. You can then step through the code one instruction at a time and verify that it works. Visual C++ allows you to manage a release and a debug version. Rachel built both versions of the code."

"Did she ... run them?"

Dillon folded both hands on his knee and stared at his knuckles unhappily. "The program writes a log file every time it runs. It includes a time stamp and the name of the user running the program, as well as a great deal of information to tell if anything went wrong. Rachel ran the release version first, at 2:46 a.m. It ran and failed in the calibration function."

"The what?"

"The computer needs to calibrate the NMR machine, scanning to find the exact resonant frequencies for all ten thousand qubits in the bio-computer."

"You don't know those already?"

Dillon shook his head. "The bio-computer is cleverly designed, but the resonant frequencies cannot be calculated theoretically. The only solution is to scan the frequency domain experimentally and find the resonant frequencies of every qubit. Then we save them in an xml file and the machine is calibrated."

Keryn felt like she was hearing a lecture in Greek. "Okay, I'm following about ten percent of this. So Rachel ran the program and ... ?"

"It failed. Twice. The third time, she ran it in debug mode and it failed again, but she evidently realized in walking through the debugger that the errors would be too difficult for her to find. She does not understand the deep structure of the program, and she made several blunders."

Keryn compressed her lips. "Why do you think she did all this?"

"I am sure she was merely trying to help. She knew I was exhausted and that I would not agree to extend the schedule. I do not know why she refuses to accept responsibility. Presumably, she is embarrassed about causing the bio-computer to be lost."

"And you're sure it has to be her?" Keryn said. "What if somebody hacked her password?"

Dillon shook his head. "Hackers are not magicians. The password encryption algorithm cannot be quickly broken by brute force unless Rachel chose some simple and obvious password, such as an English word or her name or her birthday. Assuming Rachel has a secure password, then it would not be possible for anyone to hack it."

Keryn decided she had learned enough. Everything pointed to Rachel. Method. A plausible motive. Plus the fact that nobody else had all the information needed to have done it. "Okay, Dillon, thanks for explaining everything. I think you've got enough evidence to convict. Now tell me this. What do you need in order to continue working on this project?"

"An apology," Dillon said. "She made a mistake. She left her biocomputer in the NMR machine and it leaked out. All this I can forgive. I have already forgiven it. But she also accused me of doing it myself and of lying about it." Dillon looked up and—almost—looked Keryn in the eye. "I have a good name, Keryn. I do not prevaricate. Rachel must apologize for falsely accusing me and for calling me a liar."

Keryn felt a rush of hope. She could get an apology. Maybe. Dillon had the evidence cold. She would discuss it all with Rachel. Not accusing. Just laying out the facts, all the while being empathetic and all that. She'd do the woman-to-woman empathy thing. At some point, Rachel would break down crying. Or she'd quietly admit what she had done. Keryn would not lay any blame on her. It was all understandable, of course. The time pressure. The desire to help Dillon, who had clearly been exhausted last night. Keryn would calmly put her arm around the conniving little ... around the brokenhearted, tearful Rachel. Yes, that would be nice. Rachel, busted and repentant, admitting her guilt. Keryn would help her through that, get her back working with Dillon. No recriminations.

At least not until the machine was working and they were all billionaires. Then she'd lay it all out for Grant and leave the discipline to him. Grant was a fair man. He'd take care of it.

Keryn stood up and opened the door. "Thanks so much, Dillon. I think we're done for now. Maybe you could wait over there in one of those chairs? Rachel, I'm ready to talk with you."

CHAPTER THIRTEEN

Rachel

Rachel sat down in one of the chairs in Keryn's office. She had expected Keryn to take a lot longer with Dillon. They'd been in the office for only about fifteen minutes. That was good. Keryn had probably laid it on the line for him—that because of him, they were all getting cheated out of gigabucks.

Keryn clicked the door softly shut, sat down beside Rachel, and patted her on the knee. "I'm sorry it's been such a stressful week for you."

That was a surprise. Rachel wasn't quite sure where Keryn was going with this. "So, um, what did Dillon say?"

Keryn gave her an easy smile. There was something behind that smile, and Rachel couldn't figure it out. "Rachel, I'd rather talk about you first, okay? Just kind of find out where you're at. Have you been sleeping okay this week?"

"Fine. I've been sleeping fine," Rachel said. "Dillon's the one doing all the hard work. I just sit there and give him information when he has a question. And I got on the horn to those idiots at MagTec and reamed them out pretty hard. They were giving us the runaround, and

Dillon had other things to work on, so I leaned on them till they caved."

"And what happened last night?" Keryn's voice had a soft, almost dreamy quality to it.

Rachel thought she might get to like Keryn ... eventually. She was different when it was just the two of them. "Dillon was starting to wear down. He's really been working too hard all week, but the guy is a machine, and I just let him. Until last night. Then he was making mistakes. Plus, I could see we weren't going to get it done. I wanted us to be fresh when we wrapped it. Know what I mean? One stupid mistake can cost you a lot of time. So I made him go home, and ... I guess he didn't like that."

Keryn had been nodding and repeating "uh-huh" and "I see" empathetically throughout the explanation. She patted Rachel's hand gently. "Did you know that Dillon wrote the program so that it contains something called a log file?"

Rachel felt her pulse quicken a notch. This conversation was not going the way she had expected. "I guess that doesn't surprise me. He's kind of A.R., if you know what I mean."

"Dillon says that somebody logged on last night and got the program working, and then they tested it. He has log files for three different runs. Each of those failed."

And now Rachel saw it. The whole clever little trap Dillon had set for her. Which she was *not* going to fall into. She leaned back and folded her arms across her chest. "Tell me about that. Just the facts, ma'am."

Keryn smiled at that. "Right, Joe Friday. Okay, here's what Dillon told me." She talked for several minutes, spinning out the whole string of lies exactly as Dillon had laid them out for her. Rachel thought it was all clever. She couldn't understand the motivation, but it was clever. The whole thing was set up to make it look like Rachel had done it. But there was one thing Keryn didn't know.

"... third time, the program was run in debug mode and it failed again." Keryn stopped for a moment and looked at Rachel with those big brown empathetic eyes of hers. Sweet, innocent Keryn was getting sucked into something she was incompetent to understand.

Rachel sighed deeply. "And let me guess. I'm betting these log files show my username, just like the SourceSafe history files. Am I right?"

"Um, right." A hint of uncertainty clouded Keryn's eyes. "Do you have anything you want to tell me?"

"You write mysteries, right?"

"Well ... yes." Keryn was beginning to look seriously confused.

"And you're familiar with the fact that clues often lead to false conclusions?"

A little understanding began to dawn in Keryn's eyes. "Yes, but ... I have to say the evidence is pretty conclusive here. Wouldn't you agree?"

"That depends where you sit," Rachel said. "In your chair, with the facts you have, it looks like you've Sherlocked this puppy down to one suspect, right? You're thinking that I'm the only possible person who fits the clues?"

Keryn was clearly trying to keep her nonconfrontational mask in place. "Y-yes."

Rachel leaned forward and put a hand on Keryn's shoulder. "And as a mystery writer, you know that sometimes one new clue can change everything, right?"

Keryn's face turned a couple of shades paler. "Um ... have you got a clue for me?"

Rachel nodded. "Two clues. Because, remember, we have two suspects besides me. We've got Dillon and we've got Grant. We three are the only people in the world who know the combination to get into the bio-lab. We are the only three suspects."

Keryn bit her lip. "I don't think Grant did it."

Rachel held up her index finger. "Clue number one. Grant is incompetent as a programmer. I don't think he could even write something in Visual Basic, much less Visual C++. If you set him down in front of that computer, he would not have the first clue how to compile the code, much less fix the errors. Furthermore, there's no way he could know my password to log on under my account."

"So basically, you're telling me Grant didn't do it." Keryn didn't look impressed.

"Right." Rachel smiled. "So it's either me or Dillon." She held up her second finger. "Clue number two. Dillon knows my password."

Keryn looked skeptical. "Dillon says he doesn't. But he did say you might possibly have an insecure password that maybe somebody could have hacked."

Rachel ought to have expected some stupid claim like that. "I don't have an insecure password. I can prove it for you." She grabbed a Post-it from Keryn's desk and wrote eight characters on it: *braK7bwD*.

Keryn stared at it. "That's your password?"

"Yes, and I can prove it. We'll go over to the bio-lab right now and log on to my account using that password. It's a good, secure password. You can ask Clifton or Grant or anyone. Nobody could have hacked that. But I've logged in several times with Dillon sitting right beside me. I can't type capitals and digits very fast. He could easily have watched my fingers and memorized my password. Then the whole story could have happened exactly as he played it out for you, except that he did it, not me."

"So it's your word against his." Keryn looked terribly disappointed.

"Right, and here's the problem. You're familiar with the deconstructionists?"

"Yes. I did a term paper on deconstructionism. I think they have a point, but I don't go all the way with them."

Rachel nodded. "But you agree with the basic point that two people can read the same story and find two different truths in it?"

"I happen to believe there is such a thing as absolute truth."

Rachel wasn't going to go there. Keryn was wrong about that, but she didn't want to waste breath on it now. "Okay, two people can read the same story and, because of their differing backgrounds, viewpoints, worldviews—whatever—they can read the story differently. You agree with that, right? A white Christian reads *Uncle Tom's Cabin* and is awestruck by what a wonderful inspiration Uncle Tom is to forgive his oppressor. Whereas an African-American reads it and is appalled by Uncle Tom's wretched subservient attitude that enabled the white man to keep him in bondage."

"I don't see where you're going with this." Keryn looked at her watch. "Dillon's going to be wondering what's taking so long."

"Here's my point," Rachel said. "You look at the evidence and you see that you have two suspects—Dillon and me. Whereas when I look at the evidence, viewing it through my own experience, which includes the fact that I was in my own bed last night from twelve-thirty until eight o'clock this morning, I can tell you that there is only one suspect —Dillon."

Keryn began sputtering. "But ... but ..."

Rachel put her hand up. "Listen, I don't care if you believe me or not. You've got your truth. I've got mine. I'm just saying that my truth is different from yours. My truth is grounded in my experience, which is something you can't share. You weren't in my room. You didn't see me sleeping. You can't know that I'm telling the truth. *But I can.* And my truth is that Dillon did all that stuff under my username. Why he did it, I don't know. You'd have to ask him. But I know I didn't do it."

"And what's his motive?" Keryn said. "You know how picky he is about telling the truth."

"Who knows?" Rachel said. "He didn't want to leave last night, but I made him leave. So I guess he got mad at me and came back to finish the job behind my back."

"But why would he lie about it?" Keryn said. "That's just ... ridiculous."

"How should I know?" Rachel said. "Of course it's ridiculous. But I know two things for sure. Only two people in the world knew my password last night—me and Dillon. And I didn't come back to the lab. It's a syllogism to conclude that Dillon must have. I don't usually speculate on motives, but if you want one, maybe Dillon's all hot and bothered about not giving the bio-computer to Big Brother right away. But that's a wild guess, and I don't know for sure. Nobody can read minds. Dillon's totally unreadable. If he chose to lie, he could do it with a straight face, couldn't he?"

"I guess," Keryn said. "But he wouldn't."

"You can't possibly know that," Rachel said. "Everybody has secrets. I do. You do. Dillon probably does too."

Keryn looked like somebody had just removed all the oxygen from her lungs.

Rachel wondered what kind of a nerve she'd just hit. Was there more to Keryn than she'd guessed?

Keryn cleared her throat. "What ... what will it take for you to, um, continue the work so we can all finish this project?"

Rachel folded her arms across her chest. "I want Dillon to admit he did it and explain why he tried to frame me."

"You don't want much, huh?" Keryn gave her a weak smile.

"Just that," Rachel said. "But it's nonnegotiable." She leaned back in her chair. She knew for a fact that Dillon had done it. Either Dillon would admit the truth or he wouldn't. At this point, Rachel didn't care. She had an extra vial of the bio-computer at home in a safe place. She didn't need Dillon Richard. She didn't need any of them. They needed her a whole lot more than she needed them, and that was a pretty good negotiating position, wasn't it?

Dillon

That evening in his apartment, Dillon inserted his USB flash drive into his personal laptop. It had been a trying day. Very trying. They had all gone to the bio-lab and verified that Rachel had a secure password for her user account. This eliminated all but the two of them as suspects. But Dillon knew he had not done it, and Rachel insisted she had not. After several rounds of discussions, they had all agreed that they were not making progress and decided to go home.

Rachel had repeated her claim several times that Dillon was guilty. This infuriated Dillon. He wanted his good name back. He thought Keryn believed him, but he could not be sure. Clifton had said outright that he believed Dillon. Grant had not. That stung. Dillon had worked at CypherQuanta for four and a half years, and Grant had always trusted him. Grant had always treated him like a ...

Dillon took a deep breath and blinked his eyes rapidly several times. This would not be a good time to think about his father. Not a good time at all. He stood up and took several deep breaths as his counselor had taught him. His vision clouded and his head felt dizzy and his heart was pounding. He closed his eyes and thought for a few minutes about the classification theorem for two-dimensional manifolds. It was a beautiful theorem, a very calming theorem. In a few minutes, he felt much better.

Then he remembered the way Grant had looked at him today. Pain stabbed at his heart. Until now, Grant had always treated him the way a father should treat a son. Not like—

Dillon's cell phone rang. It was Robert.

"Hello, Robert. I am sorry about not taking your call earlier. I was in a meeting."

"It's okay, buddy." Robert's voice sounded cheerful. "I wanted to tell you that we've talked to my priest again, and I think everything's going to be fine. She's doing a whole lot better, and I think it's resolved. Thanks for your concern and for listening."

"That's wonderful!" Dillon felt relieved. He had been worried that Sarah would change her mind and back out of the wedding. Women were unreliable. Highly unreliable.

"So how are you doing?" Robert said. "I'm so sorry. Here I've been spilling my guts every day, and haven't even asked what's up with you."

Dillon did not like the mental image of Robert's intestines falling out on the floor, but he knew this was just a figure of speech that Robert used frequently. It meant to explain your feelings to someone else. Dillon did not think he would ever be ready to do something like that. It seemed like a very hard thing. That was why people spoke of it in such violent terms. He walked out to his living room and sat down on his couch. "I am fine, but work is busy right now."

"Got some new orders in, then?" Robert asked.

"No."

"Working on a new project?"

Dillon did not know how to answer this question. The true answer was yes. But now the project was stalled. Furthermore, Grant did not want anybody to know about the project. Dillon felt his fingers tightening on the phone. "I have been asked not to talk about it."

"Oh." Robert's voice had a peculiar tone to it.

Dillon could not parse its meaning, but he thought he might have offended Robert. "I am sorry. I will be able to tell you more in a few weeks."

"I hope you're not going to spring it all on me at the wedding." Robert laughed. "Sorry, but I'll have other things on my mind then. Like the mystery of the female mind."

Dillon did not say anything to this. The female mind was something he would never understand. He decided to change the subject. "I am looking forward to seeing Patrick at the wedding." He liked Robert's older brother very much.

A long staticky silence. Finally, Robert said, "Patrick's not coming."

"Is he sick?" Dillon could hardly ever remember Patrick being sick.

"My folks won't let him come." Robert sounded upset. "You know how my dad is about taking him anywhere."

Dillon felt a sudden tightness in his throat. Patrick was a year older than Dillon, but he had the mind of a six-year-old. When they were young, none of the neighborhood children would play with either Patrick or Dillon, so they often played together. That was how Dillon had become friends with Robert, who was eleven years younger than Dillon. Patrick was the kindest person in the world, and it was partly because of him that Dillon had continued to believe in God after—

"So anyway, your folks are going to be there," Robert said. "And I was thinking maybe—"

"No." Dillon knew that Robert meant well, but the answer was still no.

"Just let me finish, okay?" Robert sounded edgy.

Dillon felt panic welling up inside his chest. He did not like this feeling. His counselor had explained that when he felt this sensation, he should calmly extricate himself from the situation. "Have a good evening, Robert."

"Hey, what are you doing?" Robert said.

"I am calmly extricating myself from the situation. I will talk to you later when I am calm." Dillon folded his phone and put it in his pocket. He felt very disturbed. He wished he could be like Patrick. Patrick did not get upset over such things. Patrick was the best person Dillon knew. It was not his fault that he was mentally retarded. To be retarded was not a shame. The only shame was when a family treated such things as a shame.

Dillon's heart was still beating rapidly. He went outside and locked his door and went for a walk and reviewed in his mind everything he knew about Wiles's proof of Fermat's Last Theorem. The proof was difficult and complicated, and Dillon had never been able to follow it beyond the first dozen pages. Today, he could not get past the first page.

Dillon

When Dillon returned, he felt much calmer. He went into the second bedroom of his apartment, which he used as an office, and sat down. He had followed good procedure on Friday night, and now it would pay off. All of his files were backed up onto his USB flash drive. He could continue working here, bio-lab or no bio-lab. Sooner or later, Rachel would admit what she had done and take back her accusation against Dillon, and then they could continue working together.

It would take some extra time to write a hardware emulator to behave like the NMR machine. He need only make a new concrete subclass of his abstract interface driver class and reimplement the interface. But once he completed this task, he would be able to continue development without Rachel Meyers, without the bio-computer. All because he had followed good design procedures.

A deep sense of well-being settled over him. The man who followed good design procedures could be slowed down by bad fortune, but he could never be stopped completely. Grant would be proud when he learned how well Dillon had designed the software.

Proud like a father.

CHAPTER FOURTEEN

Clifton

Late Monday afternoon Clifton returned from the bio-lab and went straight to Grant's office. He shut the door and slumped into a chair at the round table. "Grant, it's looking real bogus between Dillon and Rachel. They are still stuck at Impasse City over at the bio-lab, and Keryn's out of ideas."

Grant's eyes looked huge and hollow, like a panda bear's. "Our bigger problem is cash flow. RediChex gave us till Wednesday to put some beans in for the bean counters. Which is two days from now, if you didn't notice."

Clifton did not know what else could go wrong in his life. Maybe he should have gone to that Qualcomm interview. Except that if there was a chance—any kind of a chance—to make this baby go, he had to try for it. High risk, high reward.

"Here's what I'm thinking," Grant said. "We've got no money for payroll. So we run a snap all-hands meeting Wednesday. We send out word at eleven, set the time for eleven-fifteen."

"Dude, whoa, whoa!" Clifton held up both hands. "When you call an all-hands meeting on fifteen minutes' notice, what does everybody automatically think?"

Grant gave him a dangerous smile. "Layoffs."

"Right. And you panic the troops." Clifton was feeling a big bad lump of lead in his gut. This was horrible and getting more horrible by the second.

"Panic can work in our favor. Look, think from their point of view. They come in wondering who's getting the ax. We lay out the grim news first—we can't make payroll. Then we tell 'em about our ace in the hole and they perk right up."

"We don't have an ace in the hole. Keryn is, like, striking out major-ly." Clifton wondered if Grant was on some kind of medication that was biffing his brain.

"We'll tell them we have something in development that could make us all rich," Grant said.

Clifton shook his head. "Won't wash with the masses, Bossoroni. If we tell 'em that, we have to give details, and we can't do that. Too risky. And if we don't give details, they won't believe us."

Grant smiled. "They'll believe Dillon."

Clifton thought about that. Everybody knew Dillon was Mr. Clean. Back in December the company had paid a fifteen-thousand-dollar fine because the fire marshal had asked Dillon a question and he'd told the truth. People gave him a hard time for a month after that, but Dillon just told them he wasn't going to prevaricate for anyone, that he had to answer to the Lord, yada, yada. Dillon was the company dweebomatic, but one thing was for sure—if Dillon said he had seen the Pope playing poker with Satan, people would believe him. Dillon's word was gold.

"Here's the other thing." Grant leaned forward. "We promise no layoffs. Everyone gets paid in stock, priced at half the fair-market value. So they effectively get paid double. Plus, we tell them there's an 'event' coming soon that will enable us to go public. We won't say what that event is, but we trot out Dillon to say he's working on it, and—"

"But Dillon isn't working on it," Clifton said. "He's stuck dead in the water until Little Miss Hissy apologizes. Which she isn't—"

"He's working on it," Grant said.

Clifton stared at him. "What are you talking about? They're over in the bio-lab with Keryn right now, ignoring each other. Man, if you want an ice bath, go stand between those two for a few minutes. I say Keryn gets a medal when this is over."

"A medal's fine, but trust me. Dillon's working on it. He has a copy of the software on his machine at home and worked on it till midnight Saturday night. And he'll be at it again tonight."

Clifton stood up. "Hey, that would have been nice to know."

Grant leaned back in his chair. "I just found out myself. Dillon told Keryn this morning and she told me."

Clifton felt a surge of emotions. If the Dillon Man was still working on it, there was hope. Not much hope, but a little. But it all depended on getting Rachel back on board. Dillon could only take the software so far without having an actual factual bio-computer to test it on. Which meant Rachel needed to get started resynthesizing her qubits. And how long was that going to take? Weeks? Months?

Grant stood up too. "We'll do the all-hands meeting Wednesday. Have Dillon here exactly on time, then get him out right away. I don't want people giving him the fifth degree. He's not that great at fibbing, case you hadn't noticed."

Clifton nodded and went out. The all-hands thing was a majorly bogus risk. But what choice did they have? They had no money for payroll. No way of getting money, no backers, no nothing. They couldn't even go spin some kind of fairy tale to the bank, because the only story they could tell was too hot for human ears. Another week of this and Clifton was going to have an aneurysm.

Which was starting to sound like an improvement.

Keryn

"Y ou're going to tell them what?" Keryn's knees almost collapsed underneath her. It was Monday evening, and she was worn out after a long, horrible day of negotiations that had yielded precisely nothing.

Grant pointed to a lounge chair. "Have a seat before you fall in the pool." He turned his head. "Hey, Julia! I think Keryn needs a beer!"

"I don't need a beer." Keryn sat down. Her insides were feeling wobbly and she desperately wanted a long nap.

Julia came out with an open bottle of Heineken and gave it to her. Keryn set it on the patio without looking at it. The smell made her feel weak, unbalanced.

"Anyway," Grant said, "my mind is made up. By the way, a few people asked where you were today. I told them you're busy solving a life-and-death puzzle that could change the world. Not my fault if they thought you were home working on your book, is it?"

Keryn gave him a flimsy smile. "Listen, it's dangerously close to fraud, to pay in stock when you know—"

"Repeat after me," Grant said. "Quote—this is a forward-looking statement as defined by the Private Securities Litigation Reform Act—unquote. Standard disclaimer. Nobody reads it, but it basically means—"

"—that you have no idea what you're talking about, but you're sure hoping real hard that things work out." Keryn closed her eyes and massaged her aching temples. This was crazy. This was beyond crazy.

Julia lay down on the lounge chair next to Keryn's. "Any luck with our dynamic duo?"

Keryn shook her head. "It's hopeless. I give up. I can't make them talk to each other. This is not going to work, so let's end it now. They just sit there in the lab and glare at each other. I talk to one. I talk to the other. They say the same things every time. No change."

"Why are all geniuses such flaming idiots?" Grant said. "It's like the smarter they are, they dumber they act."

"So ... take a break," Julia said.

"What?" Keryn stared at her. She was incredibly tired right now, and she had a horrible sick feeling in her stomach.

"Take tomorrow off." Julia put her arms behind her head and a sly smile crossed her face. "All three of you."

Grant was looking like he'd swallowed a cow. "Julia, how is that going to help? Every day counts here."

Julia massaged her long, lean calves. "Right now they're stuck in a rut. It's time for something a little ... unorthodox. Keryn, when was the last time you went to the Del Mar Fair?"

Keryn shrugged. "I go with my sister and her family every year on the Fourth of July."

"Go tomorrow," Julia said. "Grant, go get Keryn some money so she can go to the fair."

Grant mumbled something and padded off into the house.

Keryn was shaking her head. "No, um, really. It's not much fun going alone. My sister can't go because Jason and Jordan have swimming on Tuesdays, and—"

"You aren't going alone," Julia said. "You're taking Dillon."

"Dillon?" Keryn laughed out loud. "That's about the last place in the world Dillon would want to go to. It's so ... proletarian. And it's huge. Dillon hates crowds."

Grant came back with a hundred-dollar bill and handed it to Keryn.

Julia held up both hands like guns and pointed them at Keryn. "They're doing an exhibit of nineteenth-century guns at the fair. That'll get Dillon in the door."

Keryn thought about that. Dillon was a gun freak. He knew everything there was to know about guns. "Okay, so he'll go look at the guns. Is there some point to this?"

"Oh, I almost forgot. You'll need to exert your womanly charms on our boy." Julia winked at her. "If I'm not mistaken, you wouldn't mind a shot at him."

Keryn just stared at her. "My womanly *what?*"

Julia rolled her eyes. "Charms, sweetie. It's time you learned to flaunt what you got."

Keryn had never felt so insulted. "I'm not going to dress like a ... skank."

"Trust me, it's fun to dress like a skank—as long as you know you're not one," Julia said. "It's time you made a power play for Dillon."

Keryn turned to Grant. "Grant, no. This is silly. This is not going to help the company."

He shrugged. "Well, no offense, but ... it might help *you.* What have you got to lose?"

Julia sat up and adjusted the straps on her bikini. "Oh, there's one other little thing."

Keryn glared at her. "If you think I'm going to do some sort of jiggle—"

"Do you like any of the rides at the fair?" Julia asked.

Keryn didn't. Mostly. "Well, there's the bumper cars. And ... The HydroSlide. Jason and Jordan love that one."

Julia pursed her lips and thought for a minute. "Be at The Hydro-Slide exactly at noon with Dillon. Can you finagle that?"

"At noon? Why?"

"Just do it." Julia chucked Keryn under the chin. "And dress your skanky best, sweetheart. Just once in your life, do something wild and risky, okay? I want some flouncing and jouncing. Now be a dear and call Dillon right now and invite him to go to the fair with you."

Something told Keryn this was going to be horrible, just horrible. She took out her cell phone, paged down to Dillon's number, stared at it for three or four thousand years, and pressed the Send button.

The phone rang twice, then picked up. "Hello, this is Dillon."

Keryn swallowed hard and then pasted a big smile on her face. She leaned forward as if she were meeting a million-dollar customer. "Hi, Dillon, it's Keryn. I was wondering if you'd like to go see that great gun exhibit at the Del Mar Fair with me tomorrow."

CHAPTER FIFTEEN

Dillon

Dillon had never been to the Del Mar Fair. He had not realized the fair had anything interesting. But after Keryn called him last night, he had checked through the Fair Special section in the Union-Tribune and discovered she was right. They were having a remarkable display of guns from the 1860s through 1890s at the fair.

"Are you sure Grant will not be upset?" he asked Keryn.

"He insisted we go." She was busy slathering sunscreen on the bare parts of her body, of which there were several.

Dillon had not realized she was quite so ... unprofessional in her life away from CypherQuanta. At work, she always wore attractive business suits. Today, she was wearing shorts and a tight shirt with a V-shaped neckline. Very immodest. Also unsafe. The sunscreen would screen out UVB radiation, protecting her from sunburn if used properly at the correct intervals. But it would not protect against UVA radiation, which caused melanoma. Highly dangerous.

"Here's our ride!" Keryn seemed in high spirits. A double-decker red bus rolled to a stop in front of them. They had parked at a place called Horsepark, which was free, and which included a free bus ride to the fair. Keryn had said it would be fun.

Dillon looked dubiously at the tall bus. The upper deck had no roof. It looked unsafe.

The line moved quickly. Dillon let Keryn get on the bus first, which turned out to be a mistake. She led the way up the steep circular stairway to the top deck. Dillon felt a rush of embarrassment. He had never noticed what attractive legs she had. He had not intended to look at her legs. Keryn would feel embarrassed if she knew he had been looking at her legs, even though it was an accident.

When they reached the top deck, Keryn stopped beside a seat bench. "You sit down first," she said. "Looking over the edge gives me the willies."

Dillon was not sure what willies were, but he slid into the seat. Keryn sat next to him, closer than he had expected. A strange feeling was building in Dillon's stomach. A pleasant feeling, yet very disquieting. He pressed against the side of the bus to give her more room.

"Great day, isn't it?" Keryn said. "Blue skies, no June gloom, perfect breeze."

Dillon nodded, but he felt dizzy in his head. He was used to feeling calm around Keryn, but today he did not feel calm. He felt ... the way Rachel made him feel when they first met. Fear gripped his heart. If he had realized this would happen, he would not have come.

The bus ride lasted for thirteen minutes. Dillon was almost panicky when they arrived. Keryn led the way down the aisle of the bus to the steep circular stairway. While following her down, Dillon discovered an interesting fact about V-shaped necklines he had not known before. As he stepped onto the sidewalk, he could feel his ears burning and was thankful for the cool breeze against his face.

At the gate Dillon learned he could not take his Swiss Army knife into the fair. A sign said that knives were a security risk. He waited in line to check it at the Will Call window while Keryn went to buy the tickets.

The woman at the window took his knife and put it in an envelope. She smiled at him. "Nice tie you're wearing, sir."

Dillon was pleased that she liked it. It was a simple patterned blue tie that matched his gray wool pants nicely. He had noticed that nobody else was wearing a tie to the fair, which seemed strange. He went back to join Keryn in line. When they went through a metal detector, Dillon had to take off his Italian leather belt and let a man run a wand over it, but they made it past the inspectors without any further problems.

As they went through the gate they met a man handing out programs from inside a cage that was being carried by another man dressed as Frankenstein. Dillon looked closely and saw there was only one man, not two. The legs of the man inside the cage were fake, and so was the upper body of the Frankenstein. The upper body of the man in the cage continued down into the legs of the Frankenstein. It was a clever costume and Dillon studied it for several minutes.

Finally, Keryn took his hand. "Come on, Dillon, you'll get double vision staring at that getup. Let's go look at those guns. It's already ten-fifteen."

Dillon followed her. They spent a pleasant hour and a half looking at the guns. Dillon explained a number of interesting features of the guns to Keryn. He had never realized before just how much she liked guns. But it was logical that she should like them, because a mystery writer needed to know about such things.

At 11:45 Keryn suddenly told Dillon she was hungry. They went back out onto the mall, which had become extremely crowded. Dillon disliked crowds and felt grateful when Keryn took his hand and led the way through. She had a nice hand, and Dillon felt warm inside his chest. It was a feeling he liked very much. He wanted to tell her so but decided it might not be appropriate.

They went past a number of garish food stands selling all kinds of outlandish foods. Fried Twinkies. Apple towers. Pan-fried bread. Roasted corn. Churros. A whole pig roasting on a spit. Hot dogs. Tacos. All of them looked highly unsanitary.

Dillon thought one of these might interest Keryn, but she looked at each of them and shook her head. "Let's keep moving!" she shouted above the racket. Dillon noticed that many of the women were dressed far more immodestly than Keryn. He did not see any men wearing wool pants or cotton button-down shirts or silk ties.

They passed a square red stand that said *Tickets* on one side and *Boletos* on the other. At last they came to a large area with many gambling games and carnival-type rides. There were dart games and many coin-pitching games. Dillon stopped to look at one of the basketball hoops. He saw that the hoop was smaller than regulation and was elliptical in shape, broader than it was deep. The geometry and physics would make it much harder to make a basket. The boy running the booth tossed the basketball to him. "Hey, Silk Tie! Take a shot for free?"

Dillon caught the basketball.

Keryn laughed. "Throw it and let's go."

Dillon threw the ball. It missed both the hoop and the backboard.

"Close! Try again!" the boy yelled.

Keryn grabbed his hand and pulled. "Come on, I'm starving. I remember last year there was something I liked around that corner."

Dillon followed. They went past some shooting games. Dillon thought they looked ridiculously easy, but Keryn pulled on his arm with both hands. "Later!" she shouted over the din of bangs, shouts, basketballs, roller coasters, and blaring music.

They turned a corner and Keryn squealed. "Oh! It's my favorite ride! Look, Dillon, have you ever ridden The HydroSlide?"

Dillon had not. He saw at once that it was a ride in which you were likely to get wet. It was not a good ride if you were wearing wool pants and polished leather shoes.

But Keryn had other ideas. She tugged on Dillon's hand and he followed. When they reached the ride, Keryn stopped and turned to Dillon. "Doesn't it look fun?"

Dillon did not think it looked fun, but he did not know how to say so nicely. "I thought you were hungry."

Keryn shrugged. "Last year they had some great ... pizza near here. I don't see it. But would you like to ride on the—"

"Yoo-hoo!" A shrill voice rang out across the mall.

Dillon turned and saw Grant and his wife, Julia. Julia was waving at them frantically. "Keryn! Dillon! Come over here!"

Dillon had never imagined he would see Grant at the Del Mar Fair. Grant wore a huge T-shirt and a baggy pair of blue jeans and a large straw hat. Julia wore ... very little. She was definitely going to get melanoma. Dillon had warned her about the dangers of excessive tanning at the first Christmas party CypherQuanta held, but she was apparently a slow learner.

Keryn pulled Dillon over to meet them. Julia's eyes were scanning Keryn up and down and she wore a large smile. Dillon did not see what was funny about Keryn, but perhaps a large smile meant something different in this social context.

"Keryn darling, you look lovely," Julia said. "Doesn't she look lovely, Grant?"

Grant nodded. "Wonderful."

Julia whipped out a camera and took a picture of Dillon and Keryn.

Dillon realized that Keryn was still holding on to his hand. He felt self-conscious.

Julia was staring at their hands and smiling. "Dillon, so nice to see you again. And ... oh my, here she comes with our tickets." Julia pointed past Dillon.

Dillon turned around and his heart made a funny thumping motion in his chest.

Rachel Meyers was coming toward them. She was wearing nothing but sandals and a tiny pair of orange shorts and a pink top that did not reach to her navel. She held two sheets of red tickets in her hands.

She was not smiling.

Rachel

Rachel ignored Dillon and Keryn and handed the tickets to Grant. "Come on, let's go on some rides!"

"Rachel, look who came to the fair," Julia said. "Keryn darling, why didn't you tell us you two were coming? We could have all driven together!"

Which was ridiculous. Rachel would not have come in the same car with Dillon. She tugged on Grant's arm. "Let's go ride something scary." She pointed to a ride labeled The Hard Rock. It was one of those twirly things that spun you around on four different axes. "That one looks fun."

"I'm game," Grant said. "Who wants to ride on The Hard Rock?"

Dillon's eyes were shining with horror.

Keryn looked queasy.

Julia put her hands on her hips. "Dear, not that one. With your neck the way it is—"

"There's nothing wrong with my neck," Grant said. "How many tickets do we need?"

Rachel squinted at the sign. "Four tickets per rider."

Grant tore eight tiny red squares from the sheet. "We're going. Julia, hold my hat."

Julia put her arms across her chest. "Grant, act like an adult. If that thing throws your neck out, at your age, you'll be—"

"I'm going." Irritation knotted Grant's bushy white eyebrows. "Keryn, can you hold my hat while I—"

"Keryn, he's not going." There was a warning note in Julia's voice that said clearly that Grant might be Keryn's boss, but Julia was Grant's.

Grant glared at Julia. "I'm going on that ride. Dillon, hold my hat."

Dillon reached out to take it.

Julia knocked it on the ground. "No, Grant. I won't have it. You're always going on about that trick knee of yours, but your neck's in worse shape. Look, there's a warning sign on that horrible ride about neck and back problems. You are not going."

Grant reached down and scooped up the hat. When he spoke, his voice was taut with anger. "Come on, Rachel, let's go get on the ride. I'll leave my hat inside the gate and—"

Julia's hand snaked out and grabbed the hat. She threw it on the ground and stomped on it.

Rachel felt embarrassed to be seeing this. She'd known Uncle Grant a long time and had never seen anyone treat him this way. Aunt Julia was just being an absolute *muggle* today.

Grant swore loudly at Julia. He seized Rachel's hand. "Let's go get in line."

"Rachel, don't you dare!" Julia shouted.

Rachel felt horrible. This was ridiculous. She let Grant drag her into line. He glared viciously ahead at the ride.

Rachel looked back and saw Aunt Julia stomping away. Keryn hurried over to the line. "Um, Grant?"

He grunted something but otherwise ignored her.

Keryn cleared her throat. "Julia said she's leaving, and it looks like she's got the car keys."

Grant swore again. He glared at The Hard Rock for several seconds, then stepped out of line. "Wait for me here, Rachel. Julia gets like this sometimes. I'll go cool her down and be back in a minute." He hurried away, leaving Rachel staring at him, wondering if she should go after him. She decided this was something they'd have to work out by themselves.

It was exactly this sort of idiocy that had made Rachel decide years ago that she didn't ever want to get married.

Keryn shook her head. "That was really silly, wasn't it?"

Rachel nodded. "Crazy."

"Who's next for The Hard Rock?" shouted the ticket taker.

The ride had ended, and a couple of dozen dazed passengers were staggering toward the exits.

Rachel stepped out of line. She'd have to wait for Uncle Grant to get back. Because there was no *way* she was riding that thing alone.

Dillon was still standing back where Grant and Julia had had the fight. Keryn took Rachel's arm. "Um, Dillon looks a little lonely over there, doesn't he?"

Rachel took a good look at him. Black polished leather shoes. Gray wool pants. A white shirt and a blue silk tie. She giggled. "He really came dressed to get down and dirty, didn't he?"

Keryn gave her a helpless shrug. "That's Dillon. He wanted to look at the gun exhibit."

Rachel gave Keryn the once-over. Twice. "You really came dressed to kill. I had no idea you had anything so ... provocative. You're showing enough cleavage to make a guy forget the multiverse. Didn't know you had it in you."

"Oh, there's a lot about me you don't know," Keryn said in an airy voice. "Come on. We'd better rescue Dillon." She began striding toward him.

A couple of barkers were talking to Dillon, pointing toward their shooting games.

Rachel hurried after Keryn. She noticed that Keryn was putting a lot of flounce in her step. Was she making a play for Dillon? That was crazy. Dillon was immune to that kind of thing. Wasn't he? Rachel ran to catch up.

"Uh-oh," Keryn said. "I think they got him."

Dillon was sitting down at a shooting booth.

Rachel felt disgusted. She hated guns and anything to do with them.

By the time they reached the booth, Dillon had already paid. It was a competition, where several people tried to shoot a set of targets. Whoever finished first won a prize. Dillon was seated next to a couple of small girls. Keryn went to stand right behind Dillon, snuggling up to him.

Rachel didn't know whether to join them or not, so she took a position behind Keryn's right shoulder.

Suddenly the competitors all began shooting at once. Rachel had a hard time following it, but Dillon was calmly firing at targets in a steady rhythm, aim and shoot, aim and shoot.

And then it was over and Dillon had won and Keryn was hugging him—in fact, she was all *over* him. Rachel came around on his other side. "Great shooting, Dillon."

He nodded at her curtly. "Yes, it was."

The man behind the counter asked Dillon what prize he wanted. He pointed to a small teddy bear. The man got it down with a long hooked pole and gave it to Dillon. Dillon handed it to one of the little girls next to him. Then he paid again.

Several minutes later Dillon had won another bear. He gave it to the other small girl, spun around on his stool, and stood up.

"Go on, Dillon!" Keryn said. "You could win one of those really big bears if you save your winnings for a few rounds."

Dillon shook his head. "It would not be fair to the others. And besides, you were hungry."

Rachel's cell phone rang and she flipped it open. "Hey, Uncle Grant, did you catch up to her?"

"Bad news, Rachel." Grant's voice sounded furious. "Julia made it to the car before I did and she was in such a hurry she backed right into a minivan. The other driver's having a shrieking match with her right now. We're ... I'm sorry, Rachel. We're not going to make it back into the fair."

Rachel started walking toward the gate. "That's terrible, Uncle Grant. I'll be right out."

"Not a good idea," Grant said. "Julia's in one of her moods right now, and it might be a few days. It's kind of embarrassing when she gets like this. Can you ... hang out with Keryn and Dillon? Have a good time and catch a ride home with them, okay?"

"Um ..." Rachel didn't think that was such a great idea. She was about to say so when the line went dead. She stared at her phone, feeling panic slice right through her body. The whole thing was ridiculous. Two grown people having a fight in front of everybody and letting it escalate out of control. Now she was stuck here with Keryn and Dillon, dependent on them to take her home. And apparently, they were here on a *date,* and she was the awkward third wheel on the bicycle.

Great, just great.

Keryn held out the two sheets of red tickets to Rachel. "We have to give these back to Grant."

"He's not coming back," Rachel said. "He ... well, Julia had an accident in the parking lot, and Grant said they're going home." She looked from Keryn to Dillon. "I guess ... I'll be seeing you tomorrow at work."

Dillon was not looking at her at all.

Keryn shook her head. "Didn't you come in Grant's car?"

"I ..." Rachel bit her lip. She had no idea how to get home from here. "I can take a taxi home."

"That's crazy," Keryn said. "It'll cost you fifty bucks. At least."

Rachel hadn't brought her wallet. Julia had told her not to bother bringing money, that Grant was paying. But it would be just way too awkward to butt in on a date, especially the way things were between her and Dillon.

Keryn touched Rachel's arm. "Listen, you two. We came here today to have fun. So let's have fun. We'll call a truce, okay? Just for today, we can forget about what happened at work. Okay, Dillon?" She grabbed his arm and clutched it. "Cease-fire?"

Dillon was looking dazed, which was natural the way Keryn was floozing all over him. "I can do that," he said.

Rachel backed away. "Um, no. I'm willing to call a cease-fire, but you guys are here on a date and ... I don't want to butt in on that."

Dillon's face showed puzzlement. "A date? That is not true, is it, Keryn?" He turned and looked at Rachel. "We came to look at guns. Keryn is interested in nineteenth-century guns."

Keryn was nodding like a monkey. "Right. Guns. That's all. Just, you know, looking at guns and ... more guns and ... a lot more guns, and then we got hungry and came over here."

So it was a half-date. Keryn thought it was. Dillon thought it wasn't. He was just so ... dense about things. Rachel tried to bite back a smile, but she couldn't help herself. She began giggling.

Keryn looked mortified.

Dillon seemed utterly confused.

Rachel covered her face with her hands and just laughed. She laughed for a long time, until she was all laughed out. At some point, she noticed that Keryn was laughing too.

Dillon was looking at them both with an expression that could have meant anything.

"So you'll stay?" Keryn finally said.

Rachel nodded. "If you'll go on some rides with me."

Keryn blanched. "I don't do scary rides."

"That's all I do," Rachel said. "Dillon, I'll join you two, but I need somebody to go on the scary rides with me."

Dillon stood thinking for a long minute. Rachel could almost see the wheels computing in his head, weighing the risk of going on an unsafe ride against the risk of sending her off on her own with no way to get home.

Finally he nodded. "I will go on the rides with you. On anything but The Hard Rock."

"Deal," Rachel said, thinking that Dillon was just too nice for his own good.

CHAPTER SIXTEEN

Keryn

They rode on The Cliffhanger first. It was a simple ride that looked like a hang glider. Three people could ride abreast on each one, and it swung you up in a big circle. No loops, no spinning, nothing fancy. It looked safe even to Keryn. Dillon rode in the middle, with Keryn on his left and Rachel on the right. They swooped up and down, round and round. Halfway through the ride, Keryn noticed that Rachel was clutching Dillon's right hand and her knuckles were white. Keryn took his other hand.

When the ride ended, their glider settled in smoothly to rest. Keryn hadn't been afraid at all. It was a tame ride. As they got off the glider, she saw that Rachel was breathing hard, and her face was bright red.

"Rachel, are you okay?" Keryn said.

Rachel took a deep breath. "I'm fine. It's just ... I'm scared of heights."

Which did not make any sense. "If you're scared of heights, why are you going on rides like that?"

Rachel was staggering just a little, but after a few paces she seemed to recover. "I'm not going to go through life running away from my fears." Her face became giddy. "What shall we ride next? Keryn, you choose!"

Keryn chose the bumper cars. She had always liked them, and it was pretty hard to get hurt in bumper cars. And Rachel wouldn't have the heights thing to worry about there. They all got in separate cars and put on the absurdly inadequate safety straps.

When the electricity started, Keryn jammed her foot to the floor. Her car wouldn't start. She spun the wheel, but she was backed up against the curb and it just would not—

"Whooheeeeee!" Somebody slammed into Keryn from the side.

Keryn's car bounced loose. She pressed the accelerator and saw Rachel roar away, waving gaily and having the time of her life. Just like a little kid. It was almost funny.

Keryn bounced off a few cars and then broke free of the pack.

Over in the corner, Dillon was whizzing around in a tight circle by himself. He wore a serious expression on his face, as if he were writing software.

Keryn cut across in front of him and swerved right sharply to bump him.

His car bounced off hers and stalled. Dillon looked shocked. Then a smile spread across his face.

"Wheeeeeeee!" Rachel sailed up from behind and slammed into Dillon's car at full speed. His car leapt away and began spinning in a tight circle. One and a half revolutions later, Dillon came roaring back. Rachel had reversed direction and was madly fishtailing her car backward, screaming in a voice that would have put a banshee to shame. She rammed into the main pack and stalled. Dillon pounded into her car and she bounced in her seat.

Dillon had a big grin now. Keryn wheeled around in a circle and sideswiped him. Dillon bounced sideways, then whipped around and roared off, snaking through the pack. Rachel followed him, whooping with glee. Keryn pursued them both but got stuck in traffic. When she finally broke through the pack, Dillon and Rachel were racing toward each other at top speed.

They met in a tremendous collision and bounced back. Rachel was laughing hysterically. Keryn drove her car into the crack between them. All three cars whacked into the end curb. Keryn's car twisted around to face Dillon and she stopped short, astounded.

Dillon was laughing.

Way too soon, the ride ended. Keryn got out of her car and found that she was laughing so hard she could hardly walk. Rachel staggered out of her car as if her legs were rubber, but she hooted and threw an arm over Keryn's shoulder. "That was fun! What are we going to ride next?"

"It's Dillon's turn," Keryn said. "Let him choose."

Dillon chose The Teacup. This was a deceptively safe-looking ride. Keryn knew from experience that you couldn't get hurt in the teacups, but you could lose your lunch. Which she still hadn't had. The three of them sat in one teacup and grabbed the center wheel. Dillon was in the middle. Keryn wedged in on his left. Rachel slid in tight against him on the right.

The ride began tamely enough. There was a little up-and-down motion and the teacup swiveled left and right.

Then Rachel swung hard on the wheel and the teacup spun full around. She shrieked like a little girl.

Keryn wished she could feel free to scream like that. To just have fun, to let go, to be ... crazy.

Rachel spun it hard again, and the teacup roared through another full circle. Keryn felt herself pressed up against Dillon. She grabbed his arm. "Having fun?" she shouted.

He took the wheel and spun it hard the other way and now they were whipping through turn after turn after turn. Rachel was screaming nonstop. Dillon was laughing out loud and turning, turning, turning. Keryn began to feel dizzy. She wished Dillon would slow down. It was fun, but it was ... too much.

They screamed through another circle and all of a sudden, Keryn knew she was in trouble. Her stomach was heaving. She leaned forward and retched. Nothing came out, but she felt horrible and she retched again.

"Keryn!" Dillon stopped spinning the wheel. He put an arm around her shoulder. "Keryn, are you all right?"

She shook her head, feeling weak. "Uh-uh."

"Rachel, no more spinning," Dillon said. "Keryn is vomiting."

Keryn covered her mouth for the rest of the ride. Finally it was over.

Keryn stumbled out of the teacup and bent over. She retched again, several times. Dry heaves. It felt terrible.

Dillon patted her back gently.

Rachel knelt beside her. "Gosh, Keryn, I'm so sorry. I didn't mean to make you sick."

"It's ... it's okay," Keryn said. "I'll be fine. Let's just ... go sit down for a bit."

Rachel and Dillon guided her out through the gates and to a bench. Rachel put her arms around Keryn's shoulders and talked quietly. Dillon went away and came back shortly with some bottled water. He twisted the cap loose. "Can you drink? Will that help?"

Keryn took a sip of water and swished it around in her mouth. The cool wetness refreshed her. "Thanks, guys. I'm ... feeling better now."

"No more rides," Dillon said. "We can go look at the gun exhibits some more and then have lunch."

"Um ... no." Keryn didn't think she could handle walking around anymore. "I think I need to be off my feet for a while. We've still got some tickets. You two go on some more rides, okay?"

"Your turn to choose, Rachel," Dillon said.

Rachel stood up and looked around. "What's left? Ferris wheels are boring. I don't like roller coasters. The merry-go-round is for little kids." She looked again at The Hard Rock.

Keryn studied the ride. It was *horrible*. There were two arms reaching out horizontally from a central axis. You locked yourself into seats in the arms and then the whole thing starting spinning around. Then the arms tilted up at an obscene angle. And the arms also spun around their long axis. *And* they rotated around a vertical axis at the center of each arm. The whole thing was grotesque.

Rachel turned her back on The Hard Rock. "There's got to be something we can go on."

"The Sleigh Ride looks fun." Dillon pointed to something that looked like a merry-go-round on steroids.

Rachel shook her head. "That's just speed. I want something ... high. High and scary."

"Try The Rocket." Keryn pointed to a tower. You strapped into chairs and they raised up a good hundred feet in the air. Then the whole thing came plunging down and braked to a stop amid a chorus of screams.

"Half a second of scare," Rachel said. "Not enough." She shaded her eyes and walked fifty yards down the pavement. When she came back, her face was glum. She hunched onto the bench beside Keryn. "Maybe we should get something to eat."

Dillon had been pacing back and forth while Rachel looked. His hard leather shoes gleamed in the bright sun. When she sat down, he kept pacing. Back and forth. Back and forth. Finally he stopped.

Reached out a hand to Rachel.

She looked up at him, her eyebrows raised in surprise.

"I will take you on The Hard Rock," he said.

Rachel's face lit up with joy. Then panic replaced it. Keryn stared at her, fascinated. Rachel was absolutely terrified of this thing. Drawn to it. Scared to death. She took Dillon's hand, and her arm was quivering. "Okay, l-let's go."

Keryn watched them walk away together and realized that somehow, someway, she had lost. Rachel, who was scared of heights, knew how to live, in a way that Keryn never would.

Dillon

Dillon had watched The Hard Rock several times by now, and he knew what to expect. He did not think it was particularly dangerous. Of course it would be unpleasant. Spinning around on four different axes would make him dizzy, and he did not like being dizzy. But the ride had been in operation for a number of days and nobody had been killed. It would be more dangerous to cross

Jimmy Durante Boulevard in the crosswalk than to ride The Hard Rock.

Furthermore, Rachel wanted to ride it and it was her turn to choose and she could not go alone because she was afraid. It was only polite to take her on the ride.

They paid their tickets and went through the gate. Rachel led the way. The seats were arranged in groups of four. The innermost of the four would experience the least centrifugal force. The outermost would experience the most. Rachel pointed to the outer one. "Do you want the good seat?"

Dillon shook his head.

Rachel jumped up into the cage and nestled into the hard plastic seat. Dillon sat beside her. Signs warned them to keep their feet in. An attendant came by and helped them pull down the thick plastic safety harness. Dillon felt trapped. He could not back out now, even if he wanted to.

A hydraulic arm pulled the top of the cage down around them, and a foot bar popped up to latch against the floorboard. Dillon rubbed his wet palms against his pant legs. A speaker began blaring loud rock music. Slowly, the arms of The Hard Rock began rotating on two axes —around the main vertical axis and around the long axis of each arm. All Dillon's weight pressed against his safety harness. The turn continued and now he was upside down, inches above the platform.

A hand fumbled for Dillon's. He twisted his head and saw Rachel. Fear covered her face. He gripped her hand.

They spun faster. The arms continued rotating on the two axes. Soon they were spinning alarmingly fast. They began to tilt upward.

Rachel screamed.

Dillon squeezed her hand. "We will be quite safe." He could not hear his voice, so he repeated the words, shouting this time. He could see Rachel's eyes, wide and white in her slick face. As they rolled forward, her hair flopped this way and that.

The arms were now pointing up at a steep angle and the centrifugal force alternately crushed Dillon's chest against the harness and his back against the seat. He felt blood rushing into his face, then out of his head. He wished the ride were over.

Then the arm began rotating on its fourth axis. Dillon felt finger-nails digging into his hand. Rachel was screaming again, so loud it hurt his ears. Now there was no predicting the motion. It had gone chaotic, and Dillon felt unseen forces sucking him first one direction then another with no discernible pattern. The sun blazed into his eyes, then disappeared. The sky, the ground, the machinery, the sun, the crowd below—all flashed past his eyes in a sickening dizzy sequence.

"Oh my gosh, Dillon, help!" Rachel cried. "This is horrible! Help me!"

Dillon could do nothing.

Her hand clutched his like a vise grip. She screamed again.

Dillon knew the ride should last for two minutes and thirty seconds. Something must be wrong. They had been swirling now for many minutes. Again and again he felt twice his body weight pressed against the safety harness, crushing the breath out of him. He hoped his tie would not get wrinkled.

After a long time, the tilt of the arms began to decrease. The rota-tion around the fourth axis stopped. The arms flattened out until they were inches above the platform, still rotating. Slowly the ride came to an end. Dillon could not believe anybody would be so foolish as to ride this terrible ride. The arms lurched to a stop. The foot stop clicked open, the cage opened, and the safety harness unlatched.

Dillon pushed up the harness with his left hand.

Rachel still clung to his right.

He stepped out, feeling woozy and dizzy and relieved that it was over. "Rachel! Are you all right?"

Rachel's face had gone completely white and a mask of sweat covered it.

Dillon pushed up her safety harness.

She lurched out of her seat and fell forward, grasping at his arms. "Oh my gosh, that was ... awful!" Rachel clung to him.

Dillon saw that most of the other riders had cleared the platform. "We have to leave, Rachel." He led the way.

She staggered along, hanging on his arm, her breath coming in deep sobs.

Somehow, they got out of the gate. Dillon helped her stumble over to where Keryn sat on the bench.

"Have a good time?" Keryn said.

Rachel collapsed onto the bench and wiped her face on the sleeve of her shirt. "That was ..." She fanned her face with her hand. "That was ... wonderful!" She seized Dillon's hand. "Didn't you love it? Let's go again!"

Which only verified something Dillon had long believed.

Women were irrational and there was no understanding them.

Rachel

Somewhere during the most horrible, blood-gushing, joyful, terrifying, exciting ride she'd ever been on, Rachel realized that she had misread Dillon. Yes, he was obsessive. Yes, he was wrapped up in rules. Compulsive, irritating, schedule-possessed.

But he was a rock.

Dillon had ridden out The Hard Rock without any kind of fear. He had something she did not have—a quiet strength. She looked up at him now, thinking how incredibly *fun* it had been to scream through the whole ride while clutching his hand. "What do you say, Dillon? What shall we go on next?"

"I need to use the men's room."

"We passed one back that way." Keryn pointed toward the main strip that led to the gate.

Dillon nodded and strode away.

Rachel sat for a minute, still trying to catch her breath after The Hard Rock. "Keryn, can I have some of your water?"

"Um, sure. I'm done with it."

Rachel took a swig from the bottle. The water was tepid. She spat it out on the ground. "Yuck! I think we need another cold one. Can I borrow a few bucks off you?"

Keryn gave her a ten, and Rachel went looking for a concession stand. She finally found one and stood in a long line. After about a six-year wait, she bought three ice-cold Aquafinas at three dollars a bottle. She left the change in the tip jar and headed back.

The Hard Rock was spinning out a fresh crop of shrieks when she walked past. She stopped to watch it. Four axes. Something inside her was burning to ride that thing again. And she would, if she could get Dillon to go with her.

She could see Dillon and Keryn sitting on the bench together on the far side of The Hard Rock. Keryn had her eyes closed and her hands behind her head, which was tilted back. Keryn was getting a little sunshine and strutting her stuff, all at the same time, all very innocent, of course. Rachel felt disgusted. Keryn was such a ... Church Lady, most of the time. Today, she had come loaded for bear, and ...

The bear wasn't looking.

Rachel suppressed a smile.

Dillon was sitting right next to Keryn. It would be so natural for him to just turn his head and take a peek at her chest. Get an eyeful of about three acres of cleavage. But he wasn't doing it. Rachel stood watching for a few minutes and Dillon kept looking straight ahead. He was talking to her. Rachel couldn't hear a thing, of course—but she could see his mouth moving, could see Keryn answering him.

Watching them, Rachel felt ... jealous. Dillon and Keryn would make a good match. Keryn was all prim and proper. Well, not so prim today, but today was an anomaly. She was putting on a different persona, and it wasn't working. Keryn probably felt like an idiot and tomorrow would go back to normal. Dillon was so old-fashioned. He wouldn't sneak a look at a woman even when she put herself out on display and practically begged him to look.

A guy like that had integrity.

Rachel felt sick to her stomach. She'd been so furious at Dillon on Saturday that it hadn't penetrated her skull that something was terribly wrong. Something did not compute.

There were certain things that you either had or you didn't have.

Like virginity. Someone like Keryn—obviously, she was saving herself for marriage, and was proud of it.

And then there was integrity. You either had that or you didn't. And Dillon had it. There just wasn't any lie in the guy. He didn't show his emotions. He had a fabulous poker face. And yet ... he couldn't tell a lie to save his life. Wouldn't tell one.

Which meant that if Dillon said he hadn't messed with her bio-computer, then there was only one possible conclusion.

Dillon hadn't messed with her bio-computer.

Rachel put her hand to her mouth, feeling suddenly nauseated. She had wasted days accusing Mr. Clean of being dirty. Meanwhile, the clock was ticking and the real work wasn't getting done. She was an idiot. A king-sized moron.

Dillon hadn't done it, any more than Uncle Grant had done it. That ought to have been obvious, but she'd let her rage do her thinking instead of her brain. Dillon couldn't possibly have done it.

Which meant that somebody else had. Somebody knew what CypherQuanta was cooking and had found a way to break in and check it out. Somebody clever enough to hack her password.

A gust of cold shivered through Rachel. She strode around The Hard Rock and hurried toward Dillon and Keryn.

Dillon looked up at her in surprise. "Rachel! Where have you been? We have been wondering where you were."

"Long line." Rachel handed Keryn and Dillon each a bottle and sat down beside Dillon. She opened her bottle and took a long, long swig. "Listen, guys, I have something to say."

Keryn's eyes narrowed. "What's up?"

Rachel took Dillon's hand and stared at it. "Dillon, I was really pissed off at you on Saturday. I mean, really mad. That's my baby in that vial. I've worked on that for six months and ... it meant a lot to me and—"

"I did not take it," Dillon said.

"Yeah, yeah, I just now had a rationality attack and figured that out." Rachel looked up at him and felt hot tears spilling up out of her eyes. "Dillon, you're ... the most honest guy I've ever met, and I'm really, really sorry I accused you of taking it. I was just so mad that I couldn't think straight. But I'm convinced now. You didn't take it. I know for sure Uncle Grant didn't do it either. And I didn't do it. You've got to believe me. I didn't do it."

Dillon's face twitched. "If that is true, then we have a problem."

Keryn looked like she was going to throw up again. "You guys are telling me somebody broke into the lab, cracked your safe, hacked your password, and ..."

"And stole most of the bio-computer," Rachel said. "I don't know how they could possibly have done all that, but they did. They made the spill look like an accident, like it had just leaked out on the floor, but I bet they took it. They tested the software and it didn't work, but they probably made a copy of that too, hoping to make it work. They could have burned a CD and walked out with all our secrets."

"Not all," Dillon said. "There was a fundamental problem with the software. It will not work."

Rachel felt her heart double-thump. "How do you know?"

He pulled his flash drive out of his pocket. "I had a backup. I continued working on it Saturday night and last night. There was a serious problem."

"What kind of problem?" Rachel had been so sure her bio-computer would work. It had to work.

"My calibration function was too slow, by a factor of about eighty thousand," Dillon said. "I have completely rewritten it using a new algorithm, and now it should take only fifteen minutes."

"How long would it have taken with the old software?" Rachel drank another swig of water.

Dillon smiled. "More than two years. The fundamental idea was wrong."

Keryn cleared her throat. "Guys, we still have a problem. The bio-computer is gone. Dillon, you could have the best calibration thingie in the world, but if it takes Rachel six months to rebuild that bio-computer, we aren't going to make it. Whoever stole it is going to come back for us and—"

Rachel leaned in close to both of them. "Well ... no. I haven't told Grant this. I haven't told anyone, because I didn't trust anyone. But I trust you two. I have another bio-computer."

"You have ... what?" Keryn's jaw dropped. "Where?"

"Shhhh." Rachel looked all around. "It's in my apartment. When I made the original, I kept back a vial of it. You know ... insurance. In case something went wrong."

Dillon's eyes gleamed. "This means we can test my software."

Rachel nodded. "But here's the thing. I don't know who to trust anymore, other than you guys. I guess I trust Grant and Clifton—mostly. But we've got a leak somewhere. Maybe Grant, maybe Clifton, maybe one of us let the cat out of the bag to one of our friends. Have either of you talked about this to anyone?"

Keryn swallowed visibly. "My brother-in-law was asking some questions the other night, but I put him off. I swear, I didn't spill it to him. Maybe he guessed."

"Don't tell him a word more," Rachel said. "What about you, Dillon? Any confessions? Is there anybody who asks you about your job?"

Dillon's face hardened. "Only my friend Robert. He is a graduate student in physics at Berkeley."

Rachel sucked in her breath. "If he asks again, tell him we've given up on the project."

Dillon shook his head. "I will not prevaricate."

Rachel bit back her exasperation. "Then don't talk to him."

"But his wedding is in August," Dillon said. "We have many things to talk about."

"Change the subject if he brings the project up," Keryn said. "Ask him if he's getting cold feet. That'll distract him."

"Cold feet?" Dillon's eyes went completely blank for several seconds. "Oh. You mean last-minute fears."

"Right." Keryn's eyes closed and her face tightened. "Do we know we can trust Julia? She's quite an operator, behind that bimbo exterior of hers."

"I don't trust her." Rachel took a deep breath. All of a sudden she was scared. "Look, I want no more leaks. Right now only the three of us know. We can't tell Grant or Clifton or Julia or anyone. If we get another leak, that'll narrow it down to one of us three."

"We have to tell them something," Keryn said. "They're going to see that you two aren't squabbling anymore."

Rachel tried to concentrate. "Okay, here's a plan."

"I am not going to prevaricate," Dillon said.

Rachel nodded. "We're not going to lie. Keryn, tell them Dillon and I made up today at the fair. Tell them ... we're working together again. Tell them Dillon's working on the software and I'm making another vial of that bio-computer, but it'll take me a month to get it finished."

"I am *not* going to prevaricate." Dillon's hand tightened on Rachel's.

"That's right, we're not going to lie," Rachel said. "Because you *will* be working on that software, which should be done in a few days. And I *will* be starting up another batch of that bio-computer—which will take a month to cook up if everything goes right."

"But that is not the whole truth," Dillon said.

"No, it isn't," Rachel said. "But it's true as far as it goes."

Dillon looked unhappy.

Keryn sighed heavily. "Listen, Dillon, in Nazi Germany people sometimes had to lie to save Jews. Like Oskar Schindler. Lives could be at stake here. If word of this leaks out, we could all end up dead, and a lot more people besides us. But we're trapped. We can't walk away from this. The genie is out of the bottle. I think we need to do what we have to. A week from now, we can tell the world the whole truth. Until then, we *have* to keep it quiet. Does that make sense?"

Dillon didn't say anything.

Rachel reached deep into her brain and pulled up one of the fragments she had heard from her cousin. "Hey, you know, there's an old Jewish principle that applies here. The rabbis call it *pikuach nephesh*. It means *the saving of a life*. When lives are in danger, it's considered okay in Jewish law to tell a lie. Mandatory, in fact."

"Who told you that?" Dillon said.

"My cousin Rivka." A wave of sadness washed through Rachel. "She's dead now, but she was studying all that before she died."

"I am very sorry," Dillon said. "How did she die?"

"Trying to save the world." Rachel felt her eyes misting. "She was kind of like a big sister to me. Anyway, she told me that most everybody agrees it's okay to kill in self-defense. So it stands to reason that it's okay to lie to protect your life. Right?"

Keryn was nodding her head. "That makes sense to me. Which means it ought to be okay to withhold the truth in order to protect your life." She put her hand on Dillon's arm. "Okay, Dillon?"

A long silence. "I am not so sure, but ... okay," he said. "For one week."

Rachel leaned forward and planted a kiss on his cheek. "You're a stud, Dillon."

CHAPTER SEVENTEEN

Grant

On Wednesday morning Grant stood at the podium in the large conference room, watching the stragglers hurry in. Nobody was ever late to an all-hands meeting announced on fifteen minutes' notice. Work had probably come to a screeching halt during the past quarter hour, but that was okay. There weren't any new machines contracted right now, so there wasn't a whole lot to do, anyway.

Clifton stood at the door with a clipboard checking off names. He nodded to Grant. "Everybody's here. Go ahead and get started."

"Where's Keryn?" somebody asked.

"Oops, she's coming." Clifton opened the door.

Keryn Wills came in holding a big stack of papers hot off the copy machine. She was wearing a nice suit in a muted green color and took a seat in the back. All around the room, everybody was looking at that stack of papers.

Clifton shut the door. "I just called Dillon and he's on his way over. Hit it, Grant."

An uneasy silence shrouded the room. Forty-odd pairs of eyes studiously avoided Grant's. He let the tension hang there for a few seconds. Best to scare them up good before giving them good news.

"Okay, people, we've had a tough little development." Grant took a pen out of his pocket and clicked it a few times. "I guess you all know San-D-Bank reneged on the contract."

A hiss of fear rippled through the room.

Grant waited for silence, then took a deep breath. "There's bad news and there's good news. I'll give you the bad news first. Lost Angels is claiming we're short on the terms for the second tranche, so they're withholding the money. Which puts us in a bad situation with the cash flow, because we spent money on those machines San-D-Bank rejected." He shook his head and put the right amount of regret into his voice. "Keryn will verify this for you, but I've been taking stock in lieu of salary for the past six months."

Heads turned to look at Keryn. She nodded. "Since last December."

"Things are about to turn around," Grant said, "but we are temporarily short on cash. Which means I need to ask you for something. In exchange for that, I'm going to give you something."

Nobody was breathing now.

Grant licked his lips. "Here's the deal, and it's a good one for you. First, there aren't going to be any layoffs. None."

A murmur of relief ran around the room.

"Second," Grant said, "I'm asking each one of you to take stock in lieu of salary for one month. Just one month, and because of the sudden nature of this announcement, I'm offering it to you at half the fair market price. Which means you get twice as much."

He waited a few seconds to let the shock of this work its way through their heads.

Bill whispered something in Jill's ear, and then they raised their hands together and started alternating words in that obnoxious way they had. "Two." "Times." "Zero." "Is." "Zero."

Nervous laughter around the room.

Grant raised his hand for silence, and he held up three fingers. "Third—and this is the kicker—we are working on a surprise technology announcement that should put us on the way to an IPO later this year."

Nancy, the frizzy-haired redhead who handled database work, stood up. "Exactly what kind of surprise are you talking about here?"

Grant was sweating. He needed Dillon *now*. "Um, I'm not at liberty to say, exactly."

All around the room, eyes narrowed. Grant could see behind those eyes, could see the inward concentration that meant that four dozen resumés would be hitting the wires by this evening. Unless his Dillon Gambit worked.

Clifton coughed and looked at his cell phone. "Hey, Grant, looks like Dillon just pulled in."

Grant nodded. He stepped back from the podium. "Um, people, stay calm for just a minute. I've asked Dillon Richard to say something."

Total silence smothered the room.

Grant could feel a bead of sweat running down the back of his head.

Footsteps outside. Hard leather shoes on linoleum.

"Dillon Dude!" Clifton pushed the door open.

Heads turned to look.

Dillon strode in, his face as expressionless as ever.

"Come on up here," Grant said.

Dillon came up and stood next to Grant. He looked down at his hands. "I ... was asked to say a few words about our financial situation."

Every eye was locked on Dillon. Grant could have stripped off all his clothes and gone running out naked, and nobody would have noticed.

Dillon took a deep breath. "I am working on a secret project that should guarantee us a number of new contracts within weeks and an IPO by the end of the year. I understand that Grant is offering each of you the same offer he made me—stock in exchange for salary for the next month. I am taking the offer." Dillon licked his lips. "If any one of you does not want the stock, please sign it over to me, and I will pay you fair market value for it. I will pay cash."

Grant's head snapped around to stare at Dillon. That last part wasn't what he had told Dillon to say. Of course, it made it just that much more believable, but if people took him up on it, Dillon would be out a boatload of money. "Say, Dillon, I'm not sure that's legitimate. Keryn, is that legal? Can he do that?"

Keryn's face was a mask of astonishment. "I ... I think so. I can't think of any reason why not. It's just ... a little unprecedented."

Grant cleared his throat. "Okay, we've got kind of a short time fuse on this, so Keryn's going to pass out the paperwork now. I'm asking each of you to sign it by close of business tomorrow. Unless you want to take up Dillon on his ... his generous offer."

All of a sudden everybody was on their feet, crowding around Keryn, grasping at the papers she was holding. Grant had been part of four startup companies, and he could smell it—IPO fever. In any company, there always came a turning point when it became clear that the beast was going to make it, that it would be going public for big bucks. That's when employees would scratch out their mothers' eyes if it got them another thousand shares.

Dillon remained standing quietly at the podium. Grant stepped up beside him. "Okay. Thanks, Dillon, that was great. You can get back to the bio-lab now." He whacked him on the shoulder. "Nice bluff. That was a stroke of genius."

Dillon just stared at him. "Bluff?"

Grant narrowed his eyes. "Do you have the beans to pay off on that offer you made?"

Dillon nodded. "Do you know what the biggest winner on the Nasdaq was in 1999?"

Grant remembered. If he'd cashed out at the end of that year, he'd have earned back thirty to one on his investment. But he hadn't cashed out. "Qualcomm."

Dillon shrugged. "And do you remember when I came to work for you?"

Grant remembered that too. December 1999. "So what are you telling me?"

"In some universes, I kept my Qualcomm stock and lost a large amount of money when the Nasdaq collapsed." A faint smile curved Dillon's lips. "But in this universe, I sold."

Grant swore softly under his breath. "You're telling me you could have financed payroll out of your own pocket for the next month? Why didn't you *say* something? We could have avoided this giveaway here."

Dillon shook his head. "It would not have been honest for me to take all the profit. This way, everybody has a fair share."

Grant wanted to shake Dillon by the scruff of the neck. Him and his confounded *honesty* could get them all killed. "You better get back to work, Moneybags. Is Rachel gonna have that bio-computer done in a month?"

"Nothing could be more certain." Dillon turned and walked quietly out the door. The door clacked shut behind him.

Clifton had a tense smile glued on his face. He came over and joined Grant. "Think they're gonna get it done?"

Grant shrugged. "The software, sure. Dillon should have that done this week. It's that bio-computer that's giving me fits. Rachel took six months to synthesize it the first time. Now she's got a month."

Clifton cracked his knuckles. "There is, like, no margin of error on that schedule. She showed me the timeline and it's mondo tight."

"She'll come through." Grant hoped it was true. Because if it wasn't, a whole bunch of nice kids were signing papers right now for some very expensive toilet paper.

Keryn

At 6:00 Keryn took a box of pizza over to see how Dillon and Rachel were doing. Rachel came outside and let her in.

Keryn laid out the food on Rachel's desk.

Rachel opened the door to the bio-lab. "Chow time, Dillon. Keryn's brought some goodies." She rolled a chair out to the desk. "Keryn, we changed the combination on the outside door so even Grant won't be able to come in. Want us to tell it to you?"

Keryn shook her head. "No. If somebody comes in and steals that bio-computer again, I don't want you thinking it was me."

Rachel shrugged. "There's nothing to steal in here. When we leave at night, Dillon copies the software to his flash drive and erases it off the computer. And the bio-computer goes home with me in my fanny pack."

"But in a few weeks, you'll have more synthesized." Keryn pulled drinks out of the paper bag and set them out on the desk. "What if somebody steals that?"

"Won't happen." Rachel shook her head. "I have a phony schedule that *says* it'll be done in a month. Reality is that it won't be done for eight weeks at the earliest. Grant would have a cow if I told him, so just smile if he asks how we're doing. Dillon's already testing the software and it looks good. I bet we'll be running Shor's algorithm tomorrow. Friday at the latest."

Dillon came out of the bio-lab wheeling a chair. He left it at the desk and went into the bathroom to wash his hands. When he came out he sat down and rubbed his neck.

Keryn handed him a plate and they all dug in. "How's the software coming, Dillon?"

He took a large bite of pepperoni and pineapple. "Very well. I am teaching Rachel how the program works now. In case something ... happens to me, she can carry on."

A chill cut through Keryn. "Nothing's going to happen to you."

"We hope not, but it is always wise to be prepared," Dillon said. "Right now I am on the critical path. If anything slows me down, the project slows down. Rachel is helping me in many small ways, and this speeds up the project."

Keryn was beginning to feel like an extra hand on a clock. "Is there anything I can do to help?"

Rachel patted her hand. "You're doing it. Thanks for bringing the food by. And for keeping the bosses happy. They are gonna be *so* surprised when we show them this thing running on Saturday."

"It might take longer," Dillon said. "It is possible we will finish as late as Monday. I will know tomorrow."

Rachel popped the tab on her Diet Coke. She opened Dillon's V-8 and Keryn's Sprite. "A toast!" she said. "To Dillon Richard, Chief Studly Officer."

Keryn raised her Sprite, but a sick feeling settled at the root of her stomach. She had helped negotiate an end to the impasse. Her reward was that she was out of the loop again.

And Rachel was right in the center of it.

~

Clifton

C lifton parked next to Keryn's car and bounded up the steps to the bio-lab. He knocked loudly several times and waited.

Footsteps inside. The door opened and Keryn stepped back. "Hey, Clifton! Come on in. There's one slice of pizza left if you want it."

Clifton didn't want pizza. He wanted news. Desperately. That crazy headhunter had called him again, and Qualcomm was asking one more time if he wanted an interview. They needed an answer tonight. Which meant Clifton needed an answer now.

He surveyed the scene. "Dudes! Grant is like majorly stressing over the schedule. We bought ourselves a month, but there isn't anything in reserve." Clifton pointed to Dillon. "You're good on the schedule, Dillon? You'll be done in a week, am I right?"

"Yes, I guarantee it," Dillon said. "If I had the bio-computer, I could be testing in a day or two and it would be done next week."

Which was all hunky-dory, but there was that massive *if* hanging up front of that sentence. Clifton jabbed a finger at Rachel. "Tell me again about your schedule, Rachel. Grant's gonna have a heart attack if it isn't done on time. Are you double sure you'll grow that new bio-computer by the end of July?"

Rachel nodded solemnly. "Tell Grant to relax. I synthesized it once by trial and error. Now I know the steps cold. I'm a hundred percent sure I'll have a bio-computer ready for testing by then."

Clifton began pacing. "The schedule looks tight."

"It is tight, but I'll make the deadline. I guarantee it." Rachel went to the bio-lab. "Do you want a demo?"

Clifton shook his head. "Not if it's going to take time away from you working."

"Well ... it would," Rachel said. "But it's okay. Half an hour isn't going to break the schedule."

Which was just the kind of attitude that broke schedules. Clifton shook his head. "Look, here's what I'd rather see. You in the lab. Dillon at the computer. Keryn making the food runs."

Keryn stood up. "Well, actually, we're done with supper. Dillon, Rachel, I think you've got work to do, right?"

Dillon rolled his chair back into the bio-lab. "We do. Rachel, you are the bottleneck in the schedule. If you run into any problems, let me know and I will help." For some reason, his face suddenly went pink.

Rachel remained seated in her chair. She pushed off from the desk and rolled into the bio-lab. "Wheeeeeee!"

Clifton could have done with a bit less fooling around and a bit more sniffing the grindstone, but he didn't want to alienate the troops. When Dillon and Rachel shut the door of the bio-lab, Clifton helped Keryn fold up the pizza box and stuff it in the trash. The trash bag was full, so he tied it off and lugged it outside to the dumpster. When he came back, Keryn was just coming out the door.

"Don't shut that!" Clifton said. "I need to call Grant, and my cell phone's battery is biffed out."

Keryn held the door and Clifton squeezed through. He looked at her pensively. "So, Keryn, whaddaya think? Is the golden girl going to make it?"

"I don't see how she can miss."

Clifton did. He could see a lot of ways. "Okay, I'll call Grant and tell him we're on track. You have a good night and write some scary stories, all right?"

Keryn nodded and headed for her car.

Clifton waited until he heard her engine start and the car pull away. He stepped to the inner door of the bio-lab and peered in.

Dillon was hunched over the keyboard typing. Rachel was doing something under the hood of the wet-lab.

Clifton tiptoed to the desk and sat down in the chair. He picked up the phone and wedged it under his chin, in case one of them came out. Then he pulled open the middle drawer of the desk and reached inside. Far inside ...

There. His fingers closed on a small device the size of a cigarette lighter. He pulled it out and slid it into his shirt pocket next to his cell phone. He eased the drawer shut and stood up, setting the phone back in its cradle.

He walked to the outer door of the bio-lab and let himself out silently. It was a long shot, but he needed to score here.

~

Clifton

Half an hour later, Clifton was driving north on Highway 5, somewhere around Carlsbad. He turned off the voice-activated electronic recorder and concentrated on traffic.

The bad news was that his crew was lying to him and Grant. For no reason Clifton could see, they were lying, pretending that Rachel was busily growing herself a new bio-computer. That was biff, but not majorly so. He could deal with his team lying. Everybody lied. Even Dillon, apparently.

The good news was that Rachel had made a backup bio-computer. Which only made sense, now that he thought about it.

The good news majorly outweighed the bad news. The only way things could go wrong was if they missed the schedule. That was the sixty-four-trillion-dollar question that Grant was asking, like every ten minutes: *"Are they gonna make the schedule?"*

And the answer was yes. They were gonna make it real soon.

Clifton pulled off at the next exit and across the overpass and drove toward the coast. He parked and got out of his car and went to look out over the Pacific Ocean.

The sun hung above the horizon, just turning to orange in the sky. It was a perfect day in paradise.

Clifton looked around and saw that, yes, he was really alone. He took out his cell phone and selected a number.

One ring and then ... "Ted Hunter."

"Hey, Ted, this is Clifton Potter."

"Clifton! Great to hear from you! Have you got a time the big boys over at Q can meet with you? Man, this is a real break, Clifton."

"Tell them I'm not interested," Clifton said.

"You ... what?" Hunter's voice trailed off. "Clifton, what is this? I went to the wall for you on this one and they finally caved."

"Hey, and I appreciate that. Believe me, I appreciate it." Clifton felt like a jerk. This was the second time Hunter had gone to bat for him, and the second time he had pulled the rug out. "Listen, I'm sorry about this, but things have changed."

"You mean, like, in the last hour?" Hunter sounded exasperated. "You said you were interested this afternoon."

"Yeah, well, something came up," Clifton said.

"Big?" Hunter said.

Clifton didn't say anything.

"Hey, not trying to get you to disclose anything, but ... if you guys at CypherQuanta need to staff up, you know who to come ask. Am I right?"

"Maybe." Clifton felt relieved that Hunter didn't sound too upset. Typical headhunter. "How many heads are you dealing these days?"

"Well, you know, the market's still a little soft. I've got about thirty names on my hot list and another fifty warm contacts. Will that do you?"

Clifton laughed. "Not a chance. Are you hooked into some kind of network?"

"Yeah, sure." Hunter's voice sounded strained. "Can you give me some kind of line on what kind of people you're interested in? Programmers? Electronics guys? Optics?"

"All those, plus some physicists," Clifton said. "Probably a lot of physicists."

"Any particular branch?"

Clifton decided he'd said enough. "I'll call you when I know more. Monday, how's that? I'll call you Monday."

"Sounds good, dude. Good luck on your IPO."

"Hey, no hard feelings on the Qualcomm thing?" Clifton said.

"I'm not gonna bleed over it, bro. Talk to you Monday."

"Gotcha." Clifton hung up and put the phone away. His hands were quivering with excitement. It had been a long time coming, but the payout on this thing was gonna be a monster.

A monster.

CHAPTER EIGHTEEN

Dillon

Dillon's phone rang at 9:13 that evening. He was working at home on his laptop and thinking about Rachel and Keryn, and his first thought was that one of them was calling. For some reason, he felt just a little breathless. Through the first three rings he waited for his heart to stop pounding. Then he went and picked up the phone. "Hello, this is Dillon."

"Yes, am I speaking to Dillon Richards?"

"Richard." Dillon shifted his weight and tried to remember the last time a telemarketer had called him. The national Do Not Call Registry kept most of them away, but there were a few loopholes.

"Oh, sorry about that, Mr. Richard. My name is Ted Hunter, and a mutual friend of mine suggested you might be interested in speaking with me."

Dillon doubted that. "Which mutual friend?"

"I'm sorry, but I need to keep that information confidential."

"I do not talk to people who will not tell me who referred them," Dillon said. "Good night, Mr.—"

"Clifton Potter."

Dillon sat down. "I know Clifton. But now you have prevaricated—"

"I'll get right to the point," Hunter said. "I advise people who are making career transitions and—"

"Clifton told you I might be interested in switching jobs?" Dillon shook his head. "No. That is a second prevarication. There is no reason he would tell you that."

"No, no, you're misunderstanding," Hunter said. "Clifton mentioned your name a couple of months ago—said you're his star player. I met him at a party and we got to talking. I understand there's a sort of crisis at your company and—"

"There was no crisis at our company two months ago."

"I'm sorry, I'm not making myself clear. I *met* Mr. Potter a couple of months ago. I've not kept in touch with him, but I have heard through the grapevine that there are problems at CypherQuanta now, and I remembered that Clifton had given me your name. Tell me, are you happy with your job?"

Dillon sat quietly trying to process all this information. He did not see the connections, and that made him feel uneasy. A person should make the proper connections when he spoke.

"Hello, Dillon, are you there?"

"If I was not here, then to whom would you be speaking?"

Hunter laughed nervously. "Hey, that's a good one, Dillon. I'm sorry about what's going on at your company, and I'd just like to let you know that I'm here to help if you need it."

"You are a headhunter."

"Right."

"Ted Hunter the headhunter." Dillon laughed out loud. "That is quite funny. Ted Hunter the headhunter." It had a nice ring to it. He wondered if Hunter had become a headhunter just so he could make a rhyme on his name. He had once known a Dr. Proctor, who was a proctologist. But Ted Hunter the headhunter was funnier.

"You're a wild and crazy guy, Dillon." Hunter cleared his throat. "I know you can't talk about internal problems at your company, but—"

"There are no internal problems at CypherQuanta."

"Oh." A long silence. "I'm sorry, maybe I've been given wrong information. Isn't it true that your payroll is processed by a company named RediChex?"

"Yes." Dillon felt sweat rolling down his sides.

"And isn't it true that CypherQuanta is missing payroll this month?"

"That kind of thing is confidential information," Dillon said. "If you tell me who told you that, I will make sure they are prosecuted."

"Um, that ... won't be necessary. I'm not interested in prosecuting anyone. I'm interested in helping you."

"I do not need help." Dillon wondered if he should just hang up. But he owed it to Grant to find out as much as possible. Somebody was spreading stories about CypherQuanta, and that somebody needed to be taken to justice.

"Are you independently wealthy, then?"

"I do not need help. Who told you about the payroll?"

In the silence that followed, Dillon realized he had just confirmed something for Hunter. That might be the point of the phone call in the first place. Ted Hunter might not be a headhunter at all. He might be a journalist. Or an industrial spy. He might be anything. He might not even be named Ted Hunter.

"Let me phrase that a little differently, Dillon. Do you see any need for some ... career options?"

"No. I am loyal to Mr. O'Connell and I intend to keep working for him until I retire."

"Even if he doesn't pay you?"

"He is paying me." Dillon realized he had just said more than he intended.

"In equity? IOUs?"

"If you would like to talk to him, I can give you his home phone number, Ted Hunter the headhunter. Would you like to talk to him right now?"

"Dillon, please. You're in a crisis and—"

"I am not in a crisis and neither is CypherQuanta."

"I understand you just lost a contract with San-D-Bank and your angel investors backed out on you."

"Who told you that?" Dillon was angry now, furious. Somebody was telling Ted Hunter the headhunter things they should not.

"Is there any chance you might have some new technology?" Hunter said.

Dillon felt his chest seize up. For a few seconds, he could not breathe. He could not think. Then he slammed down the phone and sat listening to his heart pound against his chest.

He should call Grant.

No, Grant had enough problems right now. He would panic and then he would want reassurance. He would ask when was the earliest the project could be finished, and Dillon would have to tell him it could be done next week. Or prevaricate. It was too dangerous. Dillon had promised to keep Rachel's secret and so he had to keep it.

Dillon picked up his phone and tried to think whom to call. Rachel or Keryn. Keryn or Rachel. He desperately wanted to hear Keryn's soothing voice on the line. Keryn made him feel calm. She was like a vortex of peace in a storm.

And yet he also wanted to hear Rachel's voice. Rachel was not soothing but she made Dillon feel happy. When he talked with her, he felt optimistic, excited about life. Everything seemed possible when he was with Rachel. Together, they made an excellent team. Rachel had many interesting and stimulating things to say about such things as the multiverse and quantum mechanics.

Dillon could not think which of them he should call. He had a quantum-mechanical coin flipper on his desk. It was a small electronic device that CypherQuanta salesmen used to demonstrate the physics used in quantum encryption. Inside the device were two polarizing filters set at an angle of forty-five degrees. The first allowed a single photon of light through, polarized in a particular direction. The second filter either stopped the photon or passed it through with a forty-five-degree change of polarization. One or the other, with each event happening with equal probability. This was Einstein's famous dice, which he claimed God did not throw.

If the Copenhagen interpretation of quantum mechanics was right, then Einstein was wrong and God did not know in advance what would happen.

But if the multiverse interpretation was right, then Einstein was right, because the universe split into two. In one universe, the photon passed through. In the other universe, it was stopped. God knew there would be two universes, identical in every respect except for the state of that one photon. In this picture, there were no dice, and God's fore-knowledge was preserved. That was the kind of universe Dillon believed in—a universe that made sense.

He pressed the button and somewhere deep inside, one single polarized photon was created.

∾

Keryn

Keryn had been battling writer's block for two hours when the phone rang. This was ridiculous. She never had writer's block. She taught at writers' conferences on how to avoid writer's block. Furthermore, she couldn't afford to be blocked. She had a deadline in less than two months, and she was so far behind she was practically hyperventilating.

The machine picked up. "Hello, this is Keryn Wills. I'd love to talk to you, but I'm out. Leave a message and I'll call you back as *soon* as I can."

"Girlfriend, why aren't you answering my messages?" Sunflower sounded frantic. "I swear, if you don't pick up right now, I'm going to send Kathii over there to see if you're dead."

Keryn dug her nails into her palm and snatched up the phone. "Hi, Sunflower."

"Honey, where have you *been*? You haven't answered your cell phone all day, and I left you two messages at home this afternoon."

"I ..." Keryn didn't want to admit she'd been ignoring the calls on her cell phone. "I guess I forgot to check my machine." That was true.

She'd been so eager to get to work, she just hadn't checked. "I'm sorry. Is something wrong?"

"Wrong? You're not answering my calls—that's what's wrong. Where have you been?"

Keryn's stomach contracted into a small knot. She daydreamed all the time about standing up to Sunflower, but somehow she never could do it in real life. What was wrong with her, anyway?

Rusty's voice mumbled something in the background.

"Shut up," Sunflower said. "I'm trying to get two words out of Keryn. Honey, you've been acting strange lately. Now you just tell me what's going on. Is it that man you've been seeing?"

"I ... no." Keryn felt like an idiot.

"What? Speak up. You don't sound right. Are you drunk or something?"

"I don't drink."

"Listen, there's nothing to be ashamed of having a beer once in a while. Don't lie to me. I've known you too long to lie to me. Are you getting sloshed again?"

"I'm not drinking. I'm doing fine. Everything is fine."

"Have it your way, then." Sunflower's voice cracked. "Keep your secrets. Lie to me. Booze it up." A long pause. "Are you still seeing that man? Tick, tick, tick."

Keryn didn't know what to say.

"Spill it, sister! When was the last time you saw him?"

"I saw him at work today."

"I'm not talking about work, girlfriend! When was your last date with him?"

Keryn desperately wanted to just slam the phone down. "Yesterday."

"A weeknight? You went out on a weeknight? I thought you were so busy writing."

"It was in the daytime. We went to the fair."

"The daytime? You stole away from work in the middle of the day for a secret rendezvous at the fair? Sweetcakes, tell me more!"

Keryn felt like screaming. "It wasn't any big thing. Rachel was there, and—"

"Rachel? Who's Rachel?"

Keryn took a deep breath and decided to just spill. "Rachel Meyers is a twenty-five-year-old girl genius who has the hots for Dillon and dresses like a little floozy. We all went to the fair and rode bumper cars and I got the heaves on The Teacup and then the two of them rode together on The Hard Rock while I watched. Satisfied?"

"Rusty!" Sunflower hollered. "Get on the phone and talk to this girl. She's gotten herself mixed up in some kind of a weird triangle, and I think she's drunk again."

Keryn hung up the phone, knowing that it would ring again in two minutes. Knowing she would pick it up. She put her head in her hands. She'd made things sound as crazy as she could but ...

The reality was crazier still.

Rachel

Rachel was soaking in a bubble bath, thinking about Dillon. The whole thing was absurd. She was his exact opposite. They had nothing in common. As a teenager, Rachel had spent a lot of time reading up on the Myers-Briggs personality profiles. She was an ENFP, an Extravert-Intuitive-Feeler-Perceiver. Whereas Dillon was an ISTJ, an Introvert-Sensor-Thinker-Judger. The books said an SJ could do fine with an NF, but Rachel wasn't kidding herself. There was no way in the world she could ever get along with him.

Dillon was some sort of religious whackball—she hadn't figured out what exactly yet, but it was something weird. Whereas she was ... what? She didn't know. She was nothing. Her father was a Jewish agnostic. Her mother was a fundamentalist true believer. Rachel had seen enough religious differences in her life to run away shrieking at the prospect. Growing up, she had felt split right down the middle. Home was a battlefield and she was the prize.

Which was why she had bagged on religion. A week before she was supposed to do her Bat Mitzvah, she had just bailed on the God thing. Her father wasn't religious, but a Bat Mitzvah was a big deal to him, and he had almost disinherited her. Her mother had cried for three weeks straight when Rachel told her she was glad Jesus died because she hated his guts.

Rachel still felt that way. Christians were snots, and she was just fed up with all those lies about how they were the prodigal son who came home and Jews were the self-righteous older brother doomed to die in their hypocrisy. Most of the Christians she had met were the biggest hypocrites around. She had lost her virginity one Saturday night when she was sixteen with a nice Baptist boy who sang in the choir the next day and was always doing that See-You-at-the-Pole rot. And the only difference between him and her was that he felt guilty about it and she didn't. Where was the advantage in that?

So what was it about Dillon that was dragging her toward him? It couldn't possibly work. He was her exact opposite. He was everything she wasn't.

He was everything she needed.

The phone rang.

Rachel didn't want to bother answering it. She leaned back in the water and let its bubbly fragrance soothe her.

After four rings, the machine picked up and played her message in a breathy voice. "Hi, this is Rachel and I was just thinking of you! Please leave a message and I'll get back atcha." *Beep.*

"Rachel, this is Dillon."

Rachel sat up, straining her ears. Dillon sounded ... scared. Well, maybe nervous.

"Please call me right away," Dillon said. "I think we have a problem." Then a dial tone. Something was terribly wrong. Dillon sounded totally freaked.

She could feel her heart pulsing inside her chest, could feel the sweet rush of adrenaline. Fear was kicking her right in the gut and ... she was enjoying it.

Rachel kicked the lever to start emptying the water and stepped out of the tub. She wiped her feet, grabbed her terry cloth robe, wrapped it around her wet body, and walked into her bedroom. Dillon had called barely a minute ago. She scooped up the phone and punched in his number.

He answered after one ring. "This is Dillon."

"Hi, Dillon," she purred. "I was in the tub when you called. What's up?"

Dillon told her. Ted Hunter the headhunter. RediChex. Rumors of a crisis at CypherQuanta.

"It's just a rumor," Rachel insisted. "This Ted Hunter guy doesn't know anything. He was just guessing."

"He sounded like he knew about the stock in lieu of salary." Dillon's voice sounded tight.

"Well ... at least he didn't know about our special project."

A short silence. "He ... he asked if we had any kind of new technology."

All of a sudden, Rachel thought her insides were going to melt. *Please, please no.* If one *word* of that got out ... "You didn't tell him anything, did you?"

"I hung up on him."

Rachel gasped. "Just like that? You didn't feed him some line and then hang up gracefully?"

"I just slammed down the phone. I was very upset."

"Dillon, that told him an awful lot!"

"I am sorry. I am not skilled at prevaricating."

"He didn't ask about the bio-computer, did he? Or Shor's algorithm?"

"No, of course not."

"All he asked about was new technology? That's all? Just a vague kind of fishing question?"

"He sounded like he knew more than he was saying."

Rachel shivered violently. "Dillon?"

"Yes?"

"I'm scared."

"We should talk to Keryn," Dillon said.

"I'll talk to Keryn," Rachel said. "And while I'm doing that ... could you do me a favor?"

"Anything."

"Could you ... come over for a while?"

"Come over?" Dillon sounded shocked. "Rachel, it is very late. It would not look right. Your neighbors might misinterpret."

Rachel couldn't care less what her neighbors thought. She wanted a man in the house. All night. "You could sneak in. I'll turn off my porch light. Nobody's going to know if you come over for the ... for a few minutes."

A long silence. "*I* will know," Dillon said. "I would not feel right about it."

"Dillon, I'm scared to death!"

"I could come over and sit in my car and watch your door."

"Oh, forget it. I'll just lie awake all night waiting for somebody to break in and murder me."

Dillon sighed. "Rachel, nobody is going to murder you."

"If they know about that bio-computer, they will. We're sitting on dynamite. Nuclear-powered dynamite."

"Then we should get a good night's sleep so we can finish the software. We will be testing the calibration tomorrow and factoring large numbers by Friday."

"Dillon, *please* come over!"

"I ... cannot do that. People might think something is going on."

"Fine!" Rachel snapped. "If I'm dead in the morning and that bio-computer's been stolen and the whole world economy comes crashing down, well, at least my neighbors can take comfort that nothing is *going on*." She slammed the phone down so hard she chipped a nail.

Rachel lay in bed for a minute, waiting for her heart rate to come down to normal. Finally, she went out to the living room and checked that her dead bolt was locked. She left on all the lights in the apartment and checked that all the windows were locked. When she was satisfied that the place was secure, she went back into her room and hid the bio-computer in the bottom drawer of her dresser.

Then she finished drying off from her bath and turned out the bedroom lights and crawled into bed, wishing desperately that Dillon were there. She hadn't snuggled up with a guy since her last couple of months at Caltech, and he'd turned out to be such a player, she'd felt disgusted with herself after it was all over. She'd sworn off men forever.

But she wanted a man's strong arms around her now.

Not just any man.

Dillon.

She felt safe around him. Valued. Respected.

But not loved.

It was horrible, horrible, horrible having a crush on a guy who didn't know the first thing about love.

CHAPTER NINETEEN

Grant

Grant was just getting ready to leave for work when his cell phone rang. One look at the caller ID told him it was trouble. Ron Lord, from Lost Angels. He was on the Cypher-Quanta board of directors, along with a couple of other Lost Angels. Grant sat down on his couch and flipped open his phone. "Hey, Ron, long time no see! How are ya?"

"Grant, did you just issue a special round of stock to our employees yesterday?"

Grant took a deep breath and looked out at the Pacific Ocean. "Is there some problem?"

"I don't believe you had board approval for that."

"Well, I can set your mind at ease on that question. I *know* I didn't have board approval. So if that's your question, you've got an—"

"Don't play cute with me. You need board approval and you know it."

"Actually, I don't. I wrote the Stock Option Adoption Agreement back when the board was me and Clif Potter and our lawyer." *Back before you were a bad dream, buddy.* "I have broad discretionary powers in granting stock options to employees."

"Stock *options.* You made a stock *grant.*"

Grant felt a sick jab in his gut. "Ya know, in the heat of things, I didn't think much about the distinction. Isn't there something in the charter about stock grants?"

"That's the problem, Grant. That power is reserved to the board."

Grant was sweating now. "My mistake, I guess. Listen, maybe I was hasty on that. We can get the paperwork changed. We gave everybody until close of business tonight to—"

"Grant, we're having an emergency CypherQuanta board meeting in San Clemente at ten. My office. You are going to be here. If Clifton Potter can make it too, that would be considered extra credit."

"The charter requires twenty-four hour notice in writing of a board meeting."

"And it allows for an emergency meeting with no written notice if two-thirds of the board signs a waiver document at the meeting."

"Clif Potter and I aren't going to sign any such thing."

"Grant, if you have a calculator, go ahead and work out what fraction five is out of seven. If you want to continue being employed by CypherQuanta, you'll be at the meeting to answer our questions. Mr. Potter's attendance is optional."

Grant looked at his watch. He had a bit over two hours. "Right. Thanks, Ron, I'll be there. You take care now, you hear?"

"See you at ten." The line clicked dead.

Great, just great. On top of all the fun stuff today, the board was calling him on the carpet. *Say, Grant, you don't look like you've been reamed out enough lately.*

"Grant, are you okay?" Julia plopped on the couch and scootched up to him.

"No. Got an emergency board meeting in San Clemente. Apparently, I don't have enough flaming torches to juggle."

She leaned over and nibbled on his ear. "Well, don't forget, we've got a secret weapon. So tell those goons whatever they need to hear. Next month, they'll be singing a different song."

Grant squeezed her knee and then stood up. "Right. Too bad I can't tell 'em what's in our back pocket. The only thing I hate about this thing is that making us obscenely rich is gonna make those creeps at Lost Angels obscenely richer."

"Maybe." A grim smile slid across Julia's face. "Are you thinking what I'm thinking?"

"Yeah. It may be time for the cyanide option." Grant went outside and climbed into his Lexus. The board was going to play rough today. He'd have to find a way to play rougher.

~

Keryn

Late in the afternoon, Keryn pulled out her cell phone and dialed Dillon's number, still staring at the e-mail she'd just gotten.

He answered on the second ring. "Hello, Keryn."

"Dillon, I just got a company-wide e-mail you should know about. From Grant. He's calling another all-hands meeting in fifteen minutes in the main conference room. He made it clear that all employees need to be there, which I assume means you and Rachel."

"I am busy right now."

"Then Julia called me on my cell phone right after that and she was in a flat panic. She said she just found a cryptic message from Grant on her answering machine. He had called half an hour ago while he was driving down with Ron Lord."

"Did I hear you correctly? Ron Lord? One of the board members from Lost Angels?"

"Right." Keryn's lips felt dry. "Anyway, Julia says you should make a backup of your software to your flash drive and reformat the hard drive of your computer and then leave."

"That is a strange request. Do you know what is happening?"

"Julia said to tell you *not* to ask questions, just do *exactly* what she said and then leave. And she said for Rachel to bring any lab books she has."

"Rachel does not use lab books. She keeps it all in her head." Dillon sounded disapproving.

"Then bring her head. Julia says to leave her in the parking lot—don't bring her into the building."

"This is extremely inconvenient. We just finished testing calibration. We were about to try factoring some large numbers."

"Julia said 'it' is about to hit the fan. That's a metaphor. It means—"

"I know what it means."

"Dillon ... you've got twelve minutes. Can you make it?"

"I will be a little late," Dillon said. "I am copying the latest version of the source code now."

"See you in a few minutes."

"Good-bye, Keryn." Dillon hung up.

Keryn folded her phone and sat for several minutes in her chair thinking how nice it was to hear Dillon say her name.

Keryn

At exactly 4:45, Keryn heard the door of the meeting room open. Grant walked in with a couple of men in suits. She recognized Ron Lord, one of the investors from that horrible Lost Angels group. The other man, she didn't know.

Grant walked to the podium and just stared at the assembled employees. His face looked gray and sweaty.

"Go ahead, Grant," said the man Keryn didn't recognize.

"I don't think everybody's here yet." Grant's voice sounded hoarse and raspy. "Clifton, can you check? Is Dillon here?"

Clifton got up and went outside. A slow minute ticked by. Footsteps out in the hall. Clifton Potter came back in with Bill and Jill and ... Dillon. All four sat down in the back.

Keryn found that she could not breathe.

Grant looked around the room. "As you all know, I took some drastic action yesterday to ensure that there would be no layoffs on my watch while we're going through this rough spot in our finances.

Unfortunately, the board didn't quite approve of my methods." Grant threw a poisonous look at the two men behind him.

Keryn felt a knife in her gut. She saw it coming now, as huge and horrible as a truck in the night.

Grant cleared his throat. "I've been ordered to do this by the board in an effort to save the company. The following people are notified that you are laid off, effective immediately: Ann Blodgett, Pete Cramer, Jacqui Darling ..."

A shocked hush ran around the room. Keryn was clenching her fists so tight her nails felt like they were going to snap.

"... Rachel Meyers, Ron Pettis, Clifton Potter, Dillon Richard, Renee Smythe, Chuck Tillich, Ed Vandeventer, and ... Keryn Wills." Grant looked up from the paper in his hands, and his eyes were mournful. "Those of you whose names I called, you have ten minutes to clear the building. You are advised that effective immediately, you are not to take any physical objects from your workspace, download any data, or remove anything from the building unless it happens to be on your person at the moment. The board has also asked me to resign, and I am doing so ... now."

Grant took a handwritten note out of his pocket and handed it to the board members. "I'm sorry, people. You know I did my absolute best to save the company. If any of you need references, just ... call me." Grant's voice cracked and he stepped away from the podium.

Keryn felt light-headed. She bent over, trying desperately to keep from crying. They had been so close to an IPO that would leave her set for life. Now she was laid off again. This was the second time in five months. She just couldn't face a job hunt now, while she was on deadline.

All around her, the steady buzz of voices swelled. Somebody was shouting at Mr. Lord. Grant's voice rumbled nearby, telling people to clear the building if they were laid off.

Keryn staggered to her feet and stumbled toward the exit. No, wait. She had to find Dillon.

He was in the back, and his face looked like he'd seen a corpse. When Keryn reached him, she heard Bill asking Jill who Rachel Meyers was.

Keryn grabbed Dillon's arm. "Let's get out of here."

Dillon helped her to the door. Quiet strength seemed to flow out of his arm into her hand. She loved that. Dillon was so strong, so calm.

"This way." Dillon pointed toward the exit sign.

"I need my purse," Keryn said. "It's in my office."

"Is that allowed?"

"Of course it's allowed." Keryn pulled him down the hall and into her office. Her purse was in her desk drawer. She grabbed it and a picture of Kathii and Allen and Jason and Jordan. "Come on, let's go."

Out in the parking lot, Clifton Potter was in the middle of a big crowd of people. "Okay, listen, everybody! Let's go drown our sorrows at Karl Strauss. I'm buying." He waved to Keryn. "You coming, Keryn?"

Keryn shook her head. "I ... better not. I don't drink." And besides, Rachel was parked over in the parking lot on the other side of the gully, and there was no way she could go to Karl Strauss. Everybody would want to know who she was, and that would raise some difficult questions.

"Coming with us, Dillon?" Clifton shouted.

Dillon shook his head. No explanation necessary. Dillon wasn't the most sociable guy.

Keryn clutched his arm. "Let's go tell our friend what's up."

Dillon nodded and led the way. They walked down to the bridge and across into the main parking lot. Dillon's minivan was parked in space number 314, and Rachel's Miata was right next to it.

She had the top of her car down and was stretched back with her eyes closed, her bare feet on the dashboard, listening to her CD player at high volume. "Dust in the Wind," by Kansas. Which somehow seemed fitting.

Keryn leaned down next to Rachel's car and looked back to make sure nobody had followed them over from the main crowd. "Listen, bad news, Rachel. We've been laid off."

Rachel's eyes flew open. "Who has?"

Keryn tried hard to swallow the brick in her throat. "Most of the company. You and me and Dillon and Clifton and a raft of others.

Grant just resigned. The board forced him out and they're shutting down to a skeleton crew."

"We've got to go back to the lab," Rachel said.

"The lab?" Dillon shook his head. "We cannot. That is owned by CypherQuanta. We are forbidden to go there."

Which explained Julia's request to reformat the hard drive on the lab computer. "Dillon, you brought a copy of your software, right? And Rachel, you've got your bio-computer?"

Dillon smiled. "Grant explicitly said that anything we have on our persons belongs to us."

"But ... the NMR machine," Rachel said. "We can't run the software without that."

"NMR machines are everywhere," Dillon said. He pulled his key ring out of his pocket. His flash drive dangled on the end of it. "The software is finished. We tested calibration and it works perfectly. This and Rachel's bio-computer are all we really need."

Keryn's phone rang. She checked the incoming number and flipped it open. "Hi, Grant."

"Keryn, are you doing all right?" Grant's voice sounded low and guarded.

"I'm fine. What's wrong with your voice?"

"I'm in a stall in the men's room. Listen, I'm gonna be in a debrief meeting with these clowns for a couple hours, and then I'm taking Julia out on the town to decompress, but I want to see you and our friends ASAP about ... a business opportunity. Did they bring out what Julia asked?"

"Yes."

"You know that, legally, they can't go back to the lab. Anything that's over there is a loss, is that clear?"

"We figured that out already." Keryn heard an Amtrak train approaching, and she turned and walked away toward the gully, poking a finger over her other ear.

"There's one other—" Grant's voice cut off suddenly.

Keryn heard the sound of flushing and then the call cut off. It was a good bet he'd been interrupted by the board creeps.

She put the phone in her purse and went back to join Dillon and Rachel. "Grant called."

Worry creased Rachel's eyebrows. "Did you tell him about the bio-computer?"

"On the phone? Not a chance." Keryn didn't have a lot of confidence in the privacy of a cell phone.

"What did he say?" Dillon asked.

"He said something about us meeting him to discuss a business opportunity," Keryn said. "I'm guessing he'll try to form a new company to take advantage of what we have."

Rachel gave her a strange look. "I don't think you understand, Keryn."

Keryn didn't like her condescending tone. "What don't I understand?"

Dillon put a hand on Keryn's arm. "Without CypherQuanta, we have *no* legitimate business opportunities for the bio-computer. Now the only purpose we could use it for is ... stealing."

"Or spying on people." Rachel's face glistened with sweat. "Guys, this is bad. We don't have a reason to keep working on that thing."

"Of course we do," Dillon said. "We could finish the project, announce it to the world, and sell it to the NSA. It will force people to switch to secure encryption. That will give CypherQuanta a second chance, and we could get our jobs back and save Grant from losing his investment."

"We are not going to give my bio-computer to the NSA!" Rachel snapped.

"Sell." Dillon's voice sounded even and tense. "I said sell, not give."

"I'd rather die than let Big Brother have that technology," Rachel said.

"That is absurd." Dillon's face turned red. "Rachel, you should read—"

"Guys, not now." Keryn held up two hands. "I can't handle another fight—not when I feel like somebody just kicked me in the face. Let's do something together tonight, shall we? Go to dinner maybe. Grant said he was going to do that with Julia—decompress. Let's have a good time, just the three of us."

Which was crazy, of course. Keryn didn't want three. What had *possessed* her to suggest that?

"I'm game," Rachel said. "Dillon, shall we adjourn this discussion till tomorrow? We can treat ourselves to one decent meal. How's that? What's your favorite restaurant, Keryn?"

"The Star of India just reopened in La Jolla."

Rachel grabbed Dillon's arm. "Perfect. Say yes, Dillon."

He shrugged. "Yes, with two provisos. I am driving and I am paying."

"Deal." Rachel looked up at Keryn. "Deal, Keryn?"

Keryn didn't want it to be a deal, but she didn't seem to have much choice.

"Deal," she said.

Crazy, crazy, crazy.

PART 3: DUST IN THE WIND

The opposite of a profound truth may very well be another profound truth.

Niels Bohr

CHAPTER TWENTY

Keryn

Keryn would not have guessed that parking would be so difficult on a Thursday night in La Jolla. Dillon was driving with his usual maddening precision, and they had circled for the third time from Prospect Street up to Ivanhoe to Silverado to Girard and back around again on Prospect. Keryn was wearing shoes with sensible two-inch heels, but Rachel had on a pair of four-inch spikes that would not survive a long walk. Finally Dillon decided to drop them off at the restaurant and find a parking spot farther away.

They watched Dillon drive off alone. Rachel turned and gave Keryn's dress an appraising look. "Wow, daring!"

Keryn couldn't tell if Rachel was being sarcastic. It was a basic black sheath dress that she mostly wore to awards banquets. The only thing even slightly daring about it was a smallish peekaboo slit running down from the neckline. Not a big deal. Keryn was pretty sure Dillon wouldn't be doing any peeking. By La Jolla standards, this dress was about as tame as you could get. It wouldn't draw attention to Keryn, and that was just the way she wanted it. Whereas Rachel ...

Rachel looked spectacular. The Star of India served the finest Indian cuisine in San Diego, and Rachel seemed determined to pass for a native. She was wearing a brilliant orange sari that showed a lot of skin in the back. On most women, the outfit would have looked ridiculously gaudy. Rachel made it look ... perfect.

"You look great," Keryn said, wishing she could be that bold.

Rachel smiled. "Let's get a table. Our reservations were for eight-thirty and we're a little late."

They went inside and let the maître d' find them their table. It was perfect—small and private in a little alcove in the far back corner. Rachel immediately excused herself and *tap-tapp*ed her way to the bathroom. Keryn sat at the table feeling very lonely. Ten minutes later, Dillon showed up, impeccably dressed in a charcoal suit pinstriped in light gray. He wore a white shirt and a light blue solid-color tie. He reached the table and stood there, looking puzzled at Rachel's empty seat. Keryn thought he looked terrific, for a guy with a hopelessly tame idea of fashion. A striped tie with a dash of red or yellow would—

"I'm back!" Rachel sang out. She threaded her way through the tables, turning heads all across the room.

Keryn could not imagine how a person could be so outlandish and so stunning, both at the same time. When Rachel reached the table, Dillon pulled out her chair and seated her. He sat down and looked at both of them. "This restaurant was a good idea, Keryn."

Keryn felt a rush of warmth in her chest. "I'm hoping we can forget our problems for a while."

The waiter came by and took their drink orders. Rachel asked for a bottle of Indian beer. Dillon ordered a glass of wine. Keryn got a Sprite.

They opened their menus. "Have you been here before?" Rachel said. "What's good for a vegetarian?"

"All the vegetarian dishes are marked," Keryn said. "Do you like hot food? You can order it on a scale of one to ten. I usually ask for a six."

"I'll take a nine." Rachel looked over at Dillon. "Do you like it hot too?"

"I am very sensitive to spices," he said. "I had better take a one."

It took fifteen minutes to choose their dishes and make their orders. Rachel kept changing her mind. It didn't help that she wanted to know every ingredient that went into every dish and insisted on asking the Indian pronunciation of everything.

The waiter patiently answered all of her questions and scratched her order half a dozen times.

"What part of India are you from?" Rachel asked when she finally handed him her menu.

He gave her a little half bow. "Chicago."

"Chicago." Dillon grinned as if that were extraordinarily funny. "I am from Chicago too. Maybe we were neighbors." He shook his head. "Chicago."

Keryn looked carefully around the restaurant. The lighting was dim and the mood relaxed, and the other diners were far enough away that she felt comfortable talking about CypherQuanta. "Well, guys, have you thought about what we're going to do next?"

Neither Dillon nor Rachel said anything. They looked at each other with wary eyes.

Keryn forged ahead. "I wish we could just forget about you-know-what, but I don't think we can. It's a secret for now ... I think ... but it won't be for long."

"Exactly," Dillon said. "Right now six people know about it ... and apparently one other person—whoever it was who broke into the lab. That number cannot decrease."

"Unless one of us gets ..." Keryn didn't want to say it, but it was a real possibility. They were sitting on top of a secret so valuable it could get them all killed.

Rachel shivered and leaned forward. "Are you guys as scared as I am?"

Keryn nodded. "I'm scared out of my skull."

"Isn't it ... delicious?" Rachel said. "It's like riding one of those rides at the fair, but taken to the *n*th power. I *love* this feeling."

Keryn hated it. She liked writing stories in which her characters were in terrible danger. But she didn't like it herself.

Dillon took a sip of wine. "This secret is too big for us."

Rachel leaned back and crossed her arms across her chest. "I'm not going to give it to the NSA. That defeats everything Uncle Grant has stood for all these years. That's why he founded CypherQuanta—to give people back their privacy. To take it back from Big Brother. If Big Brother tries to take this thing, I'll flush it down the toilet." She put a tiny orange handbag on the table.

Keryn hadn't noticed it yet because it blended so well with her sari. "You brought it *with* you?" she gasped. "Rachel, put that away."

Rachel pursed her lips. "Nobody's going to know what's in here."

"Put it out of sight," Dillon said. "You should have left it at home."

"I'm not letting it out of my sight," Rachel said. "Somebody stole the first one. It wasn't Grant and it wasn't Clifton, so therefore somebody else has it. I bet they don't need this one. If you want my opinion, the real danger is that somebody will get hold of your software, Dillon."

"They will not." Dillon shook his head. "I reformatted the hard drive in the bio-lab and securely erased all the relevant files on my personal laptop. There is only one copy left—on my USB flash drive."

Keryn put a hand on his arm. "Do you have it in a safe place?"

Dillon looked all around the room, then leaned close to her. "Right here on my key chain."

A heavy shroud of silence settled around them.

The waiter appeared with their plates of food and set them out. "Enjoy your meal."

When he disappeared, Dillon looked around the table. "Are you all right, Keryn? You look a little pale."

Keryn was scared to death, but she knew Dillon wasn't afraid. He would take care of them all, would set this situation straight.

Dillon tore off a chunk of the Indian flatbread and wrapped it around a chunk of lamb. "Rachel, the problem is that this secret will not go away. It will get out and then it will be too big for us to handle."

"So we'll make it public before it leaks out." Rachel wrapped a carrot in a section of bread and popped it in her mouth. Her eyes went wide. "Wow!" she gasped. "I think they gave me a twelve." She gulped a big swallow of beer.

Dillon shook his head. "We have nothing to make public. The complete system requires the bio-computer, the software, and a functioning NMR device, all integrated, tested, and ready to demonstrate the factoring of large numbers. Until we have that, we cannot hold a press conference. We would look like those scientists who announced they had performed cold fusion in the lab but were unable to reproduce the results. That would be the worst possible situation. Most people would label us fools, except for the criminals, who would consider it worth the cost of a few bullets to determine if we were telling the truth."

Keryn's throat suddenly felt horribly dry. "So you're telling me we can't hide the secret and we can't unload it either? We're hanged if we do and hanged if we don't?"

Dillon thought about that for several seconds. Keryn could almost see him parsing the sentence in his head. Finally, he nodded. "That is correct, Keryn. Our only option is to keep it secret, finish it as rapidly as possible, and give it to the governing authorities."

~

Rachel

Rachel hated hearing that kind of talk. "Dillon, that's nonsense. We've always got options."

Keryn leaned forward. "Can't we just make it go away? Rachel, you could flush the bio-computer down the toilet. Dillon, you could erase your flash drive. Then we'd be back where we were."

"That is not an option," Dillon said. "We cannot erase what is in Rachel's mind—the secret to creating the bio-computer. We cannot erase the software design from my mind. And we cannot change the fact that somebody broke into the bio-lab, tampered with my software, and stole the original bio-computer. That person knows that a secret exists that is worth trillions of dollars. When that news reaches the wrong ears, Rachel and I will be kidnapped and all that we know will be forced out of us. We *must* go to the governing authorities."

Rachel couldn't stand it any longer. "I'd rather die than go to the government."

Dillon gave her a scorching look. "You may get your wish. Unfortunately, Keryn and I would also be killed. If you will not go to the governing authorities, I will."

Rachel narrowed her eyes. "You'll look pretty silly without a bio-computer to prove your claims."

"Not for long. I will send them to speak with you."

"I'll flush it down the toilet. Big Brother won't get it."

"Then criminals will," Dillon said. "We have already established that."

Rachel glared at him. "Your problem is you see everything in black and white. Everything is a logic puzzle for you. Either/or. On or off. True or false."

"Some things *can* be reduced to two possibilities," Dillon said. "The coin lands on heads or it lands on tails."

"You're not thinking quantum," Rachel said.

"I ... what?" Dillon looked deeply offended.

"Some things can be both/and. They don't have to be either/or. A qubit can be both one *and* zero simultaneously. That's how quantum computers work."

"I know how quantum computers work. You are reasoning by analogy, and such reasoning is flawed. You have not demonstrated that our situation bears any meaningful resemblance to a quantum mechanical system. You have simply asserted without proof—"

"Guys, we aren't getting anywhere," Keryn said. "I think you're both right. If we take it public the way it is now, we'll be cold-fusioned. Then it's just a matter of whether the crooks believe us or the government—"

"Same difference," Rachel said.

"The governing authorities are not criminal." Anger flashed across Dillon's face. "They are there to help us."

Rachel could not believe anybody could be so gullible. She gaped at him, trying to come up with a truly devastating response.

"Time out, you two," Keryn held up both hands. "I'm sorry, I shouldn't have brought it up. We're not getting anywhere. So let's just drop it for a while, okay? Let's talk to Grant as soon as we can and get his thoughts. He said he wanted to discuss a business opportunity with us. Until then, how about if we forget about it and think about something fun?"

Rachel glared at Dillon for a few seconds and then realized Keryn was right. They weren't getting anywhere. They'd been strung too tight for almost two weeks. No wonder they were scratching each other's eyes out. She reached out her hand across the table. "Truce?"

"Truce." Dillon shook her hand.

Rachel drank the last of her beer and signaled to the waiter for a refill. "Say, Keryn, this Ambari is really good. Want one?"

"No."

The word came out of Keryn's mouth clipped and tight, the way Mother used to act when people offered her a drink and she got on her horrible self-righteous high horse. Rachel had never been able to resist poking Mother. "Look, we're all pretty tense tonight. Want some wine to take the edge off? We could order a bottle."

"I said *no*."

"Just curious—is that a religious thing, or—"

"Some of the people in my church drink alcohol. It's not a big deal in my personal theology."

But something was a big deal. Rachel could see it in the strained look on Keryn's face. Somehow, Rachel had struck a nerve and she didn't know why. "Any particular reason you don't drink?"

"It's very simple." A hungry look slid across Keryn's face. "It's because I'm an alcoholic."

Rachel stared at her. "*You're* an alcoholic? But you're so ..." She wanted to say *dull* but she managed not to. "You're so nice."

Keryn's face was burning now. "A lot of nice people have wretched pasts."

Rachel didn't know what to say. Finally she patted Keryn's arm. "Well, I'm sure you never killed anybody."

Keryn's face twisted as if she'd been slugged in the gut. Tears began leaking out of her eyes. She suddenly stood up, made a strange little hiccupping noise, and hurried away to the ladies' room.

Crap. Rachel hadn't seen that coming. Not in a million years. She hadn't meant to upset Keryn. She'd just been ... curious. And she'd wanted to take a little poke.

Somehow, she'd poked a boil she hadn't known was there.

Omigosh, I can be such a jerk sometimes.

Dillon's eyes lanced into her. "What have you done to poor Keryn?"

Rachel sighed deeply. She had no idea, but she'd spent hundreds of hours on a psychiatrist's couch over the years getting her head rewired. She had always thought she would have made a great shrink.

Now was her chance to find out.

CHAPTER TWENTY-ONE

Keryn

Keryn could not believe she had just cracked like that. It wasn't fair. She was stressed out, had been stressed out now for months with the new job and the book deadline and this horrible bio-computer thing and ... now that little vixen had busted her. In front of Dillon.

Keryn wiped her eyes and stared into the mirror. She looked awful. Not as awful as she felt, but awful enough.

The door creaked open. An orange sari blurred into view in the mirror.

"Keryn?" Rachel's voice was soft. "I'm sorry. I didn't mean to pry."

"It's okay." It was not okay and Keryn knew it, but she was not going to give Rachel the *satisfaction*.

Rachel took her hand and squeezed it. "I told Dillon I'd be gone awhile. If you want to talk, I'm here. And if you'd rather that I just took a long walk off a short pier, well, I can do that too, but I'm a super good swimmer, so it's not an easy way to get rid of me."

Keryn froze her with a blast of silence.

Rachel sighed. "Sorry. I'm an idiot. I'll just ... go back out there and leave you alone." She opened the door.

Keryn took a deep breath. "Wait, I'll come with you."

Rachel turned to look at her. "You don't have to."

"I want to. I'm ready." Keryn followed Rachel back to the table.

Dillon was sitting there with wide eyes. "Keryn, we can go home if you are not feeling well. I can go get the minivan—"

Keryn shook her head and sat down. "Um, maybe I could just talk a little, okay? I've got a few things to say and if I don't, I'm going to explode." Dillon might as well know what kind of person she was. He wouldn't approve of her, but she had been fooling herself, anyway, if she thought she had any kind of future with him. Eventually, she'd have to introduce him to her parents and then her whole past would come out. She couldn't run away from it forever. It was forgiven. She knew God had forgiven her. But she was still an alcoholic. Would always be one.

Rachel put a hand on Keryn's arm and stroked it gently. "You're with friends, Keryn."

Keryn swallowed the cannonball in her throat. "Okay. This is ... kind of hard. Nobody here in San Diego knows any of this. Well, except my sister. And her husband."

Dillon leaned forward. "Rachel and I are good at keeping secrets."

Keryn fumbled for her glass and fortified herself with a gulp of ice water. "My parents are a little bit weird," she said. "They're ... hippies. They never did get married. They got together in 1967. You know, the Summer of Love. Anyway, they had a couple of kids, my sister, Kathii, and me, and just hung out in Santa Cruz. They never let us call them Mom and Dad. It was always Sunflower and Rusty. They're kind of party animals. Not so much now, but when we were kids ... a lot."

Keryn bit her lip. So far Dillon hadn't freaked out. But she hadn't gotten to the bad part yet. "Anyway, I just kind of grew up thinking all that was normal. Parties every weekend. People getting drunk and throwing up in the kitchen sink. Couples sacked out in sleeping bags in the yard. By the time I was eight, they were giving me beer at parties and blowing pot smoke in my face to get me high. And I liked it. I was getting drunk by the time I was eleven. I went all the way with my boyfriend in the back of my parents' VW bus when I was fourteen. Maybe thirteen, I don't remember very well."

Keryn had her eyes closed now. It was easier to talk that way. "And it just got worse through high school. The drinking and drugs and ... boys and all that. I went to UC Santa Cruz and ... moved in with my boyfriend. We had a party every weekend that pretty much lasted the whole weekend. And in the spring of my sophomore year ..." Keryn's voice cracked. She clenched her fists tight and breathed in and out, in and out.

"One weekend we had a party at our apartment with a bunch of friends. We had a keg of beer and ... I caught my boyfriend throwing up on the coffee table. I was pretty rocked, but I got mad and told him to go do that on the balcony. I yelled at him and ..."

Keryn felt tears streaming down her face. She covered her face with her hands. "And he went out and leaned over the balcony and heaved out his guts and ..."

Keryn didn't want to say any more. Couldn't say any more.

Rachel's soft hand touched Keryn's face. "Keryn, did he ... fall?"

Keryn nodded. "The police report ruled out suicide and homicide. They said it was an accident."

"It *was* an accident," Dillon said.

"I know that, but I ... contributed to it." Keryn felt the old familiar numbness in her chest again, the cold fingers caressing her heart. If she hadn't yelled at him, he'd be alive now. She'd killed him. Simple as that.

"And that's when you ... ?"

"Right." Keryn dried her face with her napkin and opened her eyes. "My sister had just got involved with a group called InterVarsity at UCSC. She got me to come to it, and both of us decided we needed God. Kathii made me go to AA and I got cleaned up and ... I've been sober ever since. But Rusty and Sunflower still don't understand. They're so ... embarrassed that Kathii and I rejected everything they stood for. It's really hard to go home because they don't understand about the alcohol. They don't get it that one taste of beer would put me right back where I was. I used to hate them for raising me like that, but I forgave them years ago. Now I just feel sorry for them."

Keryn stared at her hands. "I don't know why I told you guys all that. It's kind of heavy, but ... I guess not everybody is what they seem to be." She risked a look at Dillon.

Stark horror covered his face.

Keryn felt completely and utterly humiliated. She had blown it. Blown it big time.

Dillon

Dillon realized that his face had given him away. Rachel and Keryn were both staring at him with strange expressions he could not parse. He did not know what social context applied in this situation, but he could not remember all the meanings of the expressions, anyway.

"Dillon, did I upset you?" Keryn said. "I'm so sorry. I shouldn't have laid all that on you. Now you know what a terrible person I am and—"

"I do not think you are terrible," Dillon said. "You did not choose the way you were raised. You made a clean break with your past. And the Lord forgave you."

"You're not disgusted with me?" Keryn asked in a small voice.

"No, why would I be disgusted with you?" Dillon's throat felt tight and his chest felt hot.

"I don't know," she said. "I just ... that expression on your face. You looked horrified."

"I ... was horrified," Dillon said in a quiet voice. "Horrified with myself."

"That doesn't make any sense," Keryn said. "I'm the one with the wretched past."

Dillon shook his head. Keryn did not understand. She could not possibly understand. Yes, her parents had given her a miserable childhood. But she had forgiven them. A person who forgave others deserved to be forgiven. Dillon's counselor had been pressing him for months on this issue. The converse was also true—a person who did not forgive others ... could not be forgiven.

The two women sat looking at him in silence. The waiter came by. "How is your meal going?"

Rachel glared up at him. "We're busy. We'll let you know when we need something."

The waiter backed away with his mouth hanging open.

Rachel leaned forward. "Dillon, maybe this is true confessions night. If you want to spill your guts, go ahead."

Dillon shivered. Why must everybody use that expression—spill your guts? It gave him a bad mental image. Highly distasteful. He had never spilled his guts to anyone. Robert did it all the time, and he said it made him feel better, but Dillon had never felt he could trust another person enough to do so, not even his counselor.

And yet ... he felt he could trust Keryn. He had always thought of her as a kind woman, and now she had spilled her guts and he found that he respected her even more. She was the type of woman who could forgive. She could be trusted.

And Rachel had shown remarkable empathy just now with Keryn. Dillon had known Rachel was not judgmental, but it was a surprise to see her behaving with genuine kindness. In another universe, perhaps she was a counselor. She would not tell Dillon he was an evil person.

Dillon looked around the restaurant and saw that they were alone. He took a deep breath and told them the one fact they needed to know in order to understand it all. "I have three brothers who are Normal."

He leaned back to let them work out the details.

Rachel and Keryn looked at each other for several long seconds and then both of them began giggling.

Dillon did not know what was so funny. He had just explained his entire terrible childhood, and they thought it was a matter for laughing?

Rachel began playing with her napkin. "Say, Dillon, I think we need a little longer true confession than that."

"Is it not obvious?" he said.

Keryn shook her head. "Pretend we're stupid. Give us the long version."

The heat in Dillon's chest expanded. His head felt light. He did not feel calm. Not calm at all. He wanted very much to talk about something calming. "There have been some interesting results on the Poincare conjecture lately."

"Dillon!" Rachel put a hand on his arm. It felt warm and made his brain tingle. "Forget the Poincare conjecture! Tell us about your three normal brothers."

Dillon's whole head felt as if it were filled with cotton candy. He thought the proof of the Poincare conjecture would have a long-lasting impact on Western history, but he could see that neither Rachel nor Keryn thought so.

Now his secret seemed to be rising up inside him, and he could not hold it down for one more second. "My brothers are all older than I am. They are Normals. One of them was student body president in high school. All of them lettered in track. My second brother also lettered in basketball and football." Dillon stopped, feeling that to say another word would make him explode.

"I bet you didn't letter in anything, did you?" Rachel said.

Dillon stared at his hands. "I was in the chess club. Normals do not join the chess club."

"And just what exactly is a Normal?" Keryn asked.

"Whatever I am not," Dillon said slowly. "Whatever my brothers are."

"Are you angry at your brothers?" Rachel asked.

"No."

"Your mother?"

"No." Dillon felt sure he would faint. It was terribly disloyal, and now he had betrayed a family confidence.

"Your father, then." Rachel's voice sounded soft and warm. "You're angry at your father."

Dillon swallowed hard. "It is a sin not to honor your father and mother."

"You hate your father," Rachel said.

Dillon felt something deep and hot rising inside him. He could not speak. He could not think. It was wrong to hate. It was a sin.

"I do not hate ..." Dillon could not say it. It was wrong to hate your father, but it was also wrong to prevaricate. He wanted to scream, to vomit. This spilling of guts was extremely painful. He put his elbows on the table and covered his face with his hands.

"When was the last time you talked to him?" Keryn said. "I know from experience that if you talk about it, you can work through it."

"Thirteen years ago."

Rachel gasped and squeezed his arm. "Dillon ... you haven't talked to your father in thirteen *years*? What do you do when you go home?"

"Sometimes you cannot go home again," Dillon said. "Sometimes there is nothing to go home to. He has been embarrassed of me since I was four years old. I was clumsy. I could never catch the football. He said I threw like a girl. I tripped and fell when I was getting my high school diploma. He refused to come to my college graduation because he did not want to be embarrassed again. I have not gone back home since then."

Keryn's eyes were gleaming. "I'm sorry, Dillon."

"I think he'd be proud of you now, if ... you'd give him a chance," Rachel said.

Dillon did not think so. He did not want to find out. He would make Grant proud of him instead. That was possible. To make his father proud of him ... that was not possible. He reached for his glass of ice water and drank. Slowly, the water chilled the rage in his heart. The rage was not gone, but now it was back the way it had been before.

In a frozen place in his heart where he could control it. He had failed. He had meant to tell them everything. But he had left out the worst part.

"Are you feeling better?" Keryn said.

"No." Dillon dared to look at her eyes. "But now you know that I am not what I seem either."

Keryn's eyes looked very warm. "Maybe nobody is. But Jesus can heal the hate, if you let him." She raised her hand and signaled to the waiter. "Check!"

Rachel's grip tightened on Dillon's hand. Her face had twisted like a knot.

Dillon did not need to know the social context to realize that she was angry. Very angry. "Rachel, is something wrong?"

She yanked her hand away. "Not at all. Let's go."

Dillon felt certain she was prevaricating, and he could not imagine why.

The waiter arrived with the check. Dillon looked at the bill. He took three fifty-dollar bills out of his wallet and handed them to the waiter. "Please keep the change. We will be staying to talk for a few more minutes."

"As you wish, sir." The waiter was smiling and looking at the bills. "Whatever you wish, sir. Have a very good evening, sir."

Rachel stood up.

Dillon did not move. "Rachel, you are upset. Please sit down."

She glared at him. "I'm ready to go home."

"I am driving and you are not," Dillon said. "Unless you intend to walk all the way home in those uncomfortable shoes, you will sit down and explain why you are angry."

Keryn leaned forward. "Rachel, I'm so sorry if I said something to upset you. Please ... let's talk about it."

Rachel's eyes flicked between the two of them. "You won't like what I have to say."

"We both had a turn," Dillon said. "It is only fair that you should take one too."

Rachel gave a loud sigh and sat down. "You're going to hate me. Both of you."

Dillon could not imagine ever hating Rachel. "Please dump your guts."

CHAPTER TWENTY-TWO

Rachel

Rachel took a sip of her Indian beer, wondering how to begin. There was no way they would understand. Finally, she said, "Wow, it's nice to hear you both had happy childhoods."

Dillon looked confused. "We did not have happy childhoods. We just told you—"

Rachel put up her hand. "That was irony, Dillon, sorry. I'm just saying, by comparison to mine, your childhoods were idyllic."

Dillon nodded.

Rachel stared into the depths of her beer, but there was nothing there. "Dillon, I told you I'm Jewish. That's half true. My father is Jewish. Not religious, just Jewish. My mother wasn't religious either when they got married. She was raised in this uptight fundamentalist church, but she rebelled and bagged religion when she went off to Princeton. She and Daddy lived together for a couple years, then they got married and started making babies."

Rachel wasn't sure how to explain the next part. She'd never understood it herself. "They had a little boy and named him Aaron. After Daddy. I've seen pictures of him. He was cute."

Dillon appeared to be holding his breath, his face was so still. Keryn's eyes were glistening.

Rachel put both hands flat on the table and studied them intently. "My brother, Aaron, died when he was six weeks old. SIDS. They never did know what caused it. But it freaked my mother out. She decided God was punishing her, so she ... decided to get right with God."

Rachel looked at Dillon and took a deep breath. "Ever notice that when somebody gets right with God, they usually get wrong with everybody else?"

"I had not noticed that," Dillon said.

"I'm sorry, Rachel," Keryn said.

"My mother became the Church Lady from hell," Rachel said. "It wouldn't have been so bad if she just picked a normal church. But she only knew one kind of church. Uptight fundie. So that's what she went back to."

"So you were raised *Christian?*" Keryn said.

Rachel gave her a twisted smile. "I wish. That would have made it simple. When I was born, Mother told Daddy that she was going to raise me 'right,' meaning her way, and Daddy told her no, I was Jewish and he'd see me dead before he saw me growing up Christian. So they fought about that for years and finally got a divorce when I was five or six—I forget exactly. I wound up in joint custody. Mostly with Mother, but every other weekend with Daddy."

"Rachel, I'm so sorry." Keryn scootched her chair over and wrapped a hug around Rachel. "That must have been horrible."

"Yeah." Rachel's voice felt thick and viscous in her throat. "Yeah, it was horrible." She daubed at her eyes with her twisted napkin. "One weekend I'd be in Sunday school learning all about how Jesus ragged on the Jews for being legalists. Then the next weekend I'd be with Daddy, and I knew he was Jewish, but he wasn't a legalist, so I got so confused. Daddy didn't even go to synagogue, so how could he be a legalist? About the only thing he did was have a Passover Seder every year. If anyone was a legalist, it was Mother."

Neither Dillon nor Keryn said anything.

"Then I'd go back to church the next week and learn about how the Jews killed Jesus, and that was really confusing because they never said which Jews. They just said Jews. It said so in the Bible. And I knew Daddy was Jewish and I was Jewish, and I knew we didn't kill Jesus."

Keryn's breath caught in her throat. "You didn't kill Jesus, Rachel."

Dillon's hands clenched on the table. "No, you did not kill him."

"And then ..." Rachel felt the anger rising in her heart again. "And then I'd go to Daddy's house the next weekend and he'd tell me about what Christians did to Jews in Europe for hundreds of years. How they killed Jews for being Christ-killers. How they said we put the blood of Christian children in our Passover matzohs."

Dillon looked like he was going to be sick.

Keryn's face had gone completely white. "How long did all this go on?"

"Till I was twelve," Rachel said. "It was a war between Mother and Daddy, and I was the prize. They fought like tigers whenever one of them came to pick me up. Then when I was twelve, Daddy secretly enrolled me in Sunday school."

"Sunday school?" Keryn said. "I think I'm missing something."

"When a girl turns twelve, she's supposed to have a Bat Mitzvah. You have to read from the Torah and the Prophets. In Hebrew. Usually, it takes months to learn to do that, to say all the prayers and stuff. Daddy did his Bar Mitzvah when he was a kid. When I turned twelve, he decided that he really wanted me to do it too. Not a religious thing. Just culture. Most synagogues have a special school that meets on Sunday mornings to train kids in Hebrew and all that. Sunday school. When Daddy put me in that, Mother went nonlinear."

"It wasn't fair, what they did to you," Keryn said.

Dillon shook his head. "It was not logical."

"I hated it," Rachel said. "It was the worst thing in the world. I was twelve years old, and I was stuck in this war zone with no way to do the right thing. The rules changed every weekend."

"And that's why you hate your mother?" Keryn said.

"I don't hate my mother. We made our peace a long time ago. I feel sorry for her."

Keryn looked confused. "But ... you call your parents 'Mother' and 'Daddy.' Sounds partial to your father."

Rachel sighed. "I identify more with Daddy than Mother. But I don't hate either one of them."

Keryn's eyes narrowed. "It sounds like you're still harboring some kind of ... grudge."

"Oh, you better believe I've got a grudge," Rachel said. "But I don't hate Mother or Daddy." She closed her eyes because she didn't want to see their faces when she told them. "It's Jesus I hate."

A gasp.

"Oh, Rachel." Keryn's voice was almost a sob. "Don't hate Jesus."

"Jesus was ... Jewish," Dillon said.

"That's why I hate him." Rachel took a deep breath. "Jesus was Jewish, but he went and started his own religion. He was always calling the Pharisees hypocrites and legalists, but they weren't! I read up on them. They were great men. They were the best Jews there were. Rabbi Hillel and Rabban Gamliel were leaders of the Sanhedrin and were good and kind men. It was the Christians who were the arrogant ones. As soon as they got the chance, they started persecuting Jews and they never quit. They called us Christ-killers and told lies about us and they murdered us. So who are the hypocrites?"

Keryn put her hand on Rachel's shoulder. "Rachel—"

"I didn't kill Jesus, but I'm glad somebody did," Rachel said. "He ruined life for every Jew who ever lived. He ruined my life. He told all those hateful stories. I heard them a hundred times. Jews are the bad guys and the Samaritan is the good guy. Jews are the wretched overseer who killed the son of the landowner and will get punished. Jews are the hypocritical older brother who didn't rejoice when the prodigal son came home. Jesus hated Jews. I *hate* Jesus!"

Shocked silence.

Rachel wiped her eyes. "So Keryn, when I hear people saying that Jesus fixes things, it just drives me right up the wall. Jesus didn't fix my life—he wrecked it."

"I'm sorry," Keryn said. "I didn't have any idea. Jesus means so much to me ... I didn't realize he'd mean something awful to you."

"It was not your fault that you were raised like that," Dillon said. "We will not talk about Jesus with you again."

"Thanks, guys," Rachel said, feeling a little better. She had known all along she'd have to tell Dillon this eventually. Tonight was probably the best possible time to get it out in the open. All of them had a dirty little secret, and who could say whose was worst?

"Well," Keryn said. "It's getting late. Maybe we'd better be going home."

Rachel saw that they were the only diners left in the restaurant. The waitstaff were busy cleaning tables and pulling linen tablecloths.

Dillon stood up. "I will go get the car and pick you ladies up outside in a few minutes." He walked outside and strode away up the street. Rachel and Keryn sat down on a couch just inside the door. They looked at each other and both of them cracked a guilty smile.

Keryn shrugged. "I guess we both shot ourselves in the kneecap, huh?"

Rachel felt an enormous lump in her throat. "I guess."

~

Dillon

D illon drove up to the curb and stopped.

The door of the Star of India opened and the maître d' ushered Rachel and Keryn out. He was staring at both of them as they walked toward the minivan.

Dillon did not like men who could not control their eyes, but there was nothing he could do to make the maître d' stop staring. He shut off the engine and hopped out to open the door for the ladies and help them in.

Rachel took his hand first and stepped up.

Dillon's heart thumped again in that strange way that seemed to happen whenever she was around. Then she was inside. Dillon helped Keryn in next. Her hand felt very warm and soothing. There was a hollow feeling deep inside his stomach that he did not understand.

Keryn settled in beside Rachel.

Dillon closed the door of the minivan and got back in the driver's seat. He buckled his seat belt and looked back to be sure the ladies were both belted. Earlier in the evening, when he had picked them both up at Keryn's house, he was forced to argue with Rachel to make her buckle up.

Dillon started the car and drove carefully down Prospect Street toward Torrey Pines Road. The streets were nearly empty. The clock on the dashboard told Dillon that it was 11:52, but he knew that this clock was nearly two minutes fast. He made a mental note to adjust it when he got home. He did not feel calm when his clocks showed different times.

A pair of headlights came zooming up from behind at an unsafe speed. They swerved into the right lane and pulled up alongside him, slowing down so that they matched his speed. As he passed under a streetlight, Dillon saw that the car was a gray Ford Taurus with dark windows.

One block ahead, the traffic light turned yellow. Dillon took his foot off the gas.

The Taurus squirted ahead, cut much too close in front of Dillon, then braked fiercely.

Dillon jammed on his brakes.

Rachel screamed.

The antilock brakes began hammering, but a minivan cannot stop as fast as a Taurus.

At the last second Dillon spun the wheel to the right.

His left front bumper nicked the back of the Taurus just before the minivan shuddered to a stop.

In the sudden silence Dillon felt his heart pounding very fast. He looked back at the ladies. "Are you hurt?"

"I'm fine," Keryn said.

"I ... I ... I'm okay too." Rachel looked like she had just swallowed a goldfish. "What happened?"

"He cut me off." Dillon looked outside.

A well-dressed man in a suit had gotten out of the Taurus. He was shaking his head and looking at his back bumper.

Dillon shut off his ignition and took the keys out. He reached into the glove compartment and took out his registration papers and proof of insurance card. "I will talk to the man. Please stay in the car."

He stepped out of the minivan and closed the door. As a precaution, he pressed the remote. All the door locks clicked. He put his keys in his pocket and turned to face the man. "I am sorry, but—"

The man in the suit had a gun pointed at him. "Give me your wallet."

Dillon stared at the gun. It was a Sig Sauer nine-millimeter pistol. He could not tell if it was a Model P225 or P226.

Three more doors of the Taurus flew open and more men jumped out. Each of them had a Sig Sauer.

"Give me your wallet!" the first man shouted.

Dillon put both hands out where the men could see them clearly. "My wallet is in my front left pocket. I am taking it out now."

He moved his left hand slowly into his pocket and eased out his wallet. He held it up to the light so the men could see it, then dropped it on the ground and stepped back several paces.

One of the men came forward and picked up the wallet. He pointed his gun at Dillon's heart. "Your car keys too. We're taking the car."

"It is not a car. It is a minivan."

"We're taking the minivan. Give us the keys now." The man looked surprisingly calm.

Dillon thought that if he himself were committing a carjacking, he would be much more nervous than these men. They must be professionals.

"My keys are in my right front pocket," Dillon said. "I am removing them now." He slowly put his hand in his pocket.

Dillon's heart was hammering in his chest and he could not catch his breath. His head felt strangely light. The women were still in the minivan. He would not allow these criminals to drive away with his friends inside. "Excuse me. I have some passengers." He stepped to the window of the minivan and tapped on the glass with his left hand. "Keryn! Rachel! Please come out! They are stealing the minivan."

Dillon stepped back two steps and slowly pulled his keys out of his pocket.

The minivan door rolled open. Rachel came out first, and her face was sweating in the dull yellow sodium lights. "Dillon, what's going on?"

"They are carjacking my minivan."

Rachel looked terrified.

Keryn came out next and her mouth was hanging open. "Dillon, they can't do this."

"They are doing it. I refuse to argue with Sig Sauer. He usually wins."

The man holding Dillon's wallet pointed his gun at Rachel. "Give me your handbag. And you there, in black. Give me your purse."

Rachel held her little orange bag out at arm's length. The man snatched it away.

Keryn took her cell phone out of her purse. "I'm keeping my phone. It's not worth anything to you." She dropped the purse on the ground and backed away.

The man picked it up, then pointed his gun at Dillon. "Now the keys, sir, if you please."

Dillon set them on the roof of the minivan and stepped back. "Keryn. Rachel. Stand behind me."

Headlights appeared three blocks back.

Two of the men jumped into Dillon's minivan. The other two leaped back into the Taurus. Both engines roared. The vehicles sped away, racing through a red light and turning left onto Torrey Pines Road toward Highway 52.

Dillon found that he had been holding his breath.

Keryn and Rachel threw their arms around him. Their bodies were shaking. Dillon thought he might fall over. His head felt detached from his body, like it was floating ten feet above the ground.

"Dillon, they got your car keys," Rachel said. "They got your flash drive."

Dillon's heart was still pounding in his chest and he could not speak. He looked all around. The headlights behind them had vanished. They were alone at midnight in La Jolla.

And Rachel's bio-computer was in the little orange handbag the men had stolen.

CHAPTER TWENTY-THREE

Keryn

Keryn had never felt so scared. She was trembling and wanted to throw up. This whole thing had turned into one of the stories she liked to write. Except that she didn't want to be inside the story. She wanted to be safely outside, twisting, twisting, twisting the plot, leaving the reader gasping with every twist until it reached that trademark Keryn Wills ending, bittersweet and clever and haunting, with a final surprise in the closing sentence.

This was clearly not going to be that kind of story. Rachel's whole body was shaking. Dillon was a shelter in the storm. His hand patted her gently on the back. "Rachel, Keryn, we are safe. They took our things, but we are alive. Now we need to call somebody to come get us. And we need to call the police."

Somewhere deep inside Keryn's brain, a neuron jiggled. Something George Smiley or somebody said in one of John le Carré's spy novels. *There are no coincidences.* "Um, Dillon? Rachel?" Keryn's voice felt shaky and weak. "I ... I'm wondering if this was just a simple carjacking."

Rachel pulled away from her and Dillon. "You're not suggesting ..."

Dillon looked completely puzzled. "Suggesting what? Those men planned this very well. They trapped us out in the open and stole our money and my minivan."

Keryn looked nervously around, wishing she could speak openly, afraid of who might be listening in the night. "That's not all they stole. I think we were followed. I think somebody knows who we are and what we ... had, and now they've stolen it. I've been telling you for more than a week that the crooks would find out about us eventually."

Rachel's green eyes were round and huge. She unclipped her cell phone from a thin belt at her waist. "I'll call Grant. He'll come get us. Oh my gosh, he's going to be so upset." She punched a button.

Keryn and Dillon leaned close. The phone rang four times and then Grant's answering machine message came on. "Hello, this is Grant O'Connell. I'm terribly sorry I missed you—"

Rachel snapped the phone shut. "Maybe he and Julia went somewhere. We can't leave a message. This is too sensitive."

"Call his cell phone," Dillon said. He pulled his own phone out of his shirt pocket. "I had better call the police. They can set up roadblocks and stop the minivan before it gets far."

Keryn didn't think that would do any good. If this was the kind of operation she thought it was, Dillon's car was parked somewhere three or four blocks away, already abandoned. The men hadn't come for the money and the minivan. They had come for the bio-computer and Dillon's flash drive on his key ring. "Go ahead and call them. We'll keep trying to get through to Grant."

Dillon stepped away a few paces.

Keryn stayed with Rachel. "Call Grant on his cell phone."

Rachel pressed some buttons and held it up so they could both hear. The line didn't even ring once but switched to voice mail right away.

Keryn felt frustrated. Grant must have turned off his cell phone. She opened her own phone. "Here, I'll call Clifton. He lives somewhere in La Jolla, doesn't he?" She selected his number in her phone list and pressed Send. It rang four times and switched to voice mail.

"Try his landline," Rachel said.

Keryn shook her head. "Clifton doesn't have a landline. He uses a cell phone for everything."

Dillon was still talking on his phone. From the sounds of things, he had some dim-witted sergeant on the line. He was reading off the vehicle identification number from his registration papers. His face looked calm, but his fists were clenched tight.

Keryn felt horrible. There was nothing Dillon could have done. You didn't argue with four men with guns.

"Who do we call now?" Rachel said. "We've gone through all the people who know our secret."

"I can call my sister," Keryn said. "She could send her husband out to pick us up."

"I could call my aunt Esther," Rachel said. "She goes to bed early, but she'd come get me."

Keryn shivered. "I think we need to stay together tonight. Kathii can put us all up. It'll be safer that way."

Fear lit up Rachel's eyes. "Okay, call her."

Keryn punched a number and heard the phone ring four times. The answering machine message started up.

Keryn knew the answering machine was right by Kathii's bed and the phone would have woken her up and she would be listening right now. "Kathii, this is Keryn, and I'm really, really scared. I was out with some—"

"Keryn, what's wrong?" Kathii sounded groggy and frantic.

Keryn felt so relieved that she had reached a real human being that she almost couldn't breathe. "Kathii! Oh, thank God you picked up! We were carjacked. I'm stranded in La Jolla with two friends of mine. Can you—"

"Of course. Hang on a second. Allen, wake up! Keryn's in trouble! Wake *up*! Keryn, where are you?"

Keryn checked the signs at the nearest corner. "We're in La Jolla on Prospect Street, just north of Torrey Pines Road."

"Allen'll come get you in a few minutes. Keryn, are you hurt? Is everyone okay?"

"Yes, we're fine, but ... we got robbed too."

A gasp. "Oh, Keryn, I'm sorry. Thank God you're alive. Did you lose much?"

Keryn felt a deep pain stab through her chest. *Only a few trillion dollars.* "Quite a bit."

"He's on the way, Keryn. Stay on the line. I'm gonna pray for you right now. Thank you, Lord, for protecting Keryn and her friends. Please, Jesus, just keep her safe until Allen gets there."

Keryn closed her eyes and clung to the sweet voice of her sister. God was going to take care of them. God had to take care of them. God could fix this awful mess they were in.

~

Rachel

Rachel felt numb in her brain. This was horrible, simply horrible.

Dillon finished talking to the cops and joined her and Keryn. Keryn still had her phone to her ear.

Now the voice of Keryn's sister was praying. Thanking Jesus.

Omigosh. Rachel clung to Dillon's arm and fought the nausea welling up inside her.

Within minutes, a white Toyota Camry turned right at the light and headed toward them.

Keryn raised her arm and waved frantically, still talking into the phone. "He's here, Kathii! Allen just turned onto our street."

The Camry passed them and flipped a U-turn and pulled up next to them. A man in his late thirties jumped out and raced to Keryn and hugged her tight. "Keryn, it's okay, it's okay. You're fine. I'm here." He patted her back, then reached a hand over Keryn's shoulder toward Dillon. "I'm Allen Russell."

Dillon shook his hand. "Dillon Richard. This is our friend Rachel Meyers."

Rachel nodded toward him.

Allen stepped back. "Okay, listen, you're all in shock. Hop in the car. Dillon and Rachel, I can take you wherever you need to go. Keryn, you're coming home to stay the night with us—don't argue."

Keryn hesitated as she placed her hand on the door handle. "Allen ... would it be possible for all of us to stay at your house?"

Allen blinked twice. "Um ... sure, Keryn. We can find room."

They all piled in. Rachel and Keryn sat in back. Dillon sat in front with Allen.

Rachel closed her eyes and saw in her mind's eye the faces of the men who had robbed them. What if they came back?

Keryn's soft hand patted Rachel's cheek gently. "We're going to be okay, Rache. God's going to take care of us."

"Right, he's done a bang-up job so far."

Keryn sucked in her breath.

Rachel realized she'd gone too far. "Sorry, that was uncalled for. I guess I'm really mad at myself for getting you into this mess. This thing has just ... exploded in our face."

"It's okay," Keryn said. "Just relax. Allen and Kathii will help us."

Rachel wasn't sure she wanted two more people in on the secret, but it didn't look like she had much choice.

A few minutes later, they took the Genesee exit off of Highway 52 and headed north into University City. It was the same exit Rachel would have taken to go home. They turned right on Governor and hung a left soon after that, and Rachel was lost. After three turns, they pulled into a driveway and sat waiting for the garage door to grind its way up.

Then they were inside and the door was shut and they were safe. Sort of.

A tall woman in a bathrobe was waiting inside the garage. She yanked open the back door of the Camry and smothered Keryn in a huge hug. "Keryn! Oh, thank God!"

It took a few minutes to get settled inside the house. Keryn and Dillon and Rachel sat in a row on the couch. Allen sat in a big leather easy chair. Keryn's sister, Kathii, went to make hot chocolate. Keryn told the whole story of the carjacking—leaving out their speculation about the carjackers' motives.

Allen nodded quietly until she finished. "I'm sorry. It was just ... bad luck."

"It was not bad luck," Dillon said.

Rachel stiffened. "Dillon."

Keryn leaned forward. "Rachel, Dillon, I think we need to tell them. It doesn't make much difference anyway. They stole ... it."

Dillon nodded. "Yes, it is out of our hands now."

Rachel felt her heart breaking. No, she didn't want to tell anyone this awful secret. But yes, it was out of their hands now. She sighed deeply. "Okay, tell them."

Dillon explained about the bio-computer and the software they had been developing. Allen's eyes grew steadily larger. Kathii came in with steaming mugs of hot chocolate. "Marshmallows, anyone?"

Nobody wanted marshmallows.

Kathii sat down on the arm of Allen's chair. "So they got the software and the bio-computer? I guess that means you're out of danger, right? I mean, now you can just call in the FBI and it's out of your hands."

"Not exactly." Dillon stood up slowly and reached into his pocket. He set the contents on the coffee table. A Swiss Army knife. A pair of fingernail clippers. Four quarters.

And a flash drive.

Rachel screamed.

The crooks were going to come back.

And next time they wouldn't ask.

They would shoot.

Keryn gasped and fell back against the couch.

"I unclipped it in my pocket before I pulled my keys out," Dillon said. "I stalled for a minute by tapping on the window and telling the ladies to come out."

Allen leaned forward and picked up the flash drive. "So ... you're telling me they only got half of what they need? They have the bio-computer but not the software to use it?"

"I am afraid so," Dillon said. "When they find out, they will come looking for us."

Rachel felt hot all over. This was unbelievable.

Keryn let out a low moan.

Dillon turned to her. "Keryn, are you all right? I am sorry, but ... it was just instinct to keep the flash drive."

Rachel was trying hard to breathe.

Keryn leaned toward Dillon, jutting her chest toward him. "Dillon, I have something to show you."

Dillon's eyebrows shot up.

Keryn slipped her thumb and forefinger inside the keyhole slit in her dress, reached down, and pulled out ...

Rachel's bio-computer.

Dillon

Dillon turned his head away, feeling deeply embarrassed. His ears had gone warm. He felt a jolt of fear, hot and molten, in his stomach. "The criminals got ... nothing." He could not believe it. "How... ?"

"As soon as I saw the guns, I knew they were going to rob us all," Rachel said. "I took out the bio-computer and was going to hide it in the car. Then the man told you to give him the keys and I knew they were going to take your car. This sari is skintight and I didn't dare try to tuck it inside and ..." She shrugged. "I couldn't think what to do. Then Keryn just grabbed it and popped it down her front and you opened the door—just that fast. I was scared to death, but I hopped out first and hoped she had time to smooth herself out."

"That was quick thinking, Keryn," Dillon said.

"Not the first time I've hid stuff down there."

Rachel snickered. "I never thought I'd say this, Keryn, but I'm really thankful you're so well-endowed."

For some reason, everybody except Dillon laughed hysterically at this. He was certain that if he understood the social context better, he would see why this was funny. Keryn's generous cleavage had saved the bio-computer. Rachel was correct that this was something to be thankful for. But why was this humorous? It made no sense at all. He would have to ask his counselor at his next appointment.

"Those crooks are going to come back for us," Keryn said.

Dillon felt dizzy. "They have my keys, my wallet, my credit cards, my driver's license, everything. They will go to my house and search it."

"Mine too." Rachel looked defiant. "They won't find anything. I don't have another bio-computer."

"If they go to my house, they won't find anything there either," Keryn said. "Just my novel, and that's backed up online. And—" She gasped and stood up. "Allen, can you run me over to my house? Smiley's there all alone."

Dillon stood up too. "No, Keryn, you cannot risk it. If they are watching your house, they will grab you or follow you back here."

"But ... Smiley." Keryn put her face in her hands. "I can't let anything happen to him."

Dillon looked at his watch. "Keryn, no. It is unsafe. Do you have a neighbor with a key who can check on your cat tomorrow?"

"Oh!" Keryn's mouth broke into a smile. "Of course! Hold on, I'll call them now."

"It is already after midnight," Dillon said.

"Not a problem." Keryn opened her cell phone and punched in a number. A short pause, and then ... "Hi, it's Keryn. Still up working on your novel?"

She listened for a couple of minutes. "Oh, I hear you, I hear you. I'm behind on mine too. Listen, I'm not able to get back home tonight, and I might be gone for a few days. Could you be a dear and take care of Smiley until I get back? I know he loves playing with Zephyr."

Another pause. "That'll be great. Big hug to Eunice and the girls. Night, night!"

Keryn closed the phone. "He was still up writing. He'll go get Smiley right now and keep him until I get back. They've got a Ragdoll cat too, so they know how to take care of him. We trade cat-sitting. I keep Zephyr for them when they go out of town."

Dillon felt impatient to deal with the real issue at hand. "This thing has become dangerous. We need to call in the governing authorities."

"I'm not going to let Big Brother have it," Rachel said. "I'd sooner flush it down the toilet."

"That'll get us killed!" Keryn said. "The crooks have been watching us. By now, they already know they didn't get what they were looking for. They'll tear our places to pieces looking for it. They're not going to give up. They'll watch Grant and Clifton until they find us. And the absolute worst thing we can tell them is that we're awfully sorry but we flushed a trillion dollars worth of bio-computer down the sewer to feed the sharks. They're not going to believe that, and they'll play hardball."

Dillon did not want to think about the next time. "We need protection. We can call the police and—"

"You talked to the cops already, didn't you?" Rachel said.

"Yes." The policeman on the phone had taken all Dillon's information in a bored tone that suggested he was probably surfing the Web at the same time.

"And did they offer to come protect you so you won't get carjacked again?" Rachel asked.

"No, of course not. We would have to tell them about the ..." Dillon leaned back and closed his eyes. It would be the worst sort of logic to tell the police about the bio-computer. The police would smile and politely promise to do something, but they would not understand what a quantum computer would mean to the world. Policemen were not stupid, but they did not study physics and encryption theory. They would take no action, but they would make inquiries, and then word would leak out. In days, instead of one group of criminals, there would be several. The police would do nothing, but the criminals would act swiftly.

"Guys, we have to go to the government," Keryn said. "Unless we want to just wait for the crooks to come back so we can hand it over nicely."

"Or terrorists," Allen said. "If terrorists got hold of this, they could shut down the economy. Sort of like a financial 9/11—and it would be global. You understand that once you shut down the flow of money, it doesn't magically start up again, right? Money flow has momentum, kind of like water flow. If you shut the valve for even a short period of time you damage the system. Catastrophically."

Rachel grabbed Dillon's arm. "That's bad, but the alternative is no better. If you give it to Big Brother, then you've got the heel of the government grinding itself into your face, forever. I can't live like that."

Dillon had read *1984*. He thought it was foolishness. But he could not make Rachel give the bio-computer to the governing authorities. If she thought Big Brother would get it, she would destroy it, and then they would all be in mortal danger. Rachel might be willing to die to keep the bio-computer away from Big Brother, but Dillon was not.

"We need Grant's opinion on all this," Keryn said. "He financed this thing. When I talked to him after the layoffs, it sounded like he had some sort of plan."

Kathii yawned. "Let's sleep on it, shall we? It's getting late, and tomorrow morning the boys and I are going to church camp."

Dillon opened his eyes. "You are going out of town?"

"Sort of," Kathii said. "Up the coast a ways. Our church is having a weekend campout. There's a nice little lagoon there, with canoeing and windsurfing and swimming and things. Allen's going to work all day and then he'll join us tomorrow evening. Keryn, were you planning to go?"

"I was going to work on my novel," Keryn said. "But I guess that's not going to happen until it's safe to go back home again. Can we ... stay here for a few days?"

Dillon shook his head. "We cannot do anything here except sit. And they will eventually learn that Keryn has a sister and coming looking here."

"Not likely," Keryn said. "Kathii and I have different last names. My only address book is in my phone, which I have right here. My neighbor won't talk to them. And if Sunflower calls and some strange man answers my phone, she'll freak out and go incoherent. I'd say we're as safe here as anywhere."

Dillon thought there might be ways for a criminal to trace Keryn to Kathii, but it would take time. "In any event, we have no transportation. My minivan is gone. Your car and Rachel's are parked in front of your house, and it is unsafe to be seen there. Somebody is probably watching your street around the clock."

"And we're broke," Rachel said. "My money, my Visa card, my license were all in that handbag."

Keryn shivered. "Mine too, in my purse. I'll have to go to the DMV and get another license tomorrow."

"Not safe," Dillon said. "They might be watching the DMV."

Allen leaned forward. "Listen, we can spot you guys some money, but I think what you really need is a break until you talk with Grant and figure out what he has in mind. How about if you join us for church camp?"

Dillon did not think that was a good idea. He did not trust churches. "What kind of church do you belong to?"

Keryn shrugged. "Nondenominational. It's a neighborhood church here in University City."

Dillon did not know what a nondenominational church was. "Is it fundamentalist? I have heard bad things about fundamentalists. I refuse to be forced into foolish arguments—"

Rachel punched him on the arm. "Hey, Dillon, chill. I'm the pagan, remember? If they're gonna try to convert anybody, it'll be me. And I'm not buying."

"Guys ..." Keryn had a strange look on her face which Dillon could not parse. "Nobody's going to try to convert either one of you. I'll tell them you're both taken, okay? But listen, I think it would be good for us to get away for a few hours. The crooks won't have a clue where we are, and we can take a break from this ... thing we're locked in. As soon as we get hold of Grant and Clifton, they can come pick us up. Okay?"

"I'm game," Rachel said. "Come on, Dillon, it'll be a blast. Ever been windsurfing? I'll teach you."

Dillon had no desire to go windsurfing. He shivered. The last place he would ever want to go was a fundamentalist church camp.

But it was also an unlikely place for criminals to come looking. It would be one step removed from this house.

Keryn and Rachel intended to go to this church camp. It would not be logical for him to be separated from them. Anyway, it would only be for a few hours—until Grant or Clifton could come pick them up.

"All right, I will go," Dillon said.

But he knew he was going to hate it.

CHAPTER TWENTY-FOUR

Keryn

In the morning Allen went off to work, and everyone else piled into Kathii's minivan with an enormous load of camping gear. Keryn wore some jeans and a T-shirt she had borrowed from Kathii. Her sister had offered clothes to Dillon and Rachel, but they declined—since they were going to be stopping at a store for supplies anyway—and so they wore the same clothes they'd worn to the restaurant last night. Jason and Jordan, who were eight-year-old twins, were bragging about how they would take a canoe and paddle it all the way to Alaska. Kathii drove up to Carlsbad, where they stopped at a Target to go shopping.

Keryn picked out some underwear and casual clothes and then tried on several swimsuits. She wanted something that would be modest, but ... not too modest. She finally settled on a one-piece Lycra suit, electric blue with white diagonal stripes. When she finished shopping, Dillon was waiting quietly in the sporting goods section reading the directions on a box containing a pup tent. Rachel was playing some sort of video game with Jason in the electronics section. Jordan was sitting on a bike, twisting an imaginary throttle, and saying, "Vroom! Vroom!"

They all went through the checkout line and Kathii paid with her Visa card. The bill was huge.

Keryn winced. "Thanks, sis. We'll pay you back as soon as this thing's over."

Kathii smiled. "Take your time. I've got no balance, so there won't be any interest on it. It's no big deal."

Keryn thought it must be nice to have a Visa card with no balance on it. They drove up to the next exit, crossed the overpass, and turned left onto a gravel road. After a long jouncing ride, they reached the campground.

It wasn't noon yet, but a few families were already there. The pastor's wife, Gloria, greeted them all and assigned them spots for two tents. Gloria was about four foot ten, and she might have been that far around too. She wore a huge pink top and flowered pants and a smile as big as her heart. Keryn always felt very welcome around Gloria.

"Who's your friends?" Gloria said, taking in Dillon's suit and Rachel's sari without showing any hint that they were dressed oddly.

"Co-workers. This is Dillon. He goes to a ..." Keryn suddenly realized she had no idea what kind of church Dillon went to. "... a Presbyterian church in Mira Mesa. This is Rachel and she's Jewish. Guys, say hi to Gloria, who pretty much runs the church when her husband isn't looking."

"How lovely to meet you!" Gloria waded into Rachel and wrapped her up in a hug.

Keryn winced. When Gloria hugged you, she left no doubt that you had been hugged. Severely.

Gloria fingered Rachel's sari. "This makes your eyes look so green! It's beautiful."

Rachel gave her a five-hundred-watt smile.

Gloria looked Dillon up and down, taking in his pinstriped suit, his silk tie, his hard leather shoes. Then she stretched out a hand. "Dillon, you've got amazing taste in clothes. I'd like you to teach my husband how to shop sometime." She wrapped up his hand in both of hers and shook it. "Welcome to camp!"

Dillon looked as if he wanted to ask whether she was a fundamentalist, but he shook her hand and even gave her a shy smile.

"Okay, guys, maybe you better get changed," Keryn said. She gave Gloria a shrug. "We went out to eat in La Jolla last night and got carjacked, so Rachel and Dillon are a little overdressed for this party. Kathii bought them some clothes, so ... I guess they'll just ... go get changed." Keryn hadn't thought much about how she was going to explain all this, and now she realized that it sounded horribly lame.

Gloria gave her a knowing smile but didn't ask any of the obvious questions. "Go on, then! Get changed, then come back and get your tent up!" She shooed them away with her hands, then turned and bellowed at the twins. "Jason! Jordan! You need to wait till you've got an adult to take you in that canoe!"

Keryn grabbed the Target bags out of the minivan. "Here, Dillon. Take this one, Rachel. There's bathrooms over there where you can get changed. I'll get started with Kathii on the tents."

Dillon and Rachel disappeared into the bathrooms. Keryn joined Kathii, who was struggling to unroll the two tents they had brought from home. They spent the next five minutes spreading them out and laying down stakes at the corners and the midpoints. Keryn rummaged around in the minivan and found a rubber hammer.

Dillon came out of the rest room carrying a bag and turned to look out at the lagoon. He had put on a pair of khakis and a polo shirt and running shoes, and he looked ... excellent.

Kathii gave Keryn a little nudge. "Sister, you better be glad I'm married or I'd be horning in on your game."

Keryn sighed. "'Fraid I already ruined my chances last night. I told him about Rusty and Sunflower and ... everything."

Kathii just looked at her. "I told Allen all that stuff on our third date and he was okay with it. Forgiven is forever."

"Yeah, well, Dillon's kind of fussy." Keryn sighed. "He likes things just so. Orderly. I'm afraid I shocked him."

"Well, just remember, it ain't over till the fat lady—" Kathii sucked in her breath. "Good heavens!"

Keryn turned to look and saw Rachel walking toward the dock

wearing a bright pink bikini. Three itty-bitty triangles of cloth. She had a trim, lithe body that made Keryn want to shriek.

"Sister ..." Kathii's voice came out in a hiss. "I think you've got competition."

Keryn felt like somebody had punched her in the stomach. "I ... no. I'm not in that game."

Kathii pinched Keryn's cheek. "Listen, I don't want to see you roll over and play dead. You always do that. I want to see you fight fire with fire."

"I am not going to prance around in three little Band-Aids."

"I'm not talking about Band-Aids," Kathii said. "But what have you got against flaunting it a little bit?"

"I think Dillon's impervious to flaunting."

"Keryn, there isn't a man alive who's impervious to flaunting. Tasteful flaunting. You've got double-Ds and that little skank is an A. Maybe halfway to a B on a good day. I call that no contest. Trust me, a little flaunting goes a long way when you outclass the competition. If you want something, you gotta fight for it."

"I'll fight, but Rachel's not fighting fair. Somebody should talk to her. That is just so ... indecent. When the men get here from work, we're gonna have a wives' revolt on our hands."

Kathii thought about that for a minute. "Well, we've got a few hours yet. I betcha Gloria will have a little chat with her by then. Look, Dillon's coming this way now. Did you see that? He didn't even look at her."

Keryn was surprised. In her experience, it was a rare guy who wouldn't at least take a quick peek.

Dillon's face was unreadable. He put his Target bag in the minivan and then came over. "Can I help with the tent?"

"Are you good at pounding spikes?" Keryn held up the hammer. "I'm not."

Dillon took it and squatted beside her. He studied the tents and then spent the next five minutes adjusting their layout so the edges were exactly parallel. He pounded in the first spike, made some fine adjustments, then went from corner to corner, pounding in the spikes rapidly.

Keryn stood watching him with one eye. With the other, she enjoyed the sight of Gloria having a quiet discussion with Rachel by the water's edge.

Kathii came back from the minivan lugging a large sackful of metal framing for the tents.

Keryn helped her spread out the tubes on the grass. She was feeling better now. Gloria would set Rachel straight, and then it would be a fair—

"Yoo-hoo!" Rachel's voice sang out.

Keryn turned to look.

Rachel was sauntering back toward them, with the twins jumping around her, looking like they had just been given a year's worth of allowance. She put her Target bag in the minivan and came up next to Keryn. "The boys want to go canoeing, and Gloria thought maybe Dillon could take them out. Would you like to do that, Dillon?"

Dillon didn't look up. "I need to help with the tents."

Kathii didn't hesitate for an instant. "We're fine, Dillon. Go ahead. The boys'll love it. We can manage here."

Dillon stood up and looked over at Keryn.

"Go," she said. "The rest of this will be easy."

Jason and Jordan came running over and began jumping around Dillon. "Can we? Can we, Mr. Richard?"

Dillon shrugged. "Okay." He still hadn't even looked at Rachel.

The boys began shrieking with glee. Each of them grabbed one of Dillon's hands and began tugging him toward the dock.

Keryn and Kathii followed to help get them launched. Kathii made a fuss about putting huge orange life vests on the boys just so. Dillon had a hard time putting his on.

Keryn wondered if he'd ever worn one before. She watched him fumble at the straps for a while and finally decided she'd better help.

"Here, let me show you." Rachel appeared from nowhere and rearranged Dillon's vest. She rethreaded the straps, cinched them down, and squared him away. "Perfect! Here, boys, I'll help you into the canoe." She gave Jason a hand in, and then Jordan.

Dillon didn't take the hand she offered. He clambered in carefully, but then his foot slipped and he nearly fell into the water. He crept forward past the boys until he reached the middle of the canoe, where he took a seat and grabbed a paddle. He turned and smiled at Jason and Jordan. "Are we ready, boys?"

"Bye, Dillon!" Keryn waved.

"Have fun, boys!" Kathii said.

"Don't you worry, we'll take good care of them!" Rachel slipped past Keryn and hopped into the tail of the canoe. She didn't have a life jacket on. "Save some lunch for us!"

She pushed off and the canoe slid silently away from the dock.

Keryn's mouth fell open and she could not even think what to say.

Rachel was already paddling away with swift, sure strokes. The boys were splashing their paddles in the water and hooting with laughter.

"I don't believe that!" Kathii's voice was shaking with rage. "Keryn, she hijacked your guy! Go get her!"

Keryn was too angry to move. That little ... skank!

Quiet laughter rippled over the dock.

Keryn turned and saw Gloria's whole frame shaking. "Well! She outfoxed us all, didn't she? Time to make some serious battle plans. I'd like to win this war before any man-flesh gets here."

Rachel

Rachel hadn't been canoeing in ages. From the way Dillon handled the paddle, it looked like he'd never done it in his life. The boys were no help. Their ropy little muscles strained at the paddles, but they were doing more splashing than anything else. Rachel pushed the canoe forward, enjoying the heat of the sun and the cool breeze. "Having fun, boys?"

Both of them shrieked in glee. Dillon kept paddling doggedly. He hadn't even looked back yet or said a word.

Rachel realized she'd made a tactical error. He was in front of her. She should have taken the front seat. But it couldn't be helped now. She had him and Keryn didn't, and that was victory enough. She had realized last night that Dillon was no fundie. She wasn't clear what he was yet, but her instincts told her he was a lot less conventional than she had thought. Which made him fair game—and a very scrumptious bit of game. Up till now, she hadn't really been trying. As of today, she was giving it her best shot.

They paddled north along the shoreline of the lagoon, then turned east when they reached the north end. When they came to the east end, they turned again south. By now Rachel was bored of hugging the shoreline, so she stuck her paddle in the water and steered them around west, on a heading across the middle of the lagoon back toward the dock.

As they reached the midpoint, one of the twins lost his paddle in the water.

Rachel leaned over and tried to scoop it up but missed. Out of the corner of her eye, she saw an orange streak.

A huge splash hit her in the face.

"Aughhh!" A boyish scream gurgled as it went underwater.

"Jason!" yelled the other boy. "Jason, get back in here!"

Rachel made a grab at Jason as the canoe swept past him, but he was thrashing so wildly it was impossible to get a grip.

"Jason!"

Dillon turned to look and his face went white—he seemed immobilized with panic.

Rachel calmly stood up and dove into the water.

Jason was churning up a regular Niagara—arms flailing like a helicopter and yelling his head off.

Rachel swam toward him in a few strokes and circled around behind him. She wrapped him up in a hug, pinning his arms. "Jason! Calm down. You're safe. I've got you. Everything's going to be fine. Just fine."

Jason was hyperventilating and crying at the same time.

Rachel wiped the water out of his face. "It's okay, Jason. You'll be fine. They'll be back with the canoe in a minute. Just settle down."

Jason finally got calmed down to a low blubber.

Rachel watched the canoe make a long, leisurely circle and head back to them. Dillon knew enough to point the canoe to one side, rather than driving it right over the top of them. Unfortunately, he didn't seem to know how to slow down. As the canoe pulled alongside them, Rachel saw that it was going too fast.

She made a grab at the side, hoping to slow it down.

Dillon leaned over and latched onto Jason's arm. Jordan reached out and got the other arm. Then physics took over. The canoe tilted and veered around sharply, and Dillon and Jordan tumbled into the water.

There followed a long minute of thrashing around while the canoe drifted away. The boys and Dillon couldn't make any kind of progress in their clumsy life vests. When Rachel was sure they were all floating safely, she corralled the paddles and swam up alongside the canoe, which was almost completely full of water.

It had been a long time since Rachel had emptied a swamped canoe, but at one time she could do it in about thirty seconds. She faced it broadside and grabbed the gunwale with both hands. Shoving the gunwale sharply beneath the water, she frog-kicked forward, pushing the canoe straight ahead and taking advantage of the water's inertia. At just the right instant, she tipped the gunwale back up to keep water from sloshing back in. She repeated this maneuver again and again in quick succession. Her timing was a little off. It took her almost a minute to get most of the water out.

She looked back to check on Dillon and the boys. "Doing okay, guys?"

"Wow, that was cool!" one of the twins shouted. "Did you see that, Mr. Richard?"

Rachel put the paddles in and then swam around to the stern of the canoe and gripped the top with both hands. She kicked up hard, pulling down with her arms in one swift move that lifted her on top of the stern, straddling the canoe and sitting on her hands. She pulled her legs inside the canoe.

Behind her, she heard the twins hollering with glee.

Rachel sat down on a bench, grabbed a paddle, and stroked the canoe around in a circle until she was gliding back to the guys. Back-paddling the last few strokes brought it to a perfect stop beside the soggy trio.

Jason and Jordan were whooping and shouting and generally having a fine time. Dillon looked a mess.

Rachel couldn't read his expression. With his help, she hauled in Jason first, then Jordan. The two of them immediately huddled in the back of the boat, shivering in the cool wind.

Rachel turned to Dillon. "Okay, you're next. Hop in."

Dillon grabbed the side of the boat and tried to haul himself in. The canoe tipped dangerously.

"Whoa!" Rachel shouted. "Hold on, you'll tip us all over. Boys, let's get on the other side and try to counterbalance it so Dillon can get in."

The three of them leaned to the other side. Dillon tried again, but he could not pull himself in. Not in a bulky life vest and a shirt and pants and shoes.

Finally Rachel shrugged. "Grab onto the end of the canoe, Dillon. I'll just have to tow you back to shore."

"Perhaps we can be of assistance?"

Rachel turned and saw another canoe gliding toward them.

Gloria sat in the back, paddling serenely, all eight thousand pounds of her. Kathii was in the front, her eyes glued on the boys. Keryn sat in the middle. She was wearing a dazzling blue-and-white swimsuit, and filling it out *wretchedly* well. As they pulled up alongside, Keryn grabbed Dillon's hand. She reached over and tugged Rachel's canoe closer, then stepped across so she had a foot in either boat. "Okay, we're stable. Pull yourself on up, big guy."

Kathii and Gloria inched to the other side of their canoe to balance it.

Keryn was not a petite woman, but she obviously worked out a lot. She had strong, firm arms and long, slim thighs and abs to die for. The only extra fat on her body was exactly where a woman would want it, and every bit of it went on display as she leaned over to help Dillon.

Rachel shivered. *Omigosh, if she ever learns to strut her stuff, it's game over.*

Dillon grabbed the side of Keryn's boat with his free hand and lunged up and inside it. He looked a horrible, soggy mess.

Kathii hopped across to Rachel's canoe and scuttled down the length of it to the twins. "You boys scared me to death! Are you okay?"

"That was fun!" Jason shouted. "Boy, Mrs. Meyers can really swim! Did you see her? She swims like a shark!"

"It's Miss Meyers." Kathii looked at Rachel and her face broke into a grateful smile. "Rachel, thank you so much."

Rachel shrugged modestly. "It was nothing."

Gloria shifted across into Rachel's canoe, and it shuddered as she plumped her frame down at the far end.

"Bye, guys!" Keryn shouted from the other canoe. "See you back at the dock!" She dug in with her paddle and accelerated away.

Alone with Dillon.

CHAPTER TWENTY-FIVE

Dillon

After getting dried and changed, Dillon came out of his tent to find that it was lunchtime. He had put on a pair of baggy swim trunks and a T-shirt but he still felt ridiculously under-dressed. Even with sunscreen, it was dangerous to expose one's skin to the sunlight in such a way. His only consolation was that he would not be the first to die of skin cancer.

Rachel would. Dillon had never seen such a small swimsuit on a grown woman. Not that he actually saw it, of course. He was doing his best not to look at her at all. The only problem was that when he was trying to not look at Rachel, Keryn somehow drifted into view. Her swimsuit covered much more of her than Rachel's did, but she had assets that Rachel did not. It was all very embarrassing. Highly immodest.

Dillon felt a strange sense of panic in his chest. He was surrounded by attractive women who seemed so ignorant of their own attractive-ness. Undoubtedly, they would be shocked and embarrassed if they knew the sort of thoughts Dillon was thinking about them. He focused carefully on his corn chips and potato salad and thought about quantum mechanics.

There was a famous experiment in physics that Dillon had seen for the first time in college. A beam of laser light was allowed to shine through two parallel slits onto a screen. If you covered up one of the slits, the light shone only through the other slit and made a fuzzy slit-shaped pattern on the screen. This suggested that light was a wave, since diffraction through slits was a property of waves.

If you uncovered both slits, then something more interesting happened. The pattern on the screen was not the simple sum of the two hazy slits. Instead, it showed a sequence of light and dark bands— an interference pattern. This proved beyond all doubt that light was a wave. The dark and light bands were caused by two waves that either canceled or reinforced each other.

Except that light could also be shown to be made of particles— photons. You could reduce the intensity of the light source until only a single photon was emitted each second, a photon that moved in straight lines like a bullet and could be seen with the naked eye or with a photomultiplier tube.

This photon could go through one slit or through the other, but of course it could not go through both. A particle could not be in two places at once. If you replaced the screen with a photographic film and waited a long time for many photons to go through the slit, you would create an image on the film—a series of alternating bands of light and dark.

That was extraordinary. You *still* got an interference pattern, even though you knew with certainty that each photon could go through only one slit or the other. The only conclusion was that the photon was a strange beast that was not quite a particle and not quite a wave. It traveled in straight lines, like a particle. But it created an interference pattern, like a wave.

A photon was a particle that could interfere with itself.

Dillon felt like this photon. When he was working with Keryn, he felt calm and peaceful, but he did not feel excited. When he worked with Rachel, he felt happy and excited, but he did not feel peaceful.

When he was around both of them together, he did not feel calm or peaceful and he did not feel happy or excited. He felt a strange and terrifying inner turmoil. In some mysterious way, it was like there were two Dillons who were interfering with each other.

It was a terrible feeling and he hated it and he did not know what to do about it. It had been bad enough last night at the restaurant, when both of them were adequately dressed.

Today at the campground, it seemed ten times worse. It was too embarrassing to speak about. Both women would be astounded and outraged if they knew how attractive he found them. Obviously, they had no idea, or they would not dress so provocatively. Dillon's whole head seemed to be buzzing, as if it were filled with hundreds of horse-flies. He chewed his food and swallowed, but he could not taste it.

Finally lunch was over. Dillon hurried to his tent and got his tooth-brush and brushed his teeth in the mildew-smelling bathroom. He had bought dental floss also, but his dentist had told him to floss only once per day—after supper—so he did not floss now. When he returned to the tents, he saw that Rachel was chasing a volleyball that one of the twins had kicked into the trees, and Keryn had gone with her sister to greet another family that was just arriving.

So Dillon walked to the dock and threw a life vest into one of the canoes and stepped in and quietly paddled away into the lagoon. He paddled all the way across and through the channel that went under Highway 5 into a smaller bay on the other side. He experimented with paddling different ways. After much practice, he found the most effi-cient way to power his canoe.

The surface of the water was still, but Dillon did not feel calm and he did not feel happy.

He felt very alone—and for the first time in his life, he did not like it.

Keryn

Around 3:00 Keryn finally heard from Grant. She had left a terse message on his cell phone voice mail that morning. "Grant, it's me. Call me as soon as you can."

When he called, he sounded nervous. "Keryn, what's up?"

She filled him in on the carjacking, taking care not to say too much over the phone. "... and we think they were after more than just our money and our car."

"Did they get the you-know-what?" Grant's voice crackled with tension.

"No."

"Where are you?"

"I'd rather not say on the phone. Where've you been all day?"

"Mexico. Julia and I decided to go to Tijuana for dinner and we stayed the night. Got a great price in the Camino Real. We're still here."

"We need to talk when you get back. Where's Clifton?"

"No idea," Grant said. "But tell me something. Did Dillon scrub that hard drive in the bio-lab?"

"Yes, of course. Julia said to reformat it, so that's what I told him to do."

"Oh crap, you gotta be kidding me. Not good enough. Any idiot with data recovery tools can read the hard drive if all you do is reformat it. You have to scrub it. You overwrite it with random ones and zeroes a bunch of times."

"I ... didn't know that. Julia said to reformat it, so I would guess that's what Dillon did."

"Julia should have told you to scrub it. Listen, you kids stay in hiding for a couple days. I don't want you out in public. I'll sneak over to the bio-lab and scrub the hard drive myself."

"You can't get in," Keryn said. A hot rush of embarrassment swept over her. "We ... we changed the keypad combination a few days ago and didn't tell you. And I'd rather not tell you the combination over the phone."

"Hey, Keryn, not to worry. That keypad lock is configured for multiple combinations. I've got one for my private use, and you can't change it."

"Oh." Keryn felt like an idiot.

"I'll get over there tomorrow morning early and scrub the hard drive. Then I'll slap the ultimate security lock on it."

"What's that?"

"A sledgehammer," Grant said. "Five or six whacks with one of those and God himself won't be able to read that hard drive."

"Talk to you tomorrow," Keryn said. "Call me as soon as Clifton turns up."

She closed the phone and stared out at the lagoon, where a distant canoe skittered across the water. Her insides felt like she'd just drunk a gallon of ice water. The hard drive in the bio-lab was not secure. And she didn't dare go near it.

~

Keryn

Keryn was playing volleyball with the twins and wondering if she ought to go say hi to Dillon. He'd gotten back from canoeing about ten minutes ago, and now he was surrounded by half a dozen men, the early arrivals from work. They were all sitting at a concrete picnic table talking, and Keryn desperately wanted to go join them.

Except Rachel was right there in the middle, still in her bikini, and Keryn didn't want to try to compete with *that*. Somebody really ought to talk to Rachel about appropriate attire.

"Keryn, we need to talk right now." Gloria's voice, behind her.

Keryn's heart double-thumped. No. Please God, no. For once, Gloria did not sound in control of the situation. Which meant she was going to pass the buck on talking to Rachel. And Keryn didn't want to deal with it.

Keryn tossed the volleyball to Jason. "Boys, I'll be back in a minute." She took a long, deep breath, and then turned to look at Gloria. "What's up?"

Gloria's face had gone tight. "There's a problem with your friends."

"I'm really sorry about that, but I don't know what to do, short of stealing her bikini."

Gloria waved her hand in the air. "It's going to be hot for another hour and then there's a marine layer coming in. Rachel's going to get cold and put on something else. Not a problem."

"Then what's the problem?"

"Just what kind of church did you say Dillon goes to?"

"Um ... why?"

Gloria shook her head. "You better come listen. This is way over my head."

They strolled over toward the table where the men were gathered. Keryn spotted Allen's best friend Jimmy, an electrical engineer who worked at SAIC. Keryn had dated him a couple of times about a year ago, but there hadn't been one tiny bit of spark.

Today, Jimmy's face was on fire. "... telling me that the Bible's wrong, is that it?"

Dillon shook his head. "No, I am telling you that the earth is 4.5 billion years old."

Keryn's stomach tightened into a cold, hard knot. She didn't know much about the whole creation-evolution debate. She hadn't grown up believing in a young earth, and she didn't think any of that mattered. But obviously it mattered to Jimmy. And Dillon.

Jimmy leaned forward. "You weren't there, so how could you possibly know that anything is billions of years old?"

"By reasoning to the best inference from the evidence at hand, which is massive."

"If you mean radiometric dating, then you're bringing in a huge number of presuppositions, none of which you can prove."

Dillon's face hardened. "Do you believe that the rules of propositional logic are incorrect?"

"Um ... no. What does that have to do with—"

"The rules of propositional logic are axioms which cannot be proved. They are precisely what you call presuppositions. Do you believe that Newton's laws are incorrect within the nonrelativistic domain?"

"Of course not, but—"

"Again, these are what you call presuppositions. Do you believe that the rules of quantum mechanics are incorrect?"

"I don't see where you're going with this."

"Clearly. Are you a Bayesian or a frequentist in your interpretation of probability?"

Jimmy's mouth was hanging open. "Hey, man, I just do the numbers."

"This is not surprising. Do you favor a foundationalist or a coherentist approach in reaching epistemological justification for your beliefs?"

A long silence while Jimmy stared at Dillon. "Dude, I'm just saying that you can't prove all your presuppositions about dating rocks."

"True but tautological. By definition, axioms cannot be proved. Which particular axiom would you remove from my noetic structure? Bearing in mind that we use those axioms every day to design bridges, power the Internet, and drive our cars?"

Jimmy's face had gone nearly purple. "Look, most of your presuppositions are fine. But you can't deny that when you do radiometric dating, you have to assume that you know how much radioactive stuff you started with and you have to assume there was no contamination over time."

Dillon shook his head. "Of course I can deny both of those statements, because they are both incorrect. Using standard isochron methods, you measure the initial conditions and age simultaneously. No assumption is necessary. Furthermore, by doing a trivial chi-squared analysis of your least-squares fit, you can test whether there was contamination of the sample. This allows you to ignore bad data and accept good data."

"So you don't believe the Bible when it says the earth is thousands of years old."

"Which verse says that?"

Jimmy hesitated. "You have to put it together from a lot of different verses."

"Which particular verses?"

"The genealogies and stuff."

"And when you do that, you presuppose that the genealogies are intended to be taken as chronological data. You also presuppose that there are no gaps in the records. You presuppose that a story about a husband named 'Man' and a wife named 'Life' is intended to be taken as a historical record of two actual persons. You are absolutely certain of these presuppositions?"

"Um ... yeah, sure."

"And based on these presuppositions, you arrive at what final number for the age of the earth?"

Jimmy shrugged. "Somewhere between six and ten thousand years."

"The simplest summation of the Biblical data, using an Ussher-like chronology, takes you to a putative creation date of 4004 B.C., which would give you an age for the earth of just over six thousand years. So where is your evidence for ten thousand? It sounds like you yourself disbelieve the Bible."

A long silence. "I suppose next you're going to tell me that Darwin was right."

"Some variant of the modern neo-Darwinian synthesis is obviously correct, but since Darwin knew nothing about DNA, genetic drift, or horizontal gene transfer, nobody would consider him to have given a full account of evolutionary processes."

Keryn couldn't stand it any longer. She wasn't following the argument very well, but she knew Jimmy was getting killed. Dillon was probably thinking that everybody in her church was a fundamentalist. And maybe some of them were, but if she didn't do something quick, this was going to turn into a shouting match.

She strolled up to the table and gave them her brightest smile. "Hey guys, who wants to play some volleyball?"

She was still wearing her electric blue swimsuit and as she leaned forward and put her elbows on the table, she was pretty sure they were all getting an eyeful, which was humiliating, but whatever. Desperate times called for desperate measures. She was not going to let them drive Dillon away.

Jimmy looked relieved to be rescued. "Volleyball? Hey, I'm in. Allen and I can be captains. Keryn, you're on my team."

Allen grinned. "I'll take Dillon."

Dillon put up both hands, palm outward. "I do not know how to play volleyball."

Allen shrugged. "Then I'll take Kathii."

Jimmy pointed at Rachel. "You're on my team too."

Rachel shook her head. Her blonde hair swished back and forth on her shoulders. "I'll sit this one out and keep Dillon company. I'm real interested in what he has to say about evolution."

Jimmy and Allen quickly finished choosing teams and they all went off to the volleyball net.

Keryn took one last look back at Dillon.

Rachel was sitting next to him on top of the picnic table, so close that there was only a sliver of daylight between them. Dillon was talking animatedly to her, looking into her eyes, gesturing with his hands.

Smiling.

CHAPTER TWENTY-SIX

Dillon

On Saturday morning, Dillon woke up at 5:00 a.m. He was sharing a tent with Allen and the twins. Allen had promised last night to take the boys fishing this morning. It took them only minutes to dress and leave the tent. By then Dillon was fully awake.

He lay in his sleeping bag wondering if Keryn's church people were going to ask him to leave. He should not have let that Jimmy person lure him into an argument yesterday. It was foolish to discuss science with a fundamentalist. Such persons did not think logically, and they took offense at people who did. Now they would throw him out.

Worst of all, Keryn must hate him.

Dillon did not want Keryn to hate him. He would still like for her to be his friend. She was not hateful like some fundamentalists. But she had not come to join him and Rachel while they talked quietly by themselves last night after supper. That probably meant she did not wish to have anything more to do with him.

The door of the tent suddenly began unzipping in a series of short, stealthy buzzes.

Dillon's heart began hammering. That would be Gloria's husband, coming to ask him to leave. Dillon's counselor had taught him to take a long, deep breath and let it out slowly in situations when people rejected him.

He tried that now, but his heart felt cold and his fists were clenching so hard that his nails bit into his hands. People did not understand him. They did not try to understand him. They would never understand him.

The beam of a tiny flashlight poked into the tent and skittered all around. "Dillon!" Rachel whispered. "Are you awake?"

Dillon felt a little flip-flop in his chest. He would not be thrown out just yet. "Yes, I am awake."

Rachel crawled all the way inside, zipped the tent shut, and raced her light all around the sides of the tent. She appeared to be wearing nothing but a long T-shirt that hugged her body tightly. "Kathii snores like you wouldn't believe. Mind if I try to catch a few Zs in here?"

"I ... that would not be appropriate." Dillon's pulse began racing. Rachel was an attractive woman wearing practically nothing. He would not be able to sleep knowing she was there. If she knew the kind of thoughts that he was thinking, she would be highly offended.

"Nobody's going to know I'm here."

"I will know."

"Well, you aren't going to tell, and neither am I, so we're good." Rachel crawled into the sleeping bag closest to Dillon, zipped it up, and scootched close to him. "I've been thinking we should get out of here."

"We should *what?*"

"Get out of this place. These people are the worst sort of fundies. We don't belong here and Grant isn't going to come get us. Let's just bail."

"We need to stay close to Keryn."

"Keryn will be fine without us. These are her people. They'll keep her safe. But I can't stand this place, and you're on the naughty list after that argument you got into yesterday. Let's ask Kathii to spot us some money and we can go rent a cheap motel room nearby and hide out till Grant gets back from Mexico."

Dillon's pulse felt like liquid fire in his veins. "I ... a motel room?"

Rachel wiggled closer and let her penlight shine on the tent floor between them. It gave just enough light so he could see her face. "Yeah. We could pay cash and give them a phony name. The crooks would never find us."

"I do not stay in motel rooms with attractive single women."

Rachel began giggling silently. Her entire body shook with suppressed laughter.

Dillon could not imagine why this was funny.

Rachel laughed for a long time. Finally she got control of herself. She reached up and tapped Dillon lightly on the nose. "You are so ... adorable! I can't believe there's a good-looking, smart, sexy guy on the planet who's still a virgin."

"I ... am not ..." Dillon's voice caught in his throat and a sudden surge of rage welled up in his stomach. He felt a rush of blood in his face and his eyes clamped tightly shut and he could not breathe.

"Dillon, are you okay? What did I just say? Omigosh, I'm so sorry." Rachel's soft hand brushed lightly down Dillon's face.

Dillon could not speak. His heart was pounding loudly on the walls of his chest, and suddenly he was ten years old again, an innocent altar boy, crying his eyes out in shock and humiliation and rage while the priest warned him never, ever, ever to tell anybody what had just happened.

Dillon's whole body was shaking.

From somewhere very far away, Rachel's voice whispered. "Dillon, did somebody ... do something to you when you were a kid?"

Dillon nodded. He had never told anybody this secret. Not even his counselor.

"Omigosh! Dillon, I am so, so sorry. Do you want to talk about it?"

Dillon did not know what to say. No, he would never dare talk about it. But ... the truth was boiling inside him, had been simmering for more than twenty years.

"Who did it? You have to talk about it. You have to, or it's going to kill you."

Dillon clamped his eyes shut.

"Was it your father? Is that why you hate him?"

Dillon shook his head.

"An uncle? Older brother? Cousin?"

Dillon could finally breathe again. "No."

"A teacher?"

"No."

"Minister?"

"No."

"Priest?"

Dillon's throat caught, and a little sob hissed out of his lungs.

"Crap, I should have guessed. And I bet he made you promise never to tell, right? On pain of burning in hell forever, right?"

"I ... do not believe in hell."

"But you did when you were a kid, didn't you? So the evil bastard held that over you and made you promise never to tell."

"Y-yes."

"It's going to kill you until you let it out. So just tell me the whole thing. Don't leave anything out. Right now, and you'll be free."

Dillon told her. The priest asking him to stay behind one day to "discuss something of importance." Locking the door. Doing the evil deed. Warning him never to tell a soul.

And then the aftermath, when Dillon refused to continue serving as an altar boy. Refused to go to church. Refused to explain why. Refused, refused, refused.

His father's quiet, stupid fury at Dillon's obstinate silence.

"And ... that's why you hate your father," Rachel said.

"I do not ... it is complicated."

"You're angry at your father."

Dillon could not say anything. It was a sin to hate his father. He did not hate his father. And yet ...

"Can you tell me what you feel?"

"Cold. Like my heart is frozen."

"Well, there's two things you need," Rachel said. "First of all, you need a good cry. Ever tried that?"

Dillon shook his head. He felt his belly tighten. Big boys did not cry, much less grown men. He would not allow it. Ever.

"Second, you need a hug. When was the last time you had a hug?"

Dillon could not remember clearly. "Maybe when I was four."

"Four years *old*?" Rachel shrieked. She covered her mouth. "Sorry, but that's way too long to go without a hug." She unzipped her sleeping bag, then reached over and unzipped Dillon's.

Before Dillon could think what to do, she was wrapping her arms around him and pulling herself toward him.

Panic raced through Dillon's veins. He was wearing nothing but a T-shirt and boxers. If Rachel had any idea what immoral thoughts were racing through his mind, she would be horrified.

The zipper of the tent door screeched up and a huge flashlight shined in.

Dillon froze.

Rachel squeaked and pulled away.

The light shone full on the two of them.

Dillon tugged the sleeping bag over his body, but he was certain whoever held the light had seen how he was dressed. How he was not dressed.

"Excuse me, but you two are being extremely inappropriate." It was Gloria's voice, and she sounded furious. "Rachel, I want you out of there right this instant."

Rachel scrambled away from Dillon and crawled out of the tent.

"Dillon, I'll speak with you after I finish with Rachel." The door zipped shut with horrible ferocity.

Dillon's face felt like it was on fire. Now they would throw him out for certain. Rachel too. They would have nowhere to go.

And Keryn would think ... Dillon did not want to imagine what Keryn would think.

It would not do to tell her he was innocent.

He had not been thinking innocent thoughts at all.

~

Rachel

Gloria tugged on Rachel's hand and led her away from the tents. When they reached the dock, she turned her flashlight off and spun around to look at Rachel. "Well? What do you have to say for yourself?"

"We were just talking."

"In your underwear? Looked like you were doing more than talking."

"I was going to give him a hug."

"He had more on his mind than a hug."

"He needed a hug. He hasn't had a hug since he was four years old."

"He—what? Are you serious?" Gloria's eyes widened. "How do you know that?"

Rachel didn't know if Gloria would believe her, but she decided to just tell the truth. She told her everything. The whole story. It took several minutes and Rachel was shivering, but she wasn't going to let Dillon get in trouble for something that wasn't his fault.

"That poor boy." Tears stood out in Gloria's eyes. "He likes you, you know."

"Don't be absurd. He's got Asperger's syndrome. He's immune to the female race."

Gloria shook her head. "He likes you. Doesn't know it yet, but he does."

"I'd have thought if there was anyone he liked, it would be Keryn. She's more his type, except she's a fundie."

Gloria's face jerked as if Rachel had slapped her. "He likes Keryn too, and he doesn't know that either. But where did you get the idea Keryn is a fundamentalist?"

"She's part of your church, isn't she? I didn't see her arguing with that Jimmy character yesterday."

"And you think that all people in our congregation are alike? Just a bunch of cookies stamped out of the same mold?"

"Well ... of course. I know you people's type."

"You like to put people in boxes, don't you?"

"I read people pretty well."

"Do you now?" Gloria closed her eyes for a minute. "And when you met Keryn, you had her pegged as some virginal goody two-shoes, right?"

"Okay, so I was wrong about her."

"And when you met Dillon, you thought he was a boring, anal-retentive geek, right?"

"I figured out pretty quick he's a Mozart."

"So you moved him from one pigeonhole to another."

"I ... do you have a point here?"

"Just that you don't like being put in a box by other people, but you do it yourself. All the time."

"I'm right most of the time."

Gloria still had her eyes closed and she seemed to be concentrating intensely. "Do you know a woman named ... Julia? A trophy wife? Lives in La Jolla?"

Rachel felt her hands go numb. "You're scamming me, aren't you? Keryn told you about Julia, didn't she?"

"And there's somebody else you've got in a box. Somebody you hate even though you don't know him. You hate him because of what people have done in his name."

"What is this, some sort of voodoo thing? You're playing mind-reader games with me? Are you some kind of carnival palm reader?"

Gloria sighed and opened her eyes. "Now you're putting me in a box."

"Are you going to throw us out of camp?"

"Of course not. You three are in danger."

"Keryn wasn't supposed to tell you that."

"Honey, it's written all over your faces."

Rachel began trembling. "I've been so scared since Thursday night. Whoever they are, they're going to keep looking till they find us."

"Well, you just stay together and I think you'll be safe. The three of you. I know you're going to think this sounds weird, but I have this ... impression that if the three of you separate, something horrible is going to happen."

Cold sweat sprang out on Rachel's body. She shivered in the chill morning air.

Gloria wrapped her up in a giant hug. "Honey, you're safe with us.

But I need you to behave yourselves. Set a good example for all the children."

"So I have to throw away my bikini."

"Heavens, no! You look wonderful in a bikini. You've already got a few of the moms in the congregation talking about how they've kind of let themselves go. About getting back into shape. I say you should wear that thing all you want. Before my metabolism went haywire years ago, I used to turn a few heads myself in a bikini."

Rachel's head felt like it was spinning. Gloria in a bikini? The mind boggled. "I ... Dillon is such a sweetie. I don't know how to help him. He's hurting and he's stuck in some pit and I just don't—"

"You have a kind heart." Gloria held Rachel out to arm's length and looked at her intently. "But you can't help someone out of a pit when you're in one yourself."

"I'm not going to come to Jesus."

"Your problem is bigger than coming to Jesus."

"What's that supposed to mean?"

Gloria shrugged her shoulders. "Honey, I have no idea."

"If you said it, you should know what it means."

"It doesn't work that way." Gloria looked at her watch. "Listen dear, people are going to be out and about soon and you need to get dressed. I've said my piece. I don't know how to help Dillon and I don't know how to help you. I have a feeling it'll come to both of you if you're open."

Rachel didn't have any idea how she was supposed to do that.

"Have a nice day, honey." Gloria began waddling back toward the tents, humming a tune under her breath.

Rachel felt so confused she didn't know what to think. A gang of ruthless criminals were out to get her. She was stuck in a horrible, boring church camp with a bunch of fundies. Dillon liked her but didn't know it, but he also liked Keryn and he didn't know that either. And she had a problem even Jesus couldn't solve.

With all that going for her, how could she *not* have a nice day?

~

Dillon

Dillon lay in his sleeping bag waiting for Gloria to come back and ask him to leave. He had been foolish to allow Rachel to come into the tent. But he could not have foreseen she would try to hug him.

While he waited, he took out his cell phone and called his home phone number. He pressed the code to access his answering machine remotely and found only one message. The police department had called last night to say that his minivan was recovered and he could pick it up at an impound yard in Point Loma. It made no sense that they had towed it all the way to Point Loma, but Dillon did not expect the police to act sensibly.

Dillon hung up and checked his watch. 5:47 a.m. His cell phone said it was 5:48. He took a minute to reset his watch to the correct time. His hair felt oily, so he pulled on his clothes and found a towel and soap and shampoo and went to take a shower in the bathroom. By 6:02 he was washed and dressed. Nobody else in the camp seemed to be up. Gloria and Rachel were not in sight.

Dillon went and sat down on the dock and stared east. The red sun hung above the horizon. His cell phone rang. He flipped the phone open. "Good morning, Grant."

"Dillon, what did you do with the hard drive?"

Dillon's heart lurched. "What hard drive?"

"The one in that computer in the bio-lab. The one you were writing all that software on."

"It is still there. I copied the data to my USB flash drive and reformatted the hard drive as Keryn told me."

"It's gone." Grant's voice sounded peculiar.

Dillon could not guess the meaning of this tone of voice. He did not know this social context at all. "How could it be gone?"

"I went in this morning to scrub the drive and smash it." Grant was breathing heavily now. "The case was open and the drive was gone."

Dillon felt like he had been punched in the face. "Rachel and Keryn and I have been together since we were laid off. None of us took it."

"Then we're screwed."

Dillon saw a picture in his mind of a giant stainless steel screw piercing each of them. He winced. "Maybe Clifton went to rescue it?"

"He doesn't know the combination to the bio-lab," Grant said. "You guys changed it, remember? And I have my own combination, but even Julia doesn't know it. Whoever ... stole the bio-computer in the first place came back and got that hard drive."

Dillon knew that a good hard-disk recovery service could recover the data on a reformatted drive. Julia had made a critical error in telling them to merely reformat the device. He could have scrubbed it or removed the hard drive, but he had not known they would be laid off when he left, and he had been too shocked afterward to think of it. That was a critical error on his part. It would have been against the rules to go back to the bio-lab, but he would have been willing to break the rules because they were foolish. Except that he had not thought of it. This was stupidity of a high order, and he had no excuse.

"Are you guys in a safe place?" Grant said.

"Yes, for now. I think they will throw us out shortly."

"How far along were you with that software?"

Dillon felt a wave of sadness wash through him. "We were ready to begin testing. We need that NMR machine from the bio-lab."

"Testing?"

Dillon realized he had just said much more than he should have.

"Dillon, listen, I don't want a direct answer on an insecure line, but I need to know if there's something important that Rachel may have forgotten to tell me."

Dillon felt sick to his core. They had deceived Grant about Rachel's backup bio-computer and now he would be angry. "Yes," he said in a quiet voice. "I am sorry, Grant, but—"

"Sorry?" Grant's voice was a yelp. "Are you telling me—no, don't tell me. I think you're telling me you need an NMR machine right now, is that correct?"

"Yes. Grant, we made a terrible mistake in not telling you."

"Actually, I'm not surprised. I should have guessed, now that I think about it. But it might turn out for the best that I didn't. If I'd known, I could have fought off the leeches. As it is ... the leeches have the shell and we've got the meat. Am I right?"

Dillon had no idea what Grant was talking about.

"What kind of NMR machine do you need?" Grant said. "Do you need any special connectors or cards or drivers to ... to test your software?"

"We were using a MagTec NMR machine with a FireWire connector," Dillon said. "And I need a computer with a FireWire port."

"I don't want you going anywhere near the bio-lab," Grant said. "For one thing, it's illegal for you to use that equipment. For another, it's dangerous. Somebody's probably watching that place."

"Then they saw you." Dillon felt a rush of fear. If anything happened to Grant ...

"Listen, nobody's gonna bother me. I don't have anything. It's you they want. You need to finish testing your ... software. I bet you can borrow an NMR machine from a university around here. I'll make some calls and get back to you on that."

"We can make some calls too. Rachel knows people at Caltech."

"No." Grant's voice sounded thick and tired. "Caltech's too obvious. Everybody knows Rachel got her Ph.D. there. Listen, you people are in danger. I want you to stay where you are and turn off all your cell phones. If your phone is on, the cell company knows where you are and the crooks could conceivably bribe somebody and track you down. Borrow a clean phone Sunday night and call me at the Camino Real Hotel in Tijuana at eleven sharp, and I'll tell you what to do next."

"Have you talked to Clifton?"

"No, I've got no idea where he is. His cell phone is turned off or he's out of service. I haven't been able to get hold of him since that all-hands meeting."

"Grant?"

"Yeah?"

"I ..." Dillon did not know how to tell Grant he loved him. "You have been like a father to me."

"Thanks, Dillon. I've always been proud of you."

An uncomfortable silence.

"Oh, say, Dillon, there's one more thing you should know."

Dillon held his breath.

Grant lowered his voice. "I looked at the manual for the keypad combination box this morning. I hadn't realized this, but there's an option to see how many combinations have been created."

"How ... how many?" Dillon was afraid to hear the answer.

"Four. You and Rachel created one. I created two of them. Somebody else created the fourth."

"Do those come with time stamps?"

"Yeah." Grant hesitated. "Two were created last December. I did those, one for me and one for Rachel. Rachel's was disabled on Wednesday morning, and another one was created at the same time."

"That was the new one Rachel and I created. I am sorry. We wanted to be able to rule you out as a suspect, and also everybody else ... in case there was another break-in."

"It's okay. You didn't show me yours and I didn't show you mine. We're even. But I wanted you to know that the other combination was created a week ago last night. Actually, a week ago this morning. At 4:45 a.m."

Dillon tried to process that. "It was created by the criminals who broke in and stole the bio-computer."

"Has to be," Grant said. "They must have been in the lab for a few hours. I don't know what it all means, but that's where we're at. Keep yourself safe, okay? I'm heading back to Mexico right now. Julia's still there, and ... I've got some things to do. Call me tomorrow night. And hug the girls, will you?"

Dillon did not think it was likely he was going to hug either Keryn or Rachel. A deep hollow filled his stomach. "I will call you if we have any trouble."

"Fine. Just turn off your phone and have the girls do the same. If *they* track you down, I can't help you. Understand?"

"Good-bye, Grant." Dillon hung up and powered off his phone and stuck it in his pocket. He felt very alone again. He was trapped in a small and shrinking box with two women he did not understand. Somebody out there was stalking him.

He did not feel calm and he did not feel happy.

Keryn

The day passed in a blur for Keryn. The morning was foggy and cool, but she kept warm playing volleyball with her many friends. Rachel had dressed decently and sat under a tree talking quietly to Dillon.

At lunch, Jimmy kept a wary distance from Dillon, which saved Keryn from having to mediate any more battles. She worried that her church friends had alienated Dillon completely. Coming to camp had been a horrible idea.

By early afternoon, the fog had burned off and the day turned fiercely hot. Rachel put on her tiny pink bikini again, and then surprised Keryn by offering to teach both her and Dillon how to windsurf.

Keryn picked it up quickly, but Dillon had coordination issues. Rachel had to give him some one-on-one coaching on his board. Keryn decided not to worry about it. Any chance she'd had with Dillon was blown anyway, now that he thought her church was packed with fundamentalists. She was never going to live that down. Dillon couldn't possibly think less of her.

She convinced herself she didn't care. If Dillon didn't like what she was, then he was the wrong guy for her. Period. End of discussion.

For a couple of hours, Keryn simply forgot her troubles and had fun. At one point, Rachel freaked out when a helicopter flew by, but it kept going straight on without slowing down or circling.

Keryn wasn't worried. The helicopter was clearly labeled with a large 8. Obviously, the Channel 8 news chopper.

Rachel was paranoid, that was all.

Late in the afternoon, a marine layer rolled in. The three of them reluctantly came in. Keryn changed into warmer clothes. Rachel put on a tight sweatshirt and some low-cut jeans over her bikini. She sat next to Dillon at suppertime.

Keryn sat with Kathii and reminded herself fifty times that she could not care less what Dillon thought about her.

After supper there were marshmallows to roast over the fire and s'mores to eat. Around 9:00 Gloria stuck a silver police whistle in her mouth and blew out a long blast. "Story time!" she bellowed.

The kids came running and gathered around her in a big circle near the fire. The adults followed, but they took care to stay on the outer fringes. Gloria's stories were famous. Or infamous. She was good at embarrassing people without meaning to. Keryn sat down with Kathii and Allen behind Jason and Jordan. *Please, please, please don't embarrass me, Gloria.*

"All right, kids," Gloria shouted. "Tonight's story is called 'The Prodigal Papa.' Who knows what the word *prodigal* means?"

Hands shot up all around the circle. A little girl named Charisse stood up and said, "It means 'bad.'"

Gloria pressed her lips together. "Does it, now?" She looked all around the circle. "How many think that's what it means?"

The show of hands she got was about as close to unanimous as a Cuban election.

"How many think that isn't what it means?" Gloria shouted.

Keryn raised her hand. Nobody else did.

Gloria pointed at her. "What does our famous author think it means?"

Keryn felt her cheeks flushing. "It means 'wasteful.'"

"We have a winner!" Gloria hooted. "A prodigal person is a wasteful person. You win a marshmallow." She took one out of a bag and tossed it toward Keryn.

It landed in the sand.

Jason lunged for it and dusted it off and ate it.

"Now then, this story has three characters," Gloria said. "The first one is the Prodigal Papa, and I'm going to play that role. Now I need two volunteers. I need a Big Brother and I need a Little Brother. Kids, who's good at acting?"

A dozen hands went up. Jason and Jordan jumped up and waved frantically. "Me! Me!"

Gloria looked around the circle and an enormous smile wreathed her huge face. "Wonderful! I see just the two I need!" She pointed toward the back. "You there, and you! Come on up! I promise you'll both win a prize for participating!" She bounded into the crowd to apply a little persuasion on her reluctant volunteers.

Jason and Jordan flounced back into the sand, complaining.

Keryn turned to see who Gloria's victims were.

Gloria came wading back through the sea of faces, clutching the arms of two very unhappy-looking campers.

Rachel and Dillon.

Crap. Keryn saw in a flash what was going to happen. She wanted to dig a hole in the sand. All the way to China.

Rachel, dressed like a little floozy, was going to be the prodigal son, Little Brother. And Dillon, stiff and shy, was going to be the uptight Big Brother. They were perfect for their roles.

And they were going to *kill* Keryn for getting them into this.

But before they did that, Keryn was going to kill Gloria.

Because no matter how bad an opinion Dillon had of her church, it was about to get a whole lot worse.

CHAPTER TWENTY-SEVEN

Keryn

Keryn wanted to run up and stop the whole thing. She wanted to, but she didn't know how. Didn't dare.

Gloria planted Dillon and Rachel behind her and turned to face the children. She apparently didn't see Keryn's wide-eyed look of dismay.

"Once upon a time there was a Jewish farmer who had a great big farm!" Gloria said. "And on this farm he had horses and cows and camels and donkeys and sheep and goats and pigs!" Gloria had a hand motion for each of these animals. The motion for pigs involved billowing her arms out in front of her to make her enormous perimeter even bigger.

"Oops!" Gloria slapped her head. "Did I say pigs? That's a mistake! Because this was a Jewish farmer, and Jewish farmers don't raise pigs. How many of you knew that Jewish farmers don't raise pigs?"

Almost nobody raised their hands. Keryn raised hers just a little. She had known that, sort of.

Behind Gloria, Rachel had a "Well, duh" expression on her face. Dillon's face was unreadable.

"And this Jewish farmer also had two sons, and they had very strange names," Gloria said. "One of them was named Big Brother and the other one was named Little Brother. And both sons worked all day long on Papa's farm, feeding all of his horses and cows and camels and donkeys and sheep and goats and pigs!" Again, the litany of hand motions.

Jason jumped up. "You said he didn't have any pigs!"

"Oops!" Gloria bellowed. "That's right, he didn't have any pigs. My mistake. So as I was saying, Big Brother and Little Brother spent their whole day feeding all those animals and telling them, 'Eat more food! Eat more food!'"

Keryn felt a rising tide of panic inside her stomach. Dillon already thought her church was a pack of fundies. Now he must be thinking the place was just too weird for words. Normally, Keryn didn't mind these whackball stories. But today she was seeing Gloria like an outsider. And she looked stupid, there was just no getting around it.

Gloria began pacing. "Now, one of those brothers didn't like spending his whole life feeding those animals. Can you guess which brother that was?"

"Little Brother!" Jordan shouted.

Gloria shook her head. "Where'd you get that idea? You must be thinking of somebody else's story. This is my story and in my story, it was Big Brother. So one day Big Brother told Little Brother that he wanted to leave that farm with all its horses and cows and camels and donkeys and sheep and goats and pigs."

"No pigs!" somebody shouted.

Gloria looked thunderstruck. "Did I say pigs? What a dummy I am! Of course, there weren't any pigs! But Big Brother was tired of telling all those animals, 'Eat more food!' every day, and he told Little Brother he wanted to ask Papa for his half of the inheritance and go far away. Who knows what an inheritance is?"

The little girl, Charisse, waved her hands in the air. "It's when somebody dies and then their children get all their money."

"That's right!" Gloria said. "You don't get an inheritance unless somebody dies. Big Brother wanted his inheritance early, because he couldn't bother to wait for Papa to die. In fact, he would have been glad for his papa to die just so he could get that inheritance. And that was a terrible thing, wasn't it? Who knows what happened next?"

Nobody ventured a guess.

Gloria smiled. "Big Brother was too afraid to ask his papa for his share of the inheritance. So he did nothing. But Little Brother got to thinking about that, and one day he went to Papa and told him he wanted his half of the inheritance right now. So what do you think Papa did? Do you think he took Little Brother over his knee and spanked him like he deserved?"

Dead silence. Anything could happen in this strange universe of Gloria's.

"No!" Gloria hollered into the night. "That silly, wasteful Prodigal Papa *sold* half of his farm and half of the horses and cows and camels and donkeys and sheep and goats and pigs, and—"

"No pigs!" shouted several of the children.

"Oops! That's right, he didn't sell any pigs," Gloria said. "But he sold the others and he got a great big bag of ... money!" Gloria held up a large bag of marshmallows. It gleamed orange in the flickering firelight.

Gloria turned around and looked at Rachel and Dillon. "Then Papa went and *gave* all that money to Little Brother." Gloria held the bag toward Rachel.

Rachel froze her with an icy glare.

Keryn wanted to die. This was too horrible for words.

Gloria yanked the bag away. "Not you, Big Brother. This money is for Little Brother." She thrust the bag into Dillon's hands.

Dillon's jaw dropped. A murmur of surprise ran around the circle.

Gloria took Dillon's elbow and pulled. "And Little Brother went on a long, long journey to a far country." She led Dillon away from the fire, threading her way through the crowd all the way to the back.

Everybody turned around so they could see.

Gloria waited while the rustle of bodies subsided to perfect silence again. Dillon towered above her, his face a mask of stone.

Keryn could not remember ever being so humiliated. Dillon was never going to speak to her again. And she couldn't blame him.

Dillon

D illon had never liked having people looking at him. He felt self-conscious around people, especially those he did not know. Whenever he found himself in a large crowd, he developed a peculiar kind of tunnel vision. His field of view closed up so that he could see only a few faces. Now, in front of a sea of darkened faces, he could not see anybody. Only the fire, and the dark shape of Rachel, backlit by the flames. He clutched the bag of marshmallows in a sweaty grip and wondered how he had gotten into this strange situation with this woman of highly dubious theology. It was bad enough that they were fundamentalists. But this foolishness was far worse.

Gloria pushed the bag of marshmallows into Dillon's hands. "Now when Little Brother got to that far country, he felt wonderfully free! Little Brother found lots of friends. One day, he threw a party for all his friends. He had food and wine and music and dancing girls, and he gave away lots of money to all his friends."

Gloria reached into the bag and grabbed a handful of marshmallows and threw them out into the crowd.

The children shrieked and dived for the marshmallows.

Dillon winced at the sound. He did not like loud noises.

"And the next day, Little Brother threw another party with food and wine and music and dancing girls, and he gave away lots of money to all his friends." Gloria threw another handful of marshmallows out at the children.

"Can you guess what he did the next day?" Gloria shouted.

"A party!" somebody hollered.

"That's right!" Gloria grabbed two handfuls. "With more food and wine and music and dancing girls and lots more money for all his friends." She heaved the marshmallows high in the air. "Little Brother was wasting all his money. Where do you think he learned how to do that?"

A stunned silence.

Gloria put her hands on her hips. "You're not thinking! What's the name of the story?"

"The Prodigal Papa," said a small girl.

"That's right!" Gloria grabbed more marshmallows and flung them at the girl. "Little Brother learned it from his Prodigal Papa!"

Dillon was sweating now. This was all wrong. Very unsound theology. Keryn was part of some bizarre cult. He would have to find some way to escape before they tried to brainwash him.

"Finally, one day, Little Brother threw another party, and guess what he discovered?" Gloria grabbed the bag and turned it upside down, emptying its contents in the dirt. "That's right, he discovered that he had spent all his money." Gloria flung the bag up in the air.

It floated down in a sad little flutter that made Dillon feel ... empty.

"Then Little Brother went to all of his friends and do you know what he discovered?" Gloria began backing away from Dillon. She motioned with her arms to those nearest Dillon. They moved back, back, back, leaving Dillon ...

Alone.

Something cold and hollow seemed to have gotten stuck in Dillon's throat. He did not like crowds. Did not like them at all. But he did not like being scorned either. Gloria went all the way back to the fire and everybody turned their backs on Dillon.

He saw that he could walk away now. If he simply went back to his tent, he would be done with this foolish story. The cold lump in his throat spread to his chest, then to his stomach.

Dillon found that he could not move. It would be wrong to leave Rachel at the mercy of this cult. But as soon as he could, he should escape with her. Even hiding out in a motel room with her would be better than this.

Gloria was pacing back and forth in front of the fire. "Little Brother went looking for a job. He couldn't find work in the city, so he went out of town to a village. He couldn't find work in the village, so he went out of the village to the farms. He couldn't find work on the farms, so he walked down the road until he came to a horrible little pigsty. And he saw some men feeding the pigs, saying, 'Eat more food! Eat more food!'"

Gloria stopped pacing and turned to look straight at Dillon, and something gleamed in her eyes. "Little Brother was a nice Jewish boy who had never touched a pig, but he was so hungry, he was so desperate for food, that he waited for those men to go away and then he jumped into that pigsty and fell down—glop—in the pig poop and he crawled past those pigs and he ate their food."

A hush settled over the crowd. Dillon felt numb all over his body. He could not imagine being so hungry that he would fight a pig for its food.

Gloria seized a thin roll of paper towels and held it up in the air. "Meanwhile, back at home, Papa bought himself a telescope. And every morning, Papa tied on his running shoes and went up on the roof of the house and set up his telescope"—she placed the tube to her eye —"and looked down the road, and guess what he saw?"

Nobody said a word.

"Nothing!" Gloria shouted. "Papa didn't see anything except horses and cows and camels and donkeys and sheep and goats and pigs."

"No pigs!" all the children shouted.

Gloria nodded and her face turned solemn. "That's right, Papa didn't see any pigs. But Little Brother did. Every day, Little Brother went down the road until he found a place that had pigs. And every day, he had to wrestle with the pigs. And every day he fell down in the pig poop. And every day he stole food from the pigs."

A great deep silence settled down on the crowd. Dillon found that he could not breathe, could not feel, could not ... think. His entire brain had gone numb. This must be what brainwashing felt like.

"Then one morning, Papa tied on his running shoes and went up on the roof and looked down the road with his telescope, and guess what he saw?"

"Little Brother!" shrieked one of the boys.

"That's right!" Gloria dropped the telescope. "Papa saw Little Brother walking down the road, and his shoes had pig poop on them and his clothes had pig poop on them and his face had pig poop on it and—"

Gloria came churning around the circle of people and barreled into Dillon at full speed.

Dillon staggered backward, desperate to keep on his feet.

Gloria threw her arms around him and engulfed him in a vast and powerful hug. Then she reached up and pulled Dillon's head down and kissed him on both cheeks. One side, then the other. Again and again and again. "Oh, Little Brother, I've missed you! Welcome home, Little Brother! Papa loves you so much, Little Brother, Papa's glad you've come home."

Something hot broke loose in Dillon's chest. He gasped and staggered to one knee, wondering what bizarre trick she had played on his mind. *It is not possible to go home again. I want to go home again. No I do not. Yes I do.*

Gloria hugged him again. "Welcome home, Little Brother! It's time for us to have a *party*!" She pulled him to his feet and led him through the people back toward the fire.

Shouts and cheers rang in his ears.

Dillon felt grateful for Gloria's thick hand leading him through the crowd because he could not see a thing through the blur in his eyes.

~

Rachel

Rachel watched Gloria leading Dillon back toward the fire. She knew this parable backward and forward. Knew what was coming next. Big Brother was the goat of this story. Which meant Gloria was going to make a fool out of her. *Omigosh, this is going to be horrible. I'm getting away from this place as soon as I can convince Dillon to get out of here.*

Gloria made Dillon stand in front. He was grinning like a monkey and ... tears were standing bright in his eyes.

Rachel stared at him, astonished. Dillon Richard, crying.

Gloria took a deep breath and turned to face the children. "So Papa called in all his friends and threw a party, with food and wine and music and dancing girls, and they roasted a nice big fat juicy pig—"

"No pigs!" the children roared.

Gloria put her hand over her mouth. "Oops, I meant a calf! A nice big fat juicy calf, and everybody was happy."

A pregnant pause. Rachel felt sure all the children were staring at her. She crossed her arms across her chest, furious. This was exactly the kind of horrible stupidity she should have expected. Keryn must have set this up.

"Oops!" Gloria said. "Did I say everybody? I meant everybody except Big Brother. Big Brother was angry when he saw what happened. He knew that Little Brother had done exactly the things he wanted to do, only he hadn't dared and Little Brother had. So Big Brother refused to go in to the party. He went out to the barn and shouted at all the animals, 'Eat more food! Eat more food!' And he went through the whole barn, feeding all the horses and cows and camels and donkeys and sheep and goats and pigs."

"No pigs!" shouted the children.

Gloria gave a sly grin. "That's right. No pigs. Big Brother stayed out in the barn feeding the animals and hollering, 'Eat more food! Eat more food!' And guess who came looking for him."

A hush. A little boy waved his hand. "Papa?"

"No!" Gloria said. "*Prodigal* Papa went looking for Big Brother. Prodigal Papa, who wasted half his farm on Little Brother and who roasted a nice big fat juicy calf out of Big Brother's inheritance. Prodigal Papa went out to the barn and saw Big Brother shouting, 'Eat more food!' at all the horses and cows and camels and donkeys and sheep and goats and pigs."

"NO PIGS!" screamed the children. "NO PIGS!"

"Oops!" Gloria rapped her forehead. "I'm sorry, I keep forgetting. No pigs. And Prodigal Papa went up to Big Brother and he said, 'Big Brother, come into the house. We're having a party for Little Brother.' But Big Brother was angry and he said, 'No, I'm not going to that party.'"

Rachel glowered at Gloria. She didn't have to pretend to be angry. She was furious. *When she gets to the part about how the Jews are all legalists, I'm going to tell her she's full of crap. Right in front of her whole idiot church.*

Gloria's face went very solemn and sad. "Then Prodigal Papa said,

'Big Brother, why won't you come to the party?' And Big Brother said, 'You know why.' And Prodigal Papa said, 'No, I don't.' And Big Brother said, 'Yes, you do.' And Prodigal Papa took Big Brother's hand and said, 'I want you to tell me.'"

Gloria's eyes were big and soft as she took hold of Rachel's hand.

Rachel wanted to scream at her that it wasn't fair that Dillon got the good role in this stupid story and she got the lousy one. Dillon was the hero and Rachel was the villain, and she hadn't even had a chance to choose.

Gloria's eyes filled with pain and her voice nearly broke when she spoke. "So Big Brother told him. 'That rotten Little Brother went and took half the inheritance and went off to a far country and had fun! He had parties with food and wine and music and dancing girls every day, and I was stuck here feeding all these horses and cows and camels and donkeys and sheep and goats so I could earn my inheritance and—'"

Gloria raised her hand and black silence fell like night.

Rachel felt hot rage in her veins. Here it came now. Big Brother represented the Jews who were going to hell because they were legalists. She had seen it coming a mile away.

Gloria's voice came out in a whispered roar. "Then Prodigal Papa said, 'What did you say? So you could earn what?' And Big Brother said, 'So I could earn my inheritance.' And then Prodigal Papa laughed. He said, 'Big Brother, you can't *earn* your inheritance! Your inheritance is free!'"

Rachel's mouth dropped open. Gloria was massively screwing with the story.

A huge smile spread across Gloria's face. "Big Brother said, 'It's ... free?' And Prodigal Papa said, 'That's right! Your inheritance is free!' And Big Brother said, 'Are you sure it's free?' And Prodigal Papa said, 'Of course it's free! There's nothing you can do to earn your inheritance. It's free, it's free, it's free!'"

Rachel felt like she'd been hit in the face. No, this was wrong, all wrong. The story did not go like—

Gloria threw her arms around Rachel. "Then Prodigal Papa gave Big Brother a big hug, and Big Brother was so happy, he starting yelling, 'Woohoo! My inheritance is free!'"

Gloria stood up on tiptoe and kissed Rachel on both cheeks, first one, then the other. Over and over. "Big Brother, I love you just the way you are! You don't have to come home, because you're already here! I love you, I love you, I love you!"

Rachel's insides felt like they were melting, and all of a sudden she couldn't see.

Gloria put an arm around Rachel and guided her over toward Dillon. She threw an arm around Dillon and squeezed them both in her vast embrace. "And Prodigal Papa killed another nice big fat juicy calf and they had another big feast, with food and wine and music and dancing girls, and everybody was happy, because Prodigal Papa got back *both* of his sons that day."

It wasn't the way the story was supposed to go at all.

Rachel wept.

~

Keryn

Somewhere in the middle of the story, Keryn couldn't stand it any more. She got up and slipped away into the darkness. She wasn't going to watch Gloria finish humiliating her friends. If she'd had any guts at all, she'd have stopped this story dead before it got started.

But that was her problem. She didn't have any guts.

She went out onto the dock and sat with her feet hanging over the edge. Her stomach felt like it was filled with boiling oil. Rachel was going to hate her forever. Dillon was going to assume she was ... like Gloria. She couldn't possibly face either of them, ever again.

Keryn sat silently for several thousand years staring out over the water. Was the story over yet? Had Dillon and Rachel taken their things and stormed away?

The dock creaked behind her.

"Are you okay?" Kathii's voice.

"Go away."

Footsteps. More creaks. Kathii sat down beside her. "Why'd you leave in the middle? Are you feeling sick? Wasn't that brilliant?"

Keryn put her face in her hands. Hot tears spilled out of her eyes. "No, I'm not sick. No, it was not brilliant. It was too stupid for words."

"What are you talking about? I was bawling my eyes out when she finished. So was Rachel. I think even Dillon went kinda shiny around the eyes."

That was impossible. "What are you talking about? Gloria humiliated them. She humiliated me. She made us look stupid."

"Us? How could she make us look stupid? She's the nutty one. Everyone knows she's nutty, but she's also kinda deep, in her own weird way."

Keryn couldn't believe Kathii was saying this. "Look, I don't want to talk about it. Have Rachel and Dillon left already?"

"No, were they planning to go somewhere?"

"After that stupid story, I expect they'd fight tigers to get out of here."

"All I can tell you is that Dillon's talking to Allen about philosophy —something about the Big Bang and the cosmological something-or-other. You know Allen likes that stuff."

"What about Rachel? She's probably hitchhiking to Mexico right this minute."

Kathii giggled. "Right this minute, she's doing some sort of aerobics dance thing with Gloria, using somebody's iPod."

"Oh heavens."

"So what are you doing out here? You walked out right in the middle."

"Maybe the fact that I was massively humiliated had something to do with it."

"Humiliated? It wasn't you up there telling the story."

"If it had been, I wouldn't have told it like *that*."

"Like what?"

"Stupid. Gloria made Christians look stupid."

"Keryn, Gloria made herself look pretty crazy, but she doesn't represent Christians. And anyway, the ending made me think."

"If I ever write a story like that, shoot me."

"Gloria's just being herself."

"Maybe she should be a little less herself."

"Maybe you should be a little more yourself."

Keryn felt a stabbing pain in her chest. "What ... is that supposed to mean?"

A long silence. "I love your books. I really do. But I just wish ..."

"We've been over this. I'm not going to bring up faith issues in my novels. That just alienates people. I don't have enough readers as it is."

"You know what I like about Dillon?" Kathii said. "Other than being so hot you could melt Frodo's Ring of Power on his chest?"

Keryn didn't say anything.

"Dillon is totally, completely Dillon."

"What else would he be?"

"And Rachel is totally, completely Rachel."

"And they're complete opposites."

Kathii leaned over and kissed Keryn on the cheek. "Maybe so, sister, but they're also completely themselves."

Keryn couldn't move.

Kathii sat quietly beside her for a few minutes. Then she stood up and padded back down the dock toward the sounds of a giant, outdoor party.

CHAPTER TWENTY-EIGHT

Keryn

S unday morning, Keryn desperately wanted to talk to Rachel and Dillon about Gloria's story, but she couldn't find an opportune moment. At breakfast, Kathii talked her into helping make pancakes. By the time she escaped cooking duty, Allen had locked up Dillon in a deep conversation about quantum mechanics and the nature of reality. Rachel disappeared in a kayak shortly before the church service, which was probably a good thing, because Gloria told an outrageous story about Jesus and Peter walking on the water and ended up getting her husband completely soaked.

By lunchtime, Keryn had chickened out. She knew she ought to talk to her friends, but she just couldn't. After lunch, she played volleyball until late in the afternoon, but her heart wasn't in it. Neither Dillon nor Rachel seemed eager to bolt. But neither of them made any effort to come talk to her, either.

After breaking camp, Dillon rode home in Allen's car with the boys, while Keryn and Rachel returned with Kathii in the minivan.

At 11:00 p.m., with Jason and Jordan safely in bed, Keryn and Rachel and Dillon and Allen and Kathii huddled around the phone in the guest bedroom in Kathii's house. Dillon dialed the number for the Camino Real in Tijuana and asked to be connected to Grant O'Connell's room. The phone rang once and then ...

"Hello." It was Grant's gravelly voice, tired and wary.

"Grant, it's me," Dillon said. "We are all here on speakerphone."

"Hi, Grant," Keryn said.

"Are you okay, Uncle Grant?" Rachel asked.

"I'm fine. I've found a lab where you guys can test the you-know-what, but they can't let you have it till Thursday. And I've got some goodies for you. I took your photos to a place here in TJ and got some driver's licenses made."

"Mexican driver's licenses?" Dillon said.

"California. Don't argue," Grant said. "They're not legal, but they look pretty good. They aren't your real names, but they are your real photos. In case you need ID. I also got you each a clean cell phone, not traceable to you, and some Visa cards. Do not drive your own cars anywhere. Do not go back to your homes. Stay incognito. Got it?"

"Grant, you're acting like we're criminals," Keryn said.

"You're the good guys, trust me," Grant said. "But there are bad guys out there who hate your guts. Next time they find you, they won't just rob you, they'll kill you."

"We should go to the governing authorities," Dillon said.

"I swear, I'll drink that thing before I let Big Brother have it," Rachel said.

"We're not gonna give it to them until we've demoed it in public," Grant said. "Then if Big Brother gets it, they can't hide the fact that they have it. Okay, time's wasting and I want to meet you guys tonight and give you your goodies. Don't use your cell phones again for any reason. Keryn, does your sister have a cell phone that I can call you at when I get across the border? I'll have you go out driving and give you directions on the fly, so we can meet somewhere safe."

Kathii handed Keryn her cell phone with the phone number displayed.

"Yes," Keryn said. "Got a pen? Here's the number." She read off the digits and Grant read them back to her.

"Okay, it'll take time for me to get across the border, even at this hour," Grant said. "Be ready to go for a drive when I call. And one more thing. Tomorrow, I want Rachel and Dillon to get separated, each of you with half the goods. In case they track one of you, they won't get the other. You can both rent cars tomorrow and just go somewhere, but don't tell each other where, okay? Keryn, you can stay wherever you are, as long as you don't go home. Any questions?"

Nobody had any.

"We will await your call," Dillon said.

"Bye, kids," Grant said. "I love you—ya know that?"

The line went dead.

Keryn

They waited for more than two hours before Kathii's cell phone rang. Keryn swallowed hard and answered it. "H-hello?"

"It's Gandalf," Grant said. "Sorry, it took a while to get back into Mordor. You guys ready to go fight the Dark Lord?"

Keryn laughed nervously. "I guess so."

"I assume you've got transportation. Wherever you are, get on Highway 5 and head north. Watch to see if anyone's following you, got it?"

"Got it."

"Call me back at this number when you get north of 52." Grant hung up.

Keryn closed the phone. "Let's go."

She climbed into the passenger seat of Allen's Camry. Allen was driving, and Dillon and Rachel were in the backseat. The garage door opened and they rolled out into the night.

"We need to head north on Highway 5," Keryn said.

Allen drove out to Governor Drive and turned right. He barreled through a yellow light when they got to Genesee. Keryn kept an eye behind them and saw nothing. No headlights, no nothing.

At Regents Road, Allen made an illegal left turn through the red light.

"Allen, please, it is not wise to do that," Dillon said.

"Nobody was watching," Allen said tightly.

"I was watching," Dillon said.

"Oh, Dillon, cut him some slack." Rachel sounded scared. "Let's just get this over with."

Allen drove down the hill and took the on-ramp onto Highway 52 west. Minutes later they were on Highway 5 heading north. Keryn pressed the dial-back button on Kathii's phone.

Grant answered on the first ring. "Any pursuit?"

"I don't think so," Keryn said. "We're heading north."

"Take the Sorrento Valley exit and wait for sixty seconds at the stop sign. Then call me." Grant rang off.

Keryn passed this on to Allen. He shrugged and moved into the left lane and pressed the accelerator until they were whizzing along at ninety. Keryn was pretty sure nobody was following them. At the Sorrento Valley exit, Allen veered across four lanes and barely caught the off-ramp. They roared down a long lane and screeched to a rest at the stop sign.

Sixty seconds passed in breathless silence. Keryn called again.

Grant picked up. "Any sign of Black Riders?"

"Nothing," Keryn said. "Nobody changed speed, nobody tried to catch our exit, nobody's come down this exit in the last minute."

"Go across the railroad tracks and turn right." Grant hung up.

Keryn shook her head. This was just too crazy. "Turn left here, Allen, then cut right and go across the tracks and then right again on Sorrento Valley Road."

Allen hit the gas and followed her directions.

"This is insane," Rachel said. "He's directing us straight to the CypherQuanta building. It's too obvious."

Keryn was sweating now. This wasn't safe.

The phone rang in her hands. She stared at it stupidly for a few seconds, then flipped it open. "This is, um, Arwen."

"Get on Highway 805 going south," Grant said. "Call me when you pass the Governor Drive exit."

Keryn flipped the phone shut. Allen was slowing down for the turn to the CypherQuanta building. "Don't turn, Allen. Go straight and take the on-ramp to 805 south."

Allen gunned the engine and roared past CypherQuanta and up the long ramp onto the highway.

Keryn had her eyes glued behind them.

Nothing but blackness. They drove in silence for a few minutes.

As they flashed past Governor Drive, Allen scowled. "He's got us driving in circles."

Keryn dialed Grant. "Me again. What's next?"

"Next exit, take a right," Grant said. "Then I want you to solve a riddle. What's the only illegal place in San Diego that Dillon approves of? I want you to go there and call me." The line went dead.

"Allen, turn right at the next exit," Keryn said.

Allen smoothly veered onto Highway 52 heading west. Again. "Crazy," he muttered.

"Okay, Grant's getting nervous," Keryn said. "He gave us a riddle. There's an illegal place somewhere in San Diego that Dillon approves of. Grant wants us to go there."

Silence.

The car roared west through the night. They passed the Genesee exit, then Regents Road.

"What do I do now?" Allen said as they approached Highway 5 for the second time that night.

Keryn shrugged. "I have no idea. Dillon, any ideas? This riddle's about you."

"There is no illegal place that I would approve of." Dillon sounded deeply offended.

"Guys, I need to know!" Allen said. "Do I take this exit north or south?"

"Straight," Rachel said. "Move left one lane and go straight."

"Into La Jolla?" Keryn said. "There's nothing illegal in La Jolla."

"Just do it."

Allen lane-shifted left and punched the gas. The Camry flew up the long ascent and merged into La Jolla Parkway and on over the pass into

La Jolla. Keryn looked back and saw a pair of headlights behind them. "Guys, there's somebody on our tail."

Allen's knuckles glared bone white in the dim glow of the dashboard. "Okay, now what? I need a little guidance here."

"Straight," Rachel said. "You guys, this is way obvious."

Keryn had her eyes on the headlights behind. They were closing. "Allen ... hurry."

Allen accelerated as they began the descent. "I need some more guidance, Rachel."

"Right lane and slow down for a right turn onto Torrey Pines Road," Rachel said.

Allen moved over one lane and began braking.

Keryn was so scared she wanted to shriek. The lights behind were catching up fast.

Rachel leaned forward. "At the next intersection, turn ... left! Now! Turn left!"

Allen swung the wheel hard and cut across two lanes into the left-turn lane. And stopped at the red turn arrow.

Brakes squealed from behind. A horn blared. The sound of skidding tires split the night sky. The headlights fishtailed past them through the green light and then veered sharply right. Finally, the loud pop of metal crunching against a traffic-light pole.

Then stark silence.

"We caused an accident!" Keryn was hyperventilating. "We have to go see if anyone's hurt!"

"That is a Taurus," Dillon said. "And I believe it is gray."

The doors of the disabled car leaped open and four men sprang out.

Holding guns.

"Go left now!" Rachel screamed. "Go, go, go!"

Allen punched the gas and roared past the red left-turn arrow onto Hidden Valley Road.

Gunshots rang out.

Keryn's fingernails were digging into her palms and her heart was thumping in her chest and she could not catch her breath. Somewhere in the back of her novelist's mind, she was taking notes furiously. *This is what it's like to be shot at.*

"Straight up the hill," Rachel said. "Don't you guys get it?"

Allen drove like a madman for a full minute before Keryn finally calmed down a little. Then she got it.

"The Mount Soledad Cross!" she said. "Grant wants to meet us up there. It's isolated and he can be sure nobody else is there."

"No, that is incorrect," Dillon said. "We have not solved the riddle."

Keryn turned to look at him. "It's the only possibility," she said. "The Cross is supposedly unconstitutional—that's what the atheists say, anyway. The city keeps losing lawsuits. Sooner or later, they're going to have to tear it down."

"I hope they do," Dillon said. "It is a violation of the separation of church and state. We have not solved the riddle at all."

Allen kept driving up the twisting hillside. "Dillon, does Grant know you don't approve of the Mount Soledad Cross?"

"I have never discussed it with him," Dillon said.

"Drive," Rachel said. "It's right up here on the left ...."

Allen slowed the car to a stop. They all stared at the small road leading to the Cross. A metal gate barred the way.

"It closes at ten." Rachel pointed at the sign.

"We were supposed to call when we got here." Keryn flipped open the phone and dialed Grant.

It answered on the first ring. "Gandalf speaking."

"Arwen here. Listen, we're at the dark gate, but it's shut. How do we—"

"Turn off your headlights and take a right and go three tenths of a mile," Grant said. "When you see three towers on your right, watch for a Dark Rider on your left." He hung up.

Keryn had no idea what that meant, but she repeated it all.

Allen cut off his lights and they crept forward along La Jolla Scenic Drive. The eerie yellow glow of the low-pressure sodium lights made the whole street look like a creepy *Nightmare on Elm Street* kind of place. They passed a trio of radio towers on their right.

A parking lot opened on their left. As they rolled past it, Keryn saw a pair of parking lights flick on and off just once. She pointed. "Stop! Back up! There's our Dark Rider."

It was a black Ford Explorer sitting in the middle of a deserted church parking lot. Allen pulled into the lot and drove slowly toward the SUV. The window on the driver's side descended. A shadowy figure sat in the driver's seat.

Allen pulled closer.

Closer.

A small penlight flicked on inside the SUV. Grant's bushy white eyebrows sprang out, sharp and clear. Behind him, Julia's anxious eyes glittered in the dark.

Allen rolled down his window and braked to a stop.

Grant tossed a packet through the window and started his engine. "Go!" he shouted. His engine revved, and he shot forward past them toward the exit of the parking lot.

Allen spun the wheel in a tight circle and hit the gas. They lurched forward and out of the lot.

Keryn grabbed the packet out of Allen's lap and clutched it to her chest.

"Crazy," Allen said again.

Nobody said anything else for the fifteen minutes it took to get home.

CHAPTER TWENTY-NINE

Dillon

Monday morning after breakfast, Dillon transferred all the phone numbers from his cell phone to the new one Grant had given him. He did not feel calm today. Grant had given him a driver's license and a Visa card in the name of Jake Scanlon. Dillon did not feel like a Jake. He felt like a fake.

Keryn sat down next to him on the couch. "Have you decided where you're going?"

"I have a friend in Berkeley, and I thought—"

"Berkeley?" Keryn narrowed her eyes. "Is that the friend who's a physicist?"

"He is in graduate school in physics. I would not call him a physicist yet."

"You were talking to him last week though, right?" Keryn was studying her hands.

"Yes, I talk to him every week."

"Listen, call me paranoid, but ... just how well do you know him?"

Dillon did not like this question. "I trust Robert completely. I have known him since he was born. His family lived next door to us in Chicago."

"Okay, I know you trust him, but I don't. Pretend he's somebody with a secret past. Pretend he's a Mafia guy. Now think. Did you ... did you tell him anything at all about the bio-computer?"

Dillon tried to recall his conversations with Robert. "I told him I was working on a special project. And ..." Dillon stood up and began pacing. He had just remembered something.

"Dillon, what's wrong?"

Dillon sighed. "Robert may have heard something. I was at the bio-lab, talking to him on my cell phone. I was about to say good-bye when Clifton came out talking loudly about Shor's algorithm."

"Remind me, what is Shor's algorithm?"

Dillon stared out the window. "It is the algorithm we use on the bio-computer to factor large numbers."

"Is there anything else Shor's algorithm is used for?"

"No." Dillon felt cold.

"Would Robert know what it is?"

"Maybe." Dillon shook his head. "Yes. He would know what Shor's algorithm is."

Keryn stood up and put a hand on his arm. "I don't think you should be going to see Robert anytime soon."

Dillon's heart skipped a beat. "I have to. He is visiting his fiancée's family in Mission Viejo this week, and I promised to drive up and meet them this weekend."

"This weekend?" Keryn's voice rose half an octave. "Dillon, you can't possibly meet these people this weekend. We won't be testing the bio-computer until Thursday, and there's no way we can hold a public demonstration of it on Friday. Not till next week at the earliest. You can't come out of hiding before then."

"I told you I have to go. I gave my word." Dillon felt sick. Robert was not the one who had leaked word of the bio-computer. He could not be.

"Dillon, if you go, you'll be putting yourself at risk. And Rachel and me. You shouldn't be out in public any more than you need to."

Dillon sat down and put his head in his hands. He had not thought of that. He was not used to this life of hiding, of prevarication.

Keryn sat beside him. "I really, really don't want you to go. Robert and his fiancée will probably be busy anyway, planning the wedding."

"That is why I need to go," Dillon said. "I am the best man."

Keryn

An hour later Keryn was driving north on Highway 5, trying to keep Dillon in her sights. Dillon had agreed to let Keryn follow him up in Kathii's car and meet Robert. If she didn't like him, Dillon would then turn around and go back to San Diego. Keryn was a good judge of character. If Robert was shady, she felt confident she would know it. Unfortunately, meeting with him meant that both she and Dillon had to come out of hiding, but Dillon had to go somewhere anyway. Grant wanted Dillon's software separated as far as possible from Rachel's bio-computer. Rachel had called her aunt, who came and picked her up.

Up ahead, Dillon's rented Dodge Caravan signaled to take the Alicia Parkway exit.

Keryn was a couple of hundred yards behind. She watched closely to see if anybody else made the same move.

Three cars took the same exit.

Keryn followed them. Her heart was hammering now. The novelist part of her brain was sitting back taking detailed notes. This was what it felt like to be in an international intrigue. She had always thought it would be *exciting*. It wasn't exciting. Part of her wanted to heave and part of her wanted to die and part of her wanted to shriek. If this were a novel, instead of real life, she'd be tempted to reach right out of the computer and wrap the mouse cord around the author's neck.

Dillon's car came to a complete halt at the end of the off-ramp. The car behind almost hit him. Either that driver was expecting a California rolling stop through the red light or he was thinking about carjacking Dillon.

If anyone tried that, Keryn would just drive up alongside and Dillon would jump in the car and ... she'd find out what a real-life car chase was like. She gripped the steering wheel so hard her fingers ached.

Dillon turned right and drove sedately down Alicia Parkway.

Keryn had a Yahoo map on the seat beside her showing exactly where they were going. There was a Denny's restaurant just off the highway. Dillon had agreed to meet Robert there and introduce him to Keryn. From there, Keryn would play it by ear.

Right now she wanted to kidnap Dillon and just take him home. Forget meeting Robert's future in-laws. Forget the stupid biocomputer. They had phony ID. Tomorrow they could be in South America or New Zealand or ... wherever. They could start a new life in a galaxy far, far away, find jobs, settle down together in a little cottage by the sea, where she could write under a pseudonym and Dillon could find some sort of techie job.

Dillon's car turned left onto Charlinda Drive and then immediately left into a shopping center. Nobody followed him.

Keryn drove on to the next light, made a U-turn, came back.

Nothing looked out of the ordinary. Dillon had parked in the main parking lot of the shopping center, not in the Denny's lot. He hadn't got out of his car yet.

Keryn parked in the Del Taco lot across from Denny's and dialed Dillon's cell phone. "I'm here. Go on in and find him. I'll watch your back."

Dillon got out of his car and locked it. He made a point of walking all the way around the minivan, looking at all four tires. A rental car that had probably been gassed and oiled and pressurized that morning.

Dillon completed his inspection and went into the Denny's.

Keryn sat watching.

A couple came out of the restaurant, each holding the hand of a small blond-haired girl.

Keryn felt an ache in her throat.

Her cell phone rang.

Keryn answered it. "Yes?"

"I have found Robert. We are in a booth in the corner."

"I'm on my way." Keryn closed the phone and hopped out. She locked the car and went into the Denny's.

A greeter assaulted her with a huge plastic smile and menu. "Table for one?"

"I'm meeting someone." Keryn pointed toward the back corner. "Those two back there." She took her time walking to the table.

Dillon was sitting with his back to the wall, talking to a tall man with sandy hair.

Keryn felt her heart racing. There had to be something she could find wrong with Robert. She did not want Dillon hanging around with him. A guy from Chicago. A guy with ties to the physics community. Was he the leak?

Dillon said something to Robert when Keryn arrived. Robert turned around and saw Keryn and stood up.

Keryn looked him in the eye. "Hi, I'm Keryn. You must be Robert."

"Glad to meet you," he said with a puppy-dog grin that was either really, really sincere or a great act. His eyes fixed on her face. "Dillon's a lucky guy."

Keryn felt her cheeks heating up. She wasn't sure what Dillon had told Robert about her, but she doubted that he had said they were an item. She stuck out her hand. "Glad to meet you."

Robert shook it and then they sat down. Dillon scooted over in the booth so Keryn had plenty of room.

Keryn studied Robert carefully, looking for something, anything wrong with him. "So ... you're getting married in August?"

Robert grinned and his eyes lit up with that special glitter that was impossible to fake. "That's right, and this is my first trip to Mission Viejo. My fiancée's got a big family and she's been wanting me to meet them all. Her little sister will be maid of honor, and she really wants to meet Dillon."

"Do you have a picture of your fiancée?"

Robert pulled out his wallet and folded out his photos. "This one. And this one."

Keryn looked at the two pictures. Robert's fiancée had a great mass of curly blond hair and startling blue eyes. And a smile that could light up the whole state of Illinois. "She's a cutie," Keryn said. "What's her name?"

"Sarah."

Keryn nodded. A guy who was in love had a special way of saying his girl's name. Robert was in love. In love bad. He was a nerdy-looking guy with a goofy grin, and Keryn would bet he was a terrible liar. Whatever else Robert was, he wasn't an enemy. She pushed the photos back to him. "Congratulations."

Robert grinned back at her. "Listen, we'd love to put you on our guest list. We just ... well, Dillon didn't tell me about you." He shot Dillon an accusing look.

Dillon didn't say anything and Keryn didn't dare look at him. She pursed her lips and looked at Robert. "I don't think Dillon can come to your family get-together this weekend."

Robert's eyes narrowed. "I would think Dillon can decide that. Listen, if you're ... worried, Sarah's sister already has a boyfriend."

"That's not the problem," Keryn said. "I can't tell you much, but Dillon's life may be in danger. Mine too, for that matter. We absolutely have to keep him in hiding for the next few days. That's the only reason I let him meet you here. But he can't be meeting a lot of people until we get something resolved, and that's probably not going to happen before the weekend."

Robert's face looked as if she'd just jabbed him with an ice pick. "What's going on? Shouldn't you call the police?"

"We're planning to," Keryn said, "but if we do it too soon, it'll be crying wolf and they won't believe us. We're waiting for the last little bit of evidence to come in. That will be Friday at the earliest, but ... more likely next Monday. You can see what kind of a bind that puts us in."

Robert looked puzzled. "I don't understand."

Which was good. The only way he could understand would be if he knew more than he should.

Dillon leaned forward. "This will all be over within a week, and then we can explain. I promise I will be there for your wedding. Nothing will keep me from that."

Robert sighed. "I'll tell the family you're sick."

"Please do not prevaricate," Dillon said.

Robert did not look happy. "You don't know Sarah's mother. She likes to be in control of things." He pulled out his backpack and rummaged around inside. Finally, he pulled out a wedding invitation. "Keryn, I'd love for you to come to the wedding. It would really make the day special. First Saturday in August. Can you make it?"

"Well ... I can try. I've got a book due in the middle of the month and I'm way behind." Keryn studied the invitation. The photo showed Robert in a suit and Sarah looking radiant. Keryn felt a tear ball up in her eye, and she brushed it away with her finger. "You two look like you were made for each other."

Robert grinned.

"There's one more thing," Keryn said. "Right now Dillon and I need to keep out of sight as much as possible. We have fake IDs, credit cards in a phony name, the works. Dillon needs a place to stay until Thursday, and I'm thinking it might be safer if you can find him a hotel room without him needing to use his bogus stuff. I'm not sure how good that ID is or how long it'll last. Can you put him in a hotel room somewhere?"

"Sure, sure!" Robert's face showed raw concern. Just that—concern. "I'll get another room in my hotel. He can stay there as long as he wants." He looked at Dillon. "You must be in a lot of trouble, buddy. Is there anything you can tell me? Anything I can do to help?"

Keryn shook her head. "Have you got some phone numbers I can reach you at?"

Robert pulled out a business card and handed it to her. "That's got my cell phone number on it. I don't remember the hotel number, but you can call Dillon when you get back to San Diego and he can give it to you."

She studied the card for a moment. The name on the card was not Robert, it was Bob. Come to think of it, he looked like a Bob, not a Robert. His last name looked utterly unpronounceable. "How do you say your last name?"

Robert grinned. "Sorry, it's kind of tricky, isn't it? Put the accent on the first and third syllables. Kaganovski. My friends call me Kaggo."

"I'd better be getting back home." Keryn stood up. "Take care of Dillon, Kaggo. And congratulations on Sarah. She's a lucky girl."

Keryn spent the long drive back to Kathii's house wondering if she was ever going to get lucky.

CHAPTER THIRTY

Rachel

"Davey's home from UCLA for the summer, so you can sleep in Rivka's old room." Aunt Esther led the way back to a small bedroom decorated in pastel pink colors.

Rachel dropped her Target bag on the floor. "Thanks for coming to get me, Auntie. Where's Davey?"

Aunt Esther shrugged. "I think he went surfing at La Jolla Shores today. Don't you have any more clothes than what's in that little bag?"

Rachel shook her head. "I ... I'm in trouble, Auntie. I didn't want to talk about it on the phone, but I can't go back to my apartment. We think people are watching it and ..." Rachel felt so exhausted and frightened she didn't know what to say. She had been trying to be strong for the last two weeks and now she was all alone and she just wanted this nightmare to be over. If she thought it would help, she'd throw the bio-computer away. But that would just make it worse. She desperately wanted a strong pair of arms to lean on. And the only strong arms she knew of had gone up to Mission Viejo. She had never felt so alone.

All at once, she had to talk to Dillon. Had to. She was going to die if she couldn't talk to him. She pulled out her phone and called.

It went to voicemail right away.

Rachel began shaking. She couldn't help it. Grant was wrong. They should have stayed together. If the crooks were going to kill her, she'd rather be with Dillon. She just couldn't do this alone.

Aunt Esther put her arms around Rachel. "Come sit down. I'll make some tea and you can tell me about it."

Rachel spent the next half hour in the kitchen explaining the whole story over a pot of tea.

Aunt Esther listened with wide eyes. She patted Rachel's hand when she told about the carjacking.

Finally, Rachel finished. She felt a little better after talking about it. But only a little.

"You like this boy, Dillon?"

Rachel smiled. She hadn't said so, but Auntie was good at picking up certain things.

"He's not Jewish." Aunt Esther made it sound like a fatal disease.

"Auntie, I'm not Jewish either. Not according to the rabbis. My mother isn't Jewish."

"I know, I know, but Jewishness is more a state of mind. You're Jewish." Aunt Esther sighed deeply. "You're welcome to come to Beth Simcha anytime you want."

It was a standing offer, but Rachel had never seriously considered it. Auntie went to some weird kind of a synagogue. Jews for Jesus or something. Daddy said they were a crock. Mother said it sounded cultish.

"You don't have to," Aunt Esther said. "I don't mean to pressure you. I just want to help."

Rachel smiled. "I'll think about it, okay? I've been ... thinking about a lot of things lately. Oh! Guess what? I decided I don't hate Jesus anymore."

"Really? That's wonderful!" Joy filled Aunt Esther's face. "People have done such horrible things to us in his name, but he's not like that at all. Yeshua was one of us."

Rachel remembered that Rivka had always been adamant that the real name of Jesus was Yeshua. Whatever. It was hard to win a debate with Rivka. Rachel usually didn't care, anyway, so she had always just agreed and changed the subject. Rachel sipped the last of her tea. "I miss Rivka so much."

Aunt Esther's eyes filled with tears. "I miss her too. She was ... doing what she loved best."

"It's been how long now? Four years?"

Aunt Esther nodded. "I haven't had the heart to change anything in her room."

Rachel cleared the cups and the teakettle from the table and put them in the sink. Aunt Esther didn't have a dishwasher, so Rachel washed them and left them to dry in the drainer. When she finished, she saw that Aunt Esther hadn't moved. Two tracks of tears gleamed on her face.

Rachel hugged her tight. "Maybe ... maybe you'll see her again, Auntie."

Aunt Esther looked up at her. "Do you believe that or are you just saying it?"

Rachel had no idea. She was so confused and mixed up right now, she didn't know what she believed and what was just California dreaming. "You believe it, Auntie, and that's enough."

"I wish you believed it too." Aunt Esther wiped her eyes.

Rachel didn't want to talk about that. Not now. Maybe not ever. She needed time to sort things out. "Could I use your washing machine? I'm almost out of clean clothes."

Aunt Esther led her back to Rivka's bedroom and opened a door in the far wall. It led into the garage. "The washer and dryer are right back here." She turned to look at Rachel and hesitated for a long time. "You're in trouble and ... Rivka would want to help you. Look and see if there's anything you can wear." Aunt Esther opened the closet. "And there's some underthings in the dresser over there."

Rachel yawned mightily. "Could I ... would it be rude if I took a nap for a while? I've had a really hard couple of weeks and I'm awfully tired."

"You go right ahead, honey."

Rachel stretched out on the bed. Aunt Esther gently closed the door.

Rachel

When Rachel woke up, she felt groggy and ratty. She had dreamed that Dillon was getting married to Keryn and she was one of the bridesmaids, and when the preacher gave that blah-blah about speaking now or forever holding your peace, Rachel had started screaming, and Jesus came down out of one of those stained-glass pictures and dragged her out of the church by the hair and stole her bio-computer and gave it to Satan.

Rachel got up and rummaged around in the dresser and closet for some of Rivka's clothes. After a long hot shower, she felt better. Rachel brushed her thick, silky hair and came out feeling almost alive. She went out to the kitchen and found Aunt Esther sitting there with a box full of things. A backpack. A wallet. Some cutoffs and T-shirts.

"What's this, Auntie?"

Aunt Esther's lip quivered. "It's all the things they sent back from Israel after Rivka ... passed. This is her backpack and some of her clothes. I've never been able to go through it all."

Rachel opened Rivka's wallet. There were pictures of Aunt Esther and Uncle David and their son, Davey. There was another picture of Rivka's biological father—Uncle Leonard—Daddy's brother. Rachel knew vaguely that Auntie had divorced him a long time ago. She didn't know the details, and she didn't want to know. Uncle Leonard had remarried several years ago, to a young bimbo who wore gaudy makeup and had been through enough surgery to start a plastics factory. There was no picture of her in Rivka's wallet.

Rachel leafed through and found an expired Visa card, a worn Blockbuster card, and ... a driver's license. Rivka was three years older than Rachel, with straight black hair, gorgeous brown eyes, and a dusky complexion. Unlike Rachel, she actually looked Jewish. The only thing they had in common was a perky nose that was decidedly not Jewish. Nobody would ever mistake either of them for Barbra Streisand.

Rachel reached in her pocket and pulled out the fake driver's license Grant had gotten for her in Mexico. It had her picture but a bogus name—Sally Swigert.

"What's that you've got, dear?" Aunt Esther stood up to look.

Rachel showed her. "My boss made it in case I needed some ID."

A VW bug roared up outside. Rachel saw a surfboard roped to the top.

"Oh my, Davey's already home." Aunt Esther scooped up all of Rivka's belongings and stuffed them back into the box. "Dear, could you put this back in Rivka's room? We'll sort through it tonight or tomorrow and throw away some of these old things. It's ... time to put the past behind us."

Rachel carried the box back to her room and plunked it on Rivka's desk. She felt oddly glad that she'd been forced to come visit Aunt Esther. Maybe, between the two of them, they could sort out the shredded pieces of their lives and make some sense of it all.

~

Keryn

On Tuesday morning Keryn called Dillon on her cell phone and made sure he was safe. He still sounded unhappy about not getting to meet Robert's fiancée. Keryn didn't care. The most important thing was to survive for the next few days.

On Thursday Rachel and Dillon would get access to an NMR machine over at Mesa College and they could finish testing and then try to run Shor's algorithm. Nobody knew how long that would take. A day or so if all went perfectly. Then Grant would arrange a press conference and the world would see the proof.

After that ... Keryn couldn't guess what would happen. The NSA would probably swoop in and grab the bio-computer. But they could not take it black. A black project, by definition, was one the world didn't know about. If the NSA used it to spy on people, well, people would know about it. There was a cure for that—the machines made by CypherQuanta. The world would be a better place and Keryn's stock would make her rich enough to quit working and write full time.

All she had to do was survive until Thursday.

Keryn decided to pass the time working on her book. She was so far behind now that there was no hope of making her deadline. She'd have to call her agent and get her to wangle an extension from her editor. Agents were good at being the bad cop.

Kathii got Keryn set up on a computer in the family room and then left to go food shopping. Keryn downloaded her files from her .Mac account on the Web and began typing. Jason and Jordan were playing a noisy game of checkers out in the living room, but within minutes, Keryn was in a universe of her own.

She kept coming back to the problem of how to kill Josh and make it look like an accident. Modern chemistry was too good. Even the tiniest traces of poisons could be detected by forensic investigators. She had been planning to use botulism, but just how believable was that?

Or did it matter? Every day things happened that were totally absurd. Ridiculous. Unbelievable. Take 9/11. Using jets as bombs. Clancy had been ridiculed for writing a scenario just like that in *Debt of Honor*. The difference between the fiction and the reality was that Clancy's idea was so much more plausible than bin Laden's.

Lots of things that happened in real life were absurdly improbable. People often did illogical things for no reason at all. Real life didn't have to make sense. But you couldn't get away with any of that in fiction. Fiction had to be plausible and logical, and it had to make sense.

"Aunt Keryn?"

Keryn turned and saw Jason standing behind her. "What is it, sweetie?"

"There's a man here who wants to innerview you."

Keryn's heart clawed its way up into her throat. "Interview me? Who would know I'm here?"

"He's at the door right now." Jason tugged on her hand. "Jordan's showing him a magic trick."

Keryn stood up. Jordan shouldn't be talking to some strange man at the door. She hurried out to the living room.

A man in a dark suit stood outside smiling at Jordan's attempts to yank a string through his neck. When he saw Keryn, he held up a badge. "I'm Special Agent Rod Greene with the FBI. I believe you're the sister-in-law of Allen Russell?"

"What's this about?" Keryn said. "How did you know I was here?" She snapped her fingers at Jordan. "Come inside right now."

"Ma'am, is there a problem?" Greene said. "Mr. Russell is being considered for a higher security clearance over at SAIC, and he listed you as one of his references. We called your home on Friday and yesterday but got no answer, so we went by your house. Your neighbor happened to be out watering his lawn."

"Since when does he water anything?" Keryn narrowed her eyes. "And his lawn is nothing but weeds."

Greene shrugged. "He told us to let you know Smiley and Zephyr are doing great together. And he guessed you were at your sister's house. So we came over here."

"We?" Keryn peered past him. "Who's 'we?'"

"My partner is Hector Gonzales. He's over at the neighbors'. They're also listed as references and—"

A Hispanic man in a suit came down the walk, shaking his head. "The Websters aren't home. Did you find Miss Wills?"

Greene nodded. "She's here." He held up a clipboard with an apologetic smile. "Is this a good time to answer just a few questions about Mr. Russell?"

Keryn had gone through this once before when Allen first went to work at SAIC. That was years ago, and the agents had spent almost an hour asking all sorts of absurd questions about Allen. "Mind if I look at your badges and call your main office?"

"Please do," Greene said. He held up his badge and picture ID for her inspection.

Keryn looked at them. She had no idea what a legitimate FBI badge should look like. This looked exactly like she imagined it should. The picture on the ID matched Greene's face.

"Here's my card, ma'am." Greene handed her a business card. "Hector, just give Miss Wills a look at your badge and your ID and give her one of your cards. She'd like to check us out."

Gonzales smiled as he showed his credentials. "Take your time, ma'am. This is our last visit before lunchtime, and our questions won't take long."

Keryn took both cards and stepped back into the house. She shut the door and twisted the dead bolt.

Jason and Jordan were staring at her with enormous eyes. "Were those real FBI men?"

"That's what I'm going to find out." Keryn went back to the family room and grabbed the phone and dialed the number on the card.

"Federal Bureau of Investigation, Security Clearance Department." It was a young female voice.

"Yes, I have two men at my door, Rod Greene and Hector Gonzales." Keryn read off their badge numbers from the cards. "Are those men in your division?"

"Yes, they're doing security clearance interviews this morning on Allen Russell. Are you Mrs. Webster or Ms. Wills?"

"Keryn Wills. Thanks, that's all I needed to know." Keryn hung up and sighed with relief. Okay, fine, so she was paranoid. But even paranoids had enemies. She had a right to—

The back patio door gritted open behind her.

Keryn spun around.

The two agents sprang inside, lunging for her.

Keryn screamed.

Agent Greene wrapped his arms around her, pinning her arms to her sides. Gonzales yanked a hood over her head.

"Get away!" Keryn stomped down hard, trying for Greene's instep.

He swore at her and lifted her off the floor.

She kicked out in the air with both feet.

Hands grabbed her ankles, lashing them together with some kind of twine.

Raw terror washed through Keryn. If they weren't real FBI agents, then she was in extreme trouble.

And if they were real FBI agents, she was in even bigger trouble.

A sickly sweet odor assaulted her nostrils.

Keryn tried not to breathe, but she knew that tactic would only last about fifteen seconds. She relaxed her body, letting her limbs go limp. She took a small, shallow breath and held it as long as possible.

Her mind began slipping, sliding away.

Relax. Play dead.

All the world went black.

~

Keryn

When Keryn came to, she felt sick and dizzy. Several slow and lazy minutes passed while she tried to get her bearings. Why was it so dark? What was that dull roar?

Slowly the world of reality pressed in around her. She could feel that her legs were tied. The men. The horrible FBI men. Or were they? Her hands were tied in front of her with rough twine.

Keryn brought both hands up to her face and found that the awful hood was gone. She raised her hands and thumped against something hollow and metallic. As the muzziness in her brain cleared, she finally realized that she was in the trunk of a car. She felt around and identified the locking mechanism. After playing with it for a minute, she realized that she was not going to unlock it.

She rolled the other way and by twisting around awkwardly, she pressed her ear up against the hard inner wall of the trunk.

Voices.

By listening hard, she could make out the voices of three men. Greene. Gonzales.

And ... Clifton Potter?

Keryn felt like somebody had shoved an icicle through her heart. Clifton! She tried desperately to make out his words, but that was impossible.

She rolled back away from the seat back and began gnawing desperately at the twine binding her wrists. Slowly, slowly, it began to come undone. Obviously, they hadn't expected her to come to so soon or they would have tied her better. At last she got the knot loose enough to slip her hands free.

Keryn took a deep breath to calm herself. She had read a news article not long ago about a kidnapping victim locked in a trunk who worked loose the taillight and stuck her hand out, eventually attracting the attention of somebody. Keryn felt around with her hands, but she couldn't see anything. She pawed for the light switch in the trunk. There!

She flicked it.

Nothing happened.

Keryn wanted to scream. Then she remembered she had put her cell phone in her pocket. Had the men found it? It had the numbers for Dillon and Rachel. Keryn held her breath and reached into her pocket. Her fingers wrapped around ... a small metallic phone.

"Thank God." Keryn brought it up to her face and flipped it open.

Blessed light nearly blinded her.

She selected the phone list and toggled down to Dillon's number. But Dillon was an hour away in Mission Viejo. Keryn sighed deeply and selected Rachel's number. Rachel was here in town. She could ... do something. Call the cops. Get the phone company to triangulate on her signal. Whatever.

Keryn pressed the Send button.

CHAPTER THIRTY-ONE

Rachel

Rachel was watering Aunt Esther's roses in the backyard when her cell phone chirped. She yanked it out and saw that Keryn was calling.

"Hi, Keryn, what's up?"

Keryn's voice came in a whisper. "Rachel! Help me! I've been kidnapped."

Rachel dropped the hose and ran into the house. "What! Say that again!"

"I've been kidnapped. I'm in the trunk of a car. We're driving somewhere."

Rachel's heart was pounding so hard, she was afraid her ribs might crack. "I'll call the cops! Do you have any idea where you are? What kind of car?"

"Wait!" Keryn's voice hissed across the line. "The men might be FBI agents."

"What do you mean, they *might* be?" Rachel fell onto the couch and put her hand on her heart, willing it to slow down.

Aunt Esther came in from the backyard. "Rachel, the hose is going full blast on the—" She gave a little shriek when she saw Rachel lying on the couch. "Oh my! Are you all right?"

"I'm freaking out! They kidnapped one of my friends. Wait, Keryn, say that all again. My aunt came in and I couldn't hear you." She motioned to Aunt Esther to come close so she could listen.

"Two men came to Kathii's house," Keryn whispered. "They said their names were Rod Greene and Hector Gonzales." She spent five minutes explaining what had happened.

"And you think they might be real FBI?" Rachel said.

"I don't know," Keryn said. "But listen! They've got Clifton in the car with them. I heard his voice up there. I can't hear what they're saying, but it's normal conversation. They're not interrogating him or anything."

Rachel wanted to puke. Clifton Potter. The *creep*. She had never liked him. This explained a lot.

Aunt Esther's face had gone white. "I'll call the police."

Rachel grabbed her hand. "Don't you dare! If the FBI are really in on this, then the cops are too, and they'll trace the call back to this address."

"Rachel, can you call Dillon?" Keryn's voice quivered with fear.

"Hang on a second." Rachel studied the buttons on the phone. Dillon had shown her the other night how to do a three-way on these gizmos. She pressed a small button labeled Conference and was rewarded with a dial tone and her phone list. Rachel toggled down to Dillon's number and pressed Send.

Three rings and then ...

"Hello, Rachel." Dillon's voice came through the line, strong and true.

"Dillon, they've got Keryn. Hold on and I'll try to patch her back in." Rachel held her breath and pressed Conference again. "Keryn, are you there?"

"I'm here." Keryn said. "Did you track down Dillon?"

"Keryn, what is happening?" Dillon's voice roared through the earpiece.

"I've been ... kidnapped," Keryn said. "I'm in the trunk of a car. There are two FBI men and *Clifton* up in the front."

"Hang on, Keryn," Dillon said. "I will be there as quickly as I can."

"Dillon, no!" Rachel shouted. "Stay where you are! There's nothing you can do down here."

Rachel heard the sound of feet running.

Dillon

Dillon raced out the door and down the hall. When he reached Robert's door, he pounded on it many times. "Robert! Open up!"

Several doors opened up and down the corridor.

Dillon kept pounding. "Robert!"

The door swung suddenly inward. Robert looked highly annoyed. "I'm trying to talk with Sarah. What's—"

Dillon pushed his way in. "I need my car keys."

Robert shook his head. "Keryn made me promise to keep them so you wouldn't go anywhere until—"

Dillon slammed the door shut. "Keryn has been kidnapped. Now give me the car keys."

"Kidnapped?" Robert stared at him. He ran to the phone and scooped it up. "Sarah, I'll call you later." He threw the phone on the cradle and went to the small refrigerator by the minibar, and pulled Dillon's car keys out of the freezer. "I'm going with you."

"Give them to me!" Dillon shouted.

"I'll drive," Robert said harshly. "You're in no state. Now move!"

Dillon jerked open the door and ran.

Robert's footsteps thudded behind him.

Two minutes later they were southbound on Highway 5. Robert slipped the minivan over into the left lane and pegged the speedometer needle to the far right. It was extremely unsafe.

Dillon did not care at all.

He cradled the phone in his hands. He had closed it when he ran to get Robert and had lost the connection. He tried to dial Keryn, but her line was busy. Likewise Rachel. He closed the phone and waited, filling Robert in on what little he knew.

After a couple of minutes, the phone rang.

Dillon flipped it open. "Keryn?"

"Dillon, I'm so scared." Keryn's voice rasped in the earpiece. "Dillon, I think ... I think it really is the FBI who took me. Don't call the cops, please. If the cops are in on this, it won't do any good to call them and they'll just track you and Rachel down. If the cops aren't in on it, the FBI will just lie to them and use them to find you."

Rachel's voice cut in. "Keryn, do you know what direction you're going?"

"No. They chloroformed me or something and ... I woke up in the trunk. I can't see a thing and ... I'm scared. Guys, listen. Get out of Dodge. Both of you. Call Grant and get as far away from here as you can. Don't try to save me. There's nothing you can do. I'm sure they've got guns, and they're probably hoping to use me to get to you. If I break the connection, don't call back and don't answer any calls from me. They'll try to trace back to you somehow."

Dillon felt dizzy and sick in his belly. He leaned forward and moaned softly.

Robert swerved into the next lane and passed a Porsche that was going a mere ninety.

"Hang on, Keryn," Dillon said.

"Be careful!" Rachel's voice sounded full of tears.

"Dillon?" Keryn's voice sounded tiny.

"Yes?" Dillon felt a buzzing in his head, and a great warmth filled his chest at the sound of her voice. "Yes, Keryn?"

"I ... if I don't see you again, I just wanted to say that ... I love you."

Dillon felt something huge rise up in his heart. He wanted to say something. Wanted to tell her that ... that she was a most excellent friend. That he admired her. That ...

"Oh my!" Keryn's voice squeaked with fright.

"Keryn, what is it?" Dillon saw a sign flash by that said *Entering Oceanside*.

"I ... we're slowing down." Keryn sounded out of breath. "We're bumping over some kind of rough road."

Dillon felt his heart crashing against his chest. "Keryn, tell them anything that will keep you alive."

"Jesus, help me!" Keryn said. "The car just stopped. I hear voices. They're getting out. Oh, Jesus, please, please, please!"

Dillon could not breathe. He simply could not breathe. Black spots danced in front of his eyes.

"I hear a key in the lock!" Keryn said. "Jesus, Jesus, Jesus!"

A thud.

A scream.

A gunshot.

Silence.

PART 4: THE GRAND ILLUSION

As I have said, there is no practical prospect of factorizing 250-digit numbers by classical means. But a quantum factorization engine running Shor's algorithm could do it using only a few thousand arithmetic operations, which might well take only a matter of minutes. So anyone with access to such a machine would easily be able to read any intercepted message that had been encrypted using the RSA cryptosystem.

David Deutsch
The Fabric of Reality, p. 216

CHAPTER THIRTY-TWO

Dillon

Dillon felt like his brain had exploded. He leaned forward and retched.

The minivan swerved violently. "Dillon!" Robert shouted. "That sounded like a gunshot!"

A scream shivered through the earpiece. "Keryn!" Rachel shouted. "Keryn, are you there?"

Nothing.

Hot tears welled up in Dillon's eyes. He closed his eyes tight and moaned.

"What's happening?" Robert shouted.

Dillon pressed the earpiece to his ear. Rachel was wailing, but there was something else.

Men's voices.

"Is she dead? Shoot her again to make sure." Clifton Potter's voice.

Another gunshot.

"Dillon, hang up!" Rachel said. "They'll trace back to us."

Dillon slapped the phone shut. He wanted to die. Right now, to die and ... go where Keryn was.

Robert braked gently to a more normal speed. "Dillon, what's going on?"

Dillon's voice cracked. "She ... they ... shot her." He fell back in the seat and wept. Evil men had killed Keryn. Sweet, innocent Keryn. A dull hollow pain welled up in Dillon's chest.

Robert swerved into the right lane and took the next exit. Dillon felt the minivan slow to a stop. Heard the engine cut off. Footsteps outside. The door yanked open.

Robert's strong arms. "Come on, Dillon. You need some air."

Dillon did not want air. He wanted to die. Life without Keryn was like ... life without air. He could not imagine living without her calm, gracious presence. Her soothing pastel colors. Her subtle perfume.

Robert unlatched Dillon's seatbelt. "Dillon, I'm so sorry."

The phone rang in Dillon's lifeless hands. He had no strength to open it.

It rang again.

Robert grabbed the phone. "The caller ID says it's from someone named Rachel. Should I answer it?"

"Yes." Dillon squeezed out a whisper. His ears seemed to be filled with a roaring sound.

Robert opened the phone. "Hello?"

Dillon vaguely heard Robert talking to Rachel. Explaining who he was, that he was a friend of Dillon, that they were just south of Oceanside.

"Hold on one second, Rachel," Robert said. The phone pressed up against Dillon's ear. "Dillon, Rachel wants you to tell her I'm not the bogeyman."

Dillon took a shallow breath. "Rachel, Robert is my best friend. He was driving me when ..." He could not say it.

"Dillon, get hold of yourself!" Rachel said. "I'm scared out of my wits and my aunt Esther is freaking out. I need you! I'm going to call Grant and tell him what happened. He'll know what to do. Are you there? Answer me, Dillon, I need you!"

"I ... I am here." Dillon felt like his body weighed a thousand pounds. "Tell me how to find you."

Rachel gave him directions to her aunt's house in Clairemont, then rang off.

Dillon closed his eyes. "Robert, we need to go to Rachel."

The door slammed. A few seconds later, Robert hopped into the driver's side. "Just tell me where, buddy."

"South on five," Dillon said.

The engine roared. "We're on the way. You just ... pray for her soul. I'll drive."

Dillon did not think it was logical to pray for someone's soul. He was not convinced there was such a thing as a soul. He leaned back and let his mind go blank.

The miles hummed by. Somewhere near the 805 fork, Dillon wiped his tears away and opened his eyes.

Robert put a big strong hand on his shoulder. "She was so right for you."

Dillon did not know what to say. He had been so blind. Robert was right. Keryn was perfect for him. He had not realized it until now, but she was perfect for him.

"The minute I saw her, I thought what a lucky guy you were," Robert said. "I could see how much she loved you."

Dillon felt numb. "Do you ... think she meant what she said?"

Robert turned to look at him. "What do you mean? What did she say?"

"Just before ... the end, she told me that she ... if she did not see me again, she wanted to say that ... she loved me. Do you think she meant that?"

"Well ... of course. I mean, you two were together, weren't you?"

"We were what?" Dillon tried to look at Robert, but all the world was a smear.

"Wasn't she your girlfriend? I just assumed ..."

"She was a good friend. I liked talking with her very much."

"And whenever you were with her, you felt like she was the only woman in the world? That you could tell her anything?"

"Yes."

"And whenever she wasn't there, you were thinking about her and wishing she would call?"

"I ... yes." Dillon wiped the tears out of his eyes. "Is ... is that what love is?"

A light pickup cut in front of them. Robert braked sharply. "Dillon, you're telling me you were in love with a gorgeous, sexy, intelligent woman and you didn't know it?"

It hit Dillon like a punch in the face. He had not known. Had not imagined. He buried his face in his hands and wept. He had not merely lost a good friend.

He had lost the love of his life.

Rachel

"Auntie, calm down, please. It's going to be all right." Rachel fumbled with the phone, finally toggled down to Grant's number. Tears stood so thick in her eyes, she could hardly see. She brushed them away madly and pressed the Send button.

On the third ring, it picked up. "Hello, Rachel," Grant said. "Everything okay?"

Rachel took a deep, deep breath and let it out slow. "N-no."

Grant swore. "I hope Dillon isn't planning anything stupid. Keryn told his friend he can't go to that thing this weekend, right?"

Rachel felt her whole insides caving in. "Uncle Grant?" Tears started rolling again. Until now, she'd been able to pretend it wasn't real. But she felt that as soon as she formed the words, it would be true. "You better sit down. Something ... awful has happened."

A muffled grunt. "Okay, I'm sitting. Now what could be so wrong? Everybody's still in one piece, right?"

Rachel sucked in her breath and started wailing.

"Rachel! What's happened? Are you hurt?"

"I'm f-fine, but ... they got K-Keryn."

"Got her? What do you mean, *got* her?"

"They kidnapped her. And ... killed her." Rachel couldn't say any more, she was crying so hard. It was true now. She had wanted so bad for it to be a lie, but it was true.

Uncle Grant sounded like he was having a seizure.

Rachel was almost hyperventilating. "Some m-men with FBI badges came and kidnapped Keryn and took her somewhere. She ... called me from the trunk of the car. Then they stopped and opened the trunk and ... shot her. And ... Clifton was there! He told them to shoot her again to make sure she was dead."

Grant's voice was husky with emotion when he finally spoke. "Rachel, this is horrible. Keryn was ... I just can't believe it." A long silence. "And ... I'm sorry I ever got you into this mess. If anything happens to you, I'll die."

"What are we going to do, Uncle Grant?"

A long silence. When he finally spoke, Grant sounded like he was going to be sick. "I think we better get out of town. All of us. Does Dillon know yet?"

"He was on the line too," Rachel said. "He heard it all."

"Tell him to get his butt back to San Diego," Grant said.

"Where are you?" Rachel said.

"Downtown in a hotel. Julia's out shopping right now. I'll track her down and we'll scoot over to the airport. I'll buy us some tickets. Meet me there as quick as you can."

"Where are we going?" Rachel said.

"I'm not sure. I'll figure it out. Call Dillon and have him meet us there."

"Uncle Grant? I'm ... really scared. Can I have Dillon pick me up here?"

"Sure. Call me when you get to the airport. Travel light. We're on the run. Bring the bio-computer."

"See you soon."

"And bring that phony driver's license," Grant said. "You can't fly without a picture ID. I'll get you a ticket in that name." He hung up.

Rachel folded the phone and put it in her pocket. "Auntie, don't worry. Uncle Grant's going to get me out of town. As soon as Dillon gets here, we're leaving."

"You should call the police." Aunt Esther was locking the window in the living room.

Rachel shook her head. "It's too dangerous. I don't trust anybody.

The FBI, or somebody impersonating them, killed Keryn. We've got to leave town. Uncle Grant is going to meet me at the airport with tickets."

"Can't the FBI track passenger names on the airline computers?"

"He'll get the tickets in phony names—the same names he put on the fake driver's licenses."

Aunt Esther went and locked the back patio door. "When is your friend coming?"

"Soon." Rachel went to Rivka's bedroom and looked around, trying to decide what she should take. She checked that the bio-computer was still in her fanny pack. But what else should she take? Underwear? Clothes? She riffled through the box of Rivka's things, but she was so scared she couldn't think. Forget packing clothes. Wherever she was going, she could buy things. She had a Visa card. Best to just travel light.

Rachel grabbed Rivka's wallet and staggered back out to the living room and sat down in Auntie's rocking chair. Slow breathing. In and out. In and out. *Think calming thoughts.*

Clifton had betrayed them. Rachel felt nauseated at the thought. How could a guy do that?

More importantly, how *had* he? Unless Rachel answered that, she might be the next one killed. Or Dillon.

Dillon. Rachel's heart began hammering as the answer fell into place. Dillon was the key. The men had kidnapped Keryn. If they knew where Keryn was, they probably knew where Rachel was, but they hadn't come for her. They came for Keryn instead. Why?

Because they already had a bio-computer.

It was so obvious, Rachel wanted to scream. Dillon was the target, not her. They had kidnapped Keryn to lure Dillon back because he had the software they needed to make the bio-computer work. Which meant that Clifton was the one who broke into the bio-lab. Clifton must have stolen the bio-computer. He had taken the software too, but then he found out it wasn't ready yet, that it was broken and he didn't know how to fix it.

Rachel closed her eyes and imagined the scene. Clifton must have seen her or Grant keying in the combination earlier that week. On

Friday night she had called him to say that they were close but were quitting for the night. Around two in the morning Clifton had just walked in and logged in under her username. He must have seen her log in once. He could have seen her password. Then he tried to compile Dillon's source code, but it failed. He found the obvious bugs, fixed them to make the code compile, but he didn't really understand the code and didn't realize that his fixes wouldn't work. He opened the safe—it had the same combination as the door—and took out the bio-computer. He tried to test the software, but the code crashed. After three tries, he gave up. He drained the bio-computer into a flask, set it up to look like it had accidentally leaked out, and left.

Then he just played dumb the next day. And now she remembered that he was always taking phone calls at weird times and going off somewhere private to talk. Which meant he was working with someone else. He'd probably bugged the office, their phones, everything. If he had some buddies in the FBI, that would explain it all. He'd offered them a few billion to help. Or something. Most people had a price, and it usually didn't have that many zeroes behind it. Rachel had heard once that seven percent of all Americans would kill somebody they didn't know for ten million dollars. For ten trillion dollars ... just about anybody could be bought.

Clifton Potter had sold his soul for a shipload of money.

That was the only explanation. Clifton knew Dillon had that flash drive on his key chain and he had tipped off his friends. The carjackers stole Dillon's car just so they could get his keys. They probably didn't even know Rachel had the bio-computer. They didn't care because they didn't need it. Dillon was the target all the time.

Rachel took the idea apart and put it back together twice in her mind. It explained all the facts. And the clincher was that Clifton was right there with them when they killed Keryn. Clifton told them to shoot her again. Clifton, in cold blood. The filthy, lying, evil *bastard*.

"Somebody's here!" Aunt Esther said.

Rachel shot out of her chair. "What kind of car?"

"It's a white minivan."

Rachel almost collapsed in relief. "That's Dillon's rental car!" She threw her arms around Aunt Esther. "I'll call you when I'm safe."

"Like fun you will. I'm coming to the airport with you."

"No, it isn't safe."

Aunt Esther was shaking, but she held Rachel's hand tight. "Rachel, honey, Yeshua will take care of me."

"He didn't take care of Keryn."

"I'll ... I'll pray for Keryn."

"And what good will that do?"

Aunt Esther put her arms around her. "Rachel, honey, if HaShem wants to raise Keryn from the dead, he can do it."

Deep bitterness filled Rachel's heart. If there was anything in the world she hated, it was blind, stupid faith.

"Honey, I'm coming with you, and that's all there is to say." Aunt Esther picked up her purse.

A knock on the door.

Rachel yanked it open.

Dillon stood there, a rock of calm.

Rachel rushed into his arms. "Dillon, I'm so glad you're here. Grant wants us to meet him at the airport."

"When?"

"Now." Rachel squeezed Dillon around the waist. "I've been so scared."

He stroked her hair gently. "I will ... do all I can to protect you."

Rachel didn't say anything. Dillon would have done anything he could to protect Keryn, too, and right now she had a bullet in her brains.

"We have to find Grant." Dillon released his hold on her.

Rachel didn't want to go anywhere. Didn't ever want to leave the quiet strength of Dillon's arms.

Aunt Esther put a hand on Rachel's back. "Let's go, already. Yeshua watched over Rivka. He'll watch over you."

Which was exactly what Rachel was afraid of.

CHAPTER THIRTY-THREE

Dillon

On the way to the airport, Dillon sat with Rachel in the middle seat of the minivan, hoping the darkened side windows would give them slightly better concealment. Rachel seemed terrified. She clung to Dillon and explained her theory about Clifton.

By the time they reached Harbor Drive, Dillon was shaking with rage. He had trusted Clifton. To betray a friend—that was evil, pure and simple. To kill Keryn for the love of money was beyond evil.

Dillon took out his cell phone and dialed Grant.

It answered after one ring. "This is Russell."

"Russell?" Dillon's heart began hammering. Who was Russell?

"Is that you, *Jake*?" Grant's voice was a dry rasp. "This is *Russell*."

Dillon realized that Russell was the name Grant would be traveling under. "Yes, this is ... Jake." He hated speaking a lie. It felt bent. Evil.

"I'm in Terminal 2, across from the American Airlines counter," Grant said. "Have you heard from my wife?"

"Julia?"

"Teresa!" Grant snapped.

"Sorry." Dillon again felt a twist in his heart. This was wrong, all wrong, this business with false names. It was wrong to prevaricate. "No, I have not heard from her. I am with ..." He tried to remember Rachel's false name. "I am with Sally. We are on Harbor, just turning in toward Terminal 2 right now. We have friends with us to help."

"Good. Walk behind them and keep your heads down. Did you bring any kind of disguise?"

Dillon felt his heart lurch. "You think they will be watching for us?"

"I have no idea what they'll be doing. I don't even know who *they* are." Grant's voice sounded tight, exhausted. "It may be just a few rogue agents—that's my guess. Or it could be the whole U.S. Army. Could be the Mafia, or foreigners, or Martians. I don't know. I'm wearing a Padres cap and some reading glasses I bought at a drugstore on the way here. And I'm hiding behind a copy of the *Union-Tribune*."

"We will be inside shortly." Dillon hung up. "Robert, no, do not park. Just drop us at the curb at the American Airlines sign."

Robert growled something and chugged to a stop at the short-term parking entrance. He lowered the window and pressed the button for a parking slip.

A minute later they had parked and were walking toward the terminal. Rachel's aunt walked in front with Robert. Dillon followed close behind Robert, keeping his head down. Rachel clutched Dillon's arm and kept her face pressed against his shoulder as if she were his girlfriend saying good-bye. Dillon felt a peculiar burning sensation in his belly.

As they crossed the drop-off lanes, a policeman turned and began walking toward them. Dillon felt his mind contract into a hard knot. He heard a whistle blow.

"Keep going," Rachel whispered. "They whistle all the time. Odds are he's whistling at some goofball who's double-parked."

Another whistle. Dillon began feeling dizzy. They reached the terminal and walked in through the automatic doors. A uniformed man appeared in front of them.

Dillon's heart felt like melted cheese.

"Carry your bags, sir?"

"No bags," Robert said. "But thank you."

"You have a nice flight, sir."

Dillon breathed again. They turned left and hugged the outer wall of the terminal, passing little shops selling San Diego sweatshirts and baseball caps and cheap paperbacks.

A newspaper rustled.

Dillon saw the bill of a Padres cap behind it. "Robert, stop. He is here."

The newspaper lowered, and Grant's bushy eyebrows peeked up at them. He pointed to Dillon and Rachel. "Sit down, quick. Have your friends stand in front of us."

Dillon sat on one side of Grant. Rachel sat on the other. Rachel's aunt and Robert took up positions that Dillon was sure told everybody in the world they were trying to hide criminals from view.

"I still haven't gotten hold of Julia," Grant said. "I don't dare leave a message. Too risky. I left her a coded text. She knows what to do if things go south on us. We discussed it." He pulled three tickets out of his pocket. "Jake Scanlon, going to Baltimore-Washington International via St. Louis on American." He looked at Dillon. "You brought your ID, I hope?"

Dillon pulled everything out of his pocket.

"You can't take that pocketknife on the flight," Grant said. "You trying to get arrested?"

"It is my letter opener," Dillon said.

"I'll keep it for you." Robert took the Swiss Army knife out of Dillon's hand and pocketed it.

Dillon held up the driver's license. "Jake Scanlon."

"What's your birthday, Jake?" Grant asked.

Dillon did not know. He looked at the card and read it off.

"Memorize that," Grant said. "Keep telling yourself, 'Jake Scanlon, Jake Scanlon.' I don't want you standing there with your mouth open when the TSA guy calls you Mr. Scanlon, okay?"

Dillon sighed. "I will try."

Grant picked the flash drive out of Dillon's hand. "You haven't made backups of this, right?"

Dillon shook his head. "This is the only copy in existence."

"How close is the software to working?" Grant asked.

"Close." Dillon did not want to say that it was finished, that all he needed was an NMR machine to verify that it could factor any large number.

"If anything happens to you, could Rachel get it finished?"

Dillon nodded. "Y-yes. Unless there is some major design flaw, any competent programmer could. Even a college student can walk through code in a debugger and verify the logic in the calibration function and—"

"All right, all right, I don't need a C++ lesson." Grant closed Dillon's fingers. "Guard this with your life, all right? When we meet up in Baltimore—"

"Meet up?" Dillon's heart thumped. "Are you not coming on our flight?"

"We're all flying separately," Grant said. "Less risky that way. They'll be watching for us. I'm sure they're expecting us to have phony names, so they'll look for a pattern. Three people flying together with the right age profile on the same flight—they'll be monitoring the computers. Rachel's flying Continental to Houston and then on to BWI. She leaves a little before you do."

"We could drive," Dillon said.

"Oh, right, spend five days driving across the country, leaving a trail of credit card transactions for gas and motels. Five days to give them time to mine the data. If there are Feds involved in this—and I suspect the bad guys have bribed a few—they'd have all the time in the world. Our only hope is to move faster than they can react. And it ain't a great hope, in case you're wondering."

"When is your flight?" Dillon said. He did not like the idea of each of them flying separately. Especially Rachel, alone with that biocomputer.

"Mine's in half an hour." Grant was talking rapidly now. "I'm going first. If anything goes wrong, I can press a couple buttons on my cell phone and send you a text message to bail out. The code word is 'Dodge'—got it? If you get a text from me with that word in it, then get out of Dodge and you're on your own. Try to make contact with Rachel's daddy. His number's in those phones I gave you. I'm flying America

West to Phoenix, then on to BWI. I'll scout the area and check for suspicious activity. When you land, turn on your cell phones right away and check for voice or text messages. If anything goes wrong, don't go into the terminal. Try to sneak down the steps off the breezeway onto the tarmac and get away somehow. We'll meet up if we can."

"Why are we going to Baltimore?" Dillon asked.

Grant turned to Rachel. "Rachel, honey, good luck. Here's your ticket. I'm gonna have to go now or I'll have a heart attack running for my flight. Make your daddy proud." He leaned over and kissed Rachel on the forehead.

Rachel hugged him fiercely. "Bye, Uncle Grant. See you when we get there. Are you going to have Daddy meet us?"

"Sure." Grant stood up, adjusted his cap down as far as he could, and strode off.

Dillon felt terribly alone. A black sheet of depression settled over his mind. This plan of Grant's seemed poorly thought out. There were many possible failure points, and the biggest problem was that Dillon did not understand Grant's purpose. What was in Baltimore and why were they going there?

~

Rachel

Rachel watched Uncle Grant stride off. She felt exhausted. "Auntie, don't you want to sit down? Here, Dillon, scootch over this way and let Auntie have your seat." She grabbed Dillon's hand and pulled him over.

Aunt Esther sat down on his other side. Robert moved to stand directly in front of Dillon. "What time are your flights?" he asked.

Rachel looked at her ticket. "An hour and ten minutes."

Dillon held up his and stared at it with a vacant expression on his face.

"Dillon, what time is your flight?" Robert said.

Dillon shook his head slowly, and a tear wandered down his face.

Rachel grabbed his ticket. "Dillon, get hold of yourself. Looks like your flight isn't for another two hours."

Robert knelt in front of Dillon and gave Rachel a savage look. "Would you mind? He's still in shock over losing her."

Which just made no sense at all. "Hey, I lost her too," Rachel said. "She was as much my friend as his."

Robert looked at her as if she were a child. "It hardly compares."

Rachel glared at him. "What hardly compares?"

Robert fished a handkerchief out of his pocket and handed it to Dillon.

Rachel wondered what kind of a geek actually carried a handkerchief in his pocket. Were they still *making* hankies? "What hardly compares?" she demanded. "You don't think I cared about Keryn? She was a good friend of mine."

Robert looked at her with an expression of disbelief. "I certainly *hope* you weren't in love with her too."

Rachel felt her jaw drop right open. Had Dillon told Robert he was in love with Keryn? Great.

An awkward silence descended on them all. Rachel felt empty and cold.

"Rachel, honey, why are you going to Baltimore?" Aunt Esther asked. "Wouldn't it be easier for your father to pick you up in Newark?"

Rachel hadn't thought of that. Uncle Grant had been in such a hurry, he hadn't really explained what they were going to do when they got there.

"I assume you're going to Fort Meade," Robert said. "Isn't that the obvious place to go?"

No. Rachel's mind refused to accept that. It made no sense at all. Uncle Grant wouldn't sell them down the river like that.

"What's in Fort Meade?" Aunt Esther said.

"The NSA." Rachel spat out the words. "No Such Agency."

"It is the logical thing to do." Dillon put a hand on Rachel's shoulder. It burned like liquid nitrogen. "If we give this thing to the governing authorities—"

"I am *not* giving it to Big Brother!" Rachel snapped. Acid fury burned in her heart. Never, ever, ever. Anyone who trusted the government was a fool. Every government abused its power. Therefore, you gave it as little power as possible and watched it like a hawk. Rachel was not going to give Uncle Sam anything with this much power.

"Rachel—"

"No!" Rachel stood up and slapped Dillon full on the face. "What part of 'no possible way' do you not get?"

He took her hand in his. "Rachel, please—"

"For the last time, no!"

"Rachel, sit down!" Aunt Esther said. "You want that people should look at you?"

Rachel flounced into her seat and turned her back on Dillon. She yanked out her cell phone and dialed information for the airport. It took her ten minutes to make a reservation in the name of Sally Swigert for a flight to Newark. She slammed the phone shut and jammed it into her pocket.

Aunt Esther knelt in front of her. "Honey, are you going home, then?"

Rachel nodded. "Daddy will know what to do. But he won't give this thing to Big Brother." She threw a scowl at Dillon, then stood up and hugged her aunt. "My flight's in Terminal 1. I'm going over there and I'll wait inside the security area. I'll call you when I get to Daddy's house."

Aunt Esther held her tight. "Go with Yeshua. I'll be praying for you."

Rachel kissed her fiercely on the cheek. "Thanks, Auntie." She marched away without looking back at Dillon.

CHAPTER THIRTY-FOUR

Dillon

Dillon stood up to follow Rachel.

Robert moved to block his way. "Dillon, she's not going to go to the NSA."

Dillon felt like he had swallowed a ten-star pepper from the Star of India. Heat burned in his heart. "That woman is so ... infuriating."

Robert shook his head. "Reminds me of Sarah. She's Irish, you know. Kind of hotheaded."

"So why are you marrying her?" Dillon did not understand what any man could see in a woman like that.

Robert smiled. "I guess ... opposites attract. She's a lot of things I'm not. Sarah kind of completes me. I don't know what I'd do without her. She's so lively, so ... fun."

Dillon slumped down into his chair and looked at his watch. "My flight leaves in an hour and forty minutes." Despair washed over him. What was the point of going to Baltimore now? He had the software but no bio-computer. If they caught him, he was dead. His only hope was that bio-computer. And Rachel's only hope, whether she liked it or not, was his software. If they caught her, they would kill her too. He and she were two halves of a puzzle, and neither half had any value without the other.

Rachel's aunt put a hand on Dillon's arm. "Dillon, I'm Rachel's aunt Esther. I'm sorry she didn't formally introduce us."

"Dillon Richard." He put out his hand. "Actually, for the time being I am Jake. Fake Jake until I can get rid of this ... thing."

"You two need each other," Esther said. "You and Rachel."

Dillon nodded. "I am no good without her. She is no good without me."

"You know why she's so angry, don't you?" Aunt Esther had a strange expression on her face.

Dillon sat trying to parse this social context for a quarter of a minute, then shook his head. "I am not good at understanding people."

Esther smiled. "Dillon, honey, it's as plain as anything. She *likes* you."

"Likes me?" Dillon did not see the point of this comment. "I like her too—most of the time. She is a good friend, when she is not acting like a moron."

"Dillon, don't be dense. She's attracted to you." Esther pinched his cheek. "And I can see why. You're everything she isn't. She's flighty—you're a rock. She's one of those right-brained wonders—you're left-brained as all get out. Plus, you're a handsome devil."

Dillon felt a hot current in his cheeks. "I am not handsome."

"You're humble too. Even better."

Dillon did not want to contradict her anymore. He sat there trying to understand this puzzle.

Esther shook her head. "I'm terribly sorry about the other girl. Were you going together long?"

"I ..." Dillon swallowed hard. "We were not going together."

Robert squatted down beside him. "Actually, you already said it, ma'am. Dillon's kind of dense about women. He didn't know he was in love with Keryn. And he had no clue she liked him."

Esther collapsed in laughter.

Dillon could not imagine what was so funny.

"Oh, Fakey Jakey, you are such a case!" Esther wiped her eyes. "If you weren't in so much danger, I'd take you home and frame you. Good heavens, you're telling me you've had two beautiful young girls after you and you didn't have a clue?"

Dillon stared at her. "You are telling me ..."

"You didn't notice?"

"I am sorry," Dillon said. "I have been trying to learn more about social contexts."

"Social what?" She looked at him with an expression Dillon could not read.

Robert grinned at her. "Dillon has a funny kind of autism, ma'am. Asperger's syndrome. It means he's not completely human, the best I can tell. We always thought he was just weird when we were kids, but ... they diagnosed him a couple years ago, and he's had a counselor helping him learn the language the rest of us speak. He's getting better at figuring us out, but you've got to understand, he just thinks about things in his own way. He's a genius, trust me—just not about reading people."

Esther pursed her lips in thought for a couple of minutes. "If I could make a suggestion here, there's an angry and hurting young woman heading to Newark in about ... forty-five minutes, and I think you two need each other. And not just because of those wretched computer things either. She could help heal your heart, and ... you might heal hers too."

Robert stood up. "Dillon, she's right. It's no good you going to Baltimore without her. For better or worse, you need to be with Rachel." He yanked on Dillon's arm.

Dillon stood up. "But—"

Esther jumped to her feet and slapped him hard on the buttocks. "Go, you silly goose! Run!"

Robert pulled on Dillon's arm. Dillon followed him out into the bright sunshine.

The two of them ran.

Dillon

When they got to Terminal 1, Dillon raced to the United Airlines desk. There were a dozen people in line, and he had thirty minutes to make the flight. Robert stood waiting beside him, fidgeting and looking around anxiously.

"Is something wrong?" Dillon said.

"I'm just thinking." Robert turned his head to both sides, eyeing those around them. "You'll be buying a second ticket for almost the same time and under the same name as the one Grant bought you. If some crook bribed me to watch the computers, that would be a red flag."

Dillon knew that a red flag meant a danger signal. "It will be much worse if I use my real name. But I cannot do that, because I do not have my driver's license. The carjackers stole it."

Robert looked all around them, then slipped his hand into his pocket. He drew his hand out and gave Dillon his wallet. "Use my driver's license and my Visa card. Just study the signature on the card and try to scribble like I do."

"I ... I cannot do that." Dillon felt a vise grip on his heart. "I have dark hair and you have light hair."

Robert grinned at him. "Not to worry. Nobody looks like their driver's license. We're both nerdy white males. I'm a little taller than you and a little heavier. It's close enough."

"I am eleven years older than you."

"I don't see a date stamp on your forehead. But the big problem is you're a lot better looking."

"Robert, I cannot do this. What if they ask why I do not look like my picture?"

"They won't. Nobody ever looks like their picture," Robert said. "So beat them to the punch. Give them an ironic smile and ask if you look like your picture."

"What?" Dillon stared at him. "That is foolish."

"Try it. I guarantee it'll work. Stay here in line alone. I'll wait by security." Robert strode away.

Dillon's heart was jackhammering against his ribs. This was insanity. But Robert was right that he could not buy another ticket under the name of Jake Scanlon. He might be caught if he used Robert's ID, but he would certainly be caught using Jake's. The line dwindled slowly, and there were only twenty minutes till flight time when his turn came.

Dillon strode to the counter and held up Robert's license and Visa card. "Round trip to Newark with no specific return date. No bags. I would like to get on the 1:10 flight if I possibly can. My father had a heart attack an hour ago and ... he may not last till I get there tonight."

Dillon tasted bile in his throat. This was prevarication. In a just universe, he would now be struck by lightning.

"I'm sorry about your father, sir. I'll see if there's room on that flight." The woman took Robert's Visa card and began typing furiously. Then she picked up Robert's driver's license and looked at Dillon.

A thin sheet of icy sweat covered his back. He had no idea how to give an ironic smile. "Do I look like my picture?"

"Yes, sir, but you look much better in person," she said in a practiced tone that told Dillon she had answered this question five hundred times. "Sign here and hurry, sir. Your flight leaves in fifteen minutes."

Dillon signed something that looked like R-squiggle K-squiggle, grabbed his ticket, and ran.

When they reached security, Dillon handed Robert his wallet and got in line. Robert looked in the wallet and gave Dillon his license. "You'll need this to get through security." Then he gave Dillon his Visa card too and thumped him on the arm. "Good luck, buddy. On ... everything." He turned and hurried away.

Dillon shoved the license and credit card into his pocket and waited.

The security agent took his ticket and peered at it. "Where you going today, sir?"

"Newark. My father had a heart attack and I am trying to get there before ..." Dillon's voice cracked. He could not finish this prevarication.

"My God, I'm so sorry." The agent looked at Robert's license, looked at Dillon, scribbled something on the ticket, and then shoved everything back to him. "Hope you get there in time, my friend."

Dillon hurried to the shortest line. He put his cell phone and flash drive and fingernail clippers in a tub and sent them through the X-ray machine.

It suddenly occurred to him to wonder how Rachel was going to get that bio-computer through the X-ray machine. It was in her fanny pack, which she could not wear through security. He scanned the area beyond the machines but saw nothing. Had they detained her? He checked his watch. The flight was certainly boarding already. He would have to run to catch the flight.

He walked through the scanner slowly, arms well away from his body. No lights, no beeps, no suspicious glances. Dillon reclaimed his pocket contents and checked his ticket. Gate 22. Six minutes. He ran.

Seven minutes later he reached the gate.

A flight agent was standing all alone, holding a microphone. "Last call for Flight 524 to Denver."

Dillon handed her his ticket and held up Robert's driver's license.

She waved away the license, scanned his ticket, and handed it back to him.

Dillon strode down the breezeway and into the plane. He looked at his ticket. Seat number 8A. It was the first row behind first class. The flight attendant greeted him. "Please take a seat, sir. We'll be leaving momentarily."

Dillon nodded and rushed to his seat. It was a window seat. He turned around and craned his neck, hoping to catch sight of Rachel. Nothing. Given her height, that was not surprising. But what if she was not on the plane? What if they had caught her at security?

The intercom buzzed with static. "Ladies and gentlemen, we'll be leaving momentarily. Please fasten your seat belts and make certain all your luggage is stowed securely in the overhead bins or under the seats in front of you."

Dillon listened carefully to all the instructions, then buckled his seat belt and settled in for takeoff.

The plane did not move.

The intercom buzzed again. "Ladies and gentlemen, this is your captain speaking." A low chuckle. "Seems we have a special announcement for a *very* special young lady. This message comes to you from a young man in love."

More static, and then ...

"Sally, this is Jake. Please, please, please forgive me."

Dillon's head shot up, and every hair on his body quilled out like a porcupine. That was his voice coming over the intercom. *His voice.*

"Sally, I was wrong. I'm sorry for what I said ... and I'll do anything to get you back. Please forgive me. I ... I want you to share my life. Sally, please take me back." The voice broke.

Whoops rang out all up and down the aisles. A woman shouted, "Take him back, Sally!" An old man hollered, "Throw the bum out!" More laughter. Another woman shrieked, "Sally, if you don't want him, I'll trade you for mine!"

Hoots of laughter. Dillon could not understand what was happening. That was his voice, begging Rachel to take him back. Somebody was trying to draw her out. Somebody who knew Rachel was on this plane. Under the name Sally Swigert. Sweat poured down his sides. He wanted to shout a warning, but that would only give him away too.

Please, Rachel, do not take me back.

But when we get to Newark ... please take me back.

The laughter continued for close to a minute. Rachel did not appear. She must have noticed that the fake Jake did not use grammatical constructions at all like Dillon.

Two men in suits came through the curtain from first class. One of them held a picture of Rachel out to Dillon and his two seatmates. "We're FBI. Have any of you seen this woman?"

Dillon shook his head. He did not believe this man was with the FBI. These were criminals. Well-financed criminals who could impersonate the governing authorities and trick the airlines into letting them delay a flight and search a plane.

The man moved on to the next row. "FBI. Have you seen this woman?"

Dillon leaned back in his seat and tried to breathe. It was possible that these were the very men who had murdered Keryn. Heat seared his eyes. If he could know that for certain, then he would smash their faces right now. But he could not know it for certain.

One thing he did know for certain. They would find Rachel. There was no possible way she could evade capture. They would take her off the plane. Would take the bio-computer.

Would kill her.

Hot fear roiled in Dillon's stomach. He had not been able to save Keryn. He could not save Rachel either, but ...

He would not let her die alone.

When they dragged her screaming down the aisle, Dillon would block their way and fight them.

And let the devil take the software.

Dillon unbuckled his seat belt and waited.

CHAPTER THIRTY-FIVE

Rachel

After Rachel had left Dillon and Robert, she had run all the way to Terminal 1 in a white fury. Dillon was such a ... wimp! Ready to go to the government every time there was trouble. That was not acceptable. Not acceptable at all. The line at the ticket counter had a dozen people in it, and Rachel only had forty-five minutes before her flight. She didn't want to wait, so she walked up to a guy in a Princeton shirt near the head of the line and threw a flirty smile at him. "Hi, mind if I cut in with you? I'm late for my flight and ... oh my gosh! Are you at Princeton too?"

"I'm ..." He looked her up and down and grinned. "Yeah."

She touched his arm. "Oh, that is so cool! What's your major?"

"Philosophy."

"Really? Like, wow! I'm in math. What do you think of Gödel's Theorem?"

His eyes opened wide and then his grin broadened. "I'm undecided."

Rachel giggled as if that were original. She had a well-practiced giggle for airhead moments like this. "You are so funny! Oops, it's your turn!"

He looked over at the counter. "You go ahead of me. You're in a hurry."

Rachel backed toward the ticket agent and blew the guy a kiss. "Thanks, you're a stud!" She spun around and pulled out her driver's license. "I'm Sally Swigert," she said. "No relation to Jimmy Swaggart."

The agent picked up the license and typed in her name. "May I see your credit card?"

Rachel pulled out her Visa card and handed it to him. Minutes later, she had a seat in row 37 and a ticket. She hurried toward the security checkpoint. Fear shot an arrow through her heart.

The X-ray machines! She could not put the bio-computer in her fanny pack through the X-ray machines. But she couldn't carry it in her hand either.

Rachel hesitated just a minute and then hurried past the security line into the ladies' room. She locked herself in a stall, opened her fanny pack, took out the bio-computer, and stared at it. They would make her empty her pockets before going through. Unfortunately, Keryn's stick-it-in-the-bra trick wasn't an option. Rachel put her foot on the toilet, lifted one leg of her jeans, and shoved the bio-computer down her sock. She flushed the toilet, zipped shut her fanny pack, and went out.

Ten minutes later, she was through security and still had almost thirty minutes before flight time. They'd be boarding soon. Rachel decided to do like Uncle Grant and buy a bit of disguise. She stopped in one of the little shops and bought a thin blue silklike scarf and some horrible pink sunglasses and a huge sweatshirt with a picture of a panda bear on the front and the words *San Diego Zoo*. At the next bathroom, she ducked into a stall and recovered her bio-computer from her sock and put it in her fanny pack. She covered her hair completely in the scarf and pulled on the sweatshirt, which was so big it made her feel like a walking tent. Finally, she put on the sunglasses and went to check herself in the mirror.

It wasn't much, but it would have to do. The important thing was that she had neutered her hair. That was the first thing people noticed, her blond hair. Now it was buried under blue silk. The sweatshirt made her look fat.

Rachel checked her watch and saw that she now had only fifteen minutes till her flight. Time to rock and roll. She grabbed her ticket out of her back pocket and strode out.

As she approached the gate, Rachel paused to reconnoiter. Just to be sure. There was a ticket agent with a microphone announcing which rows could enter. Rachel's row had already been called, so all she had to do was walk up there and—

A man in a dark suit.

He was standing near the gate and he was not holding a ticket. In his hand he held something. A stiff piece of paper that looked like a five-by-seven photo. He was wearing dark glasses and studying passengers as they walked past the ticket agent.

And Rachel thought she had seen him before. He had a mole next to his nose. The last time she'd seen a man with a mole like that, he'd been standing under a streetlight pointing a gun at Dillon.

He was one of the carjackers.

Rachel stuffed her knuckles into her mouth to keep from screaming. Her head felt so light that she thought she would faint. She didn't dare look around to see who else was there. Didn't dare turn and run. After fifteen seconds of jagged panic, she decided that the only thing she could do was leave.

Slowly, Rachel turned around. She looked at her watch, then began walking with a determined pace back toward the exits. They had tracked her. She had reserved a ticket by phone less than an hour ago, and they had detected it. How? Nobody knew Sally Swigert from Adam. Uncle Grant said the ID was safe.

A sick feeling filled her stomach. Of course. She was an idiot. They had checked the computers and seen that two tickets were bought in the same name on two different airlines. That tipped them off that Sally Swigert was a person of interest.

Which meant that both her tickets were useless. They would have put agents at both gates to watch for her. If she got on either plane, they'd take her and kill her.

Rachel ducked into the nearest rest room and hid in a stall. It was still ten minutes till her plane took off. She waited fifteen minutes, just to be sure. Then she ducked out and hurried toward the exits. She didn't see anyone in dark suits, or anyone holding stiff pieces of paper. When Rachel reached the exit of the terminal, she breathed in deeply. Freedom. Thank goodness for fresh air. For life. She looked at her watch. Grant was safely away and Dillon's flight would go out in forty-five minutes.

Dillon.

All of a sudden she wanted his strong, calm presence. Dillon wasn't afraid. He was being stupid about going to the government, but ... even Uncle Grant was being stupid about that. She didn't have to go. Anytime she felt like it, she could break the vial and all the king's horses and all the king's men couldn't put Humpty together again. Dillon couldn't stop her. She could make him listen. Make Uncle Grant listen.

Though Rachel hated to draw attention to herself, she started to run. She was sweating by the time she reached Terminal 2 but she didn't want to take off her sweatshirt. Even if it was a crummy disguise, it was all she had.

She found an ATM just inside the terminal. Her Sally Swigert Visa card was the kind that let you take a cash advance. She got the limit, five hundred dollars. Which would probably cover a flight to the East Coast. Uncle Grant had said Dillon was flying American Airlines through St. Louis to BWI. Rachel bit her lip.

And decided.

She reached into her pocket and pulled out the driver's license of her dead cousin, Rivka Meyers. The license had expired last October. Rachel got in line clutching the license and cash and waited.

The ticket line was horrible, and it took twenty-five nerve-wracking minutes to get a ticket on Dillon's flight. The idiot at the counter gave Rivka's license a careful examination that lasted a full five milliseconds before he gave her a ticket. Rachel had twenty minutes to make the flight. If she called Dillon on his cell phone, he could stall the people at the gate, but she didn't want to risk him calling attention to himself. She'd just have to hurry. She found a bathroom and did her trick with the bio-computer in the sock again.

At security, the agent inspected Rachel's license closely. His face tightened. "I'm sorry, but this license expired last October."

"I *know*." Rachel looked down at her shoes repentantly. "Last night I was out with friends in the Gaslamp and we got robbed. My God, I was so *scared*! I thought for sure he was going to shoot one of us. I lost my license and all my credit cards and ... I'm going to Johns Hopkins to start my residency in ophthalmology tomorrow, and my mother convinced me to just use my old license from when I was studying here at UCSD. I'm sorry. I know it was wrong." She brushed away a real tear that had formed in her eye. "I'm gonna be an eye surgeon, and I really need to get back to Baltimore before tomorrow."

A long silence while the security guy studied her closely. "What's the name of the hospital you'll be working at?"

"The Wilmer Eye Institute. I'll be in the Pediatric Eye Disease Center. Kids with strabismus, amblyopia, things like that."

Another long silence.

Rachel sighed. "I'm so sorry, I knew this was a bad idea. I can go to DMV this afternoon and then catch a flight tomorrow and hope the airline doesn't screw me over too bad for changing the ticket."

The agent shook his head. "They'd kick my butt up the escalator and down if they knew I'm doing this, but ... you're obviously not a terrorist. Go on, catch your flight. And you get a new license tomorrow, all right?"

"Thank you so much! You're so kind. And I will. First thing."

Rachel got through the X-ray machines without a problem, but now it was five minutes before her flight. It took her two precious minutes to find a bathroom and get the bio-computer out of her sock.

Then she ran.

She made the gate just as they were shutting the door.

Waving her ticket, Rachel raced up to the ticket agent. "Sorry!" She grinned at him. "You know how long the line in the rest room is."

He nodded sympathetically. "Hurry! They're almost ready to push back from the gate."

Rachel ran through the door and down the breezeway and into the plane. This flight was only half full. The aisles were clear and people stared up at her as she rushed past them toward her seat. She found her row, plunked into the window seat, and buried her nose in the in-flight magazine.

She heard the dull *thunk* of the main door being closed. There followed a pause, and then the doors *whoosh*ed open again.

"Ladies and jellybeans, this is your captain speaking. I know it isn't Valentine's Day, but there's a very persistent young lady on board who wants to say something to a lucky young man."

Rachel found that she was holding her breath.

"Jake, it's me—Sally! Please, I'm sorry. I'm such a jerk. I want you back. I'm sorry for what I said. Jake, I'm crazy about you and I want to go wherever you go. Take me back and I'll never leave you again."

Rachel thought she was going to get airsick right there. It was her voice. *Her voice.*

A chorus of whistles greeted this. "Go for it, Jake!" "Take her back!"

Rachel waited for Dillon to call out, but nothing happened.

Shortly, two men came down the aisles showing pictures of Dillon and asking if anyone had seen him. When they reached her row, Rachel took a good look and shook her head earnestly.

Cold fingers of fear caressed her body. It was a photo of Dillon taken at the Del Mar Fair with Keryn. Rachel saw right away that this was the same photo that had been used for Dillon's phony driver's license. It had been cropped down tightly for the license, but Dillon wore the same squinting-into-the-sun half smile.

Only one person in the world could have given them that photo.

Uncle Grant.

CHAPTER THIRTY-SIX

Dillon

When he reached Denver, Dillon found a quiet spot and called Grant's cell phone. No answer. He tried Rachel's phone. Still no answer. Finally, he tried Julia.

Three rings and ...

"Hello?" Julia sounded frantic.

"Julia, this is Dillon. Where are you?"

"Dillon, what's going on? Are you in the Caymans already?"

"I am in Denver." Dillon's throat felt tight. "What are you talking about?"

"I was out shopping and forgot to turn on my cell phone. When I got back, Grant was gone. I tried to call him and found that he'd left me a voice mail saying that you were all flying to the Caymans."

"The Caymans? No." Dillon did not want to believe this. "Grant met us at the airport and bought us tickets to Baltimore. He got on a flight just ahead of us."

"What's happening? Why are you all leaving?"

Dillon realized that she did not know. His voice buckled. "They ... kidnapped Keryn." He turned toward the corner and let the tears flow. "Rachel and I were on the phone with her and ... they shot her."

Julia shrieked and then began crying.

Dillon waited until they both calmed down. "Rachel was supposed to be on my flight, and they came for her, but she was not there. I do not know where she is."

"Where are you going?" Julia said.

"Newark. Rachel's father teaches at Rutgers."

"Call me when you get there, honey. Something's fishy."

"Julia?"

"Are you thinking what I'm thinking?"

"If Grant is going to the Caymans, then he has been ... prevaricating."

"Oh, Dillon, I'm sure there's a reasonable explanation."

Dillon's fingers were clutching the phone so tightly it hurt. Yes, there was a reasonable explanation. There was only one reasonable explanation. Grant was in league with the criminals.

"Dillon, are you there?"

"If Rachel calls you, tell her ... I am sorry and that I want to make peace with her."

"Call me when you get to Newark."

Immediately after Dillon hung up, it occurred to him that it was possible that the person he had just spoken with was not really Julia.

∽

Rachel

Rachel sat with her face turned toward the window all the way to St. Louis, trying to grapple with the horrible truth.

Uncle Grant had betrayed her. Betrayed them all. There was no other explanation. He had been running a giant con on them the whole time. It was evil—that's what it was. He had let them kill Keryn. Had put Dillon and Rachel on separate flights. Why? So they could be taken separately, with no fuss? It didn't make sense. Was Julia in on it? Clifton?

Rachel couldn't be sure. Grant had claimed he couldn't get hold of Julia, but she might have been waiting for him at the gate. *While he was meeting with me and Dillon and giving us his sweet talk and lies.* There was no proof he was going to Baltimore. He and Julia could be out of the country by now. As for Clifton ...

Everything Rachel knew about Clifton, every point she thought she had against him, could be explained away. She didn't know for sure he had broken into the bio-lab—that was inference based on the assumption that it couldn't be Uncle Grant. She didn't know with certainty that Clifton had stolen the hard drive from the computer or added a new alarm combination on the door. She had deduced it from what Grant had told her.

Furthermore, she couldn't even trust her own ears. Sure, she had heard Clifton over the phone, telling them to shoot Keryn. But she had heard her own voice on the intercom of the plane begging Dillon to take her back. Somebody had some really good speech-synthesis gear. Good enough so it sounded real over a scratchy plane intercom. They had faked her voice, and they might just as well have faked Clifton's over Keryn's cell phone. And they could probably fake Dillon's. Rachel took out her phone and stared at it. She could not use it when she landed. How could she trust the voice on the other end? Grant and his accomplices could spoof anybody, and she would have no way of knowing.

A cold hard knot formed in Rachel's belly. She closed her eyes and pretended to be asleep, but she did not think she would ever sleep soundly again.

∾

Rachel

Rachel had a tight connection in St. Louis and had to run to catch the second leg of her flight. She wanted to call somebody, anybody, but she had no idea whom she could trust.

Nobody bothered her on this flight. There weren't any agents showing pictures of Dillon. Nobody doing phony speech-synthesis tricks to fake her voice. When she reached the Baltimore-Washington airport, she took stock of her cash. She had five dollars and change. A look at her watch told her that she had landed twelve minutes after she would have if she'd gone to Newark.

Rachel took out her cell phone and wished she dared call home. But what if they were already there, waiting for her to call, with Daddy duct-taped to the chair? She would have no way to authenticate—

The phone rang in her hand. The caller ID said it was Dillon, but that didn't mean a thing. If they'd captured Dillon, they could spoof him. It rang again. Again.

Rachel took a deep breath and opened the phone. "Yes?"

"Rachel, please do not hang up. I am sorry for making you angry. We are in terrible trouble. The criminals are impersonating FBI agents and they can synthesize our voices."

"So how do I know you're Dillon?"

"We will have to authenticate both ways," Dillon said. "I will ask a question only you can answer. Quickly now, what is the only illegal place in San Diego that I would approve of?"

Rachel backed out of the foot traffic to a quiet corner. "I don't know. If you're really Dillon, then it isn't the Mount Soledad Cross, because it violates separation of church and state."

"Good. I believe you are really Rachel. Now authenticate me."

Rachel closed her eyes and thought for several seconds. "Who did I take a dive for?"

"Jason. He wore a lot of orange. You wore ... a little pink."

Rachel laughed. "Okay, you're Dillon. Where are you?"

"We will have to talk in riddles, Rachel. I am assuming they can listen in on this conversation."

Rachel checked again that nobody was watching her, then turned back toward the corner. "Okay, let's make this simple. I don't need to know where you are, because I don't have any money so I can't go anywhere. The Visa and driver's license Grant gave me are probably compromised. I've got another ID they don't know about, but I've only got five bucks cash. You'll have to come to me, and I can't tell you where I am."

Silence for thirty seconds.

"I am assuming you are in an airport," Dillon said. "There are hundreds around the country and each has a unique three-letter designator. San Diego is SAN. Los Angeles International is LAX. Do not tell me the three letters for your airport. Just tell me if you know what they are."

Rachel stared at her ticket. BWI. "Yes."

"All right, you need to think of three words. Each word starts with one of the three letters. Do not tell me the words. Just give me a clue that only I would know so I can guess each word."

Rachel thought for a few seconds. "How many brothers do you have, Dillon?"

"Three."

"No, you have a fourth one. What's his first name? That's the first clue."

A long silence. Rachel hoped it was obscure enough, but not too obscure.

"If Gloria is his papa, then I know the answer," Dillon said.

"You're good. Second clue. I have a friend who went through AA twelve years ago. Last name."

"That one is easy."

"Third clue." Rachel closed her eyes and concentrated, but she could not think of a word that started with I. She'd have to improvise. "There's somebody I used to hate a whole lot—more than anybody in the whole world."

"Used to?"

"Right, but ... not anymore. First letter of the first name. Take the letter before that in the alphabet."

"Fine, I know where you are. Are the concourses labeled with letters?"

Rachel looked at the nearest gate and saw that it was labeled C24. "Yes."

"Then I need one more letter for your concourse. I'll come there and meet you at your gate."

Concourse C. "Okay, what was my favorite ride at the fair? Remember?"

"How could I forget? It had three words."

"Third letter of the third word," Rachel said.

"Can you find somewhere to hide?" Dillon asked. "When I get there, I will call you. Be ready with another authenticator question."

"Bye, Dillon."

"Good-bye, Keryn." Dillon hung up.

Rachel closed the phone, wondering why Dillon had called her Keryn. She walked down the concourse, looking for a bathroom. By the time she found one, three gates away, she had guessed the answer.

Rachel locked herself in a stall, closed the lid on the toilet, and sat down.

And smiled.

~

Dillon

D illon had excellent luck and needed only ninety-two minutes to buy a ticket and make the flight on Continental direct from Newark to BWI. He came out on Concourse D and spent ten minutes navigating to Concourse C. He sat down in a quiet corner and pulled out his cell phone. During the short flight, a gnawing fear had been growing in his mind.

Grant had warned him that the authorities could trace the locations of cell phones. Dillon was not sure if this was true, but it seemed clear that the criminals were in collusion with the authorities or using them somehow. Therefore it was probable that they could listen to his phone conversations and plausible that they could also vector in on him and Rachel. In that case ...

He had walked into a trap. He would join Rachel and then they would be taken.

If that were true, Dillon did not see how they could escape. Whoever was pursuing them seemed to have vast knowledge. They could search airline reservation records. They could mobilize FBI men, real or fake. They could probably tap and trace cell phone conversations.

And yet both he and Rachel had somehow evaded them. So far. Was it luck or ... something else?

Dillon did not know and he did not care. While he had been talking to Rachel on the phone, he had suddenly realized something.

Whenever he heard Rachel's voice, his heart did strange things inside his chest. When she said his name, it was like ... magic. He had not been able to think of anything but Rachel on the long flight across the country. Rachel's enthusiasm for life. Rachel's brilliant mind. Rachel's dazzling smile.

She was completely different from him. An agnostic, whereas he believed in God. An extreme extrovert, whereas he was a complete introvert. Creative, disorganized, intuitive, whereas he was methodical and organized and analytical. She had everything he needed, and he had all that she lacked.

And he did not care about any of those things. All that he cared about was that when he looked into her light green eyes, he felt an instant and deep connection with her mind.

There was only one explanation, and it terrified Dillon.

He was in love with Rachel. Had been in love with her since the day he met her. He had not known this or he would have run the other direction as fast as possible. It was foolish to fall in love with somebody so different. Furthermore, he had also been in love with Keryn. A part of him was still in love with her, even though she was now ... gone.

He did not understand how this was possible. Rachel and Keryn were as different as two women could possibly be. If he was in love with both of them, then love was a dangerous and illogical thing. And he was not the man he had thought he was. He was no man of logic, of reason.

He was Dillon Richard, double-minded man, unstable in all his ways. All along, there had been two Dillons inside him, each passionate for one woman, interfering with each other and creating turmoil in his soul. Dillon did not like that at all. He could not trust his own heart. Why then should Rachel trust him?

Dillon shook his head. He did not have time to unlock this riddle. He selected Rachel's number and waited.

"Hello?" Rachel's eager voice, or an excellent imitation.

Dillon did not trust his ears any longer. "What animal is *not* on Papa's farm?"

"Pigs," Rachel said. "What three words should you have told Keryn?"

Dillon froze. It seemed ... sacrilegious to talk about Keryn now. To talk about her with Rachel. To force the Keryn-Dillon to interfere with the Rachel-Dillon.

"You're not Dillon, are you?" Rachel said.

"I ..." Dillon's voice caught in his throat. "I ... love you."

A little sigh. "Okay, you *are* Dillon. Where are you?"

Dillon looked at the gate nearest him. "In your concourse, near Gate 7."

"I'll be right there." Rachel hung up.

Dillon found he could not sit still. He got up and began pacing back and forth, watching for men in dark suits. Five minutes passed and Rachel did not appear. Dillon found the waiting unbearable. An image formed in his mind. Prodigal Papa, up on his roof, wearing running shoes, scanning the road with a telescope, looking for Little Brother.

Dillon's mouth suddenly felt very dry. He found a water fountain and took a long drink. Looked down the concourse.

Looked up the concourse.

Saw movement.

A girl in a huge panda-bear sweatshirt and a blue scarf, holding a fanny pack in her hand.

Dillon began walking toward her.

Recognition lit up her eyes. She quickened her pace.

Dillon hurried forward.

Rachel broke into a run.

Dillon raced toward her, arms spread wide.

Rachel jumped.

Dillon caught her in an enormous hug and staggered backward.

"Oh, Dillon, I missed you."

Dillon squeezed her slender frame. "Please do not leave me ever again."

"I have something for you," Rachel said. "Look at me."

Dillon looked down into her face.

She lunged up and kissed him.

A great wall of heat seared up through Dillon's chest.

He had never kissed a woman before.

It was excellent.

~

Rachel

Rachel wanted to stay here in Dillon's arms forever, but she didn't dare. "Dillon, people are staring at us. We'd better go sit somewhere and figure out what to do next."

"We do not have time to sit. Whoever is after us can trace our calls. They may be closing in on us now."

"I'm starving and my blood sugar's getting low. They didn't feed me anything on the plane and I'm broke. Take two minutes and buy me something to eat."

Dillon released her. In less than two minutes, they found a place that sold pizza at outrageous prices. It didn't have pepperoni and pineapple. Dillon got pepperoni. Rachel got pineapple and mushrooms and gave him her pineapples. They began walking toward the exit.

"What are we going to do?" Rachel said. "Grant sent us here but I think he was trying to screw us over while he got out of the country."

"I called Julia during my layover in Denver. I do not know if it was really her or the criminals. She said Grant told her to join him in the Caymans. She sounded confused."

"The ... Caymans?"

"Yes. Offshore banks," Dillon said. "It is an excellent place for money laundering and tax shelters. There are many wire transfers in and out."

Rachel felt her heart lurch. That pretty much proved it. "If ... Grant was planning to start a life of crime, he could ... go there and steal a few million." *The bastard.*

"He could steal a few billion." Dillon's face was sweating now. "Enough to pay his accomplices any amount of money."

"But this isn't making sense," Rachel said. "We've got the bio-computer and the software. When he saw us off, he didn't make any attempt to get them from us. So why would he send us here while he went to the Caymans? He's got nothing and he'd be crazy to trust those crooks to steal it from us and hand it over to him."

Dillon just looked at her. "How do we know he has nothing?"

"Because he ..." Rachel didn't want to say, *because he told me so.* That was so stupid it stank.

"Here is a possible scenario," Dillon said. "Grant went into the bio-lab and tried to run the software that night of the break-in. It was no break-in. He had the combination. He knew the combination of the safe too. He compiled the software—"

"Doesn't work." Rachel shook her head and bit into her pizza. "Grant doesn't know Visual C++. There's no way he could have fixed your bugs and got it to compile."

"But Julia could," Dillon said.

"She ... what?" Rachel nearly dropped her pizza.

"Before he started CypherQuanta, Grant owned a software company. One of his programmers was Julia. She has a degree in Cognitive Science."

"I ..." Rachel stared at him. "She told me that, but I wasn't even sure what it was. It's a branch of psychology, isn't it?"

"Psychology, computer science, artificial intelligence. Julia was an expert in designing human interfaces. She was very good in C++."

"Omigosh!" Rachel felt like she'd just found out her parents weren't her parents.

"There was some sort of scandal," Dillon said. "Grant's wife left him and then he married Julia. She went back to UCSD to study Russian literature and has not written a line of C++ in years, but ..."

"But it's like riding a bike, right?"

"Good programmers do not forget," Dillon said. "I have heard that Julia was extremely good."

Rachel felt like she'd been stabbed in the face. "So Grant and Julia went to the lab together, tested the software, and kept the bio-computer, leaving a small amount of it to make it look like an accident. Why?"

"I do not know." Dillon looked utterly lost.

"All right, we'll leave that for now," Rachel said. "Their main goal was to get filthy rich. Which they are now going to do. They have the bio-computer. Grant got the hard drive from the computer after we all got laid off. Which means he engineered the layoffs himself, to get rid of us. It gave him an excuse to leave the country. He took the hard drive and told us it was already gone."

Dillon was looking unhappy. "So you are telling me he had both the bio-computer and the software? And not satisfied with that, he hired some men to rob us? That does not make sense."

"Okay, so it's got some holes in it. Maybe he wanted to make sure we couldn't take anything to the government when we found out he had disappeared. But we agree that Grant's behind all this, right?"

"Something is wrong." Dillon's voice sounded strained.

"I'm sorry." Rachel was worn out. Exhausted. "If you don't like it, come up with a better theory."

"No, I mean, something is wrong over there." Dillon's eyes pointed over Rachel's left shoulder.

Rachel squatted down to tie her shoe and stole a peek behind her.

A man in a gray suit was talking into a cell phone and staring right at Dillon.

Rachel's heart slammed into overdrive. The pursuit had caught up with them. "Pretend we're fighting and chase me," she whispered. She stood up and slapped Dillon hard in the face, then stalked away.

Dillon's footsteps pursued her.

Rachel began running, hoping that Dillon would have the sense to follow.

At the end of the concourse, she jumped onto the escalators and raced down the steps and past baggage claim. She ran through the doors and out into the humid, sweltering night.

A line of taxis sat waiting.

Rachel ran up to the head of the line. "Taxi!"

A dark man in a turban flashed a row of crooked white teeth at her. He looked Indian or Pakistani or whatever. "And where is it you are wishing to be going?"

"D.C." She had no idea where she wanted to go, but she had to tell him something. "The Grand Hyatt."

He held the back door for her.

Dillon raced up. "Rachel, please!"

Rachel slid in and scooted over.

Dillon jumped in and yanked the door shut.

The driver looked at them, astonished. He tapped on the window. "Ma'am, are you wishing—"

"Drive!" Rachel screamed. "Now!"

The driver hopped around to the front seat and jumped in. "As you are wishing."

The cab lurched away.

Rachel looked out the back window and saw two men in suits race up to the taxi behind them. "Dillon ..."

"I see them." Dillon's voice sounded like death.

Rachel buried her face in her hands. This was too much. Too crazy. She couldn't spend the rest of her life running away from men in suits.

"Ma'am, are you feeling well?" asked the driver.

"No." Rachel didn't know how she felt. Exhausted. Terrified. Used up. She opened her fanny pack and took out the bio-computer.

"What are you going to do?" Dillon's voice was tight.

Rachel began rolling down the window. "I'm going to let it get smashed on the freeway. I can't take this anymore."

"Then we are both dead."

"You don't know that."

"They killed Keryn. They will not hesitate to kill us."

"How do we know that was Keryn on the phone?"

Dillon sighed. "Just before the gunshot, do you remember what she said?"

Rachel remembered. "She was ... crying to Jesus."

"That is her authenticator. Keryn would do that."

Rachel knew he was right. "Dillon, I don't want to die."

"Please roll up the window."

Rachel rolled it up. "We don't have any options."

"Grant now has a bio-computer and our software," Dillon said. "He has an excellent programmer to help him test it. The device will almost certainly work, and if it does not, the comments in my code are clear enough that Julia will be able to fix it. They are going to use it, Rachel. And their accomplices are going to ensure we are dead. We have to alert the authorities."

"Nobody would believe us," Rachel said. "Most people think this kind of technology is thirty years away."

Dillon didn't say anything.

Rachel felt sick to her stomach. "You want me to take it to the government? Just hand it over to them?"

Dillon took Rachel's hand in his. "Rachel, I will not tell you what to do. It must be your decision. Right now there are two men behind us and they have accomplices. They are well-funded and we are not. They have already killed Keryn. They intend to kill us and take what we have. They do not need it. Grant already has both a bio-computer and the software. If we destroy your bio-computer and my flash drive, they will kill us anyway. They do not want what we have. They want us dead because of what we know. We cannot keep running and we cannot hide."

"What if those guys behind us *are* the authorities?"

"They are in league with Grant. Would Grant collaborate with the authorities? Would the authorities allow him to go to the Caymans? Do you seriously believe our government would try to kill us when they could simply arrest us and confiscate what they want? Those men are criminals."

Rachel's heart was beating a ragged rhythm in her chest.

"Rachel, if I die, I will go to be with the Lord. And with ..." Dillon let out a deep sigh.

With Keryn. Rachel shut her eyes tight. She didn't believe in an afterlife. There was no way to prove such a place existed.

Of course, there was no way to prove such a place *didn't* exist, either.

Being an agnostic cut both ways.

Well, *crap.*

The bottom line was simple. If those men caught up with them, Keryn would get Dillon, or else nobody would. Probably nobody, but ...

Keryn couldn't lose and Rachel couldn't win.

Without protection, she was going to die. And nobody would protect her unless they believed she had a real, working quantum computer.

Rachel put the bio-computer back in her fanny pack and pulled out her phone.

"What are you doing?" Dillon asked.

Rachel dialed 4-1-1 and asked for the National Security Agency.

The words were bitter on her tongue.

But they were a whole lot better than dying.

CHAPTER THIRTY-SEVEN

Dillon

Late the next afternoon, Dillon finished testing. He and Rachel had been assigned two scientists to validate their claims. Dr. Weinberg was an orthodox Jewish mathematician in his mid-fifties with a thick untrimmed beard and a habit of talking very fast. Dr. Narain was much younger, probably Dillon's age, a skinny physicist who never seemed to blink and who spoke in a Mississippi accent.

"I am ready." Dillon rubbed his eyes and threw an encouraging smile at Rachel. She seemed tense. Dillon wondered whether she hoped it would succeed or fail.

Dr. Weinberg handed Dillon a CD. "Okay, here's the drill, my friend, and I'm hoping it works out for you, because this would be extraordinary, just extraordinary, if it's real. On this CD you'll find an ASCII file with six integers, each having a length between one hundred eighty and five hundred digits. What I want you to do is use your device to factor those integers."

Dillon nodded and started up the software. A text window popped up asking him to type in a number to be factored. Dillon opened the file on the CD and selected the first number. He copied and pasted it into the text window of his program and hit the Enter key.

The computer began logging the various stages in Shor's algorithm as it executed them.

Dillon felt sweat sliding down his sides.

Weinberg stood up and began pacing.

Narain leaned back and watched the screen.

A hand reached across the table and clutched Dillon's.

He took it and held it. A flush of excitement filled his veins. Whatever happened, whether the machine worked or not, he had discovered something of great value.

Dillon picked up his glass of ice water and drank deeply. He was tired, very tired. The people here at the NSA had been suspicious last night when Rachel called them with her strange and wandering tale about a quantum computer. But it did not take long for one of them to track down Rachel's former professor at Caltech, who told them that Rachel was indeed working on nanoconstruction problems when she had left Caltech. So when the taxi pulled up outside, armed marines surrounded them and spirited them into the building. The two men who had been chasing them in the taxi apparently did not even take the Fort Meade exit. So after spending the night here on site, this morning Dillon and Rachel had—

A hiss of breath.

Dillon turned to look and saw that his program had finished executing and had printed out two integers, each more than filling the width of the text window.

Dr. Weinberg pulled out a slip of paper with the correct answer printed out. He rapidly compared the numbers, muttering digits under his breath as his finger moved across the page. When he reached the end of the second number, he turned and reached out to shake Dillon's hand. "Congratulations."

Dillon backed away and pointed to Rachel. "Please shake her hand, not mine. She did all the hard work."

Rachel stood up and came and shook his hand and Dr. Narain's. Her eyes were glistening.

Weinberg picked up the phone and began dialing, talking all the while. "If you don't mind, I'd like to have one of our colleagues come watch the next one."

"Of course," Dillon said.

"Hello, Michael," Weinberg said. "Yes, the machine factored the first number correctly, a hundred eighty digits, and it chewed them up and spit out the answer. It looks like a winner, so maybe you'll want to come down and watch. I think you'll be impressed." He put the phone down. "All right, now let's see how you do on the next one. Two hundred twelve digits—that's about thirty-five times harder than the first one, if you were using a conventional algorithm."

Dillon ran the software again and fed it the two-hundred-twelve-digit number, and they waited.

"Who's coming to see this?" Rachel asked.

"My ... colleague Michael King," Dr. Weinberg said. "Really, this is quite phenomenal, wouldn't you agree, John?" He turned to Dr. Narain.

Narain nodded. "I don't understand the biology, but it seems to work. Explain to me again how you constructed so many qubits in this bio-computer."

Rachel went to the whiteboard and began drawing a complicated schematic of a cell. She drew in a double helix and an arrow labeled *mRNA* pointing to a blob labeled *tRNA + ribosome*. "I discovered a large class of proteins with slightly different magnetostatic properties, depending on the precise sequence in one stretch of base pairs. I guessed that—"

"It's finished." Weinberg whipped out his paper and rapidly checked the answer. He shook his head and grinned. "You realize that you just broke the record for the largest number ever factored?"

"Who had the record before?" Dillon asked.

Weinberg gave him a quiet smile. "You did. You set it ten minutes ago. The previous record before that was one hundred seventy-four digits. It took over thirteen thousand MIPS-years of computing power."

The door opened, and a small dark-haired man with a neat goatee stepped in.

Weinberg waved his piece of paper. "Michael, they've just factored a two-hundred-twelve-digit number into two primes. This is really quite amazing. That's about seven hundred bits and—"

"Excellent." Michael came over and shook hands with Rachel. "I'm Dr. Michael King. Dr. Meyers, it's an honor to meet you. And Dr. Richard." He shook hands with Dillon. "Now I should like to challenge your little computer to something a bit more difficult. Shall we skip straight to the five-hundred-digit problem?"

Dillon ran the program again and pasted in the last number from Weinberg's text file.

The program began churning out lines of text, logging the progress of Shor's algorithm.

They sat in silence now. Weinberg and Narain both seemed rather nervous. Dr. King leaned back in his chair, studying Rachel and Dillon and saying nothing.

Dillon poured himself more water.

Rachel bit her lip and looked like she might be about to cry.

"We're not monsters, Dr. Meyers," Dr. King said. "We solve problems. Very difficult problems. I have no doubt that you would enjoy—"

"I'm not going to come work for you," Rachel said.

"Of course." Dr. King gave her a soothing smile. "I've gathered you don't particularly admire us. Quite all right. You're well within your rights as a citizen to feel that way. Free speech and all that." He turned to look at Dillon. "And you're quite a programmer, from what I hear, Dr. Richard. Tell me more about yourself."

Rachel looked ready to bolt for the door.

Dillon had no idea what to say. This agency was part of the governing authorities, put here to maintain order. Honest people had nothing to fear from the governing authorities. It would be challenging and interesting to work for the NSA. But Rachel did not feel that way, and therefore Dillon found himself in a quandary. He had realized last night that Rachel helped complete him. They were wildly different, and yet in those differences they had strength. He did not think he would want to work here if Rachel did not.

"Dr. Richard?" Dr. King gave him a reassuring smile. "You're with friends."

Dillon shrugged. "I am an electrical engineer. I know quantum encryption and programming and a few other things."

"Would you ever consider—"

Weinberg's breath caught.

They all turned to look.

Two enormous numbers filled several lines of the text window. Weinberg pulled out his paper and compared answers, meticulously running his finger across the lines. Finally, he turned and nodded. "Another record, Michael. Really, this is more than extraordinary. It's a miracle. Give thanks to HaShem."

Michael was smiling now. He lifted the phone and punched in a number. "Monica? Bring me my laptop, if you would."

Dillon wondered what this could be about.

Michael set down the phone and began drumming his fingers on the table.

Two minutes later, a tap at the door. A young woman came in with a laptop and handed it to Michael.

He smiled up at her. "Thanks, Monica." He pulled a small flash drive out of his pocket and stuck it into the USB port. He copied a file onto the flash drive and ejected it. "Dr. Richard, I have a number here which I suspect your machine will not be able to factor."

"How many digits?" Dillon said.

"Nearly eight hundred."

Dillon plugged the flash drive into his computer and started up his software. He copied over the number, which filled up nearly ten lines of text.

The software began working.

"I'm afraid this may take a while," Michael said. "Coffee, anyone? Doughnuts?"

Dillon did not want to go anywhere. "Why do you have an eight-hundred-digit number on your laptop?"

Michael shrugged. "A pet project of mine. Tell me, how are the Padres doing this year?"

Dillon had no idea. He never followed professional sports. But it did not make sense that a man like Michael King would have a pet project of factoring an eight-hundred-digit integer. Until an hour ago, even a hundred-eighty-digit number was outrageously difficult.

Dr. Weinberg paced back and forth, muttering a strange chant under his breath. Dr. Narain did not move at all, but fixed his eyes on Rachel in a way that annoyed Dillon. Michael King sat rocking in his chair, clenching a pen in his hands. His knuckles were so white they reminded Dillon of bones.

The minutes ticked by. Dillon wondered if the device would run out of qubits. In theory it had nearly ten thousand, but—

Dr. King leaned forward and stared at the screen.

Dillon turned to look and saw that the number had been neatly factored into two.

Dr. King did not take a piece of paper out of his pocket. Instead, he transferred the results onto a file on his flash drive and brought it back to his laptop. He opened up the program *Mathematica* and used it to multiply the two numbers. *Mathematica* quickly spit out the answer. Dr. King then subtracted the original number, which gave a result of zero. He laughed softly and picked up the phone and called Monica to come get the laptop.

Dillon was staring at him. "Did you not already know the answer?"

Dr. King shook his head. "It was ... how shall we say this? It was ... a grand challenge problem. I didn't know the answer, but *Mathematica* verifies that your machine solved it correctly. As you know, multiplication is a trapdoor function. Easy to go through one way, very difficult to come back the other way."

A grand challenge problem? Dillon could not imagine who would present such a challenge.

Monica came back in and retrieved the laptop, picking it up almost reverently.

Rachel leaned across the table, and her eyes were black with anger. "Whose key was that?"

"I don't think you want to know the answer to that question," Dr. King said.

"What are you talking about?" Dillon said.

Rachel stood up and jabbed a finger at Dr. King. "You just cracked somebody's PGP key, didn't you? You did it with my technology, and you better believe I want to know who you're spying on."

Dr. King shook his head. "I'm terribly sorry, but that information is restricted."

Rachel scowled at him. "Dillon, let's go. I'm not going to let him jerk us around like this."

Dr. King sighed. "Dr. Meyers, you're quite a woman—did anyone ever tell you that?"

"Don't sweet-talk me!" Rachel strode to the NMR machine. "Come on, Dillon, let's just—"

"Dr. Meyers." Dr. King took a pair of reading glasses out of his shirt pocket and polished them on his tie. "I realize you despise what we do here, but we have a job—protecting the security of the United States. As it happens, you may be at risk if you step outside this building."

The words hung in the air.

Rachel pursed her lips and leaned against the whiteboard. "I suppose you're going to offer to make all my problems disappear, right? You'll give me a new name, new face, new ... boobs. Stick me in the Witless Protection Program."

"Something a bit better than that, but you have the basic idea—that we will guarantee your safety. In addition, we're prepared to offer you and Dr. Richard a large sum of money. Fair market value in exchange for a device of extreme importance to the United States and its citizens. And in exchange"—he held his glasses up to the light—"for a certain amount of discretion from you."

"Discretion?" Rachel asked.

"Secrecy. As I have said, we can guarantee your personal safety and a comfortable sum of money. But the value of your machine is sharply dependent on the fact that others do not know of its existence. In particular, there is a certain terrorist, whose PGP key you have just helped us crack. We do not wish for him to know that his communications are now an open book to us."

"Which terrorist?" Rachel said. "Hillary Clinton?"

Dr. King laughed curtly. "Dr. Meyers, for the record, I am a registered Democrat. Furthermore, the National Security Agency's activities are directed against foreign powers and agents of foreign powers."

"Which terrorist?"

"The Fourth Amendment strictly prohibits us or any other government agency from spying on U.S. citizens without a search warrant. Of course, the Patriot Act eases those restrictions a bit, but in any event the President's Intelligence Oversight Board ensures that we comply with all regulations."

"Which terrorist?"

Dr. King shrugged his shoulders. "We have certain documents you could sign that would make it possible for me to answer that question."

Dillon leaned forward. "Documents?"

"Swearing you to secrecy on pain of prosecution for espionage," King said. "I'm sure you've signed nondisclosure agreements in your work."

"Of course," Dillon said.

"Think of these as NDAs with a ridiculously long prison sentence attached as the penalty for violating them."

"What if we don't sign?" Rachel said.

Dr. King held up both hands in the air. "You have that option. But we are offering you protection outside these walls as part of the deal. And a sizable sum of—"

"You can't hold us prisoner here," Rachel said. "If we want to leave, we'll leave."

Dillon sighed. "Rachel, if we leave here without protection, whoever was pursuing us will ... find us. We cannot escape them."

"Precisely," Dr. King said. "Whereas, we can offer you a rather complete protection package."

Rachel slumped into a chair. "What do you think, Dillon? Are you going to sign?"

Dillon did not see any choice. "Yes."

Rachel's eyes gleamed. Two small teardrops leaked down her cheeks and shattered on the table. She stared at Dr. King for a long time. Finally, she sighed. "All right, I'll sign. But first you tell me, who was that terrorist?"

"As a matter of formality, you'll need to sign the papers before I can give you a name. But you know perfectly well which terrorist we want more than any other."

Dillon felt his heart lurch.

"You're just throwing crap in our eyes," Rachel said.

"What a charming visual, Dr. Meyers."

Dillon leaned forward. "Are ... will you be able to catch him now?"

"Only time will tell. The trail has gone rather cold. Fortunately, nobody is perfect. At some point, our friend will make a mistake and the trail will warm up again. And the gentleman in question has hundreds of comrades using encrypted communications. We'll soon be reading their mail and preparing a surprise for each one of them. A very well-deserved surprise, complete with seventy virgins—or perhaps seventy-two—theological opinions differ."

Dr. King picked up the phone and dialed. "Monica? If you could bring those documents down now, I believe our guests are ready to sign." He paused. "Yes, have them wait." He set down the phone. "It'll be just a few minutes. I believe you'll be quite pleased with what we're prepared to do for you."

~

Rachel

Rachel could not believe she had agreed to sign. She felt like puking. She had always thought that she would rather die than give the NSA her bio-computer. But it was a lot harder to be high-minded after hearing your friend screaming to Jesus in the last half-second before some evil bastard blew her brains out. "Dr. King? Could I talk to Dillon alone for a minute?"

"Of course." Dr. King stood up and led Dr. Weinberg and Dr. Narain out.

Dillon was looking at her with wide eyes. "Are you feeling all right, Rachel?"

"I'm totally freaking out," Rachel said. She walked over and sat down next to Dillon. "Listen, they're going to offer us a ton of money.

New identities. New lives. We'll never be able to see our friends and family again. No phone, no e-mail, no letters."

Dillon appeared to be in physical pain. "I will ... never be able to see Robert's children. To meet his wife."

"That's right. And what I was thinking ..." Rachel took Dillon's hand in both of hers. "Listen, it'll be a whole lot easier on both of us if we've got someone along from our old life."

Dillon looked up at her sharply and his mouth hung open.

Rachel laughed. "Don't look at me like that. I know how you feel about me."

Dillon's face colored.

"You called me Keryn on the phone yesterday. And when I kissed you, you kissed back. You're an amateur, but I bet you'd learn quick with a little coaching."

"Rachel." Dillon's voice wavered. "You are an attractive woman. But I think we have some serious differences."

"Differences make life interesting. I'm yin. You're yang. I'm fire. You're ice. I'm quantum mechanics. You're gravity."

His eyes clouded. "I ... it has been an extremely difficult week."

Rachel reached up and stroked his face. "You had some serious differences with Keryn too."

Dillon's face was unreadable.

"It's been a horrible week for both of us." Rachel got out of her chair and sat on Dillon's lap. "We're going to miss her, both of us. There'll always be a hole in our hearts where she was. But ... we're alive and we've got a lot of years ahead of us. We can't live in the past."

Dillon's whole body began shaking.

Rachel didn't know quite what to do. Empathy had never been her strong suit.

Something wet fell on her hand.

She tilted her head and kissed the tears rolling down Dillon's cheeks. "It's okay, Dillon. Let it out."

Dillon wrapped his arms around her and wept.

For several long minutes, they sat like that.

Finally Rachel grabbed a napkin from the tray of drinks on the table. "Here, blow your nose." She wiped his face and kissed his eyelids.

His eyes fluttered open. He took the napkin and blew his nose and threw it on the table.

A tap at the door.

Rachel could not imagine a worse time for an interruption. She stalked to the door and jerked it open.

Michael King stood there with a bland smile on his face. "I've got those papers for you to sign."

Rachel wanted to punch his infuriating little lights out. "I told you we wanted some privacy."

"You said nothing of the sort. You said you wished to talk for a minute. It has been several minutes."

Rachel put her hands on her hips and glared at him, wondering if he'd been listening in the whole time. She wouldn't put it past him.

Dillon came up beside her. "I believe we are both ready to sign." His throat sounded a little hoarse, and his eyes were red, but his face was a blank wall.

Dr. King nodded. "I hope you'll find that we have several attractive options for you." He held up a thick sheaf of paper. "It will take some minutes to explain the details."

Rachel

In fact it took over an hour. Dr. King explained in great detail the requirements for secrecy and the penalties for violating them. Rachel nodded vaguely through them all. Basically, she couldn't tell a soul anything—couldn't ever hint that there was a bio-computer or that large integers could be factored. Failure to comply ... blah, blah, blah ... would result in prison sentences approximately twice the age of the universe ... yada, yada. That was the stick.

The carrot was rather nicer than Rachel had guessed. She was being paid a flat fee of $53.2 million. She had no idea who came up with that number or how it was calculated. Dr. King gave her a long explanation about the commercial value of "the product" and something called a "mortality factor" that accounted for the fact that her odds of living to commercialize the product on her own were about the same as getting struck by lightning on the way home from winning the lottery.

Dillon was getting a fee of $14.7 million for the software. Apparently, they thought he hadn't worked as hard. Whatever.

In exchange for that, the United States Government and its agents promised to take all reasonable actions to keep them both alive ... Yakkity-yak. Rachel had a sick feeling in her stomach. What did *reasonable* mean? But she didn't see any better options. Walking loose from here with an out-of-date driver's license and five dollars in cash wasn't all that appealing.

Dillon signed.

Rachel signed and then slapped the pen down on the table, hoping she wouldn't regret this. She leaned over and kissed Dillon on the ear. "Guess we're rich, Little Brother."

Michael King gathered all the papers together and gave them both a polished smile. "Now then, that's taken care of. I believe I have a pleasant little surprise for you. Some visitors."

Rachel narrowed her eyes. "Who?"

King opened the door. "Some parties interested in your achievement. Experts in the field. Please come with me."

Rachel felt a rush of fury in her veins. It was bad enough to sell her soul. Now she was going to have her brains picked clean by the vultures.

Dillon patted Rachel's hand. "Rachel, relax. He said it would be a pleasant surprise."

They followed Dr. King down the hall and around a corner.

He stopped at a door and smiled at them both. "A private little suite where I hope you'll be more comfortable."

Rachel doubted that very much. She wanted to turn and run.

King knocked at the door.

The knob rattled and the door swung inward.

Grant and Julia stood there.

Rachel screamed.

CHAPTER THIRTY-EIGHT

Grant

Grant hadn't known what to expect, but a scream was low on his list. "Rachel, what's wrong?" He stepped forward.

Rachel slapped him. "You ... filthy bastard!"

Grant staggered back, clutching his face. "Ouch, what's all this about?"

Michael King stepped in. "Oh dear, this won't do, Dr. Meyers. You should be celebrating your new-found wealth together—old friends who've come through a tight spot and are still in one piece."

"Rachel, won't you come in and talk?" Julia said. "We've had quite an upsetting couple of days."

Rachel was staring at them both, looking bewildered.

Dr. King took Rachel's arm and led the way into the room. "Rachel, please be assured that Grant and Julia have done you no harm. Come along, Dillon. I hope you'll be able to contain your enthusiasm a bit better than the impetuous Dr. Meyers."

Grant took Julia's hand and limped back into the suite. He heaved himself into an overstuffed chair. Julia sat protectively on the arm of the chair and draped herself above him.

Rachel and Dillon sat in chairs across from Grant, giving him the kind of look usually reserved for dead rats and live congressmen.

"Very good, then!" Dr. King said. "It seems we may have a slight failure to communicate among you friends. Let me invite you all to discuss things as adults." He pointed to the bar. "And may I suggest a round of refreshments? You are all, as of today, quite wealthy." King bowed himself out and shut the door.

"What happened at the airport yesterday?" Dillon said.

Grant shook his head. "I went to my gate and got on my plane. It was America West to Phoenix. Just before takeoff, a couple of men with FBI badges came on the plane and down the aisle with my picture. When they found me, they asked me to come off the plane."

Rachel's mouth fell open in the shape of a tiny O.

Dillon looked expressionless, but his eyes bored into Grant.

Grant's heart began racing at the memory. "Guys, I thought I was dogmeat. I knew that FBI impersonators had killed Keryn. I was sure they were going to kill me too, but what could I do? I didn't have any weapons. Nothing. So I went." Grant felt hot all of a sudden. He leaned back and started shaking.

Julia bent down and fanned him. "They escorted him off the plane and took his cell phone. We think they used it to call me. You know, they have some amazing software these days that they can program to sound like anybody's voice. Over a phone, you can't tell the difference from the real thing anymore. Anyway, that's the only way I can think that they left that ridiculous message on my voice mail about going to the Caymans. I didn't know what to do. I've never been to the Caymans, and it just didn't smell right. Then Dillon called me from Denver and I knew something was awfully wrong."

Dillon's face relaxed. "So that was the real you I talked to?"

"That was her," Grant said. "About fifteen minutes after you called her, who showed up at her hotel but a couple of nice men with FBI badges."

"They tracked the phone," Rachel said.

"Apparently." Grant felt incredibly stupid. "I'm sorry, guys. I spent a lot of money in Mexico to get those fake licenses for you. The Visa cards are real. The cell phones—I thought they were secure, or what passes for secure in this crazy world."

"So you both got arrested?" Rachel asked. "Were they real FBI?"

"We don't think so," Julia said. "They brought Grant to join me and kept us locked up in our hotel room for a few hours. Then one of them got a call on his cell phone. They bolted out of there like they were on fire. We were scared to death—didn't know whether to stay or run. Not thirty seconds later, men from the Hostage Rescue Team came charging in with guns. They were the real thing, and after they debriefed us, they kept us under guard overnight and then put us on a plane with a couple of bodyguards to come out here, for our own safety. Dr. King met us and told us you two had come in too."

Rachel had a strange look on her face. "Sorry, but something isn't computing here." She leaned back in her chair and put her feet up on the seat. "How much did you get for signing the NDA, Uncle Grant?"

"A bit over eleven million," Grant said. "Plus, they promised to put heat on the board of CypherQuanta. This Michael King guy dug up some dirt on Lost Angels. Turns out there's a way to push them out completely, because they violated the terms of our contract. I'm gonna get my company back free and clear with an exclusive contract to make encryption devices for Uncle Sam. They guarantee purchases of a couple of thousand machines right off the bat. In this economy, that gives us a lot of stability. And I can sell to any other customers I can drum up."

Rachel's face had gone a light shade of green. "With certain restrictions, right?"

"Well ... yes." Grant shrugged. He'd had to compromise on that, but when it was a question of staying alive, a guy could bend a little. "Anything I sell to a private or foreign entity will have a backdoor in it that lets the Feds take a peek. Same rules as for wiretapping—they need a court order. And I can't say a word to anyone about Rachel's bio-computer. Which means we ain't gonna scare the world into buying billions of our machines, but hey, we're alive. And the world gets privacy from everyone except ... Big Brother." He gave Rachel an apologetic shrug. "Sorry. It was that or get eaten by the big bad wolf."

Rachel looked like she was going to have a stroke.

Grant didn't see what her gripe was. She was getting more money than he was, by a long shot. "Guys, the only explanation I can see is that Clifton sold us down the river to the Mafia or someone. He's been acting real suspicious ever since this thing started. He's been getting phone calls he won't explain. Somehow he must have gotten the combination to the bio-lab. I bet he was the one who stole Rachel's bio-computer. After the layoffs, he disappeared, and so did that hard drive. We're down to one suspect and Clifton's it, the little weasel."

Julia leaned over and put her hand on Grant's shoulder. "I never did like the way he always talks to my chest. It's like I haven't got a head."

Dillon looked sick.

Rachel had her face buried in her hands as if she were trying to erase the whole world.

Grant didn't think he blamed her. Thanks to Clifton, they could all have been killed.

Rachel came and knelt beside Grant. "I'm sorry for slapping you. I ... we thought you betrayed us."

"Don't mention it," Grant said. "We've all kind of had double vision lately. After a while, you don't know who to trust." He sighed deeply. "I guess it won't take long for the Feds to track Clif down. I hope they throw him in the slammer for life."

A knock at the door.

Nobody moved.

It opened and Michael King stepped in, smiling at them all benignly. "Oh, very good. It appears that peace has broken out again. Excellent." He turned back to the hallway. "Clifton, come along. Don't be shy."

Grant thought he was going to have a heart attack.

Clifton Potter shambled into the room, looking guilty as sin. "Hi, guys," he said in a small voice.

King stepped to the door, beaming. "Very well, then. I'll just leave you all to smooth over any minor misunderstandings."

Clifton

Clifton took a chair and scanned the circle. This was going to be gnarly. All four of them looked pretty chafed. Which was only natural, considering what a wally he'd been. "I'm sorry, guys," he said.

Grant was glowering at him. "I take it you're responsible for all this mess?"

Clifton couldn't look at him. "I ... guess so. I didn't mean to. It just kind of ... happened."

"You just kind of accidentally kidnapped Keryn?" Rachel said.

Clifton felt like she'd taken a hammer to his face. "Whoa, dudes and dudettes. I don't know what you think I did, but kidnapping was never on the menu."

Julia glowered at him. "Oh. Well, suppose you tell us what you did, then."

Clifton took a deep breath. "I didn't ask for that headhunter to call me. He just called, out of the blue."

"Ted Hunter the headhunter?" Dillon said.

"Dillon Dude, you score!" Clifton said. "He said that was his name, anyway. Had a really spiff interview lined up at Qualcomm and asked was I interested." Clifton didn't want to look at Grant. "Ordinarily, I wouldn't be, ya know. Only wallies go around job-hopping. But the last couple weeks haven't exactly been ordinary, know what I mean?"

Clifton saw from their faces that they knew. "Anyway, so I said maybe. I didn't say yes and I didn't say no. I kind of stalled them. I figured if Dillon Man and Rachelette hit the big pony, then there was no way I'd be interested in the Q. But if they struck out, well, I might as well keep my options open."

Dillon looked like he was getting it now. "So you broke into the bio-lab that Friday night?"

"Bingo!" Clifton jabbed a finger at him. "Dillon Man gets another point. I didn't really break in. That first day we all went over there, I snarfed the keypad combination by just watching Grant push the buttons. Same thing with Rachel's password and the safe combination a couple days later when Rachel was showing me everything. You guys really need to work on your paranoia. Anyway, Friday night, after

Dillon and the Rache Woman went home, I just went over to have a look. Rachel had sworn on the phone it was ready to test. All I wanted was to know whether that software was gonna come up winners or losers."

"Did you leak that bio-computer or did you steal it?" Rachel asked.

Clifton felt like an idiot. "It leaked. It was an accident, and I didn't find out till the next day. I loaded it into the NMR machine and compiled the software and fixed a couple glitches in Dillon's code. They were just minor things. I got the code to build and run, but it wouldn't calibrate. I walked through it in debug mode and finally realized I was just wallying around so I decided to bail and come back the next day. But I was afraid you guys would guess I'd been in there and change the lock, so I figured I had to add in my own keypad combination. Then it took me forever to find the manual for the security system. Rachel hid it in the filing cabinet."

"I *cleaned* my desk," Rachel said. "I didn't hide anything."

"Took me two hours to find it," Clifton said. "Then when I left, I forgot to put the bio-computer back in the safe."

"And you had put it in upside down to begin with and probably loosened the top enough so it leaked on the floor," Rachel said.

"A point to Goldilocks!" Clifton said. "I biffed things up bad. I'm sorry, dudes."

Grant cleared his throat. "What else did you do?"

Clifton looked up, mystified. "What *else*? Wasn't all that bad enough? That got Rachel and Dillon setting fire to each other's shorts, and I just sat there and couldn't say a thing. We lost time and it was my fault."

"And you stole the hard drive?" Grant said.

Clifton's heart thumped in his chest. "Stole it? No way! I rescued it."

"Meaning what?" Dillon said.

"Meaning, after I took the crew over to Karl Strauss, I got to thinking that our prize software was sitting unattended in the bio-lab. Oh yeah, by that time I knew Rachel had a spare copy of the bio-computer. Sorry, guys, but I spied on you. I left a recording gizmo in the lab. So I knew we had to secure that hard drive, even if it was just slightly illegal. I drove over there and grabbed the hard drive and stuck it in my safe deposit box. I did that for you, Grant. I figured you paid for that software, and I was gonna keep it safe for you."

Grant's eyes narrowed. "It would have helped if you'd told me."

"Couldn't get hold of you," Clifton said.

"I was a little out of commission that night," Grant said.

"He was stone drunk." Julia bent over and kissed his bald head. "The wisest thing he could have done under the circumstances."

"Gotcha," Clifton said. "When I got home and told Cindy what happened with the layoffs, she said we ought to go down to Baja and drown our sorrows in some surfing. So we drove down that night and camped out for a few days and caught some waves."

"Who's this Cindy?" Rachel said.

"My lady."

"His girlfriend," Grant said. "Why didn't she come out here?"

Clifton shrugged. "She wasn't invited. We got back to La Jolla last night and found some gentlemen eager to invite me out for some, quote—discussions of mutual interest—unquote. Sounded bogus, but they turned out not to be interested in my opinion of the matter. Meaning, they gave me no choice. So I flew out this morning with one of them babysitting me. Biff dude. Couldn't crack a smile to save his wife."

"So basically, you can't account for about five days." Grant looked as if somebody had stolen his Lexus.

Clifton didn't understand what the problem was. "Hey, I'm just saying—"

"Uncle Grant, it's okay," Rachel said. "I believe him."

"Well, I don't." Grant scowled at Clifton. "There's a hole a mile wide in his story."

"Clif, how much did you get for signing the NDA?" Rachel said.

"Almost as much as Grant," Clifton said. "Just over seven million. Pretty sweet, plus I keep all my stock in CypherQuanta and Lost Angels is out in the cold and we're back in business selling widgets to Uncle. Life could be worse."

Grant shook his head. "There's a whole lot that isn't explained yet. There's a carjacking, a kidnapping, a murder, my arrest, and a whole bunch of harassment that somebody's got to take the blame for. If it isn't Clifton, then I'd like to know who it is."

The phone rang.

Rachel picked it up and listened for several seconds, then slammed it down. "That was Michael King. He says he'd like to come by and answer Grant's questions."

Clifton felt violated. "You mean that King dude's been listening in on all this?"

"Surprise, surprise," Rachel muttered.

A knock at the door.

Clifton leaned back in his chair. Grant and Julia didn't move.

Another knock, more insistent.

"Come on, Dillon." Rachel grabbed his hand and tugged him toward the door. "Let's go scratch out that bastard's eyes."

Clifton watched them walk together to the door, holding hands. It hadn't occurred to him until now that maybe they were an item. *Spiff*.

Before they reached the door, it swung open.

Standing there, wearing a light blue silk dress, was Keryn Wills.

CHAPTER THIRTY-NINE

Dillon

Dillon had been hit in the head once by a baseball bat in grade school. He should have been standing behind the backstop, but he was not paying attention to the game, and when Lizzy Robles swung and missed and the bat flew out of her hands, he did not see it.

But he felt it.

The school nurse gave him an ice pack on his head and shone a light in his eyes and called his mother and she came and took him home. Dillon spent the rest of the day in a haze. His head ached and there was a deep pain in his chest and he got dizzy when he tried to stand.

Seeing Keryn alive again made Dillon feel like that.

He heard Rachel scream.

Saw Keryn step toward him, her eyes shining.

Felt his legs turn as unstable as jelly.

A great roaring sound filled his ears.

He could not tell which direction was up.

Keryn threw her arms around him.

The smell of her perfume pierced his heart.

She pressed her soft and warm lips to his and kissed him.

Dillon felt like somebody had put a blowtorch to his brains.

From somewhere far away, Rachel was saying, "Omigosh! Omigosh!" over and over.

Behind it all, Michael King was chuckling softly. "I take it we're witnessing the reunion of *friends?*"

Keryn broke off the kiss, and then her cheeks turned bright red. "Oh! Dillon, I'm so sorry. I didn't mean ..."

Dillon kissed her back.

It was more than excellent.

~

Keryn

Keryn held Dillon for a long time, crushing him to herself, bawling her eyes out. She had lost him once. She was never going to lose him again.

Finally, she heard Grant's gravelly voice. "Let me look at her, Dillon."

Dillon's strong arms released their grip.

Rachel clutched Keryn's arm. "Thank goodness you're alive, Keryn."

"Sweetheart, we thought you were dead," Julia said.

"She looks pretty alive to me," Clifton said. "Somebody explain to me what happened to her."

"I ..." Keryn suddenly felt weak. "I think I'd better sit down."

They led her into the suite and everybody sat down. Keryn sat next to Dillon and took his right hand in both of hers.

Rachel sat on his left, very close to him.

For once, Keryn didn't care what Rachel did. The way Dillon had kissed her told her that any competition from Rachel was over. Way over.

Michael King had discreetly disappeared.

Rachel leaned right up against Dillon. "Keryn, we were so scared!

We heard you scream over the phone and then a gunshot and then ... nothing."

Keryn felt the same rush of terror that had slugged her in the gut when it happened. "When they opened the trunk, I screamed. Then one of them shoved a sock in my mouth. Another one fired his gun into the dirt. Then they took out this laptop and played a recording that sounded an awful lot like Clifton telling them to shoot me again. They fired into the ground again, and then ... they put some chemical over my nose and I passed out."

Dillon squeezed her hand. "So Clifton was not there?"

"Of course I wasn't there." Clifton sounded insulted.

Keryn shivered. "There were three men, all in suits."

"Were they FBI?" Rachel asked.

"I ... don't think so," Keryn said. "When I came to, I was in a hotel room with a doctor and nurse and some military-looking guys. Apparently, somebody had rescued me while I was unconscious. I haven't gotten a straight story from anybody yet on what happened. Early this morning, a federal marshal came and escorted me to the airport and flew out here with me. He was awfully nice, but he couldn't tell me anything I didn't know. He said we were coming here for my safety."

"Thank God they found you," Dillon said.

She smiled at him shyly. "Dillon, they explained all about what the bio-computer will do for them. They offered me a little over four million to sign some secrecy papers. I'll ... I'll be able to quit my job and write full time."

"Hold on, everyone," Rachel said. "Something really sucks with this story."

Everybody looked at her.

Keryn didn't see what could be wrong with being alive and having four million dollars.

Rachel took Dillon's hand and held it in hers. "They told me and Dillon we'd have to go into hiding. That we'd have to get plastic surgery and live in Wyoming or somewhere and never talk to our family again."

Keryn gasped. "Never? They ... nobody told me that. I thought we could just ... go free."

"Nobody told me that either," Grant said. "I'm going to be running CypherQuanta. Right, Clif?"

Clifton nodded. "If those wallies are jerking us around—"

The door swung open without a knock and Michael King ambled in. "Ah, very good, it seems that all is now righteousness and peace among our merry band."

CHAPTER FORTY

Rachel

Rachel had never hated anyone as much as she hated Michael King. "You ... you lying, evil bastard!"

Dr. King raised his eyebrows. "My dear Rachel, flattery will get you nowhere."

She picked up her can of Coke and threw it at him.

He made no move to dodge.

The can hit him in the chest. Coke splashed onto his suit.

He flicked off little droplets with his fingers. "Really, perhaps you might want to invest in some anger management classes. I'm told you can well afford the cost."

"You've been spying on us all, haven't you?" Rachel shouted.

"Spying?" A wounded look spread across Dr. King's face. "Dr. Meyers, whatever gave you that idea?"

Rachel wanted to spit on him. "How about if I tell you a little story, shall I?"

King nodded calmly. "Please do. I'm sure we all enjoy a good story, even if it is mere fiction." He threw a benevolent smile toward Keryn. "Not meaning to cast aspersions, of course."

"Once upon a time, there was a certain Big Brother," Rachel said. "And he learned through his web of contacts that Little Brother was developing technology he might be interested in. So he made sure that Little Brother got into deep financial water. He pulled strings to get a key customer to pull out of a signed contract."

Grant's face had gone pale.

Rachel sat down on the coffee table. "Naturally, Little Brother took desperate measures to bring the technology to completion. Big Brother didn't have a search warrant, so he sent a headhunter to pulse Little Brother." Rachel turned to look at Clifton. "He made an offer nobody in their right mind could refuse. But Little Brother refused it. Big Brother now had probable cause to tap Little Brother's phones. Then he watched to see what Little Brother would do."

Dr. King wasn't saying anything. He stood leaning against the wall with an amused smile on his face.

Rachel scowled at him. "Quicker than anybody would have imagined, Little Brother got his new technology working. Big Brother pulled more strings, and all of a sudden, Little Brother had a financial collapse. Big Brother sent out his hired guns to steal Little Brother's technology, but he didn't try very hard, because stealing it would be illegal and would raise a stink. So he scared the wits out of Little Brother. He let Little Brother go tearing around town making midnight runs and getting shot at with blanks. He let Little Brother buy phony ID and new cell phones, and all the while Big Brother was watching every move. He was tapping Little Brother's calls, using the GPS in his phone to keep tabs on him, watching him with spy cameras in robotic planes. When the time was right, Big Brother decided to scare Little Brother straight. So he kidnapped Little Brother and faked his murder."

Keryn sat with her mouth open, staring at Rachel. A thin sheen of sweat covered her forehead.

Rachel stood up and jabbed her finger at Dr. King. "Big Brother knew that if things got too hot, Little Brother would break down and offer the technology to Big Brother. But there was a problem. Little Brother had a little sister named Goldilocks who didn't want to sell, and nobody could make her sell. So Goldilocks had to be chased across the country. Big Brother could have caught Goldilocks anytime he wanted, but he didn't. He chased her and chased her, just hard enough to scare her to death, until finally she went to Big Brother of her own free will and sold it to him."

Rachel glared at Dr. King. "How does that sound?"

King gave her an innocent smile. "An outlandish story, Dr. Meyers. Completely outlandish. And conveniently unfalsifiable."

"It explains all the facts," Rachel said.

"It gives that appearance, as all unfalsifiable hypotheses do, but it's missing one essential element."

Rachel put her hands on her hips. "Namely, what?"

"Motive," Dr. King said. "If this mythical Big Brother were so powerful, he could steal whatever he wanted with much less trouble. There is no conceivable motive for Big Brother to undertake this"—he flicked his fingers in the air—"preposterous scheme."

"Yes, there is." Dillon stood up.

Rachel stared at him, astonished.

Dillon's face was a mask of fury.

~

Dillon

Dillon rolled up the nondisclosure agreement he had signed a few hours earlier. He wanted to punch Michael King in the face, but he did not think that would help matters. He stepped up to King and handed him the documents. "I have changed my mind. I do not want to sign these."

King gave him a half smile. "Regrettably, that option is no longer open to you. You have already signed them. I have an official copy in my office."

"Suppose I want my signature back?" Dillon said. "Suppose I am experiencing buyer's remorse?"

"First, let me point out that you are a seller, not a buyer," King said. "Second, there is no cooling-off period in sales of this nature."

"If I walk outside this building and hold a press conference—"

"Then you will be prosecuted to the fullest extent of the law," King said. "The documents you signed prohibit you from making any public disclosure of the nature of the sale."

Dillon felt rage surging through his veins. "That is all? You will not have me kidnapped or killed?"

Dr. King shook his head. "Unfortunately, operations of that nature are prohibited now. I do sometimes wish for the good old days, but ... no, you would not be killed. Waterboarded, to be sure, but there would be no messy corpses. It simply creates too much paperwork."

Dillon had never felt so betrayed. Everything Rachel had said was true. They had been manipulated by the governing authorities. Big Brother had ... prevaricated. Not merely to buy their machine but also their silence in perpetuity. That was unacceptable. Highly unacceptable.

"Please have a seat, Dr. Richard," King said. "There is no reason to—"

Dillon turned on his heel and strode toward the door.

"Excuse me, but where do you think you're going?" Dr. King said.

Dillon yanked open the door. "I am going to tell the truth."

A slow smile spread across King's face.

Dillon could not understand the social context of this smile. Dr. King should be terrified. His entire scam had been designed to force them all into this pact of silence. But the pact was wrong. It was evil. Rachel's deepest fears had proved true. Big Brother would be able to spy on whomever it wished, and nobody would know. Dillon could not accept this. He would have to tell the truth. To do otherwise was to prevaricate.

"That wouldn't be wise, I'm afraid," Dr. King said.

Dillon stared at him. If they sent him to prison, then he would go to prison.

Dr. King turned and pointed toward Rachel and Keryn. "It would be a pity if you spread a malicious tale about your own government and found yourself isolated from such friends as these for the next fifty years."

Dillon's heart felt like it was trapped in a vise.

"Dillon, it's not worth it." Keryn hurried past Dr. King and clutched Dillon's arm. "Please. Don't throw your life away on this. We don't have any proof."

Dillon wavered. Was it possible he was mistaken? It was true that he had no proof that Dr. King had done any of the things Rachel had accused him of. All the facts fit Rachel's story, but ... those same facts had also seemed to convict both Grant and Clifton. The facts had seemed to prove that Keryn was dead. A hypothesis that fit the facts perfectly was not enough. There might always be a new fact that broke the hypothesis.

Rachel staggered toward Dillon. "I ... I think Keryn's right. We don't have any proof. They've set things up so we'll never have any proof. We'll look like one of those idiot conspiracy theorists. Don't put yourself in jail when it won't accomplish anything. Let's just ... go."

"Is it safe?" Dillon asked. "Out there?"

Dr. King smiled. "If you trust this outlandish tale of Miss Meyers', then you will be perfectly safe 'out there.' If you trust me instead, then I will say only that I personally guarantee your safety 'out there,' so long as you abide by our agreement. You are free to go wherever you like."

Rachel grabbed his arm and tugged. "Let's get out of here. Now."

"Go where?" Dillon said. "We may be rich on paper, but we do not have any cash."

Rachel turned to Dr. King. "I assume you were planning to find us a hotel for the night?"

"Of course, of course," Dr. King said. "I meant to tell you when I came in. We've already made arrangements at a place I'm sure will be suitable for you all. I've taken the liberty of sending for a limousine."

"A limousine?" Rachel said. "Isn't that a little excessive? It must create a lot of ... paperwork."

"Not at all. The cost will be deducted from your new-found wealth. But I'm sure you'll agree that it is worth the price. A visit to the Grand Hyatt is best experienced with a bit of flair."

CHAPTER FORTY-ONE

Dillon

D illon found it hard to go to sleep that night. The day had brought many surprises. He had woken up this morning not knowing if the bio-computer would work, not knowing why Keryn was murdered, not knowing who had pursued him and Rachel across the country.

Now he knew the answers to all these questions.

The bio-computer worked perfectly. Keryn was not dead but alive. Rachel and he were no longer pursued.

The entire episode was a grand illusion, designed to drive them all willingly into the arms of the governing authorities. Michael King would deny this, hiding behind his bland smile, but it was the best inference from the data.

The proof was trivial. Dr. King had given them no new identity, no special protection. Why? Because he himself had architected the whole vile charade. They were perfectly safe because he was no longer a danger to them. That was the only way he could have assured them of their safety now.

Dillon had yet more proof. Dr. King had even known the exact destination Rachel had given the taxi driver when they fled the BWI airport—this hotel, the Grand Hyatt in Washington, D.C. That could not be a coincidence. Somehow, Michael King had spied on them even in the taxi.

Dillon felt sick at heart. The governing authorities were supposed to protect the citizens, not prevaricate to them. This was evil, and he had signed a sworn statement to keep it secret. If he violated the confidentiality of his agreement, terrorists would go free, while he himself would be deprived of his freedom and his friends.

All his world was now bent, and how could he unbend it?

Dillon

T he next morning, Dillon woke up early. A terrible confusion clouded his mind. He showered and dressed and went down to the lobby. A large part of the floor of the lobby was cut out so that he could see down to a shallow pool in the lower level. A grand piano sat on a small island in the pool. The atrium was twelve stories tall, lit by skylights in the roof. Light filled the whole interior. Darkness filled Dillon's soul.

Dillon looked up at the rows of windows, all the way up. Behind each window, a hidden room, secrets. People were like that too. They hid secrets that you could never know, however long you studied them from the outside. Clifton had deceived them all after the break-in, saying nothing when he could have ended the controversy at once. Keryn had a secret past that nobody would ever have guessed. Rachel, Grant, Julia—each of them was different on the outside than the inside.

The governing authorities were supposed to be honest and open, but they were not. In order to do good, they had done great evil.

Dillon found that he could not breathe, could not think. He got a map at the desk and went outside the hotel and walked down 10th Street toward the Mall. He passed Ford's Theatre, where President Lincoln was shot. He passed the FBI Building and the Justice Department, both dedicated to a justice Dillon would never have faith in again.

When he reached Constitution Avenue, he turned right and walked toward the Washington Monument. He desperately wanted to see the city from above. To change his perspective. He found his way to a little booth on 15th Street that sold tickets. None were on sale. The tickets were free, but they had all been given out for the day. Dillon checked his watch. Already past 9:00. The booth opened at 8:00.

He wandered aimlessly back down the Mall in the direction of the far-off Capitol. On his right he saw the National Air and Space Museum. Dillon went inside and passed through the security line. He walked underneath the original airplane flown by the Wright brothers. Saw the Spirit of St. Louis, flown by Lindbergh across the Atlantic. Peered inside the window of a couple of the earliest capsules ridden by astronauts into space.

None of it gave him any joy. Machines were wonderful things, able to make life easier and more interesting. But people were more wonderful. People were more important than things or ideas. Souls were more precious than gold. If he had learned anything in this whole sorry episode, it was that.

He now had more money than he had ever imagined. Yet he felt impoverished. He did not have love in his heart. He did not know the first thing about love. He had thought, for a moment, that he was in love with Keryn. Then he had thought he was in love with Rachel. But something was wrong, and that thing was himself. He was a double-minded man.

He, Dillon Richard, was bent. How could this have happened? All his life he had pursued the straight way. Even so, he was bent. Only a bent man could be in love with two different women. Only a bent man would have double vision. He was no better than Michael King, who had deceived them all. In fact, he was worse, because he had deceived himself.

Dillon sat in a chair and tried to think how he had gone wrong. He could not blame this on his Asperger's syndrome. That would be a prevarication. An easy way to evade responsibility. He was what he was because of his decisions. Every decision he had ever made had been a turning point in the great maze of the multiverse. He was the sum of a vast welter of decisions. If he was wrong now, it was because he had made wrong decisions. He could undo the wrong in his life by unmaking his wrong decisions.

But which ones?

Dillon's cell phone rang. He took it out and saw that Julia was calling. He flipped open the phone. "Good morning, Julia."

"Dillon, honey, where are you? Grant and I knocked on your door before we came down to brunch, but you didn't answer."

"I am not hungry."

"That's okay, honey. I just wanted to make sure you hadn't been kidnapped or killed or kissed or anything. Where are you?"

"In the National Air and Space Museum."

Julia laughed. "Why am I not surprised? Listen, why don't you come join us?"

Dillon did not want to deal with a complicated situation right now. "Are you with Rachel and Keryn?"

"No. Rachel's probably still sleeping. Keryn was here earlier, but she's gone up to her room. You need to come back to the hotel, Dillon. We have some things to talk about."

Dillon sighed. If only he had some time to himself, he could straighten out his bent universe.

"Dillon, are you coming? Grant really needs to see you."

Dillon stood up. "I can be there in about fifteen minutes."

"That'll be wonderful, dear. Ta-ta!" Julia hung up.

Dillon put his phone away and began walking. His own problems would have to wait. Grant needed him. If he owed anyone allegiance, it was Grant, who had been like a ... like a father to him.

Dillon swallowed a great lump in his throat and began walking.

Keryn

Keryn had brunch with Grant and Julia and Clifton in the Grand Café on the lower level of the hotel. She didn't know where Rachel was, and she didn't care. But Dillon was another matter. She really, really wanted to talk to him.

Grant and Clifton were already making plans for the new and vastly better-financed CypherQuanta. There were board members to get rid of. Facilities to rent. Production schedules to set up. Keryn was not much interested in all this. She intended to quit her job and write full time. Julia said little during the meal, but she kept catching Keryn's eye from across the table and winking at her.

After they finished, Clifton went back to his room to get some paper and pens for further brainstorming. Grant sat in a chair near the fountain. Julia caught Keryn's elbow. "That was a lovely dress you were wearing yesterday. I'd love to get some photos of you wearing it. Something to remember this trip by."

Keryn sighed and felt her insides melt. It would be awesome to have a photo of herself in the dress she'd been wearing when Dillon first kissed her. Of all the horrible things that had happened in the last couple of weeks, that was the one good thing. She hurried up to her room and changed.

Down in the lobby, Julia had her camera ready. "Just have a seat at the piano, dear."

Keryn took off her shoes and stepped across the four-foot gap onto the island. She edged around and sat down on the piano bench. It was an old-fashioned player piano, with an actual paper tape loaded up.

Julia waved. "Just look over here, dear, and I'll shoot a few frames."

Keryn looked over her right shoulder and smiled dutifully.

Julia's camera flashed.

"Oh, that was marvelous." Julia stepped to her right. "Now just look this way."

Several flashes later, Keryn saw Dillon coming down the escalator. He was dressed very nicely in a thick cotton shirt and wool pants and a red tie. Obviously, the NSA people understood his tastes pretty well, but they'd goofed on the tie.

Julia turned. "Oh, there you are, Dillon. You look wonderful. I think I've finished with Keryn, so perhaps you could just step across there and join her."

Keryn's heart speeded up a notch.

Dillon looked at Grant and Julia, then he looked at Keryn and stepped across the gap onto the island.

"Just ... there on the piano bench. I'd like to get a few of you two together. Keryn, make a little room for him." Julia winked at her.

Keryn scooted to her left.

Dillon came and sat beside her.

"Now just a few shots. Look this way and smile!" Julia moved a bit farther away from them. The lens on her camera zoomed out. "And ... here we go." A flash. "Just one more." Another flash.

Julia closed her camera. "Very good! Thank you so much. I'll just be on my way. I'm sure you both have a lot to talk about." She slipped onto the escalator and rode up toward the lobby.

Keryn sat there feeling like an idiot. She smiled at Dillon. "I didn't see you at breakfast."

"I ... went for a walk." Dillon's voice sounded thick.

"Just a walk?"

"I had some thinking to do."

Keryn had been doing a lot of thinking herself. Self-conscious, she looked down at the piano keys. "I'm feeling really hurt that ... our own government treated us that way. It's like ... it's like finding out your parents are a couple of stoners."

A long silence. "Yes, that is exactly how it feels."

Keryn looked up at Dillon's face. His eyes were closed and a tear had fully formed in each eye. It must be ten times worse for him. He had always had so much trust in the government.

She suddenly realized what she wanted to do. Something crazy. Something forward. Something she'd never have been bold enough to do until now.

"Hold still, don't move." Keryn reached up a finger to his left eye and let his tear flow onto her finger. She did the same with his right eye. Then she leaned up and kissed his cheek gently. "Dillon, you've really changed lately, haven't you?"

He nodded, eyes clamped shut.

"I like that. I liked the old Dillon, but I like the new one more. I like that you're still growing and changing. I realized something when those men kidnapped me. Can I tell you about that?"

Dillon opened his eyes. "Yes."

"I thought I was going to die. I thought they were going to kill me and I'd be going to see Jesus."

Dillon bit his lip. "I was terrified for you."

"I was terrified too," Keryn said. "Not so much afraid of dying. I was ... afraid of missing out on knowing you." She took Dillon's hand in hers. "Afraid of not having you as my friend. Of never telling you how much I care about you. I hope you don't think I'm horribly forward, but ... it broke my heart when I thought I'd never be able to tell you I love you."

Dillon's face reddened and he looked down at his hands.

Keryn was sure she'd blown it. Too fast. Way too fast.

Dillon tightened his grip on Keryn's hand. "When I heard the gunshot on the phone, I ... thought you were gone to be with the Lord." He sighed deeply. "And I wanted to go there too."

Keryn felt a surge of joy in her heart.

Dillon looked like he was going to faint. "I ... I talked to Robert, and he helped me understand something." Dillon's Adam's apple rose and fell several times.

"What was that?"

"That I ... that I love you, Keryn."

Keryn felt like she had on the day she came to Jesus, the day her whole life changed. "Really?"

"Yes, really." The look on Dillon's face showed some deep emotion that Keryn could not fathom.

"Dillon, did you ever see the movie *Casablanca*?"

He shook his head.

She raised his hand to her lips and kissed it. "You should see that movie sometime. The last line is one of my favorites."

"How does it go?"

"'I think this is the beginning of a beautiful friendship.'"

"You kissed me yesterday," Dillon said. "Did you ... mean that?"

"Yes. Did you?"

Dillon's eyes clouded. "Yes, but ..."

Keryn just looked at him. "But what?"

"Yoo-hoo!"

Keryn spun around to look across the shallow pool.

Rachel Meyers was standing on the other side, wearing a thin T-shirt and short shorts. And no bra. She waved cheerily. "Hi, guys? Mind if I join you?"

The words froze on Keryn's lips. *Yes, I mind, you little skank. Get lost.*

Rachel stepped down into the pool and began wading through the knee-deep water toward them.

Rachel

That morning Rachel had slept late and ordered room service for breakfast, then had lain down again on her bed. She felt worn out. The last couple of days had been just too much. Her cell phone rang.

It was Clifton. She ignored it. After four rings, it went to voice mail. A few seconds later, he called again. Rachel groaned and flipped it open. "What *is* it, Clifton?"

"Hey, Rache, where are you?" Clifton's voice was a thin whisper.

"On my bed, *trying* to get some rest."

"Can you see the lobby from your room?"

"What are you whispering for?"

"Just take a look. A word to the wise." Clifton hung up.

Rachel stood up and went to look out of her window. Her room was on the sixth floor, looking down into the lobby. She could see the registration desk. A bellman wheeled a luggage cart across the floor toward the exit. Rachel's eyes followed him. He crossed over the bridge and waved at a man and a woman on the piano bench on that cute little island in the blue, blue pool.

Rachel blinked twice and squinted them into focus. Keryn and Dillon were sitting there, talking. Bad news. Very bad news.

Rachel whirled and strode toward the door. There was no time to be fancy. Keryn was all duded up in that gorgeous silk dress. A regular vision of loveliness. Great, just great. But Rachel was not going to lie down and play dead.

Dillon wanted a vision of loveliness. Fine, she'd give him a vision. She'd give him double vision. Rachel kicked off her pants and put on a pair of short shorts. The NSA people knew her tastes.

Rachel ran out the door and down to the elevator. The Grand Hyatt had some of the slowest elevators in the world. Rachel waited impatiently. When the elevator finally showed up, she jumped in and punched the button for the lobby.

Her heart was thumping in her chest. This was idiotic. This was not how she operated. A strong, independent woman didn't throw herself at a guy like some ... cave woman. But there wasn't time for finesse. Keryn was putting all her chips on the table. If Rachel wanted to be in the game, she had to do the same. That was stupid, but it was reality.

If Keryn wanted a cat fight, then meow. *And watch out for my claws.*

An eternity later, the elevator arrived at the lobby level.

Rachel looked down to the lower level and saw Keryn holding Dillon's hand in both of hers. Disgustingly lovey-dovey. Rachel saw that if she took the escalator, they would see her coming. That was not the way to make her entrance. Next to the escalator was a set of stairs that went down to one of the restaurant cafés. Rachel took the steps and went to the café. She asked the waiter for a table for one by the pool. He seated her and handed her a menu.

When he disappeared, Rachel stood up and wedged her way past the barrier to the edge of the pool. She waved her arms at Dillon and Keryn. "Yoo-hoo!"

Dillon and Keryn turned to look at her.

"Hi, guys? Mind if I join you?" Rachel stepped down into the pool and began wading across. The water felt wonderfully cool and refreshing.

She heard shouts and laughter from the café behind her, but she ignored them.

Keryn was shooting her full of laser beams with her eyes.

Dillon was staring at her with that unreadable look on his face.

Rachel didn't care. She was going to roll the dice and see how it came up. Maybe she'd win and maybe she'd lose, but for sure Keryn was going to win unless Rachel gave her some competition.

Rachel staggered the last few feet and clambered up onto the platform. "Hey, how are you? I saw you two looking lonely over here and just thought I'd join you and liven things up."

Keryn gave her a look that would have frosted a nuclear reactor. "We were discussing ... us."

Rachel sat down on Dillon's right side. "Good idea. I'd like to discuss us too. What say, Dillon? Shall we discuss us?"

Keryn spluttered. "I don't think—"

"Yes," Dillon said. "Maybe we should."

Rachel dared to breathe again. She hadn't won, but at least she was in the game. It was time to be reckless, to risk it all on one throw. She leaned up against Dillon and planted a kiss on his cheek. "Look, I'll be honest, Dillon. Might as well put my cards on the table. I'll show you mine and you show me yours. Okay?"

Dillon nodded.

"And I'll show mine," Keryn said.

"Fine." Rachel saw that Keryn had hold of Dillon's left hand, so she grabbed his right. "Look, here's the thing. Dillon, you really light my candles. When I'm around you, I feel just ... really right. I'm hot for you and I think you're hot for me. Am I right?"

Dillon was getting that Bambi-in-the-headlights look in his eyes.

"I kissed you a couple days ago," Rachel said. "And you kissed me back. Was that honest or were you just being polite?"

"It was ... honest," Dillon said.

"And yet you're sitting there holding hands with Keryn," Rachel said. "Is that honest?"

Keryn's face went rigid. "Rachel, this is really inappropriate."

"Please stop it, both of you," Dillon said.

"Time to stop dithering around, Dillon," Rachel said. "You can't have it both ways. Not anymore. You've been toying with the hearts of the fair young maidens way too long. Time to choose."

Keryn lifted Dillon's hand to her lips. "Choose me, Dillon. We were made for each other. You know it and I know it."

Rachel snickered. "You were made for each other like 'bore' and 'ing.' Face it, Keryn, you're dull. I say Dillon needs an opposite. He's a south pole. I'm a north. Together we make beautiful magnetism."

Keryn's face turned white. "Dillon, you believe in God and she doesn't. How would you ever work out that difference?"

Rachel shook her head. "Dillon, you believe in the Big Bang and evolution and she doesn't. She's a fundie and neither of you are ever going to change. Not in five billion years, you won't."

Keryn clutched Dillon's hand to her chest. "Dillon, you're going to have to choose."

Rachel reached up and ran her fingers through his hair. "That's right, Dillon. Time to choose. You've been on the fence way too long."

Dillon's face showed a storm of conflict. He seemed to be trying to say something, but no words came out.

"Perhaps I can be of assistance," said a voice behind Rachel.

CHAPTER FORTY-TWO

Dillon

Dillon turned to look. At the edge of the pool stood Dr. Michael King. He wore a three-piece suit, and he was smiling like a professor who knew all the answers.

Dillon did not have any answers. He did not know how he could have allowed this to happen. He was truly in love with Keryn. He was truly in love with Rachel. He was a double-minded man, and however he turned, he would do wrong to one of them. That was a terrible thing to do to a woman. He had not meant to, had not even seen this coming. But now the moment had come and he must choose.

He could not simply try one for a while and then decide. If he rejected that one, the other would no longer be interested. Dillon did not know much about women, but he was certain that no woman would accept being a second choice.

"Your problem is that you want two excellent things and you can have only one," Dr. King said. "In earlier times, this would have been settled by marrying them both." He shook his head sadly. "Alas, that option is no longer permitted to men of good will. How unfortunate.

The net effect is that you, Dillon, must choose one of these extraordinary women."

Dillon felt Rachel and Keryn squeeze each of his hands.

"On the one hand," Dr. King pointed to Keryn, "we have the talented and wonderfully well-endowed Keryn Wills. A charming woman of faith, though perhaps her beliefs are naïve and primitive as compared to yours. She is intelligent—a writer of mystery novels, I believe?"

Dillon nodded. "She is an extremely good writer."

"Of course. I'm told that her novels pack a surprise all the way to the very last word. A remarkable mind. And"—he began pacing—"a soothing influence on you. When the turbulence of life overtakes you, Dillon Richard, as it will even in your new-found wealth, Keryn will be there to have and to hold, to nurture you, to make it right again. You will rarely argue with her, because she is warm and soft and accommodating. She is a well-trimmed cottage, a white picket fence, clean sheets, and a warm bed. With her, you will find a straight and unbent marriage, but never a boring one."

Dillon felt Keryn's hand squeezing his tight. It felt soft and warm to his touch.

"Yet, on the other hand ..." Dr. King pointed to Rachel. "We have the brilliant and fiery Rachel Meyers. She is a woman of genius, as we are all too well aware. There might have been a Nobel in her future, had she chosen some more prosaic field of endeavor. She is a dynamic woman, one who will always engage your mind and, if I am one to judge a woman, also your animal passions."

Dillon felt his ears growing hot.

"Oh no, nothing to be ashamed of, Dillon Richard!" Dr. King shook his head. "I believe even the wise King Solomon had a few words to say on the goodness, indeed the excellence, of love." He paused a moment to straighten his tie. "Rachel will be a most stimulating and exciting companion for you should you choose to accept her. Your fine mind will never lack for interesting discussions on any topic you should care to name, whether it be the nature of reality, or the Poincare conjecture, or"—he winked at Dillon—"the ever-intriguing multiverse. You will often argue with Rachel. And worse! You will even fight—nasty, tumultuous, emotional fights. From which you will quickly recover and find, remarkably, that your love has grown deeper and more complex. Rachel is a disorganized house, a wild garden, a roaring fire, and a bearskin rug. With her, you will have a fiery marriage, but never an impossible one."

Rachel's hand gripped Dillon's with heat he had never imagined.

Dr. King gave a sad shrug. "Alas, you must choose one or the other. There is no middle ground. You could refuse them both, but"—Dr. King looked at Keryn and then at Rachel with admiration—"who would be so foolish? Both would make an excellent choice. I know you, Dillon Richard, possibly better than you know yourself. I foresee great joy and great pain with either woman. Joy in having the one. Pain in having lost the other. The joy will outshine the pain in either case. But only if you choose. If you refuse both, or if you dither, then all is as it was before you met them, and that was a dark and cold life."

Dillon shivered. He had not known he was in darkness until he saw the light of Keryn's smile. Nor had he known he was cold until he felt the heat of Rachel's lips.

"Very well, then, the hour has come." Dr. King locked his hands behind his back and smiled serenely at Dillon. "Your present life is the sum of all your past choices. Your future life hangs on this choice before you now. Knowing that you cannot fail to choose well, how, then, do you choose? Will it be the warm and soothing Keryn Wills? Or will it be the fiery and exciting Rachel Meyers?"

Dillon could not imagine how he could possibly choose. It was like choosing between quantum mechanics and general relativity. Dr. King had said it all perfectly. Dillon saw that he must choose. He wanted so desperately to choose Keryn. He wanted so desperately to choose Rachel.

Dr. King shook his head. "Bad form, Dillon. Bad form. Indecision may yet spoil your life. Let me propose a solution that is eminently fair. A means of choosing that both women must admit is completely without bias."

Dillon's throat felt terribly dry. "What solution?"

Dr. King turned toward the chairs and gestured to Grant, who was still seated near the fountain. "Mr. O'Connell, could I trouble you for the use of one of those demonstration devices you use for your excellent sales presentations?"

Grant stood up and reached into his pocket. He pulled out a quantum coin-flipper.

Dr. King strode over to him and took it. "A marvelous device, this. With odds that are mathematically perfect, it throws the dice Einstein insisted God could never throw. Press this button and the universe will choose for you. Call it God if that hypothesis is your preference. Call it karma. Or call it blind, stupid fate. Call it what you will, but press the button and your choice will be made. Should it land heads, why then, take the divine Ms. Wills for your true love. Should it land tails, without delay take the extreme Dr. Meyers to your heart. And if the multiverse represents the true nature of reality"—King gave them all a broad smile—"then this quantum event will create two universes. In each universe, you will take one of the two. Quite literally, you will have the best of both worlds."

Dr. King stepped onto the island and set the coin-flipper before Dillon. "Are you ladies agreeable? Is this not a solution made in heaven, or the best approximation to it?"

"No possible way," Keryn said.

"Not on your life," Rachel said.

Dillon did not know what to say.

Julia came running down the escalator. For a moment, Dillon was afraid she would make things worse by suggesting her own preposterous idea. But she did not. Instead, she took Grant's hand and pulled him over to the edge of the pool.

Clifton followed them. "Dude, you have like the ultimate spiff deal here. You can't go wrong."

"Clifton, shut up," Julia said. "Grant, maybe you could give Dillon a little fatherly advice."

Grant did not look like he wanted to give any fatherly advice.

In that moment, something clicked into place for Dillon, and he understood what he truly wanted to do.

He stood up and grabbed the quantum coin-flipper.

He threw it into the pool.

Dr. King's eyes bulged. "Dillon, I hardly think that is—"

"Please go to hell, Dr. King," Dillon said. "From now on, we will make our own decisions, in our own time, without interference from you. Is that clear?"

Dr. King's mouth fell open, and he stared at Dillon for a moment. Then he stepped off the island and walked past Grant and Julia and Clifton. His shiny leather shoes *click-clack*ed all the way across the tiled floor to the escalator. Dillon watched him until he disappeared.

"Dillon, you the man! That was awesome!" Clifton said. "But, dude, you still have to make a choice."

"No, I do not have to make a choice," Dillon said. "Not this minute. That would be foolish. We have all just survived a crisis and we are in shock. Rachel has had her life's work stolen. Keryn has survived a kidnapping and pretended murder. I have just learned that the governing authorities have abused my trust. Each of us needs time to regain our equilibrium."

Julia had a funny expression on her face that Dillon could not parse. "Girls, I think Dillon's right. I mean, let's face it, he hardly knows either one of you, and you barely know him. Maybe you all need to give each other a little space. What do you think?"

Rachel squeezed Dillon's right hand. "Good idea."

"Sounds smart to me," Keryn grabbed his left hand.

"And furthermore, there is one other person I must get to know before I can make any such decision," Dillon said.

Clifton's eyes were bulging. "Someone *else*? Dude, who else have you been stringing along?"

Dillon looked down at his hands and slowly pulled them away from both women.

"Myself."

PART 5: DOUBLE VISION

When you come to a fork in the road, take it.

Yogi Berra

CHAPTER FORTY-THREE

Rachel

On the last weekend in July, Rachel sat in her aunt's car, wondering why she had agreed to come. "It looks like a church."

"It *is* a church on Sundays. We rent it from the Baptists. Today it's a synagogue." Aunt Esther hopped out of the car. "Davey, tuck in your shirt. Rachel, come on, we'll be late."

Rachel slowly got out and stared up at the building. A church. She had known that Aunt Esther's congregation, Beth Simcha, met in a church. She just hadn't expected it to look like ... a *church*.

Davey tucked in most of his shirt and clipped a blue yarmulke with white lettering onto his helmet of curly black hair. He ambled off to join a circle of teenage boys in untucked shirts and baggy pants.

Rachel wished she had asked Dillon to come with her. He was such a ... rock. Somebody she could lean on. She did not want to go inside a church alone, even if it was functioning as a synagogue. It had been a full month since all the craziness in Washington, D.C. After coming back to San Diego, she had spent a lot of time talking with Aunt Esther. Reading some books Dillon recommended. Thinking.

She had finally decided she was never going to get anywhere by just talking and reading and thinking. So here she was. Already it looked like a bad idea.

"*Shabbat shalom!*" said a voice behind her.

Rachel turned to look.

A huge bear of a man was coming toward Aunt Esther. He had a thick black beard streaked with gray and wore a satin yarmulke and an enormous smile. Blue and white ritual fringes hung from beneath his suit jacket.

Rachel gawked at him.

"*Shabbat shalom,* Rabbi Shaul. This is my niece Rachel." Aunt Esther beckoned to her. "Rachel, come meet the rabbi."

Rachel suddenly felt like an idiot. She was wearing the same tie-dyed shirt she'd worn the day she met Dillon, and she realized that she must look very ... frivolous.

The rabbi came around the front of the car. "I'm Shaul," he said. "Welcome to Beth Simcha." He appeared to be about Daddy's age, and he had warm eyes that seemed to look right into Rachel's.

Rachel shook hands with him. His enormous paw swallowed her entire hand. "G-glad to meet you."

"They'll be starting the music soon," Rabbi Shaul said. "Are you a dancer like your cousin Rivka?"

Rachel didn't know what to say to that. She was an excellent dancer, but she didn't think her kind of dancing would set well in a synagogue. "Maybe."

"A firm *maybe.*" Rabbi Shaul smiled at her. "We can work with a *maybe.* I have a few *maybes* in my own heart."

"Rachel, come along!" Aunt Esther said.

Rachel went. Inside, she was given a bulletin and hugged by a woman who looked like she was about eight hundred years old. She told Rachel she had been praying for her all week.

Rachel didn't know how to respond to that.

A bass guitar began thrumming inside the sanctuary. "Rachel, they're starting!" Aunt Esther tugged at her arm.

Rachel followed her through a pair of double doors and stopped short, gaping.

On the stage was a full band. Drums. A bass. An electric guitar. A saxophone. A couple of singers. Behind a synthesizer stood an enormous young man with piercing black eyes that marked him clearly as Rabbi Shaul's son.

There wasn't a single cross in sight. Behind the band stood an ark. An honest-to-God ark holding a Torah scroll. In front of the stage, a circle of women had gathered.

The drummer tapped out a starting four-count and the band began playing and the women began dancing. The music sounded very Jewish, and the dance looked like a traditional sort of circle dance.

Aunt Esther led Rachel midway down the left aisle to a seat. Up front there was a computer projection system to display the words of the song. It was a Hebrew song, but Rachel did not remember any Hebrew. She closed her eyes and let the music wash over her.

It was typical Jewish music, happy and sad, both at the same time. Like the qubit, which could be zero and one, both at the same time. Like these people, Christians and Jews, both at the same time.

Rachel wished she could understand the words. The music seemed to be seeping inside her skin. It was Jewish through and through, and yet ...

And yet she was sure they did not play music like this in most synagogues. Rachel felt the music caressing her soul. When the song finally ended, Rachel opened her eyes. The dancers returned to their seats. Was that *it*? Disappointment cut through her.

The band switched to a faster rhythm, Yemenite, very spicy. Rachel's foot began tapping. Some of the dancers went back to the front. Rachel closed her eyes. Again, the words were Hebrew, the melody haunting. An ineffable sadness welled up in her heart. This was her music, her language, her rhythm.

When the song ended, Rachel felt more alive than she had in a long time. Some of the dancers returned to their seats, smiling. Others stayed in front. The keyboard player began a new song, this one slower, an Eastern European melody. This time the words on the screen were in English. They looked like they came from the Bible, more or less.

The Lord is my Rock,

The Lord is my Rock,
The Lord is my Rock,
In Him will I trust.

The Lord is my Strength,
The Lord is my Strength,
The Lord is my Strength,
In Him will I trust.

Rachel felt all the breath go out of her body. She *needed* a rock in her life. Needed a fixed point. Like Dillon.

But Dillon was not enough. No guy could be enough. Because, basically, everybody was in the same boat. Everybody was part of the multiverse, making decisions, drifting this way and that, splitting and resplitting in a billion different directions. Everybody was fragmented, partly yes and partly no. Everybody was maybe.

Everybody except God. That was the theory, anyway. God was supposed to be the Ultimate Ground of Being, the Ancient of Days, the One.

Could she buy into that?

Rachel sank down onto her pew and closed her eyes. She honestly didn't know.

Maybe yes.

Maybe no.

Maybe maybe.

She sat quietly for a few minutes trying each of those on for size.

At the end of that time, without knowing quite how she'd decided, Rachel realized that she had.

She stood up and walked quietly outside, blinking in the bright July sun.

She had got past hating Jesus. She had even got past hating Christians.

But this wasn't her place and these weren't her people.

Her place was Israel. She'd never been there. Now, all of a sudden she wanted to go. Maybe for a short visit. Maybe a lifetime.

She had the money to do whatever she wanted. And she wanted to go see the land of her fathers.

The only question was whether Dillon wanted to go with her.

~

Dillon

"Y ou're sure you want to do this?" Robert looked concerned. "I can do it myself, if you're not—"

"I am sure." Dillon hopped into the passenger seat of Robert's rented minivan. "Anyway, I am looking forward to seeing your brother."

Robert jumped into the driver's side. "Hey, thanks for buying his airline ticket. That was really ... generous."

"Trust me, it was nothing."

Robert started the engine. "So ... are you looking for a new job yet?"

"No."

They drove in silence until they reached the freeway. Robert merged in with traffic, heading north toward John Wayne Airport. "You really can't tell me anything about what happened back east last month?"

"I am sorry."

Robert turned on the radio. "How's Keryn doing? I'd love to have her come to the wedding this weekend, if she can make it."

"She has a book due two weeks from today, and she is working extremely hard."

Dillon felt a sharp longing to talk to Keryn. And Rachel also. He had not seen either of them since they'd arrived home a month ago, though he had talked to each of them on the phone once or twice per week. He was glad he had taken time to sort out his life, and he felt sure they were also glad. He did not think a relationship was something that would be harmed by a little distance and a little time.

He had quit his job at CypherQuanta. It felt strange not going to work every day, but he had spent a pleasant month doing nothing and getting to know himself better. And this week he had kept busy helping Robert. The wedding was only three days away, and there were still many things to do.

Robert said nothing more until they reached the airport. Dillon's pulse was racing. Fear clogged his throat. He should not have come. Robert could have come alone. Now it was too late to back out.

Robert parked in the lot nearest the terminal, and they got out. Dillon wiped his sweating hands on his blue jeans. The cloth felt coarse. He did not like blue jeans, but he thought they would help. He was also wearing a short-sleeved knit shirt and no tie. And running shoes. Robert had helped him buy the clothes.

"We're a little late," Robert said. "Are you *sure* you want to do this?"

Dillon started walking toward Terminal A. "We should hurry."

When they reached the terminal, the automatic doors *whoosh*ed open. There was a large baggage claim area directly in front of them. Dillon checked the Arrivals screen and saw that the flight from Chicago had gotten in a few minutes late.

"The escalator is that way." Robert began walking toward it.

Dillon followed him.

"There's Patrick!" Robert pointed toward a tall man near the top of the escalator.

Patrick had a wide smile, and he was wearing a Cubs cap and holding tightly to a large G.I. Joe action figure. The toy was more than thirty years old. Dillon could remember playing with it when he was six. Patrick still took it everywhere he went. That embarrassed his parents very much, but Patrick did not know that.

Behind Patrick on the escalator was an older couple in their mid-sixties. It had been a long time since Dillon had seen them, and he almost did not recognize them. The woman had a hand on Patrick's shoulder. The man was leaning down, speaking into the woman's ear.

The escalator was packed. Dillon and Robert stood near the rest rooms, waiting.

Patrick staggered when he reached the bottom of the escalator.

"Patrick!" Robert shouted and ran forward.

"Bobby!" Patrick found his footing and raced toward Robert. They collided violently. The G.I. Joe flew out of Patrick's hands and skittered across the floor toward Dillon.

Dillon picked it up and walked toward them.

The man and woman caught up to Patrick. The man shook hands with Robert. The woman's eyes fell on Dillon. She gave a little shriek and tugged at the man's arm, pointing.

Dillon kept walking.

The man looked at Dillon. Astonishment filled his eyes.

Dillon reached the group. His hands suddenly felt weak. The G.I. Joe fell on the floor.

"Dillon!" Patrick shouted.

The woman screamed.

Dillon threw his arms around the man.

The man's body shook as if he had been slugged in the face.

"I ... love you, Dad," Dillon said.

His father let out a sound like a sob. "My boy's come home! My boy's come home at last!"

Dillon wept.

~

Keryn

Keryn woke up to the sound of the phone ringing. She did not want to face the phone. Yesterday, she had slammed out forty-five pages, more than eleven thousand words, to finish her novel by her deadline. She had not even spell-checked it. At 3:00 a.m. she had e-mailed the wretched beast to her editor and collapsed into bed. It was probably horrible, the worst piece of drivel she'd ever written, but it didn't matter. She had made her deadline. After all, it was only supposed to be a first draft.

The answering machine in her office picked up and played her recording. After the beep, Sunflower's voice broke in. "Sweetheart, it's me. You haven't called in ages and you're not answering your phone and I'm just *frantic*. I know you're listening. Either that or you're dead.

If you don't pick up that phone right now, I'm going to call the cops to come find your body."

Keryn smiled. Sunflower was such a sweetie. She meant well. Really. But she wasn't going to set the terms for their relationship anymore. If that meant the cops came busting in on Keryn, well, that's just the way it would be. She'd call when she was rested. The last six weeks had been a horrible rush, but she had finished her book on time without the humiliation of asking for an extension.

"All right, then, I'm really calling the cops right ... now. Really." Sunflower's voice sounded deflated. "Bye, honey."

The machine clicked off.

Keryn rolled over and tried to go back to sleep. The next thing she knew, the phone rang again. This time it was her editor.

"Keryn, this is Janey. I read through it just now, and I *love* it! Wow! Excellent, really excellent. There are just a *couple* of little problems I want to discuss with you. Call me when you get a—"

Keryn grabbed her bedside phone. "Hi, Janey, sorry! I was up so late last night, it was early when I went to bed. Do you really like it?"

"It's ... *wow*. Way different from your usual style, though. This isn't the story line you put in the proposal."

"No, but ... sometimes things change."

"Keryn, this is *way* different. Kind of farfetched too. Not your usual reality fiction. Don't get me wrong, I *like* it. But listen, it's stepping quite a bit outside your brand. Would you mind very much if we published it under a pseudonym?"

Keryn hadn't thought about that. "I guess I'm okay with that."

"A *male* pseudonym? Marketing thinks it would fly a lot better that way. Women writers don't usually do a science kind of backdrop."

"Whatever makes it fly." Right now Keryn was too tired to care.

"One other thing," Janey said. "The ending's a little ambiguous. Our readers like to see a bit more ... resolution. You can't just leave the most important thread untied."

Keryn closed her eyes and reminded herself to be firm. "The ending *has* to be ambiguous. The book is *about* ambiguity. I'm not sure I can do better than that."

"Try. Okay?"

Keryn pursed her lips. "Listen, I'm really tired right now. I'll *think* about it, but I think it works the way it is, and I'm going to leave it like that unless some serious inspiration falls out of the sky."

"Keryn, are you feeling well? You're usually a little more ..."

"Malleable?"

"I was going to say 'team player.'"

"Maybe I've finally figured out that I'm the captain of the team."

A long silence from Janey.

Keryn waited it out.

"Okay, I know you need your beauty sleep, so I'll let you go. Talk to you later. I am *really* excited about this. It could be your breakout book."

"Bye, Janey." Keryn hung up and went out to the kitchen to get a drink of water. Already she was having second thoughts. Maybe Janey was right. For sure the ending could be improved a bit. But Janey wasn't going to dictate it. Keryn would figure it out herself or not at all.

The phone rang again as she was heading back to her bedroom. That had to be Janey.

I should apologize. No way am I going to apologize. Oh Lord, I'm such a mess.

Keryn went into her office and scooped up the phone on the third ring. Then she saw the caller ID and her insides twisted into a hard, cold knot. "Oh ... hello, Dr. King."

"Keryn, I'll get right to the point. You are not going to publish that novel. Do I make myself clear?"

Keryn sat down in her chair and pressed the Record button on her fancy new phone. "This is Keryn Wills, and I'm speaking with Dr. Michael King of the National Security Agency. Dr. King, I don't speak with anyone unless they consent to be recorded. Do you consent to be recorded?"

For a long moment, the sound of silence. "Keryn, it is a felony if you publicly identify me or my employer."

Keryn rocked back and forth a couple times to calm her heart. "Fine, I realize that. But you listen up, all right? Dillon did a little checking, and we know for a fact that, one, your name is not Michael King and, two, you do not really work for the NSA."

A quiet laugh. "Ah, very good, very good. I'm glad we've got that little *prevarication* out in the open."

"I'm assuming you work for one of those secret government agencies that officially don't exist?"

"If it's any comfort, Dr. Weinberg and Dr. Narain actually do work for the NSA, and—"

"We know that. Do you consent to be recorded?"

"Yes, since I apparently don't exist, fine. But getting back to my main point, you are not going to publish that novel."

"I know the rules," Keryn said. "I didn't give any description of anything inside the NSA. From what I wrote, you'd never know I'd even been inside the building."

"Yes, you managed that rather well. But that's not the problem. You've violated your NDA."

Keryn pulled up the last page of her manuscript. "Excuse me, but did you bother to read the author's note at the end of the book?"

A short silence. "Hold on, I'm looking now."

"I'll save you the trouble," Keryn said. "It reads, 'This is a work of fiction and is not meant to represent actual events or characters.' Which means that I assert that none of it really happened. How does that violate my NDA?"

"It is painfully close to the actual events. You've managed to change a few details, but—"

"Tell you what," Keryn said. "I just talked to my editor and she loves it. Well, except for the ending. Now you want me to call her up and say that a man who isn't named Michael King and who doesn't work for the National Security Agency doesn't want her to print that story?"

"Yes, that's exactly what you are going to do."

"And Janey's going to ask why, and I'll just tell her Mr. No-Name from the No-Such-Agency has decided that the story line is, quote— painfully close to the actual events—unquote. Am I understanding you correctly?"

Long silence. "Keryn, we do not want people to believe that

conventional encryption techniques might be insecure. There are too many people who don't trust us already, and—"

"I wonder why that might be."

Dr. King cleared his throat. "The bottom line is—"

"No, excuse me, but I'll decide what the bottom line is." Keryn leaned forward. "I am going to print that story just as it stands. Even my editor thinks it's farfetched. And it is. Nobody is going to believe that story has anything remotely to do with reality. Oddly enough, it's too close to the facts to be believable. That's just one of life's little ironies, isn't it?"

"Keryn—"

"If you have a problem with that, take me to court," Keryn said. "You'll look like an idiot and I'll get a ton of free publicity." She slammed down the phone and turned off the recording.

Oh, Lord, I hope I handled that right.

The phone rang. Keryn saw from the caller ID that it was Michael again. She leaned far back in her chair and crossed her arms. Let him try to mess with her.

The machine picked up and her recording played. Michael's voice came on. "Keryn, I apologize if I was a little brusque. Please excuse me. I'll send you some flowers as a small token of my—"

The doorbell rang.

Keryn gasped. That had to be the cops. Sunflower had actually called the cops. Keryn raced to her bedroom and threw a bathrobe on over her nightgown. Her hair was a wretched, horrible mess, but there wasn't time.

The doorbell rang again.

Keryn dashed out to the living room and flung open the front door. "I'm okay, I'm okay. Everything's—"

A flower delivery man stood there holding a bouquet of roses and a clipboard. "Delivery for Keryn Wills. Can you sign for this?"

Keryn covered her mouth with her hands. Thank God it wasn't the cops, but this was almost as bad. Michael King was playing with her head. He was manipulating her again, the little slimeball. He had to have ordered those flowers at least an hour ago. Whatever game he was running, she wasn't going to play.

"Sorry," Keryn said. "I can't accept it."

The delivery man gaped at her. "He said you might refuse, so he asked me to insist that you at least read this card."

Keryn slipped the card out of the envelope and studied it suspiciously. It had a gorgeous picture of a bluish-colored galaxy. She flipped the card open. It was handwritten in block letters.

Roses are red,
The multiverse is blue.
In one world I chose Rachel,
But in this world ... I choose you.

Love, Dillon

WANT TO GO ON ANOTHER ADVENTURE?

Dillon Richard's best friend is Bob Kaganovski.

When Bob finishes his Ph.D., he gets a job with NASA and winds up on the first expedition to Mars.

Bob's a bit paranoid, and he doesn't trust Valkerie Jansen, the gorgeous astronaut that NASA has forced onto the team at the last minute. Bob thinks Valkerie is mentally unbalanced, possibly even dangerous.

Which is just too bad, because Bob's falling in love with her.

Can Bob survive Valkerie's charms?

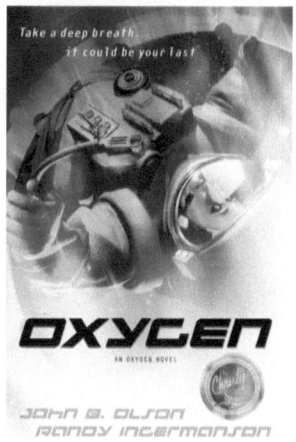

IF YOU ENJOYED THIS BOOK...

A note from Dillon Richard: "Word-of-mouth is the most powerful marketing force in the multiverse. If you enjoyed reading my adventures with Keryn and Rachel, I would appreciate you rating this book and leaving a review. Even if you write only a sentence or two, it will help alert people to the dangers of trusting people like Michael King."

Thank you so much! I appreciate you!

ABOUT THE AUTHOR

Randy Ingermanson got his Ph.D. in theoretical physics from the University of California at Berkeley.

For no good reason, Randy would rather make up stories about imaginary people than do honest work. This is a serious character defect, but he's not a bit sorry.

Randy is not Aspie, but he's not Normal either, and he fights many of the same battles as Dillon does when trying to understand those pesky social contexts.

If you'd like to get an e-mail alert whenever Randy has a new book out, or whenever he's running an especially good deal on one of his books, then feel free to sign up here:

RandyIngermanson.com

Or follow Randy on social media:

facebook.com/RandyIngermansonFiction

amazon.com/author/randyingermanson

bookbub.com/authors/randy-ingermanson

goodreads.com/randyingermanson

First edition, Bethany House Publishers, 2004

Second e-book edition, Ingermanson Communications, Inc., 2013, Ingermanson.com

Second print edition, Ingermanson Communications, Inc., 2018, Ingermanson.com

Cover illustration and design by Markus Designs.

ISBN: 978-1-937031-22-0

✹ Created with Vellum

STANDARD DISCLAIMER

AUTHOR'S NOTE

This is a work of fiction and is not meant to represent actual events or characters. However, the physics ideas in this book are real and so are the applications to encryption and decryption.

If Rachel's bio-computer could be built, then there would be two Xtreme effects that should worry us all:

1) Every e-commerce website using "secure" encryption would be exposed to any criminal with a quantum computer.

2) The government would be able to read even the RSA-encrypted e-mail of private citizens. (It can already read any unencrypted e-mail.)

There is no strong reason to believe that Rachel's bio-computer exists. There is no way to prove it doesn't. Her explanation of how she constructed it is purely fictitious—plausible only at "the hand-waving level" that we physicists use when speculating. However, many physicists believe that quantum computers will someday be as powerful as Rachel's.

I wrote *Double Vision* in the summer of 2003 and it was published the following year. The story is set during the summer of 2004, seven years before Osama bin Laden was killed by SEAL Team Six.

I have no idea whether quantum decryption technology had anything to do with bin Laden's capture. If it did, that fact would be classified several miles above my pay grade.

But if a quantum computer had existed in 2004, it seems likely to me that the US government would have done everything possible to get it and keep its existence secret. And someone like Michael King would have argued that this was the most righteous thing it could possibly do.

CypherQuanta is fictitious, but the machines it builds—one-qubit quantum encryption devices—are commercially viable now. The first quantum-encrypted bank transfer was made in Vienna by Bank Austria

Creditanstalt on April 21, 2004, using a quantum key distribution device built by id Quantique.

Multi-qubit quantum computers also exist but are not nearly as advanced as Rachel's. Shor's algorithm was published in 1994 by Peter Shor of AT&T. It was demonstrated in the lab in 2001 on a seven-qubit quantum computer by Isaac Chuang of IBM. The technology used was essentially the same as the NMR qubit that Rachel used.

As of this second edition of *Double Vision*, a 512-qubit quantum computer is commercially available from D-Wave, which specializes in quantum computing.

The largest integer factored by a general method using conventional computers at the time of the first edition of this book was a 174-digit number (RSA-576) reported on December 3, 2003. As of this second edition of *Double Vision*, the current record is a 232-digit number (RSA-768) that required two years of effort using hundreds of machines. Results were reported on December 12, 2009.

The National Security Agency has a budget that is classified, but the agency is believed to be the largest single employer of mathematicians in the world. You can decide for yourself how much you trust the NSA.

I wrote this book while working at a startup high-technology company in San Diego. Three of my co-workers there often asked me to put them in a novel. Ted Hunter, Monica, and Michael King all have names suspiciously similar to these co-workers. However, all resemblance ends there and the characters are nothing like the real people. Thanks to Edd, Monika, and Mike for your friendship.

If you'd like to know more about Dillon's friend Bob Kaganovski, you might enjoy the Mars novels I co-authored with John Olson: *Oxygen* and *The Fifth Man*.

If you're interested in Rachel's cousin Rivka, then you might like to read my time-travel novels *Transgression, Premonition,* and *Retribution.*

SNEAK PEEK AT OXYGEN

AN EXPLOSION ON THE WAY TO MARS

Halfway to the Red Planet, an explosion leaves the four-member crew of the Ares 10 with only enough oxygen for one.

Valkerie Jansen, the ship's doctor, is tough, beautiful, and has an uncanny knack for survival.

Bob Kaganovski, the ship's mechanic, is paid to be paranoid -- and he's good at it. He's worried that Valkerie is mentally unbalanced, possibly even dangerous.

Which is just too bad, because Bob's falling in love with her.

Meanwhile, NASA is trying to figure out who should live and who should die, when there's only enough oxygen for one.

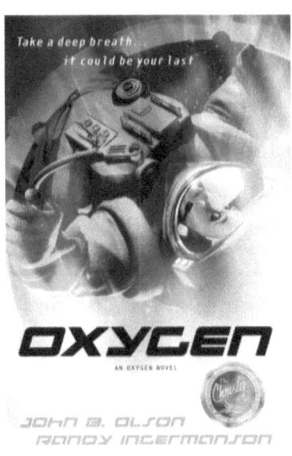

JOHN B. OLSON
RANDY INGERMANSON

CHAPTER 1

Valkerie woke up screaming. A viper bat clung to her face with fish-hook claws, smothering her with its thin, leathery body. She tore at her face, but the creature had dug in too deep. She could already feel its venom burning into her lungs, constricting her chest in a long, convulsive cough. Struggling for control, she traced the contours of her face with tingling fingertips. Slowly, the clinging creature melted into her skin, fading back into the world of dreams.

The nightmare gradually faded, giving way to a new, more gripping terror. Valkerie was wide awake now. There was no such thing as a viper bat. But she still couldn't breathe.

Valkerie flung herself from the camping cot and thudded to the floor. She lay on her back, gasping for breath. She was hyperventilating, but the burning in her lungs grew worse. An acrid stench filled the cabin—the smell of sulfur dioxide—SO_2.

No... Valkerie rolled over and fought her way up onto her hands and knees. This couldn't be happening. The volcano couldn't be venting. It was supposed to be dormant. Sleeping like a baby. Dim red light filtered in through the cabin window, illuminating a large duffel bag in the middle of the room. She crawled slowly toward the bag, struggling through the coughs that wracked her body.

Squeezing her eyes shut against the pain in her cramping muscles, Valkerie inched forward until she felt the heavy canvas. She dug underneath a metallic thermal suit and pressed her breather to her face. Her lungs choked shut at the rush of acidic gas. *Idiot!* She flung the mask across the room. Gina-Marie had warned her about the filter, but Valkerie had insisted it would be good for one more trip.

Her mind raced. If Mount Trident was venting, the whole valley could be filled with sulfur dioxide. She had to get out of there. Fast.

Valkerie tried to stand, but the room spun out of control. She crashed onto the floor, hitting her head hard on the edge of the cot. A cloud of ringing light sparkled in her mind. Her muscles relaxed, and she gave herself to the tide of darkness that washed gently across her senses. *Sleep. No more experiments. Sleep.*

An image crept into her mind. A large plastic bag filled with new sample tubes. Was it still sealed? She couldn't remember.

Groping her way forward, Valkerie swept her hands across the floor. A smooth surface crinkled at her touch. She lunged at the bag, poked a trembling finger through the heavy plastic, and pressed her lips to the hole. The air tingled in her lungs with burning sweetness.

She curled around the bag, hugging it to her body, breathing life through the ragged wound. Gradually, the needles that prickled at her consciousness started to recede, but she knew it wouldn't last. The air in the bag was getting stale.

Valkerie took one last breath and staggered to her feet. Her jeep! It was just outside. She lurched to the cabin door and pushed her way out into the night. The air hit her in the face like a blast of hot tear gas. Gagging on the foul gases, she stumbled blindly forward, clinging to consciousness.

Heaving herself into the seat of the jeep, she turned the key. The starter whirred and the engine coughed to life, but then died immediately. *Idiot!* Valkerie smashed her fist against the dash. The jeep couldn't run without oxygen any more than she could.

A wave of nausea wracked Valkerie's body. Her muscles were cramping again. She fell across the seat and reached into the glove box for her knife. *Pliers.* They would have to do.

Valkerie crawled out of the jeep and threw herself on the ground by the jeep's front tire. Taking off the cap of the air valve, she crushed its metal tip with the pliers. After a few seconds of twisting and squeezing, she heard a faint hiss.

Valkerie chomped down on the rubber valve and sucked in a desperate breath. The air was black with the taste of rubber, but anything was better than SO2. When her lungs were full, she clamped down on the valve with the pliers. Breathe, clamp, breathe, clamp. She held each breath as long as she could before letting it out.

The tire went flat way too soon. Valkerie crawled to the next tire and repeated the process. Then the next tire and the next. After she had sucked the last ounce of air from the spare, she took off running across the clearing. The valley was rugged and wide. She knew she couldn't make it out on foot, but if she could just get above the blanket of heavy gases she might have a chance.

Halfway across the clearing, Valkerie fell reeling to the ground. Red thunderbolts stabbed at her brain. A sparkling haze shrouded her vision as she fought her way to her feet. The heavy gases were thicker close to the ground. She had to stay upright. Walking on tiptoe, she made her way to the edge of the clearing, looking up at the night sky to keep her nostrils elevated.

Valkerie stumbled into a limbless old pine and crashed to the ground. Too dizzy to stand, she crawled on her hands and knees to a young pine with limbs closer to the ground.

The rough branches cut her face and tore at her nightgown as she climbed. Valkerie lost her grip and fell, crashing into the branches below. She pulled herself up and kept climbing. Higher and higher through the darkness, until slowly, her head began to clear.

"Thank you. Thank you ..." Valkerie breathed in and out to the cadence of the simple litany that filled her mind. The sparkles in her eyes were fading. Below her feet, tendrils of mist danced in the moonlight, flowing along the envelope of the deadly gas cloud.

The valley reflected an angry red glow. Valkerie looked up at the peak that loomed above her. If the venting continued long enough, the gases might rise higher than she could climb. But that was the least of her worries.

She closed her eyes and wrapped her arms around the tree, hoping Professor Henderson was wrong. His solemn voice echoed in her mind: *"If it starts venting, get out. Fumarolic venting almost always presages a major eruption."*

~

Wednesday, August 15, Year One, 9:30 A.M.
Bob

Bob Kaganovski had shampoo in his eyes when the decompression alarm went off.

He grabbed the suction hose and ran it frantically over his face and eyes. Footsteps pounded outside the shower.

"Decompression!" shouted Josh Bennett, mission commander of the Ares 10. "Get to the EVA suits now! We've got about fifteen minutes."

Bob popped open the Velcroed shower door and grabbed a towel. Fear knotted his gut. Only fifteen minutes! He stepped out of the shower and swiped a towel across the soles of his feet, drying them just enough so he wouldn't kill himself on the stairs.

He ran through a corridor to the steep circular stairway that led down to Level 1 of the Habitation Module. The decompression alarm beeped once every two seconds. The interval was keyed to cabin pressure. When it got down to vacuum, the beeps would merge into one steady drone. If he wasn't in his suit by then, he wouldn't hear it. For one thing, sound wouldn't travel in a vacuum. For another, he'd be dead.

Bob slipped and slithered down the metal staircase. Josh lay on the floor, with both his legs already stuffed into the lower half of his EVA suit. Bob yanked open the door of his locker and pulled out the heavy upper half of his suit.

It fell on the floor in a heap.

"Easy!" Josh said. "Don't panic. I'll give you a hand—"

"I've got it." Bob grabbed it and heaved. *Who designed this beast?* Fifty years of research, and the thing still weighed over eighty pounds. Normally, somebody was supposed to help you into an Extra-Vehicular Activity suit. But in an emergency, you could do it yourself. In theory.

Bob latched the upper half of the suit to a stability rack and laid out the lower half on the floor. He grabbed a MAG—NASA-speak for a diaper—and taped it on.

The beeping of the alarm increased in tempo.

Now for the hard part, the LCG—Liquid-Cooled Garment—a Spandex pair of long johns with feet, encased in a clunky water-cooled nightmare of tubes and gizmos. Bob struggled furiously to pull it over his damp skin. Minutes passed.

Josh was almost all of the way into his suit by the time Bob got his LCG on. "How you doing with that thing?" Josh asked.

"I'm getting there." Bob wiped the sweat out of his eyes.

"We're down to eight minutes." Josh fastened the inner connectors at his waist, then the outer ones. "Need some help before I put on my gloves?"

Bob stuck both feet into the legs of the EVA suit and pushed in. His feet slid home into the boots and he pulled the pant legs up to his waist. "Okay, give me a hand up."

"Better hurry." Josh put on his Snoopy cap and adjusted his comm mikes. "The air's getting thinner." He pulled Bob to his feet. "Just climb up into your top. Nothing to it."

Right. Bob clumped over to his top, turned, and tried to squat. Which was almost impossible wearing the pants.

"Drop the pants," Josh said. "I need to pressurize, okay?" He pulled his helmet and gloves out of his locker.

I'm on my own now. Bob let go of the circular metal ring that ran around the belt of the pants. He squatted and tried to back in underneath the suit. Which was practically impossible for a guy almost six feet tall. Josh had it easy—he was five inches shorter and a lot more limber. Bob pushed up into the suit. The thing was the mother of all turtleneck sweaters, fifteen layers of everything from Teflon to Nomex to who-knows-what. Halfway up, his head got stuck.

His heart was hammering now, three beats for every beep of that blasted alarm. He backed down and tried again.

And got stuck again. *Force it.* He pushed harder. Harder.

The suit popped loose from the stability rack. He staggered forward, but the heavy pack pulled him back. He teetered, lost his balance, and fell on the suit's backpack with his legs pinned beneath him.

Stuck! Bob tried to roll onto his side, but he couldn't move. His head and arms were tangled inside the suit. His legs began cramping. He was trapped like a turtle on its back. Except a turtle would at least have its head out of the shell. The alarm beeped fainter, faster. Sweat poured down his face. *So this is what the Apollo 13 boys felt like. Dogmeat.*

Minutes passed. The beeps merged into a single tone. Quieter. Quieter.

Off.

Hysterical laughter echoed in the small room. Bob felt strong hands grab the upper half of his suit and begin tugging.

"Congratulations. You're dead!" Josh slowly manhandled Bob out of his turtle-shell prison.

Bob opened his eyes and saw Josh with his helmet and gloves off, grinning like a maniac.

The airlock door opened and two med techs walked in. "The exercise is over," said the first one, a cute redhead with dangly earrings. "That's six times in a row you've killed yourself, Bob. You've got the record." She and Josh helped him to his feet.

The other tech grinned. "Don't sweat it, bro. You're supposed to break records, right? That's what they pay you for—to go where no man has gone before." He and Josh helped Bob step out of the lower half of his suit.

The redhead shook her head, making her earrings dance like wild men. "Okay, now let's check you over. Any parts broken?"

"I'm fine," Bob said.

It took the techs ten minutes to peel off his Spandex underwear and MAG diaper and check him over for damage. Bob stood there, buck naked, barely noticing them. He'd been in this program too long to bat an eye at the indignity of the medigeeks' inspections. But if he couldn't pass the EVA drill ...

"You're fine, Dr. Kaganovski," said the redhead. "Next time take it slower and dry off a little better." She turned to Josh. "How's the splint on your wrist holding up?"

He shrugged. "Hey, it's just a hairline. No sweat."

"Yeah, well, take my advice and don't buy another motorcycle." She walked out of the room with the other tech.

"Yes, Motherrrr." Josh flexed his wrists and revved an imaginary bike. "Hey, Kaggo, you want to run another exercise before lunch?"

Bob looked at his watch. "We don't have time. The psych test is coming up."

"Psych test?" Josh raised an eyebrow.

"At eleven," Bob said. "Didn't you read your e-mail?"

Josh just looked at him.

"Don't tell me you weaseled out of it." They walked out of the Hab and into the locker room. Bob went to the sink and began rinsing the last of the shampoo from his hair. "Lex and Kennedy are gonna spit bile if you're the only one who doesn't have to take it."

"Nobody told me anything about a psych test." Josh stepped into his street pants. "Lex is doing T-38 proficiency training this morning. And Kennedy's running docking sims over in SES."

Bob's heart double-thumped. He went to his street-clothes locker and began dressing. "Let me see if I've got this straight. The klutz of the crew has to go have a happy chat with the shrinks, while the rest of you get to play?"

"You're not a klutz," Josh said. "You just need a little more time—"

"What do you call a guy who can't even get dressed without hurting himself?" Bob yanked on his pants and plopped down on the bench. "Seventeen months till lift-off, and they're getting nervous, that's what I think. They've still got time to unload me, bring in someone else who knows his head from a hole in the ozone."

"Just can it, will you?" Josh sounded angry. "Listen up. You know who's the most important guy on the crew? Read the mission architecture document. The flight engineer, that's who. The ace mechanic. Scotty. That would be you, in case you've forgotten."

"Mechanics are a dime a dozen."

"Yeah, right, and monkeys can do brain surgery." Josh finished tying his shoes. "You're the best mechanic in the Ares program. Anything goes wrong out there, it's you who's going to fix it, and everybody knows it. So what are you worried about?"

"Flight surgeons, that's what. They want a change. I can smell it."

"Then blow your nose. I don't care who wants a change. My main priority is getting to Mars and back with my crew alive. As long as I'm commander on this mission, you're my number-one mechanic. Got it?"

"So what's the deal with the psych test, then?" Bob jammed his feet into his shoes. "What do I tell these guys?"

"Shrinks are all alike," Josh said. "They're afraid of a repeat of the Mir fiasco. Just figure out what they want to hear and tell it to 'em."

"Oh, right," Bob said. *And what do they want to hear?*

"You'll do fine." Josh whacked Bob on the shoulder. "Believe me, you haven't got a thing to worry about."

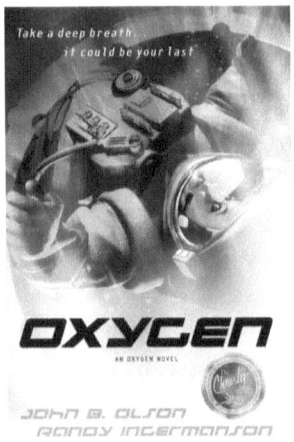

SNEAK PEAK AT TRANSGRESSION

WHAT IF ...?

What if you were studying for your Ph.D. in archaeology and decided to take a break from your crummy life for the summer by working on an archaeological dig in Israel?

What if you met a great guy in Jerusalem who happened to be a world-famous theoretical physicist working on a crazy idea to build a wormhole that might make time-travel possible ... someday?

What if he had a nutball colleague who turned the theory into reality — and then decided to use YOU as a guinea pig to make sure it was safe?

What if the nutball had a gun and went on a crazy, impossible mission to hunt down and kill the apostle Paul?

It's A.D. 57 when Rivka Meyers walks out of the wormhole into a world she's only studied in books. Ancient Jerusalem is awesome! Rivka can't believe her friend Ari Kazan's theory actually worked. But when she runs into Ari's wacko colleague, Damien West, in the Temple, Rivka starts to smell a rat.

When Ari discovers that Damien and Rivka have gone through a wormhole that's on the edge of collapse, he has to make a horrible choice: Follow them and risk never coming back — or lose the woman of his dreams forever.

PROLOGUE

Rivka

Rivka Meyers knew something was wrong when she bumped into a wall that wasn't there.

"Ow!" She tugged at the virtual reality headset she had worn for the past half hour. "Dr. West?" she said. "How do I get this thing off?"

No response.

She fumbled with the straps at her chin. "Dr. West? Are you there? Hello?"

The buckle popped loose in her hand. She pulled off the headset and blinked. The lab was much darker than she remembered, and it smelled musty. Why hadn't she noticed that before?

The game had defocused her vision. While she waited for her eyes to adjust, she put her hand against the wall. It felt rough, stony. *Like limestone,* said something deep inside her archaeologist's brain.

But that was impossible. She was in the back part of a physics laboratory. Rivka suddenly felt dizzy, nauseated.

"Dr. West, what's going on?" she asked in a loud voice. "I'm done playing your computer game." Her voice echoed oddly in the stillness.

"Dr. West!" She was shouting now, angry. What kind of a prank was he playing? She didn't like it, and she wanted out. Now.

Rivka turned her head in a slow semicircle, studying her surroundings. In one direction, she could see light from a rough-cut entrance. In the other direction—total darkness. She sniffed. It smelled like...a cave. But it couldn't be. Not on the third floor of a physics building in downtown Jerusalem.

"God, help me!" It wasn't a prayer—just a figure of speech. Maybe it wouldn't hurt to try the real thing.

Lord...help me get back to the lab. I need to find Ari...

A bead of sweat ran down her back. Did she really want to see Ari again, after what he had said last night?

A footstep scuffled at the lighted end of the room. A deep male voice said something muzzy and indistinct.

Thanks, Father. Rivka turned to look.

Right away, she saw that it wasn't Ari. Nor Dr. West. At the moment, she didn't care. Any human being would be welcome. "Excuse me!" she shouted in English and began walking toward the man. "Could you tell me how to get to Ari Kazan's lab?" She repeated this in Hebrew.

The light grew better as she got closer to him. He wore a black beard and rough garb much like a Bedouin's...but different. Rivka couldn't quite place his costume, although she had been in Israel for over a month now and had thought she had seen everything: Arabs in checkered *kaffiyehs,* Hasidic rabbis in black fur hats, Druze villagers in baggy shirts and pants, *sabra* girls in string bikinis. This man might well be the janitor or just as easily the department chairman.

The man squinted in her direction. The nearer Rivka came to him, the more she slowed. Finally, she stopped. "Hello?" she said. *"Shalom? Salaam?"*

He said something in a language she didn't recognize. The vowel usage reminded her vaguely of Syriac—a notion so ridiculous that Rivka almost laughed out loud. Syriac had been a dead language for centuries.

A little smile formed on the man's face as he stared at her. His gaze ran up and down her body, seeming to peel away her T-shirt and cutoffs. His eyes lit up with an evil glow that needed no translation.

Rivka's heart double-thumped, then began a tap dance of panic in her chest. She stepped backward, clutching the virtual reality headset in her hands as though it were a shield. "Dr. West!" she shouted. "Help!"

The man chuckled softly. He took a step toward her, his hands held out to either side to cut off her escape.

"Who are you?" Rivka asked in a loud voice that grated in her own ears. She stepped back again. *"Mi attah?"* She couldn't remember how to say it in Arabic.

The man took another step toward her.

Rivka backed rapidly away from him. "Don't you dare touch me!" she said. "I'm an American! *Ani Amerikait!*" The words sounded foolish, but she had read somewhere that you had a better chance if you kept talking and put up a fight.

The man gave a yellow smile and kept advancing, catlike.

Rivka stepped back again, and the headset in her hand clunked against something hard. A wall. Her mind spun wildly now, out of control. The man was only a few paces away. Desperate, she lunged forward and screamed, "Get away from me!"

She threw the headset at his face and dodged to her left.

He batted the flimsy missile away with a hairy paw and scooted to his right, keeping between her and the exit. His eyes glowed with animal pleasure. He took another step.

Rivka pulled a key out of her pocket and clenched it tightly. Improvise! Fight! She kept moving sideways, maneuvering for room. *Please, Father, save me!*

The man feinted forward. She skittered sideways, tripped over a huge bump on the ground, staggered. Then her foot stepped on a marble-sized pebble, and her leg shot out from under her. She landed hard on her back in the dirt. Her key dropped into the loose dirt somewhere nearby.

The man grunted in triumph and rushed at her.

She dug her hands into the soft dust for balance and timed her kick perfectly.

Almost perfectly. At the last instant, he twisted his hips. Not much, but enough.

Her sandal thudded into a very solid thigh. The shock ran up her leg and into her spine. "No!" she screamed, and began kicking her feet in the air like windmills.

His hands snaked at her ankles, caught them, locked them in an iron grip. He laughed softly and forced her feet to the ground. He pinned them down with one enormous hand and leaned forward. Rivka smelled his vinegary breath.

She slashed wildly with her left hand, scratching at his eyes. He jerked his head away.

Point-blank, Rivka flung a handful of fine dust into his eyes. He screamed, clawed at his face. Suddenly, Rivka's legs came free.

She rolled away from him. He lunged blindly for her, coughing, spitting.

She scrambled up, grabbed another handful of dust, and pitched it into his gaping mouth.

He choked and fell on his face.

Rivka turned and ran. "Ari!" she screamed. "Help!"

She raced outside into the sunlight, sprinted madly through a dark grove of trees with gnarled branches. Her heart pounded in her chest. Her ragged breath rasped in her ears. Was he following? Faster! Tears fogged her eyes. Her leather sandals tore at her feet. Trying to look back over her shoulder, she tripped and fell. Dust flew up all around her.

Coughing, she clambered to her feet and dared to look back. The man was nowhere in sight.

Rivka panted until she caught her breath. Her left wrist throbbed from the fall. She massaged it while she squinted into the trees, afraid that the man might be lurking in the shadows.

Nothing happened.

Finally, she turned around to get her bearings.

She blinked twice and then stared.

Across a small valley massive stone walls rose. Herodian masonry. Jerusalem limestone. Towering white walls. It looked like...

But that was impossible. She closed her eyes, breathed deeply three times, and opened them again. *Absurd.* Had she gone loony or something?

Rivka had visited the Temple Mount twice and studied hundreds of pictures during three years of graduate school. But she had never seen it looking like this.

So pure.

So spotless.

So new.

~

www.ingramcontent.com/pod-product-compliance
Lightning Source LLC
Chambersburg PA
CBHW051510250626
47156CB00001B/43